SERPENT & DOVE

SERPENT & DOVE

SHELBY MAHURIN

HARPER TEEN
An Imprint of HarperCollinsPublishers

HarperTeen is an imprint of HarperCollins Publishers.

Serpent & Dove
www.epicreads.com
Library of Congress Control Number: 2019939331
ISBN 978-0-06-287802-1 — ISBN 978-0-06-297710-6 (special ed)
ISBN 978-0-06-297113-5 (intl ed)
Typography by Sarah Nichole Kaufman
20 21 22 23   PC/LSCH   10 9 8

First Edition

To my mom, *who loves books,*
to my dad, *who gave me the confidence to write them,*
and to RJ, *who still hasn't read this one*

SERPENT & DOVE

PART I

Un malheur ne vient jamais seul.
Misfortune never arrives alone.
—French proverb

THE BELLEROSE

Lou

There's something haunting about a body touched by magic. Most people first noticed the smell: not the rot of decay, but a cloying sweetness in their noses, a sharp taste on their tongues. Rare individuals also sensed a tingle in the air. A lingering aura on the corpse's skin. As if the magic itself was still present somehow, watching and waiting.

Alive.

Of course, those stupid enough to talk about such things ended up on the stake.

Thirteen bodies had been found throughout Belterra over the past year—more than double the amount of years prior. Though the Church did its best to conceal the mysterious circumstances of each death, all had been buried in closed caskets.

"There he is." Coco motioned to a man in the corner. Though candlelight bathed half of his face in shadow, there was no mistaking the gold brocade on his coat or the heavy insignia around his neck. He sat rigid in his chair, clearly uncomfortable, as a scantily-clad woman draped herself across his plump midsection. I couldn't help but grin.

Only Madame Labelle would leave an aristocrat such as Pierre Tremblay waiting in the bowels of a brothel.

"Come on." Coco motioned toward a table in the opposite corner. "Babette should be here soon."

"What sort of pompous ass wears *brocade* while mourning?" I asked.

Coco glanced at Tremblay over her shoulder and smirked. "The sort of pompous ass with money."

His daughter, Filippa, had been the seventh body found.

After her disappearance in the dead of night, the aristocracy had been shaken when she'd reappeared—throat slashed—at the edge of L'Eau Mélancolique. But that wasn't the worst of it. Rumors had crawled through the kingdom about her silver hair and wrinkled skin, her cloudy eyes and gnarled fingers. At twenty-four, she'd been transformed into a hag. Tremblay's peers simply couldn't understand it. She'd had no known enemies, no vendettas against her to warrant such violence.

But while *Filippa* might've had no enemies, her pompous ass of a father had accumulated plenty while trafficking magical objects.

His daughter's death had been a warning: one did not exploit the witches without consequence.

"Bonjour, messieurs." A honey-haired courtesan approached us, batting her lashes hopefully. I cackled at the brazen way she eyed Coco. Even disguised as a man, Coco was striking. Though scars

marred the rich brown skin of her hands—she covered them with gloves—her face remained smooth, and her black eyes sparkled even in the semidarkness. "Can I tempt you to join me?"

"Sorry, darling." Adopting my smarmiest voice, I patted the courtesan's hand the way I'd seen other men do. "But we're spoken for this morning. Mademoiselle Babette will be joining us shortly."

She pouted for only a second before moving on to our neighbor, who eagerly accepted her invitation.

"Do you think he has it on him?" Coco scrutinized Tremblay from the top of his bald head to the bottom of his polished shoes, lingering on his unadorned fingers. "Babette could've been lying. This could be a trap."

"Babette might be a liar, but she isn't stupid. She won't sell us out before we pay her." I watched the other courtesans with morbid fascination. With cinched waists and overflowing bosoms, they danced lithely amongst the patrons as if their corsets weren't slowly suffocating them.

To be fair, however, many of them weren't wearing corsets. Or anything at all.

"You're right." Coco dug our coin pouch from her coat and threw it on the table. "It'll be after."

"Ah, *mon amour*, you wound me." Babette materialized beside us, grinning and flicking the brim of my hat. Unlike her peers, she swathed as much of her pale skin as possible with crimson silk. Thick, white makeup covered the rest—and her scars. They snaked up her arms and chest in a similar pattern to Coco's. "And for ten more golden *couronnes*, I would never *dream* of betraying you."

"Good morning, Babette." Chuckling, I propped a foot on the table and leaned back on my chair's hind legs. "You know, it's uncanny the way you always appear within seconds of óur money. Can you smell it?" I turned to Coco, whose lips twitched in an effort not to grin. "It's like she can smell it."

"*Bonjour*, Louise." Babette kissed my cheek before leaning toward Coco and lowering her voice. "Cosette, you look ravishing, as usual."

Coco rolled her eyes. "You're late."

"My apologies." Babette inclined her head with a saccharine smile. "But I did not recognize you. I will never understand why such beautiful women insist on masquerading as men—"

"Unaccompanied women attract too much attention. You know that." I drummed my fingers against the tabletop with practiced ease, forcing a grin. "Any one of us could be a witch."

"Bah!" She winked conspiratorially. "Only a fool would mistake two as charming as you for such wretched, violent creatures."

"Of course." I nodded, tugging my hat even lower. While Coco's and Babette's scars revealed their true natures, Dames Blanches could move through society virtually undetected. The russet-skinned woman on top of Tremblay could be one. Or the honey-haired courtesan who'd just disappeared up the stairs. "But the flames come first with the Church. Questions second. It's a dangerous time to be female."

"Not here." Babette spread her arms wide, lips curling upward.

"Here, we are safe. Here, we are cherished. My mistress's offer still stands—"

"Your mistress would burn you—and us—if she knew the truth." I returned my attention to Tremblay, whose obvious wealth had attracted two more courtesans. He politely rebuffed their attempts to undo his trousers. "We're here for him."

Coco upended our coin pouch on the table. "Ten golden *couronnes*, as promised."

Babette sniffed and lifted her nose in the air. "Hmm . . . I seem to remember twenty."

"What?" My chair plummeted back to the ground with a bang. The patrons nearest us blinked in our direction, but I ignored them. "We agreed on *ten*."

"That was before you hurt my feelings."

"Damn it, Babette." Coco snatched our coin away before Babette could touch it. "Do you know how long it takes us to save that kind of money?"

I struggled to keep my voice even. "We don't even know if Tremblay *has* the ring."

Babette merely shrugged and extended her palm. "It is not my fault you insist on cutting purses in the street like common criminals. You would earn thrice that sum in a single night here at the Bellerose, but you are too proud."

Coco took a deep breath, hands curling into fists on the table. "Look, we're sorry we offended your delicate sensibilities, but we agreed on ten. We can't afford—"

"I can hear the coin in your pocket, Cosette."

I stared at Babette incredulously. "You *are* a goddamned hound."

Her eyes flashed. "Come now, I invite you here at my own personal risk to eavesdrop on my mistress's business with Monsieur Tremblay, yet you insult me like I'm a—"

At that precise moment, however, a tall, middle-aged woman glided down the staircase. A deep emerald gown accentuated her flaming hair and hourglass figure. Tremblay lurched to his feet at her appearance, and the courtesans around us—including Babette—swept into deep curtsies.

It was rather odd, watching naked women curtsy.

Grasping Tremblay's arms with a wide smile, Madame Labelle kissed both his cheeks and murmured something I couldn't hear. Panic spiked through me as she looped her arm through his and led him back across the room toward the stairs.

Babette watched us out of the corner of her eye. "Decide quickly, *mes amours*. My mistress is a busy woman. Her business with Monsieur Tremblay will not take long."

I glared at her, resisting the urge to wrap my hands around her pretty neck and squeeze. "Can you at least tell us what your mistress is buying? She must've told you *something*. Is it the ring? Does Tremblay have it?"

She grinned like a cat with cream. "Perhaps . . . for another ten *couronnes*."

Coco and I shared a black look. If Babette wasn't careful, she'd soon learn just how *wretched* and *violent* we could be.

The Bellerose boasted twelve luxury parlors for its courtesans to entertain guests, but Babette led us to none of these. Instead, she opened an unmarked thirteenth door at the end of the corridor and ushered us inside.

"Welcome, *mes amours*, to the eyes and ears of the Bellerose."

Blinking, I waited for my eyes to adjust to the darkness of this new, narrower corridor. Twelve windows—rectangular, large, and spaced at regular intervals along one wall—let in a subtle glow of light. Upon closer inspection, however, I realized they weren't windows at all, but portraits.

I traced a finger down the nose of the one nearest me: a beautiful woman with luscious curves and an alluring smile. "Who are they?"

"Famed courtesans of years past." Babette paused to admire the woman with a wistful expression. "My portrait will replace hers someday."

Frowning, I leaned closer to inspect the woman in question. Her image was mirrored, somehow, her colors muted, as if this were the back of the painting. And . . . holy hell.

Two golden latches covered her eyes.

"Are those *peepholes*?" Coco asked incredulously, moving closer. "What kind of macabre freak show is this, Babette?"

"Shhh!" Babette lifted a hasty finger to her lips. "The eyes and *ears*, remember? *Ears*. You must whisper in this place."

I didn't want to imagine the purpose of such an architectural feature. I *did*, however, want to imagine a very long bath when I returned home to the theater. There would be scrubbing. Vigorous scrubbing. I could only pray my eyeballs survived it.

Before I could voice my disgust, two shadows moved in my periphery. I whirled, hand flying to the knife in my boot, before the shadows took shape. I stilled as two horribly familiar, horribly unpleasant men leered at me.

Andre and Grue.

I glowered at Babette, knife still clenched in my fist. "What are *they* doing here?"

At the sound of my voice, Andre leaned forward, blinking slowly in the darkness. "Is that . . . ?"

Grue searched my face, skipping over my mustache and lingering on my dark brows and turquoise eyes, freckled nose and suntanned skin. An evil smile split his face. His front tooth was chipped. And yellow. "Hello, Lou Lou."

Ignoring him, I glared pointedly at Babette. "This wasn't part of the deal."

"Oh, relax, Louise. They're working." She flung herself into one of the wooden chairs they'd just vacated. "My mistress hired them as security."

"Security?" Coco scoffed, reaching into her coat for her own knife. Andre bared his teeth. "Since when is voyeurism considered security?"

"If ever we feel uncomfortable with a client, all we do is knock twice, and these lovely gentlemen intervene." Babette pointed lazily toward the portraits with her foot, revealing a pale, scarred ankle. "They are doors, *mon amour.* Immediate access."

Madame Labelle was an idiot. It was the only explanation for such . . . well, idiocy.

Two of the stupidest thieves I'd ever known, Andre and Grue infringed constantly on our territory in East End. Wherever we went, they followed—usually two steps behind—and wherever *they* went, the constabulary inevitably did too. Big and ugly and loud, the two lacked the subtlety and skill necessary to thrive in East End. And the brains.

I dreaded to think what they would do with *immediate access* to anything. Especially sex and violence. And those were perhaps the *least* of the vices happening within these brothel walls, if this business transaction served as any example.

"Do not worry." As if reading my thoughts, Babette cast the two a small smile. "My mistress will kill them if they leak information. Isn't that right, *messieurs?*"

Their grins vanished, and I finally noted the discoloration around their eyes. Bruises. I still didn't lower my knife. "And what keeps them from leaking information *to* your mistress?"

"Well . . ." Babette rose to her feet, sweeping past us to a portrait down the corridor. She lifted a hand to the small golden button next to it. "I suppose that depends on what you're willing to give them."

"How about I give *all* of you a knife in the—"

"Ah, ah, ah!" Babette pressed the button as I advanced, knife raised, and the golden latches over the courtesan's eyes flipped open. Madame Labelle's and Tremblay's muffled voices filled the corridor.

"Think carefully, *mon amour*," Babette whispered. "Your precious ring could be in the very next room. Come, see for yourself." She stepped aside, finger still pressing the button, allowing me to stand in front of the portrait.

Muttering a curse, I stood on my tiptoes to see through the courtesan's eyes.

Tremblay wore a path through the plush floral carpet of the parlor. He looked paler here in this pastel room—where the morning sun bathed everything in soft, golden light—and sweat beaded along his forehead. Licking his lips nervously, he glanced back at Madame Labelle, who watched him from a chaise longue by the door. Even sitting, she exuded regal grace, neck straight and hands clasped.

"Do calm yourself, Monsieur Tremblay. I assure you I will obtain the necessary funds within the week. A fortnight at most."

He shook his head curtly. "Too long."

"One might argue it is not nearly long enough for your asking price. Only the king could afford such an astronomical sum, and he has no use for magic rings."

Heart lurching to my throat, I pulled away to look at Coco. She scowled and dug in her coat for more *couronnes*. Andre and Grue pocketed them with gleeful smirks.

Promising myself I would skin them alive after I stole the ring, I returned my attention to the parlor.

"And—and if I were to tell you I have another buyer in place?" Tremblay asked.

"I would call you a liar, Monsieur Tremblay. You could hardly continue boasting possession of your wares after what happened to your daughter."

Tremblay whirled to face her. "Do not speak of my daughter."

Smoothing her skirts, Madame Labelle ignored him completely. "Indeed, I'm rather surprised you're still in the magical black market at all. You do have another daughter, don't you?"

When he didn't answer, her smile grew small and cruel. Triumphant. "The witches are vicious. If they learn you possess the ring, their wrath on your remaining family will be . . . unpleasant."

Face purpling, he took a step toward her. "I do not appreciate your implication."

"Then appreciate my threat, *monsieur*. Do not cross me, or it will be the last thing you ever do."

Smothering a snort, I glanced again at Coco, who now shook with silent laughter. Babette glared at us. Magical rings aside, this conversation might've been worth forty *couronnes*. Even the theater paled in comparison to these melodramatics.

"Now, tell me," Madame Labelle purred, "do you have another buyer?"

"*Putain.*" He glared at her for several long seconds before grudgingly shaking his head. "No, I do not have another buyer. I've spent *months* renouncing all ties with my former contacts—purging all inventory—yet this ring . . ." He swallowed hard, and the heat in his expression flickered out. "I fear to speak of it to anyone, lest the demons discover I have it."

"You were unwise to tout any of their items."

Tremblay didn't answer. His eyes remained distant, haunted, as if he were seeing something we couldn't. My throat constricted inexplicably. Oblivious to his torment, Madame Labelle continued ruthlessly. "If you hadn't, perhaps dear Filippa would still be with us—"

His head snapped up at his daughter's name, and his eyes—no

longer haunted—glinted with fierce purpose. "I will see the demons burn for what they did to her."

"How foolish of you."

"I beg your pardon?"

"I make it my business to know the business of my enemies, *monsieur.*" She rose gracefully to her feet, and he stumbled back a half step. "As they are now also your enemies, I must offer a piece of advice: 'tis dangerous to meddle in the affairs of witches. Forget your vengeance. Forget everything you've learned about this world of shadows and magic. You are wildly outmatched and woefully inadequate in the face of these women. Death is the kindest of their torments—a gift bestowed only to those who have earned it. One would think you'd have learned that with dear Filippa."

His mouth twisted, and he straightened to his full height, spluttering angrily. Madame Labelle still loomed over him by several inches. "Y-You cross the line."

Madame Labelle didn't shrink away from him. Instead, she ran a hand down the bodice of her gown, utterly unfazed, and withdrew a fan from the folds of her skirt. A knife peeked out from its spine.

"I see the pleasantries are over. Right, then. Let us get down to business." Spreading the device in a single flourish, she fanned it between them. Tremblay eyed the knife point warily and conceded a step. "If you wish me to relieve you of the ring, I will do so here and now—for five thousand gold *couronnes* less than your asking price."

An odd choking noise escaped his throat. "You're mad—"

"If not," she continued, voice hardening, "you will leave this place with a noose around your daughter's neck. Her name is Célie, yes? La Dame des Sorcières will delight in draining her youth, in drinking the glow from her skin, the gleam from her hair. She will be unrecognizable by the time the witches finish with her. Empty. Broken. Just like Filippa."

"You—you—" Tremblay's eyes bulged, and a vein appeared on his shiny forehead. "*Fille de pute!* You cannot do this to me. You *cannot*—"

"Come now, *monsieur*, I do not have all day. The prince has returned from Amandine, and I do not want to miss the festivities."

His chin jutted obstinately. "I—I do not have it with me."

Damn it. Disappointment crashed through me, bitter and sharp. Coco muttered a curse.

"I do not believe you." Striding to the window across the room, Madame Labelle peered down. "Ah, Monsieur Tremblay, how could a gentleman such as yourself leave your daughter to wait outside a brothel? Such easy prey."

Sweating profusely now, Tremblay hastened to turn out his pockets. "I swear I don't have it! Look, look!" I pressed my face closer as he shoved the contents of his pockets toward her: an embroidered hand cloth, a silver pocket watch, and a fistful of copper *couronnes*. But no ring. "Please, leave my daughter alone! She is not involved in this!"

He made such a pitiful sight that I might've felt sorry for

him—if he hadn't just dashed all my plans. As it were, however, the sight of his trembling limbs and ashen face filled me with vindictive pleasure.

Madame Labelle seemed to share my sentiment. She sighed theatrically, dropping her hand from the window, and—curiously—turned to look directly at the portrait I stood behind. Tumbling backward, I landed squarely on my ass and bit back a curse.

"What is it?" Coco whispered, crouching beside me. Babette released the button with a frown.

"Shhhh!" I waved my hands wildly, motioning toward the parlor. *I think*—I mouthed the words, not daring to speak—*she saw me.*

Coco's eyes flew open in alarm.

We all froze as her voice drifted closer, muted but audible through the thin wall. "Pray tell me, *monsieur* . . . where is it, then?"

Holy hell. Coco and I locked eyes incredulously. Though I didn't dare return to the portrait, I pressed closer to the wall, breath hot and uncomfortable against my own face. *Answer her,* I pleaded silently. *Tell us.*

Miraculously, Tremblay obliged, his vehement reply more dulcet than the sweetest of music. "It's locked away in my townhouse, you *salope ignorante*—"

"That will do, Monsieur Tremblay." As their parlor door clicked open, I could almost see her smile. It matched my own. "I hope for your daughter's sake you aren't lying. I will arrive at your townhouse at dawn with your coin. Do not keep me waiting."

THE CHASSEUR

Lou

"I'm listening."

Sitting in the crowded patisserie, Bas lifted a spoonful of *chocolat chaud* to his lips, careful not to spill a drop on his lace cravat. I resisted the urge to flick a bit of mine at him. For what we had planned, we needed him in a good mood.

No one could swindle an aristocrat like Bas could.

"It's like this," I said, pointing my spoon at him, "you can pocket everything else in Tremblay's vault as payment, but the ring is ours."

He leaned forward, dark eyes settling on my lips. When I irritably brushed the *chocolat* from my mustache, he grinned. "Ah, yes. A magic ring. I have to admit I'm surprised you're interested in such an object. I thought you'd renounced all magic?"

"The ring is different."

His eyes found my lips once more. "Of course it is."

"Bas." I snapped my fingers in front of his face pointedly. "Focus, please. This is important."

Once, upon arriving in Cesarine, I'd thought Bas quite handsome. Handsome enough to court. Certainly handsome enough to kiss. From across the cramped table, I eyed the dark line of his jaw. There was still a small scar there—just below his ear, hiding in the shadow of his facial hair—where I'd bitten him during one of our more passionate nights.

I sighed ruefully at the memory. He had the most beautiful amber skin. And such a tight little ass.

He chuckled as if reading my mind. "All right, Louey, I shall attempt to marshal my thoughts—as long as you do the same." Stirring his *chocolat*, he sat back with a smirk. "So . . . you wish to rob an aristocrat, and you have, of course, come to the master for guidance."

I scoffed but bit my tongue. As the third cousin twice removed of a baron, Bas held the peculiar position of being part of the aristocracy, while also *not* being part of it. His relative's wealth allowed him to dress in the finest fashions and attend the fanciest parties, yet the aristocrats couldn't bother to remember his name. A useful slight, as he often attended said parties to relieve them of their valuables.

"A wise decision," he continued, "as twits such as Tremblay utilize layers upon layers of security: gates and locks and guards and dogs, just to name a few. Probably more after what happened to his daughter. The witches stole her during the dead of night, didn't they? He'll have increased his protections."

Filippa was becoming a real pain in my ass.

Scowling, I glanced toward the patisserie's window. All manner of pastries perched there on glorious display: iced cakes and sugar loaves and *chocolat* tartlets, as well as macarons and fruit danishes of every color. Raspberry eclairs and an apple *tarte tatin* completed the display.

Out of all this decadence, however, the enormous sticky buns—with their cinnamon and sweet cream—made my mouth truly water.

As if on cue, Coco threw herself into the empty seat beside us. She thrust a plate of sticky buns toward me. "Here."

I could've kissed her. "You're a goddess. You know that, right?"

"Obviously. Just don't expect me to hold your hair back when you're puking later—oh, and you owe me a silver *couronne*."

"Like hell. That's my money too—"

"Yes, but you can weasel a sticky bun out of Pan anytime. The *couronne* is a service fee."

I glanced over my shoulder at the short, plump man behind the counter: Johannes Pan, pastry extraordinaire and halfwit. More important, however, he was the close personal friend and confidant of Mademoiselle Lucida Bretton.

I was Mademoiselle Lucida Bretton. With a blond wig.

Sometimes I didn't want to wear the suit—and I'd quickly discovered Pan had a soft spot for the gentler sex. Most days I only had to bat my lashes. Others I had to get slightly more . . . creative. I shot Bas a covert look. Little did he know, he'd committed all sorts of heinous acts to poor Mademoiselle Bretton over the past two years.

Pan couldn't handle a woman's tears.

"I'm dressed as a man today." I tucked into the first bun, shoving half of it into my mouth without decorum. "'esides, 'e prffers"—I swallowed hard, eyes watering—"blondes."

Heat radiated from Bas's dark gaze as he watched me. "Then the gentleman has poor taste."

"*Ick.*" Coco gagged, rolling her eyes. "Give it a rest, will you? Pining doesn't suit you."

"That *suit* doesn't suit you—"

Leaving them to bicker, I returned my attention to the buns. Though Coco had procured enough to feed five people, I accepted the challenge. Three buns in, however, the two had turned even my appetite. I pushed my plate away roughly.

"We don't have the luxury of time, Bas," I interrupted, just as Coco looked likely to leap across the table at him. "The ring will be gone by morning, so it has to be tonight. Will you help us or not?"

He frowned at my tone. "Personally, I don't see what all the fuss is about. You don't need an invisibility ring for safety. You know I can protect you."

Pfft. Empty promises. Perhaps that was why I'd stopped loving him.

Bas was many things—charming, cunning, ruthless—but he wasn't a protector. No, he was far too worried about more important things, like saving his own skin at the first sign of trouble. I didn't hold it against him. He *was* a man, after all, and his kissing had more than made up for it.

Coco glared at him. "As we've told you—*several* times—it

grants the user more than invisibility."

"Ah, *mon amie*, I must confess I wasn't listening."

When he grinned, blowing her a kiss across the table, her hands curled into fists. "*Bordel!* I swear, one of these days I'm going to—"

I intervened before she could slash open a vein. "It renders the user immune to enchantment. Sort of like the Chasseurs' Balisardas." My gaze flicked to Bas. "Surely you understand how useful that might prove to me."

His grin vanished. Slowly, he reached up to touch my cravat, fingers tracing where it hid my scar. Chills erupted down my spine. "But she hasn't found you. You're still safe."

"For now."

He stared at me for a long moment, hand still raised to my throat. Finally, he sighed. "And you're willing to do whatever it takes to procure this ring?"

"Yes."

"Even . . . magic?"

I swallowed hard, threading my fingers through his, and nodded. He dropped our clasped hands to the table. "Very well, then. I shall help you." He glanced out the window, and I followed his gaze. More and more people had gathered for the prince's parade. Though most laughed and chatted with palpable excitement, unease festered just beneath the surface—in the tightness of their mouths and the sharp, quick movements of their eyes. "Tonight," he continued, "the king has scheduled a ball to welcome his son home from Amandine. The entire aristocracy has been invited—including Monsieur Tremblay."

"Convenient," Coco murmured.

We all tensed simultaneously at a commotion up the street, eyes locking on the men who emerged through the crowd. Clad in coats of royal blue, they marched in rows of three—each *thump, thump, thump* of their boots perfectly synchronized—with silver daggers held over their hearts. Constables flanked them on either side, shouting and marshaling pedestrians to sidewalks.

Chasseurs.

Sworn to the Church as huntsmen, Chasseurs protected the kingdom of Belterra from the occult—namely, the Dames Blanches, or the deadly witches who haunted Belterra's small-minded prejudices. Muted anger pounded through my veins as I watched the Chasseurs march closer. As if *we* were the interlopers. As if this land hadn't once belonged to *us*.

Not your fight. Lifting my chin, I mentally shook myself. The ancient feud between the Church and witches didn't affect me anymore—not since I'd left the world of witchcraft behind.

"You shouldn't be out here, Lou." Coco's eyes followed the Chasseurs as they lined the street, preventing anyone from approaching the royal family. The parade would soon start. "We should reconvene in the theater. A crowd this size is dangerous. It's bound to attract trouble."

"I'm disguised." Struggling to speak around the sticky bun in my mouth, I swallowed thickly. "No one will recognize me."

"Andre and Grue did."

"Only because of my voice—"

"I won't be reconvening anywhere until after the parade." Dropping my hand, Bas stood and patted his waistcoat with a salacious grin. "A crowd this size is a glorious cesspool of money, and I plan on drowning in it. If you'll excuse me."

He tipped his hat and wove through the patisserie tables away from us. Coco leapt to her feet. "That bastard will renege as soon as he's out of sight. Probably turn us in to the constabulary—or worse, the Chasseurs. I don't know why you trust him."

It remained a point of contention in our friendship that I'd revealed my true identity to Bas. My true name. Never mind that it'd happened after a night of too much whiskey and kissing. Shredding the last bun in an effort to avoid Coco's gaze, I tried not to regret my decision.

Regret changed nothing. I had no choice but to trust him now. We were linked irrevocably.

She sighed in resignation. "I'll follow him. You get out of here. Meet us at the theater in an hour?"

"It's a date."

I left the patisserie only minutes after Coco and Bas. Though dozens of girls huddled outside in near hysterics at the prospect of seeing the prince, it was a man who blocked the doorway.

Truly enormous, he towered over me by head and shoulders, his broad back and powerful arms straining against the brown wool of his coat. He too faced the street, but it didn't look as if he was watching the parade. He held his shoulders stiffly, feet planted as if preparing for a fight.

I cleared my throat and poked the man in the back. He didn't move. I poked him again. He shifted slightly, but still not enough for me to squeeze through.

Right. Rolling my eyes, I threw my shoulder into his side and attempted to wedge myself between his girth and the doorjamb. It seemed he felt *that* contact, because he finally turned—and clubbed me square in the nose with his elbow.

"Shit!" Clutching my nose, I stumbled back and landed on my backside for the second time that morning. Treacherous tears sprang to my eyes. "What the hell is *wrong* with you?"

He extended a swift hand. "My apologies, *monsieur*. I didn't see you."

"Clearly." I ignored his hand and hauled myself to my feet. Brushing off my pants, I made to shove past him, but he once again blocked my path. His shabby coat flapped open at the movement, revealing a bandolier strapped across his chest. Knives of every shape and size glinted down at me, but it was the knife sheathed against his heart that made my own drop like a stone. Gleaming and silver, it was adorned with a large sapphire that glittered ominously on its hilt.

Chasseur.

I ducked my head. Shit.

Inhaling deeply, I forced myself to remain calm. He presented no danger to me in my current disguise. I'd done nothing wrong. I smelled of cinnamon, not magic. Besides—didn't all men share some sort of unspoken camaraderie? A mutual understanding of their own collective importance?

"Are you injured, *monsieur?*"

Right. Today, I was a *man*. I could do this.

I forced myself to look up.

Beyond his obscene height, the first things I noticed were the brass buttons on his coat—they matched the copper and gold of his hair, which shone in the sun like a beacon. Combined with his straight nose and full mouth, it made him unexpectedly handsome for a Chasseur. *Irritatingly* handsome. I couldn't help but stare. Thick lashes framed eyes the precise color of the sea.

Eyes that currently regarded me with unabashed shock.

Shit. My hand shot to my mustache, which dangled off my face from the fall.

Well, it'd been a valiant effort. And while men might be proud, women knew when to get the hell out of a bad situation.

"I'm fine." I ducked my head quickly and tried to move past him, eager now to put as much distance as possible between us. Though I'd still done nothing wrong, there was no sense in poking fate. Sometimes she poked back. "Just watch where you're going next time."

He didn't move. "You're a woman."

"Well spotted." Again, I tried to shove past him—this time with a bit more force than necessary—but he caught my elbow.

"Why are you dressed like a man?"

"Have you ever worn a corset?" I spun around to face him, reattaching my mustache with as much dignity as I could muster. "I doubt you'd ask such a question if you had. Trousers are infinitely more freeing."

He stared at me as if I'd sprouted an arm from my forehead. I glared back at him, and he shook his head slightly as if to clear it. "I—my apologies, *mademoiselle*."

People were watching us now. I tugged fruitlessly at my arm, the beginnings of panic fluttering in my stomach. "Let me *go*—"

His grip only tightened. "Have I offended you somehow?"

Losing my patience completely, I jerked away from him with all my might. "You broke my ass bone!"

Perhaps it was my vulgarity that shocked him, but he released me like I'd bitten him, eyeing me with a distaste bordering on revulsion. "I've never heard a lady speak so in my entire life."

Ah. Chasseurs were holy men. He probably thought me the devil.

He wouldn't have been wrong.

I offered him a catlike smile as I inched away, batting my lashes in my best impression of Babette. When he made no move to stop me, the tension in my chest eased. "You're hanging out with the wrong ladies, Chass."

"Are you a courtesan, then?"

I would've bristled had I not known several perfectly respectable courtesans—Babette not necessarily among them. Damn extortionist. Instead, I sighed dramatically. "Alas, no, and hearts all over Cesarine are breaking for it."

His jaw tightened. "What's your name?"

A wave of raucous cheers spared me from answering. The royal family had finally rounded the corner to our street. The Chasseur turned for only a second, but it was all I needed. Slipping behind a group of particularly enthusiastic young girls—they shrieked the prince's name at a pitch only dogs should've heard— I disappeared before he turned back around.

Elbows jostled me from all sides, however, and I soon realized I was simply too small—too short, too slight—to fight my way through the crowd. At least without poking someone with my knife. Returning a few elbows with my own, I searched for higher ground to wait out the procession. Somewhere out of sight.

There.

With a jump, I caught the windowsill of an old sandstone building, shimmied my way up the drainpipe, and pulled myself onto the roof. Settling my elbows on the balustrade, I surveyed the street below. Golden flags with the royal family's crest fluttered from each doorway, and vendors hawked food at every corner. Despite the mouthwatering smells of their *frites* and sausages and cheese croissants, the city still reeked of fish. Fish and smoke. I wrinkled my nose. One of the pleasures of living on a dreary gray peninsula.

Cesarine embodied gray. Dingy gray houses sat stacked atop one another like sardines in a tin, and crumbling streets wound past dirty gray markets and even dirtier gray harbors. An ever-present cloud of chimney smoke encompassed everything.

It was suffocating, the gray. Lifeless. Dull.

Still, there were worse things in life than dull. And there were worse kinds of smoke than chimney.

The cheers reached a climax as the Lyon family passed beneath my building.

King Auguste waved from his gilt carriage, golden curls blowing in the late-autumn wind. His son, Beauregard, sat beside him. The two couldn't have looked more different. Where the former was light of eyes and complexion, the latter's hooded eyes, tawny skin, and black hair favored his mother. But their smiles—both were nearly identical in charm.

Too charming, in my opinion. Arrogance exuded from their very pores.

Auguste's wife scowled behind them. I didn't blame her. I would've scowled too if my husband had more lovers than fingers and toes—not that I ever planned to have a husband. I'd be damned before chaining myself to anyone in marriage.

I'd just turned away, already bored, when something shifted in the street below. It was a subtle thing, almost as if the wind had changed direction mid-course. A nearly imperceptible hum reverberated from the cobblestones, and every sound of the crowd—every smell and taste and touch—faded into the ether. The world stilled. I scrambled backward, away from the roof's edge, as the hair on my neck stood up. I knew what came next. I recognized the faint brush of energy against my skin, the familiar thrumming in my ears.

Magic.

Then came the screams.

WICKED ARE THE WAYS OF WOMEN

Reid

The smell always followed the witches. Sweet and herbal, yet sharp—too sharp. Like the incense the Archbishop burned during Mass, but more acrid. Though years had passed since I'd taken my holy orders, I'd never acclimated to it. Even now—with just a hint of it on the breeze—it burned all the way down my throat. Choking me. Taunting me.

I loathed the smell of magic.

Sliding the Balisarda knife from its place by my heart, I scanned the revelers around us. Jean Luc shot me a wary glance. "Trouble?"

"Can't you smell it?" I murmured back. "It's faint, but it's there. They've already started."

He pulled his own Balisarda from the bandolier across his chest. His nostrils flared. "I'll alert the others."

He slipped through the crowd without another word. Though he also wore no uniform, the crowd still parted for him like the Red Sea for Moses. Probably the sapphire on his knife. Whispers followed him as he went, and some of the more astute revelers looked back at me. Their eyes widened. Realization sparked.

Chasseurs.

We'd suspected this attack. With each passing day, the witches grew more restless—which was why half my brethren lined the street in uniform, and the other half—the half dressed like me—hid in plain sight within the crowd. Waiting. Watching.

Hunting.

A middle-aged man stepped toward me. He held a little girl's hand. Same eye color. Similar bone structure. Daughter.

"Are we in danger here, sir?" More turned at his question. Brows furrowed. Eyes darted. The man's daughter winced, wrinkling her nose and dropping her flag. It hung in midair a second too long before fluttering to the ground.

"My head hurts, Papa," she whispered.

"Hush, child." He glanced down at the knife in my hand, and the tight muscles around his eyes relaxed. "This man is a Chasseur. He'll keep us safe. Isn't that right, sir?"

Unlike his daughter, he hadn't yet smelled the magic. But he would. Soon.

"You need to vacate the area immediately." My voice came out sharper than I'd intended. The little girl winced again, and her father wrapped an arm around her shoulders. The Archbishop's words reared in my head. *Soothe them, Reid. You must instill calm and confidence as well as protect.* I shook my head and tried again. "Please, *monsieur,* return home. Salt your doors and windows. Don't step out again until—"

A piercing scream cut through the rest of my words.

Everyone froze.

"GO!" I thrust the man and his daughter into the patisserie behind us. He'd barely stumbled through the door before others raced to follow, heedless of anyone standing in their way. Bodies collided in every direction. The screams around us multiplied, and unnatural laughter echoed from everywhere at once. I tucked my knife close to my side and barreled through the panicked revelers, tripping over an elderly woman.

"Careful." I gritted my teeth, catching her frail shoulders before she fell to her death. Milky eyes blinked up at me, and a slow, peculiar smile touched her withered lips.

"God bless you, young man," she croaked. Then she turned with unnatural grace and disappeared into the horde of people rushing past. It took several seconds for me to register the cloying, charred odor she left in her wake. My heart dropped like a stone.

"Reid!" Jean Luc stood in the royal family's carriage. Dozens of my brethren surrounded it, sapphires flashing as they drove frenzied citizens back. I started forward—but the throng before me shifted, and I finally saw them.

Witches.

They glided up the street with serene smiles, hair billowing in a nonexistent wind. Three of them. Laughing as bodies fell around them with the simplest flicks of their fingers.

Though I prayed their victims weren't dead, I often wondered whether death was the kinder fate. The less fortunate woke without memories of their second child, or perhaps with an insatiable appetite for human flesh. Last month, a child had been found without its eyes. Another man had lost his ability to sleep. Yet another spent the rest of his days pining after a woman no one else could see.

Each case different. Each more disturbing than the last.

"REID!" Jean Luc waved his arms, but I ignored him. Unease rapped just beyond conscious thought as I watched the witches advance on the royal family. Slowly, leisurely, despite the battalion of Chasseurs sprinting toward them. Bodies rose like marionettes, forming a human shield around the witches. I watched in horror as a man lunged forward and impaled himself on the Balisarda of one of my brothers. The witches cackled and continued contorting their fingers in unnatural ways. With each twitch, a helpless body rose. Puppeteers.

It didn't make sense. The witches operated in secrecy. They attacked from the shadows. Such conspicuousness on their part— such *showmanship*—was surely foolish. Unless . . .

Unless we'd lost sight of the bigger picture.

I charged toward the sandstone buildings to my right for a perch to see over the crowd. Gripping the wall with shaking fingers, I forced my limbs to climb. Each pitted stone loomed higher and higher than the last—blurry now. Spinning. My chest tightened. Blood pounded in my ears. *Don't look down. Keep looking up—*

A familiar mustachioed face appeared over the roof's edge. Blue-green eyes. Freckled nose. The girl from the patisserie.

"Shit," she said. Then she ducked out of sight.

I concentrated on the spot where she'd disappeared. My body moved with renewed purpose. Within seconds, I hauled myself over the ledge, but she was already leaping to the next rooftop. She clutched her hat with one hand and raised her middle finger with the other. I scowled. The little heathen wasn't my concern, despite her blatant disrespect.

I turned to peer below, clutching the ledge for support when the world tilted and spun.

People poured into the shops lining the streets. Too many. Far too many. The shopkeepers struggled to maintain order as those nearest the doors were trampled. The patisserie owner had suc- ceeded in barricading his own door. Those left outside shrieked and pounded on the windows as the witches moved closer.

I scanned the crowd for anything we'd missed. More than twenty bodies circled the air around the witches now—some unconscious, heads lolling, and others painfully awake. One man hung spread-eagled, as if shackled to an imaginary cross. Smoke billowed from his mouth, which opened and closed in silent screams. Another woman's clothes and hair floated around her as if she were underwater, and she clawed helplessly at the air. Face turning blue. Drowning.

With each new horror, more Chasseurs rushed forward.

I could see the fierce urge to protect on their faces even from a distance. But in their haste to aid the helpless, they'd forgotten our true mission: the royal family. Only four men now sur- rounded the carriage. Two Chasseurs. Two royal guards. Jean

Luc held the queen's hand as the king bellowed orders—to us, to his guard, to anyone who would listen—but the tumultuous noise swallowed every word.

At their back, insignificant in every way, crept the hag.

The reality of the situation punched through me, stealing my breath. The witches, the curses—they were all a performance. A *distraction*.

Not pausing to think, to acknowledge the terrifying distance to the ground, I grabbed the drainpipe and vaulted over the roof's edge. The tin screeched and buckled under my weight. Halfway down, it separated from the sandstone completely. I leapt—heart lodged firmly in my throat—and braced for impact. Jarring pain radiated up my legs as I hit the ground, but I didn't stop.

"Jean Luc! Behind you!"

He spun to look at me, eyes landing on the hag the same second mine did. Understanding dawned. "Get down!" He tackled the king to the carriage floor. The remaining Chasseurs dashed around the carriage at his shout.

The hag glanced over her hunched shoulder at me, the same peculiar grin spreading across her face. She flicked her wrist, and the cloying smell around us intensified. A blast of air shot from her fingertips, but the magic couldn't touch us. Not with our Balisardas. Each had been forged with a molten drop of Saint Constantin's original holy relic, rendering us immune to the witches' magic. I felt the sickly-sweet air rush past, but it did nothing to deter me. Nothing to deter my brethren.

The guards and citizens nearest us weren't so lucky. They

flew backward, smashing into the carriage and the shops lining the street. The hag's eyes flared with triumph when one of my brethren abandoned his post to help them. She moved swiftly—far too swiftly to be natural—toward the carriage door. Prince Beauregard's incredulous face appeared above it at the commotion. She snarled at him, mouth twisting. I tackled her to the ground before she could lift her hands.

She fought with the strength of a woman half her age—of a *man* half her age—kicking and biting and hitting every inch of me she could reach. But I was too heavy. I smothered her with my body, wrenched her hands above her head far enough to dislocate her shoulders. Pressed my knife to her throat.

She stilled as I lowered my mouth to her ear. The blade bit deeper. "May God have mercy on your soul."

She laughed then—a great, cackling laugh that shook her entire body. I frowned, leaning back—and froze. The woman beneath me was no longer a hag. I watched in horror as her ancient face melted into smooth, porcelain skin. As her brittle hair flowed thick and raven down her shoulders.

She stared up at me through hooded eyes, lips parting as she lifted her face to my own. I couldn't think—couldn't move, didn't know if I even *wanted* to—but somehow managed to jerk away before her lips brushed mine.

And that's when I felt it.

The firm, rounded shape of her belly pressed into my stomach.

Oh, God.

Every thought emptied from my head. I leapt backward—away from her, away from the *thing*—and scrambled to my feet. The screams in the distance faltered. The bodies on the ground stirred. The woman slowly stood.

Now clothed in deep bloodred, she placed a hand on her swollen womb and smiled.

Her emerald eyes flicked to the royal family, who crouched low in their carriage, pale and wide-eyed. Watching. "We *will* reclaim our homeland, Majesties," she crooned. "Time and time again, we have warned you. You did not heed our words. Soon, we will dance atop your ashes as you have our ancestors'."

Her eyes met mine. Porcelain skin sagged once more, and raven hair withered back to thin wisps of silver. No longer the beautiful, pregnant woman. Again the hag. She winked at me. The gesture was chilling on her haggard face. "We must do this again soon, handsome."

I couldn't speak. Never before had I seen such black magic—such desecration of the human body. But witches weren't human. They were vipers. Demons incarnate. And I had almost—

Her toothless grin widened as if she could read my mind. Before I could move—before I could unsheathe my blade and send her back to Hell where she belonged—she turned on her heel and disappeared in a cloud of smoke.

But not before blowing me a kiss.

Thick green carpet muffled my footsteps in the Archbishop's study hours later. Ornate wood paneling covered the windowless walls of the room. A fireplace cast flickering light on the papers strewn across his desk. Already seated behind it, the Archbishop gestured for me to sit in one of the wooden chairs opposite him.

I sat. Forced myself to meet his gaze. Ignored the burning humiliation in my gut.

Though the king and his family had escaped the parade unscathed, many others had not. Two had died—one girl at her brother's hand and the other at her own. Dozens more bore no visible injury but were currently strapped to beds two floors above. Screaming. Speaking in tongues. Staring at the ceiling without blinking. Vacant. The priests did what they could for them, but most would be transported to the asylum within a fortnight. There was only so much human medicine could do for those inflicted with witchcraft.

The Archbishop surveyed me over steepled fingers. Steely eyes. Harsh mouth. Silver streaks at his temples. "You did well today, Reid."

I frowned, shifting in my seat. "Sir?"

He smiled grimly and leaned forward. "If not for you, the casualties would have been much greater. King Auguste is indebted to you. He sings your praises." He gestured to a crisp envelope on his desk. "Indeed, he plans to hold a ball in your honor."

My shame burned hotter. Through sheer willpower, I managed to unclench my fists. I deserved no one's praise—not the king's, and especially not my patriarch's. I had failed them today. Broken the first rule of my brethren: *Thou shalt not suffer a witch to live.*

I had suffered four.

Worse—I'd actually—I'd wanted to—

I shuddered in my chair, unable to finish the thought. "I cannot accept, sir."

"And why not?" He arched a dark brow, leaning back once more. I shrank under his scrutiny. "You alone remembered your mission. You alone recognized the hag for what it was."

"Jean Luc—"

He waved an impatient hand. "Your humbleness is noted, Reid, but you mustn't assume false modesty. You saved lives today."

"I— Sir, I—" Choking on the words, I stared resolutely at my hands. They fisted in my lap once more.

As always, the Archbishop understood without explanation. "Ah . . . yes." His voice grew soft. I looked up to find him watching me with an inscrutable expression. "Jean Luc told me about your unfortunate encounter."

Though the words were mild, I heard the disappointment behind them. Shame reared and crashed within me once more. I ducked my head. "I'm sorry, sir. I don't know what came over me."

He heaved a great sigh. "Fret not, son. Wicked are the ways of women—and especially a witch. Their guile knows no bounds."

"Forgive me, sir, but I've never seen such magic before. The witch—it was a hag, but it . . . changed." I stared down at my fists again. Determined to get the words out. "It changed into a beautiful woman." I took a deep breath and looked up, jaw clenched. "A beautiful woman with child."

His lip curled. "The Mother."

"Sir?"

He rose to his feet, clasping his hands behind him, and began to pace. "Have you forgotten the sacrilegious teachings of the witches, Reid?"

I shook my head curtly, ears burning, and remembered the stern deacons of my childhood. The sparse classroom by the sanctuary. The faded Bible in my hands.

Witches do not worship our Lord and Savior, nor do they acknowledge the holy trinity of Father, Son, and Holy Spirit. They glorify another trinity—an idolatrous trinity. The Triple Goddess.

Even if I hadn't grown up in the Church, every Chasseur learned the witches' evil ideology before taking his vows.

"Maiden, Mother, and Crone," I murmured.

He nodded approvingly, and warm satisfaction spread through me. "An embodiment of femininity in the cycle of birth, life, and death . . . among other things. 'Tis blasphemous, of course." He scoffed and shook his head. "As if God could be a woman."

I frowned, avoiding his eyes. "Of course, sir."

"The witches believe their queen, La Dame des Sorcières, has been blessed by the goddess. They believe she—*it*—can shift into the forms of the trinity at will." He paused, mouth tightening as he looked at me. "Today, I believe you encountered La Dame des Sorcières herself."

I gaped at him. "Morgane le Blanc?"

He nodded curtly. "The very same."

"But, sir—"

"It explains the temptation. Your inability to control your

basest nature. La Dame des Sorcières is incredibly powerful, Reid, particularly in that form. The witches claim the Mother represents fertility, fulfillment, and . . . sexuality." His face twisted in disgust, as if the word left a bitter taste in his mouth. "A lesser man than you would have succumbed."

But I wanted to. My face burned hot enough to cause physical pain as silence descended between us. Footsteps sounded, and the Archbishop's hand came down on my shoulder. "Cast this from your mind, lest the creature poison your thoughts and corrupt your spirit."

I swallowed hard and forced myself to look at him. "I will not fail you again, sir."

"I know." No hesitation. No uncertainty. Relief swelled in my chest. "This life we have chosen—the life of self-restraint, of temperance—it is not without difficulties." He squeezed my shoulder. "We are human. From the dawn of time, this has been men's plight—to be tempted by women. Even within the perfection of the Garden of Eden, Eve seduced Adam into sin."

When I said nothing, he released my shoulder and sighed. Weary, now. "Take this matter to the Lord, Reid. Confess, and He will absolve you. And if . . . in time . . . you cannot overcome this affliction, perhaps we should procure you a wife."

His words struck my pride—my honor—like a blow. Anger coursed through me. Hard. Fast. Sickening. Only a handful of my brethren had taken wives since the king had commissioned our holy order, and most had eventually forsaken their positions and left the Church.

Still . . . there had once been a time I'd considered it. Yearned for it, even. But no longer.

"That won't be necessary, sir."

As if sensing my thoughts, the Archbishop continued warily. "I needn't remind you of your previous transgressions, Reid. You know very well the Church cannot force any man to vow celibacy—not even a Chasseur. As Peter said, 'If they cannot control themselves, let them marry: for it is better to marry than to burn with passion.' If it is your wish to marry, neither your brothers nor I can stop you." He paused, watching me closely. "Perhaps the young Mademoiselle Tremblay will still have you?"

Célie's face flared briefly in my mind at his words. Delicate. Beautiful. Her green eyes filled with tears. They'd soaked the black fabric of her mourning gown.

You cannot give me your heart, Reid. I cannot have it on my conscience.

Célie, please—

Those monsters who murdered Pip are still out there. They must be punished. I will not distract you from your purpose. If you must give away your heart, give it to your brotherhood. Please, please, forget me.

I could never forget you.

You must.

I shoved the memory away before it consumed me.

No. I would never marry. After the death of her sister, Célie had made that very clear.

"'But I say therefore to the unmarried and widows,'" I finished, my voice low and even, "'it is good for them if they abide even as I.'" I stared intently at my fists in my lap, still mourning a future—a family—I'd never see. "Please, sir . . . do not think I would ever risk my future within the Chasseurs by entering into matrimony. I wish nothing more than to please God . . . and you."

I glanced up at him then, and he offered me a grim smile. "Your devotion to the Lord pleases me. Now, fetch my carriage. I'm due at the castle for the prince's ball. Folly, if you ask me, but Auguste does spoil his son—"

A tentative knock on the door halted the rest of his words. His smile vanished at the sound, and he nodded once, dismissing me. I stood as he strode around his desk. "Come in."

A young, gangly initiate entered. Ansel. Sixteen. Orphaned as a baby, like me. I'd known him only briefly throughout childhood, though we'd both been raised in the Church. He'd been too young to keep company with me and Jean Luc.

He bowed, his right fist covering his heart. "I'm sorry to interrupt, Your Eminence." His throat bobbed as he extended a letter. "But you have a correspondence. A woman just came to the door. She believes a witch will be in West End tonight, sir, near Brindelle Park."

I froze. That was where Célie lived.

"A woman?" The Archbishop frowned and leaned forward, taking the letter. The seal had been pressed into the shape of a rose. He reached into his robes for a thin knife to open it. "Who?"

"I don't know, Your Eminence." Pink tinged Ansel's cheeks. "She had bright red hair and was very"—he coughed and stared at his boots—"very beautiful."

The Archbishop's frown deepened as he flicked open the

envelope. "It does not do to dwell on earthly beauty, Ansel," he chided, turning his attention to the letter. "I expect to see you at confession tomor—" His eyes widened at whatever he read there.

I stepped closer. "Sir?"

He ignored me, eyes still fixed on the page. I took another step toward him, and his head snapped up. He blinked rapidly. "I—" He shook his head and cleared his throat, turning his gaze back to the letter.

"Sir?" I repeated.

At the sound of my voice, he lurched to the fireplace and hurled the letter into the flames. "I am fine," he snapped, clasping his hands behind his back. They trembled. "Do not worry yourself."

But I did worry. I knew the Archbishop better than anyone— and he didn't shake. I stared into the fireplace, where the letter disintegrated into black ash. My hands curled into fists. If a witch had targeted Célie like Filippa, I would rip it limb from limb. It would beg for the flames before I finished with it.

As if sensing my gaze, the Archbishop turned to look at me. "Assemble a team, Captain Diggory." His voice was steadier now. Steelier. His gaze flicked back to the fireplace, and his expression hardened. "Though I sincerely doubt the validity of this woman's claim, we must uphold our vows. Search the area. Report back immediately."

I placed a fist over my heart, bowed, and moved toward the door, but his hand snaked out and caught my arm. It no longer trembled. "If a witch is indeed in West End, bring it back *alive*."

Nodding, I bowed once more. Resolute. A witch didn't need all its limbs to continue living. It didn't even need its head. Until burned, witches could reanimate. I'd break none of the Archbishop's rules. And if bringing back a witch *alive* would ease the Archbishop's sudden distress, I would bring back three. For him. For Célie. For *me*.

"Consider it done."

THE HEIST

Lou

We hastily donned our costumes in Soleil et Lune that night. Our safe haven and haunt, the theater's attic provided an endless repository of disguises—gowns, cloaks, wigs, shoes, and even undergarments of every size, shape, and color. Tonight, Bas and I strolled in the moonlight as a young couple in love—clothed in the rich, sumptuous fabrics of aristocrats—while Coco trailed behind as an escort.

I snuggled into his sinewy arm and cast him an adoring look. "Thank you for helping us."

"Ah, Louey, you know how I dislike that word. *Help* implies I'm doing you a favor."

I smirked, rolling my eyes. "God forbid you do anything from the goodness of your heart."

"There is no goodness in my heart." Winking roguishly, Bas pulled me closer and leaned down to whisper in my ear. His breath was too warm against my neck. "Only gold."

Right. I elbowed him in a seemingly innocent gesture and shifted away. After the nightmarish parade, we'd spent the greater part of the afternoon plotting our way through Tremblay's defenses, which we'd confirmed after a quick jaunt past his townhouse. Bas's cousin lived near Tremblay, so hopefully our presence hadn't roused suspicion.

It'd been just as Bas described: a gated lawn with guard rotations every five minutes. He assured me additional guards would be posted inside, as well as dogs trained to kill. Though Tremblay's staff would probably be asleep when we forced entry, they were an additional variable over which we had no control. And then there was the matter of locating the actual vault—a feat that could take days, let alone the few hours before Tremblay returned home.

Swallowing hard, I fidgeted with my wig—blond and piled high with pomade—and readjusted the velvet ribbon at my throat. Sensing my anxiety, Coco touched her hand to my back. "Don't be nervous, Lou. You'll be fine. The Brindelle trees will mask the magic."

I nodded and forced a smile. "Right. I know."

We lapsed into silence as we turned onto Tremblay's street, and the ethereal, spindly trees of Brindelle Park glowed softly beside us. Hundreds of years ago, the trees had served as a sacred grove to my ancestors. When the Church had seized control of Belterra, however, officials had attempted to burn them to the ground—and failed spectacularly. The trees had regrown with a vengeance. Within days, they'd towered above the land once more, and settlers had been forced to build around them. Their magic still reverberated through the ground beneath my feet, ancient and unchanged.

After a moment, Coco sighed and touched my back again. Almost reluctantly. "But you *do* need to be careful."

Bas whipped his head around to face her, brows furrowing. "Excuse you?"

She ignored him. "There's something . . . waiting for you at Tremblay's. It might be the ring, but it might be something else. I can't see it properly."

"What?" I lurched to a halt, spinning to face her. "What do you mean?"

She fixed me with a pained expression. "I told you. I can't *see* it. It's all hazy and unsettled, but something is definitely there." She paused, tilting her head as she considered me—or rather, as she considered something I couldn't see. Something warm and wet and flowing just beneath my skin. "It *could* be malevolent, but I don't think whatever it is will harm you. It's—it's definitely powerful, though."

"Why didn't you tell me this before?"

"Because I couldn't see it before."

"Coco, we've been planning this *all day*—"

"I don't make the rules, Lou," she snapped. "All I can see is what your blood shows me."

Despite Bas's protests, Coco had insisted on pricking our fingers before we'd left. I hadn't minded. As a Dame Rouge, Coco didn't channel her magic through the land like me and the other Dames Blanches. No, her magic came from within.

It came from blood.

Bas raked an agitated hand through his hair. "Perhaps we should have recruited another blood witch to our cause. Babette might have been better suited—"

"Like hell," Coco snarled.

"We can trust Babette as far as we can throw her," I added.

He regarded us curiously. "Yet you trusted her with knowledge of this critical mission—"

I snorted. "Only because we paid her."

"Plus, she owes me." With a look of disgust, Coco rearranged her cloak against the crisp autumn breeze. "I helped her acclimate to Cesarine when she left the blood coven, but that was over a year ago. I'm not willing to test her loyalty any further."

Bas nodded to them pleasantly, plastering on a smile and speaking through his teeth. "I suggest we postpone this conversation. I don't fancy being roasted on a spit tonight."

"*You* wouldn't roast," I muttered as we resumed our stroll. "You're not a witch."

"No," he conceded, nodding thoughtfully, "though it would be useful. I've always thought it unfair you females get to have all the fun."

Coco kicked a stray pebble at his back. "Because persecution is a real treat."

He turned to scowl at her, sucking on the tip of his forefinger, where her pinprick was still barely visible. "Always the victim, aren't you, darling?"

I elbowed him again. Harder this time. "Shut up, Bas."

When he opened his mouth to argue, Coco gave him a feline smile. "Careful. I still have your blood in my system."

He looked at her in outrage. "Only because you forced it from me!"

She shrugged, completely unabashed. "I needed to see if anything interesting would happen to you tonight."

"Well?" Bas glared at her expectantly. "Will there?"

"Wouldn't you like to know?"

"Unbelievable! Pray tell, what was the *point* of allowing you to suck my blood if you weren't planning on sharing—"

"I've already told you." She rolled her eyes, feigning boredom and examining a scar on her wrist. "I only see snippets, and the future is always shifting. Divination isn't really my forte. Now, my aunt, she can see thousands of possibilities with just a taste—"

"Fascinating. You can't imagine how much I enjoy these cozy little chats, but I'd rather *not* learn the specifics of divining the future from blood. I'm sure you understand."

"You were the one who said it would be useful to be a witch," I pointed out.

"I was being chivalrous!"

"Oh, please." Coco snorted and kicked another pebble at him, grinning when it hit him squarely in the chest. "You're the least chivalrous person I know."

He glared between us, trying and failing to quell our laughter. "So this is my reward for helping you. Perhaps I should return to my cousin's, after all."

"Oh, shut it, Bas." I pinched his arm, and he turned his baleful look on me. I stuck my tongue out at him. "You agreed to help us, and it's not like you aren't pocketing your share. Besides, she just had a drop. It'll be out of her system soon."

"It'd better be."

In response, Coco flicked a finger, and Bas cursed and jolted as if his pants had caught fire. "That *isn't funny*."

I laughed anyway.

Too soon, Tremblay's townhouse loomed before us. Built of pretty pale stone, it loomed over even its richly crafted neighbors, though it gave the distinct impression of opulence gone to seed. Green crept steadily up the foundation, and the wind whipped dead leaves across the gated lawn. Brown hydrangeas and roses dotted the flowerbeds—beside an outrageously exotic orange tree. The spoils of his black-market trade.

I wondered if Filippa had liked oranges.

"You have the sedative?" Bas whispered to Coco. She sidled up beside us and nodded, extricating a packet from her cloak. "Good. Are you ready, Lou?"

I ignored him and grabbed Coco's arm. "You're *sure* it won't kill the dogs?"

Bas growled impatiently, but Coco silenced him with another flick of her finger. She nodded once more before touching a sharp fingernail to her forearm. "A drop of my blood in the powder for each dog. It's just dried lavender," she added, lifting the packet. "It'll make them sleep."

I released her arm, nodding. "Right. Let's go."

Raising the hood of my cloak, I stole silently to the wrought-iron fence lining the property. Though I couldn't hear their footsteps, I knew the others crept after me, keeping close to the shadows of the hedgerow.

The lock on the gate was simple and strong, crafted from the same iron as the fence. I took a deep breath. I could do this. It'd been two years, but surely, *surely*, I could break one simple lock.

As I examined it, a shimmering gold cord drifted up from the ground and wrapped around it. The cord pulsed for only a second before snaking around my forefinger as well, linking us. I sighed in relief—then took a deep breath to steel my nerves. As if sensing my hesitation, two more cords appeared and floated to where Coco and Bas waited, disappearing into each of their chests. I scowled at the fiendish little things.

You can't get something for nothing, you know, a loathsome voice at the back of my head whispered. *A break for a break. Your bone for the lock . . . or perhaps your relationship. Nature demands balance.*

Nature could piss off.

"Is something wrong?" Bas edged forward cautiously, his eyes darting between me and the gate, but he couldn't see the golden cords as I did. The patterns existed solely within my mind. I turned to look at him, an insult already rising to my tongue.

You worthless coward. Of course I couldn't love you.

You've already fallen in love with yourself.

And you're terrible in bed.

With each word, the cord between him and the lock pulsed brighter. But—no. I moved before I could reconsider, twisting my forefinger sharply. Pain lanced through my hand. Through clenched teeth, I watched as the cords vanished, returning to the land in a whirl of golden dust. Savage satisfaction stole through me as the lock clicked open in response.

I'd done it.

The first phase of my job was complete.

I didn't pause to celebrate. Instead, I hastily swung the gate open—careful to avoid my forefinger, which now stuck out at an odd angle—and stepped aside. Coco streaked past me toward the front door, Bas following closely behind.

Earlier, we'd determined that Tremblay employed six guards to patrol the house. Three would be posted inside, but Bas would see to them. He had quite a skill with knives. I shuddered and crept onto the lawn. My outdoor targets would suffer a much kinder fate. Hopefully.

Not even a moment had passed before the first guard rounded the townhouse. I didn't bother hiding, instead throwing my hood back and welcoming his gaze. He spotted the open gate first and immediately reached for his sword. Suspicion and panic warred on his face as he scanned the yard for something amiss—and spotted me. Sending up a silent prayer, I smiled.

"Hello." A dozen voices spoke within my own, and the word came out strange and lovely, amplified by the lingering presence of my ancestors. Their ashes, long absorbed by the land until they *were* the land—and the air and the trees and the water— thrummed beneath me. Through me. My eyes shone brighter than usual. My skin glowed lustrous in the moonlight.

A dreamlike expression crossed the man's face as he looked at me, and the hand on his sword relaxed. I beckoned him closer. He obliged, walking toward me as if in a trance. Only a few steps away, he paused, still staring at me.

"Will you wait with me?" I asked in the same strange voice. He nodded. His lips parted slightly, and I felt his pulse quicken under my gaze. Singing to me. Sustaining me. We continued staring at one another until the second guard appeared. I flicked my gaze toward him and repeated the whole delicious process. By the time the third guard came around, my skin glowed brighter than the moon.

"You've been so kind." I extended my hands to them in supplication. They watched me greedily. "I'm so sorry for what I'm about to do."

I closed my eyes, concentrating, and gold exploded behind my eyelids in an infinite, intricate web. I caught one strand and followed it to a memory of Bas's face—to his scar, to the passionate evening we'd spent together. A trade. I clenched my hands into fists, and the memory vanished as the world tilted behind my eyelids. The guards fell to the ground, unconscious.

Disoriented, I opened my eyes slowly. The web dissipated. My stomach rolled, and I vomited into the hedge of roses.

I probably would've stayed there all night—sweating and puking at the onslaught of my repressed magic—had I not heard the soft whine of Tremblay's dogs. Coco must've found them. Wiping my mouth on my sleeve, I mentally shook myself and crept toward the front door. Tonight was not the night for squeamishness.

Silence cloaked the inside of the townhouse. Wherever Bas and Coco had gone, I couldn't hear them. Creeping farther into the foyer, I took stock of my surroundings: the dark walls, the fine furniture, the countless trinkets. Large rugs in tawdry patterns covered mahogany floors, and crystal bowls, tasseled pillows, and velvet poufs littered every surface. All very boring, in my opinion. Cluttered. I longed to rip the heavy curtains from their rods and let in the silver light of the moon.

"Lou." Bas's hiss emanated from the stairwell, and I nearly

jumped out of my skin. Coco's warning reared to life with terrifying clarity. *There's something waiting for you at Tremblay's.* "Quit daydreaming, and get up here."

"I'm technically *night* dreaming." Ignoring the chill down my spine, I half sprinted to join him.

To my surprise—and delight—Bas had found a lever on the frame of a large portrait in Tremblay's study: a young woman with piercing green eyes and pitch-black hair. I touched her face apologetically. "Filippa. How predictable."

"Yes." Bas flicked the lever, and the portrait swung outward, revealing the vault behind. "Idiocy is oft mistaken for sentimentality. This is the first place I looked." He gestured to the lock. "Can you pick it?"

I sighed, glancing down at my broken finger. "Can't you pick it instead?"

"Just do it," he said impatiently, "and quickly. The guards could wake up any moment."

Right. I shot the golden cord spreading between myself and the lock a nasty look before going to work. It appeared quicker this time, as if waiting for me. Though I bit my lip hard enough to draw blood, a small groan still escaped as I snapped a second finger. The lock clicked, and Bas swung the vault open.

Inside, Tremblay had stacked a slew of tedious items. Pushing aside his seal, legal documents, letters, and stock, Bas eyed the pile of jewelry beyond them hungrily. Rubies and garnets, mostly, though I spied a particularly attractive diamond necklace. The entire box glittered with the golden *couronnes* lining its walls.

I swept it all aside impatiently, heedless of Bas's protests. If

Tremblay had been lying, if he *didn't* have the ring—

At the back of the vault lay a small leather album. I tore it open—vaguely recognizing sketches of girls who had to be Filippa and her sister—before a gold ring tumbled out from between the pages. It landed on the carpet without a sound, unremarkable in every way except the flickering, nearly indiscernible pulse that tugged at my chest.

Breath catching in my throat, I crouched to pick it up. It was warm in my palm. Real. Tears pricked at my eyes, threatening to spill over. Now she'd never find me. I was . . . safe. Or as safe as I'd ever be.On my finger, the ring would dispel enchantments. In my mouth, it would render me invisible. I didn't know why—a quirk of the magic, perhaps, or of Angelica herself—but I also didn't care. I'd break my teeth on the metal if it kept me hidden.

"Did you find it?" Bas stuffed the last of the jewelry and *couronnes* into his bag and looked at the ring expectantly. "Not much to look at, is it?"

Three sharp raps echoed from downstairs. A warning. Bas's eyes narrowed, and he crept to the window to peer out at the lawn. I slipped the ring onto my finger while his back was turned. It seemed to emit a soft sigh at the contact.

"Shit!" Bas turned, eyes wild, and all thoughts of the ring fled my mind. "We have company."

I ran to the window. The constabulary swarmed across the lawn toward the manor, but that wasn't what made genuine fear stab at my stomach. No, it was the blue coats that accompanied them.

Chasseurs.

Shit. Shit, shit, *shit*.

Why were *they* here?

Tremblay, his wife, and his daughter huddled next to the guards I'd left unconscious. I cursed myself for not hiding them somewhere. A clumsy mistake, but I'd been disoriented from the magic. Out of practice.

To my horror, one of the guards had already begun to stir. I had little doubt what he would tell the Chasseurs when he regained full consciousness.

Bas was already moving, slamming the safe shut and hauling the portrait back into place. "Can you get us out?" His eyes were still wide with panic—desperate. We could both hear the constables and Chasseurs surrounding the manor. All the exits would soon be blocked.

I glanced down at my hands. They were shaking, and not just because of the broken fingers. I was weak, *too* weak, from the exertion of the evening. How had I let myself become so inept? The risk of discovery, I reminded myself. The risk had been too great—

"Lou!" Bas grabbed my shoulders and shook me slightly. "Can you get us out?"

Tears welled in my eyes. "No," I breathed. "I can't."

He blinked, chest rising and falling rapidly. The Chasseurs shouted something below, but it didn't matter. All that mattered was the decision made in Bas's eyes as we stared at one another. "Right." He squeezed my shoulders once. "Good luck."

Then he turned and dashed from the room.

A MAN'S NAME

Reid

Tremblay's townhouse reeked of magic. It coated the lawn, clung to the prone guards Tremblay attempted to revive. A tall, middle-aged woman knelt beside him. Redheaded. Striking. Though I didn't recognize her, my brethren's whispers confirmed my suspicions.

Madame Labelle. Notorious courtesan, and mistress of the Bellerose.

Surely she had no business here.

"Captain Diggory."

I turned toward the strained voice behind me. A reedy blonde stood with her hands tightly clasped, an expensive wedding band glinting on her ring finger. Frown lines marred the corners of her eyes—eyes that currently burned holes in the back of Madame Labelle's head.

Tremblay's wife.

"Hello, Captain Diggory." Célie's soft voice preceded her as she stepped around her mother. I swallowed hard. She was still clothed in mourning black, her green eyes stark in the torchlight. Swollen. Red. Tears sparkled on her cheeks. I longed to close the distance between us and wipe them away. To wipe this whole nightmarish scene—so like the night we'd found Filippa—away.

"Mademoiselle Tremblay." I inclined my head instead, keenly aware of my brethren's eyes. Of Jean Luc's. "You look . . . well."

A lie. She looked miserable. Afraid. She'd lost weight since I last saw her. Her face was drawn, pinched, as if she hadn't slept in months. I hadn't either.

"Thank you." A small smile at the lie. "You do too."

"I apologize for these circumstances, *mademoiselle*, but I assure you, if a witch is responsible, it will burn."

I glanced back at Tremblay. He and Madame Labelle were bent close together, and they appeared to be in harried conversation with the guards. Frowning, I stepped closer. Madame Tremblay cleared her throat and turned her indignant eyes on me.

"I assure you, sir, you and your esteemed order are not necessary here. My husband and I are God-fearing citizens, and we do not abide witchcraft—"

Beside me, Jean Luc bowed his head. "Of course not, Madame Tremblay. We are here only as a precaution."

"Though your guards were unconscious, *madame*," I pointed out. "And your home reeks of magic."

Jean Luc sighed and shot me an irritated look.

"It *always* smells like this here." Madame Tremblay's eyes narrowed, and her lips pressed into a thin line. Displeased. "It's that beastly park. It poisons the entire street. If it weren't for the view of the Doleur, we would move tomorrow."

"My apologies, *madame*. All the same—"

"We understand." Jean Luc stepped in front of me with a placating smile. "And we apologize for the alarm. Usually, robberies fall under the constabulary's jurisdiction, but . . ." He hesitated, smile faltering. "We received an anonymous tip that a witch would be here tonight. We'll just do a quick sweep of the premises, and you and your family may safely return to your home—"

"Captain Diggory, Chasseur Toussaint." The voice that interrupted was warm. Smooth. Intimate. We turned as one to see Madame Labelle striding toward us. Tremblay hurried to follow, leaving the disoriented guards behind. "We've just spoken with the guards." She smiled, revealing bright white teeth. They nearly glowed against her scarlet lips. "The poor dears don't remember anything, unfortunately."

"If you don't mind me asking, Helene," Madame Tremblay said through clenched teeth, "what business do you have here?"

Madame Labelle turned to her with polite disinterest. "I was passing and saw a disturbance, of course."

"Passing? Whatever were you doing in *this* part of town, dear? One would expect you might have, ah, *business* to attend to on your own street at this hour of night."

Madame Labelle arched a brow. "You're quite right." Her smile widened, and she glanced at Tremblay before returning his wife's icy stare. "I *do* have business to attend to."

Célie stiffened, bowing her head, and Tremblay hastened to intervene before his wife could respond. "You are, of course, welcome to question my staff yourselves, good sirs."

"Don't worry, Monsieur Tremblay. We will." Glaring at him for Célie's sake, I raised my voice to the constabulary and Chasseurs. "Spread out and form a perimeter. Block all exits. Constables, partner yourselves with a Chasseur. If this *is* a witch, do not allow it to catch you defenseless."

"It isn't a witch," Madame Tremblay insisted, glancing around anxiously. Lights in neighboring townhouses began to flicker on. Already a handful of people had appeared by the broken gate. Some wore nightclothes. Others wore finery similar to the Tremblays'. All wore familiar, wary expressions. "It's just a thief. That's all—"

She stopped abruptly, her eyes flicking toward the townhouse. I followed her gaze to an upstairs window. A curtain moved, and two faces peered out.

One of them was familiar, despite the wig. Blue-green eyes—vivid even at a distance—widened in panic. The curtain snapped shut.

Satisfaction spread through my chest, and I allowed a grin. *Let justice roll on like a river, and righteousness like a never-failing stream.*

"What is it?" Jean Luc looked toward the window too.

Justice.

"They're still here—a man and a woman."

He drew his Balisarda with a flourish. "I'll dispatch the woman quickly."

I frowned, remembering the woman's mustache. Her baggy trousers and rolled shirtsleeves and freckles. The way she'd smelled when she'd crashed into me at the parade—like vanilla and cinnamon. Not magic. I shook my head abruptly. But witches didn't always *smell* evil. Only when they'd been practicing. The Archbishop had been clear in our training—every woman was a potential threat. Even so . . . "I don't think she's a witch."

Jean Luc lifted a black brow, nostrils flaring. "No? Surely it isn't coincidence we received a tip on this particular night— before these particular thieves robbed this particular home."

Scowling, I looked back at the window. "I met her this morning. She—" I cleared my throat, heat creeping up my cheeks. "She didn't seem like a witch."

The excuse fell flat, even to my own ears. Célie's eyes burned on my neck.

"Ah. She can't be a witch because she didn't *seem* like one. My mistake, of course."

"She was wearing a mustache," I muttered. When Jean Luc scoffed, I resisted the urge to flatten him. He knew Célie was watching. "We can't discount Brindelle Park next door. It's possible the man and woman are simply thieves, despite the circumstances. They could deserve prison. Not the stake."

"Very well." Jean Luc rolled his eyes and marched toward the door without my order. "Let's hurry this up, then, shall we? We'll interrogate the two of them and decide—prison or the stake."

Gritting my teeth at his insolence, I nodded to the constabulary, and they hurried after him. I didn't follow. Instead, I kept my gaze trained on the window—and the rooftop. When she didn't reappear, I crept around the side of the house, waiting. Though

Célie's presence was an open flame on my back, I did my best to ignore it. She'd wanted me to focus on the Chasseurs. That was what I needed to do.

Another moment passed. And another.

A small cellar door obscured by hydrangeas flew open to my right. Jean Luc and a man with amber skin barreled out of it, knives flashing in the moonlight. They rolled once before Jean Luc landed on top, knife pressed to the man's throat. Three constables burst from the cellar door after them with handcuffs and rope. Within seconds, they had his wrists and ankles bound. He snarled and twisted, shouting a tirade of curses. And one other word.

"Lou!" He pulled uselessly at his bonds, face purpling with rage. One of the constables moved to gag him. "LOU!"

Lou. A man's name. It figured.

I continued on, still searching the windows and roofline. Sure enough, I soon spotted a slight shadow moving up the wall. Slowly. I looked closer. This time, she wore a cloak. It parted as she climbed, revealing a dress as fine as Madame Tremblay's. Probably stolen. But it wasn't the dress that seemed to cause her problems.

It was her hand.

Each time it touched the wall, she drew it back sharply, as if in pain. I squinted, trying to locate the source of the problem, but she was too high. *Much* too high. As if in response to my fear, her foot slipped, and she plummeted several feet before catching herself on a window ledge. My stomach dropped with her.

"Oi!" I rushed forward. Footsteps sounded as the Chasseurs and constabulary closed in behind me. Jean Luc shoved the bound man to the ground at my feet. "You're surrounded! We already have your boyfriend! Come down now before you kill yourself!"

She slipped and caught herself again. This time, her wig tumbled to the ground, revealing long brown hair. Inexplicably furious, I lurched forward. "Come down RIGHT NOW—"

The man managed to work the gag from his mouth. "LOU, HELP ME—"

A constable wrestled to gag him once more. The woman paused at his voice, perching in a window, and glanced down at us. Her face lit with recognition when she saw me, and she lifted her good hand to her forehead in mock salute.

I stared at her, dumbfounded.

She'd actually *saluted*.

My hands curled into fists. "Go up and get her."

Jean Luc scowled at the command, but he still nodded. "Chasseurs—with me." My brethren surged forward, drawing their Balisardas. "Constables—on the ground. Don't let her escape."

If the other Chasseurs questioned why I remained on the ground, they said nothing. Wisely. But that didn't stop the constabulary's curious stares.

"What?" I snapped, glaring at them. They hastily resumed staring at the roof. "Was anyone else inside?"

After several long seconds, one of them stepped forward. I

vaguely recognized him. Dennis. No—Davide. "Yes, Captain. Geoffrey and I found someone in the kitchen."

"And?"

Another constable—presumably Geoffrey—cleared his throat. The two shared an anxious look, and Geoffrey swallowed hard. "She escaped."

I expelled a harsh breath.

"We think she's your witch, though," Davide added hopefully. "She smelled like magic, sort of, and—and she poisoned the dogs. They had blood on their maws, and they smelled . . . strange."

"If it helps, she was, well—*scarred*," Geoffrey said. Davide nodded earnestly.

I turned toward the roof without another word, forcing myself to unclench my fists. To breathe.

It wasn't Davide or Geoffrey's fault. They weren't trained to handle witches. And yet—perhaps *they* could explain their incompetence to the Archbishop. Perhaps they could accept the punishment. The shame. Another witch free. Another witch left to plague the innocent people of Belterra. To plague Célie.

Through a haze of red, I trained my eyes on the thief.

Lou.

She would tell me where the witch went. I would force the information from her, no matter what it took. I *would* fix this.

Even with her injured hand, she still managed to outclimb the Chasseurs. She reached the roofline before the others had even cleared the first story. "Spread out!" I roared to the constabulary. They scattered at my command. "She has to come down somewhere! That tree—cover it! And the drainpipes! Find any-thing she could use to make an escape!"

I waited, pacing and seething, as my brethren scaled steadily higher. Their voices drifted down to me. Threatening her. Good. She consorted with witches. She deserved to fear us.

"Any sign?" I called to the constabulary.

"Not here, Captain!"

"Not here either!"

"None, sir!"

I bit back an impatient growl. Finally—after what seemed an eternity—Jean Luc hoisted himself over the rooftop after her. Three of my brethren followed. I waited. And waited.

And waited.

Davide shouted behind me, and I whirled to see the bound thief halfway to the road. He'd somehow worked the ropes from his feet. Though the constables sprinted toward him, they'd spread themselves too far across the yard on my orders. Biting back a curse, I leapt after him, but Jean Luc's shout made me falter.

"She's not here!" He appeared back at the roofline, chest heaving. Even from a distance, I could see the anger in his eyes. It matched my own. "She's gone!"

With a snarl of frustration, I scanned the street for the man.

But he too had disappeared.

ANGELICA'S RING

Lou

I could still hear the Chasseurs as I sprinted down the street, staring at the place where my feet—and my legs and my *body*—should've been. They couldn't understand where I'd gone. I hardly understood it myself.

One second, I'd been trapped on the roof, and the next, Angelica's Ring had burned hot on my finger. *Of course.* In my panic, I'd forgotten what the ring could *do*. Without stopping to think, I'd slid the ring off my finger and stuck it in my mouth.

My body had vanished.

Climbing up the townhouse with an audience and two broken fingers had been difficult. Climbing down with an audience, two broken fingers, and a ring clenched between my teeth—invisible—had been almost impossible. Twice I'd almost swallowed the thing, and once I'd been certain a Chasseur heard me when I torqued my broken fingers.

Still, I'd done it.

If the Chasseurs hadn't thought I was a witch before—if by some miracle, the guards hadn't squealed—they certainly suspected it now. I'd need to be careful. The copper-haired Chass knew my face, and thanks to Bas's idiocy, he also knew my name. He would search for me.

Others far more dangerous might hear and begin searching for me too.

When I was far enough away to feel relatively safe, I spat the ring from my mouth. My body immediately reappeared as I slid it back on my finger.

"Neat trick," Coco mused.

I whirled at the sound of her voice. She leaned against the dirty brick of the alleyway, eyebrow arched, and nodded to the ring. "I see you found Tremblay's vault." When I glanced toward the street, hesitating, she laughed. "Don't worry. Our muscled blue friends are currently tearing Tremblay's townhouse apart brick by brick. They're far too busy looking for you to actually find you."

I chuckled but stopped quickly, looking back at the ring with awe. "I can't believe we actually found it. The witches would riot if they knew I had it."

Coco followed my gaze, brows furrowing slightly. "I know what the ring can do, but you've never told me why your kin revere it. Surely there are other objects more—I don't know—powerful?"

"This is Angelica's Ring."

She stared at me blankly.

"You're a witch." I returned her befuddled stare. "You haven't heard the story of Angelica?"

She rolled her eyes. "I'm a red, in case you'd forgotten. Forgive me for not learning your cultic superstitions. Was she a relative of yours or something?"

"Well, yes," I said impatiently. "But that's not the point. She was really just a lonely witch who fell in love with a knight."

"Sounds dashing."

"He was. He gave her this ring as a promise of marriage . . . then he died. Angelica was so devastated that her tears flooded the land and created a new sea. L'Eau Mélancolique, they called it."

"The Wistful Waters." Coco lifted my hand, scorn giving way to grudging admiration as she examined the ring. I slid it off my finger and held it out to her in my palm. She didn't take it. "What a beautiful, terrible name."

I nodded grimly. "It's a beautiful, terrible place. When Angelica had cried all her tears, she threw the ring into the waters and herself after it. She drowned. When the ring resurfaced, it was infused with all sorts of magic—"

Raucous voices sounded from the street, and I stopped talking abruptly. A group of men passed by, singing a pub song loudly and off-key. We shrank farther into the shadows.

When their voices faded, I relaxed. "How did you escape?"

"Through a window." At my expectant stare, she grinned. "The captain and his minions were too concerned with you to notice me."

"Well, then." I pursed my lips and leaned against the wall beside her. "I suppose you're welcome. How did you manage to find me?"

She lifted her sleeve. A web of scars marred her arms and wrists, and a fresh cut down her forearm still oozed. A mark for every bit of magic she'd ever done. From the little Coco had taught me about Dames Rouges, I knew their blood was a powerful ingredient in most enchantments, but I didn't understand it. Unlike Dames Blanches, they weren't bound to any laws or rules. Their magic didn't demand balance. It could be wild, unpredictable . . . and some of my kin even called it dangerous.

But I'd seen what the Dames Blanches themselves could do. Filthy hypocrites.

Coco arched a brow at my appraisal and rubbed some blood between her fingers. "Do you really want to know?"

"I think I can guess." I sighed and slid down the wall to sit on the street, closing my eyes.

She joined me, her leg resting companionably against my own. After a few seconds of silence, she nudged me with her knee, and I forced an eye open. Hers were unnaturally serious. "The constabulary saw me, Lou."

"What?" I lurched forward, eyes fully open now. "How?"

She shrugged. "I waited around to make sure you escaped. I was lucky it was the constabulary, really. They nearly pissed down their legs when they realized I was a witch. Made climbing out the window easier."

Shit. My heart sank miserably. "Then the Chasseurs know too. They're probably already looking for you. You need to get out of the city as soon as possible—tonight. Now. Send word to your aunt. She'll find you."

"They'll be looking for *you* now too. Even if you hadn't disappeared without a trace, they know you've consorted with a witch." She leaned forward and wrapped her arms around her knees, heedless of the blood on her arm. It smeared her skirt red. "What's your plan?"

"I don't know," I admitted quietly. "I have Angelica's Ring. It'll have to do."

"You need protection." Sighing, she took my good hand in her own. "Come with me. My aunt will—"

"Kill me."

"I won't let her." She shook her head fiercely, and the curls around her face bobbed. "You know how she feels about La Dame des Sorcières. She'd never help the Dames Blanches."

I knew better than to argue, instead sighing heavily.

"Others might. It would only be a matter of time before one of your coven stabbed me in my sleep—or turned me over to *her*."

Coco's eyes flashed. "I'd tear out her throat."

I smiled ruefully. "It's my own throat I'm worried about."

"So what then?" She dropped my hand and pushed to her feet. "You're just going back to Soleil et Lune?"

"For now." I shrugged as if unconcerned, but the movement felt too stiff to be convincing. "No one but Bas knows I live there, and he managed to escape."

"I'll stay with you."

"No. I won't let you burn for me."

"Lou—"

"No."

She huffed impatiently. "Fine. It's your own neck. Just . . . let me mend your fingers, at least."

"No more magic. Not tonight."

"But—"

"Coco." I stood and took her hand gently, tears pricking my eyes. We both knew she was stalling. "I'll be fine. It's just a couple of broken fingers. *Go.* Take care of yourself."

She sniffed, tipping her face back in a losing effort to contain her tears. "Only if you do."

We hugged briefly, neither of us willing to say goodbye. Goodbyes were final, and we would see each other again someday. Though I didn't know when or where, I would make sure of it.

Without another word, she released me and melted into the shadows.

I hadn't even left the alley when two large figures stepped in my path. I cursed as they pushed me none too gently into the alley wall. Andre and Grue. Of course. Though I struggled against them, it was pointless. They outweighed me by several hundred pounds.

"How you doing, sweet thing?" Andre leered. He was shorter than Grue, with a long, narrow nose and far too many teeth. They crowded his mouth, yellow and chipped and uneven. Gagging at his breath, I leaned away, but Grue buried his nose in my hair.

"Mmm. You smell good, Lou Lou." I smashed my head into his face in response. His nose crunched, and he staggered backward, swearing violently, before lunging for my throat. "You little bitch—"

I kicked his knee, simultaneously elbowing Andre in the gut. When his grip loosened, I darted toward the street, but he caught my cloak at the last second. My feet flew out from under me, and I landed on the cobblestones with a painful thud. He kicked me over to my stomach, pinning me there with a boot on my spine.

"Give us the ring, Lou."

Though I twisted beneath him to upset his balance, he only pushed harder. Sharp pain radiated up my back. "I don't have—" He reached down before I could finish, smashing my face into the ground. My nose cracked, and blood spurted sickeningly into my mouth. I choked on it, stars bursting in my eyes, and fought to remain conscious. "The constabulary busted us, you asshole!" An unpleasant realization dawned. "Was it *you*? Did you bastards snitch?"

Grue snarled and rose to his feet, still clutching his knee. His bulbous nose bled freely down his chin. Despite the blinding pain, vindictive pleasure stole through me. I knew better than to smirk, but it was hard—*so hard*—to restrain myself.

"I ain't no snitch. Search her, Andre."

"If you touch me again, I swear I'll rip out your fucking eyes—"

"I don't think you can issue threats, Lou Lou." Andre yanked my hair back, extending my throat, and caressed my jaw with his knife. "And I think I'll take my time searching you. Every nook and cranny. You could be hiding it anywhere."

A memory surfaced with crystalline focus.

My throat over a basin. Everything white.

Then red.

I exploded beneath him in a blur of limbs and nails and teeth, clawing and biting and kicking every bit of him I could reach. He stumbled backward with a cry—his blade nicking my chin—but I didn't feel the sting as I swept it aside. Didn't feel anything—the breath in my lungs, the tremble of my hands, the tears on my face. I didn't stop until my fingers found his eyes.

"Wait! Please!" He forced them closed, but I kept pressing, curling my knuckles beneath the lids and into the sockets. "I'm sorry! I—I believe you!"

"Stop!" Grue's footsteps pounded behind me. "Stop, or I'll—"

"If you touch me, I'll blind him."

His footsteps stopped abruptly, and I heard him swallow. "You—Just give us something for our silence, Lou. Something for our trouble. I know you pinched more than a ring from that knob."

"I don't have to give you anything." Backing toward the street slowly, I kept one hand pressed firmly against Andre's neck. The other remained lodged in his eyeball. With each step, sensation returned to my limbs. To my mind. My broken fingers screamed. I blinked rapidly, swallowing the bile in my throat. "Don't follow me, or I'll finish what I started here."

Grue didn't move. Andre actually whimpered.

When I reached the street, I didn't hesitate. Shoving Andre toward Grue's outstretched arms, I turned and fled to Soleil et Lune.

I didn't stop to stanch the bleeding or set my fingers until I was safe in the theater's rafters. Though I didn't have any water to wash my face, I smeared the blood around a bit until most of it was on my dress instead of my skin. My fingers were already stiff, but I bit down on my cloak and set the bones anyway, using a piece of boning from a discarded corset as a splint.

Though exhausted, I couldn't sleep. Every noise made me flinch, and the attic was too dark. A single, broken window—my only means of entry—let in the moonlight. I curled up beneath it and tried to ignore the throbbing in my face and hand. For a brief moment, I contemplated climbing to the roof. I'd spent many nights up there above the city, craving the stars on my cheeks and the wind in my hair.

But not tonight. The Chasseurs and constabulary were still searching for me. Worse, Coco was gone and Bas had abandoned me at the first sign of trouble. I closed my eyes in misery. What a rotten mess.

At least I'd procured the ring—and *she* hadn't found me yet. This thought alone gave me enough comfort to eventually drift into an uneasy sleep.

TWO NAMED WRATH AND ENVY

Reid

The clashes of swords filled the training yard. Late-morning sun bore down on us—chasing away the autumn chill—and sweat poured from my forehead. Unlike the other Chasseurs, I hadn't discarded my shirt. It clung to my chest, wet fabric chafing my skin. Punishing me.

I'd let another witch escape, too distracted with the freckled thief to realize a demon had been waiting inside. Célie had been devastated. She hadn't been able to look at me when her father finally steered her inside. Heat washed over me at the memory. Another failure.

Jean Luc had been the first to discard his shirt. We'd been sparring for hours, and his brown skin glistened with sweat. Welts covered his chest and arms—one for every time he'd opened his mouth. "Still thinking about your witches, Captain? Or perhaps Mademoiselle Tremblay?"

I smashed my wooden sword into his arm in response. Blocked his counterstrike and elbowed him in the stomach. Hard. Two more welts joined the others. I hoped they'd bruise.

"I'll take that as a yes." Doubling over to clutch his stomach, he still managed to smirk up at me. I obviously hadn't hit him hard enough. "I wouldn't worry. Everyone will forget the townhouse fiasco soon."

I clenched my sword until my knuckles turned white. A tic started in my jaw. It wouldn't do to attack my oldest friend. Even if that friend was a miserable little—

"You did save the royal family, after all." He straightened, still clutching his side, and grinned wider. "To be fair, you also humiliated yourself with that witch. I can't say I understand it. Fatherhood isn't particularly my taste—but the thief last night? Now *she* was a pretty little thing—"

I lunged forward, but he blocked my advance, laughing and punching my shoulder. "Peace, Reid. You know I jest."

His jests had grown less funny since my promotion.

Jean Luc had arrived on the church's doorstep when we were three. Every memory I had included him in some form or another. Ours had been a joint childhood. We'd shared the same bedroom. The same acquaintances. The same anger.

Our respect had also once been mutual. But that was before.

I stepped away, and he made a show of wiping my sweat on his pants. A few of our brethren laughed. They stopped abruptly at my expression. "Every jest holds truth."

He inclined his head, still grinning. Pale green eyes missing nothing. "Perhaps . . . but does our Lord not command us to lay aside falsehood?" He didn't pause for me to answer. He never did.

"'Speak truth, each one of you,' he says, 'for we are members of one another.'"

"I know the scripture."

"Then why silence my truth?"

"You talk too much."

He laughed harder, opening his mouth to dazzle us with his wit once more, but Ansel interrupted, breathing heavily. Sweat matted his unruly hair, and blood flushed his cheeks. "Just because something *can* be said doesn't mean it *should*. Besides," he said, risking a glance at me. "Reid wasn't the only one at the parade yesterday. Or the townhouse."

I stared at the ground resolutely. Ansel should've known better than to intervene. Jean Luc surveyed the two of us with unabashed interest, sticking his sword in the ground and leaning against it. Running his fingers through his beard. "Yes, but he seems to be taking it particularly hard, doesn't he?"

"Someone ought to." The words left my mouth before I could stop them. I ground my teeth and turned away before I could do or say anything else I'd regret.

"Ah." Jean Luc's eyes lit up, and he straightened eagerly, sword and beard forgotten. "There's the rub, isn't it? You disappointed the Archbishop. Or was it Célie?"

One.

Two.

Three.

Ansel looked between us nervously. "We all did."

"Perhaps." Jean Luc's smile vanished, and his sharp eyes

glinted with an emotion I wouldn't name. "Yet Reid alone is our captain. Reid alone enjoys the privileges of the title. Perhaps it is fair and just for Reid alone to bear the consequences."

I threw my sword on the rack.

Four.

Five.

Six.

I forced a deep breath, willing the anger in my chest to dissipate. The muscle in my jaw still twitched.

Seven.

You are in control. The Archbishop's voice drifted back to me from childhood. *This anger cannot govern you, Reid. Breathe deeply. Count to ten. Master yourself.*

I complied. Slowly, surely, the tension in my shoulders eased. The heat on my face cooled. My breath came easier. I clasped Jean Luc's shoulder, and his smile faltered. "You're right, Jean. It was my fault. I take full responsibility."

Before he could respond, the Archbishop stepped into the training yard. His steely eyes found mine, and I immediately fisted my hand over my heart and bowed. The others followed.

The Archbishop inclined his head in response. "As you were, Chasseurs." We rose as one. When he motioned for me to come closer, Jean Luc's frown deepened. "Word has spread throughout the Tower of your foul mood this morning, Captain Diggory."

"I'm sorry, sir."

He waved a hand. "Apologize not. Your toil is not in vain. We shall catch the witches, and we shall burn their pestilence from the earth." He frowned slightly. "Last night was not your fault." Jean Luc's eyes flashed, but the Archbishop didn't notice. "I am required to attend a matinee performance this morning with one of the king's foreign dignitaries. Though I do not condone theater—for it is a vile practice befitting only vagrants and scoundrels—you will accompany me."

I wiped the sweat from my forehead. "Sir—"

"It wasn't a request. Wash up. Be ready to leave within the hour."

"Yes, sir."

The unnamed emotion in Jean Luc's eyes bored into my back as I followed the Archbishop inside. It was only later—sitting in the carriage outside Soleil et Lune—that I allowed myself to name it. Allowed myself to feel the bitter sting of regret.

Our respect had once been mutual. But that was before the envy.

A MUTUALLY BENEFICIAL ARRANGEMENT

Lou

By the time I woke the next morning, dusty rays of sunlight shone through the attic window. I blinked slowly, lost in the pleasant moment between sleeping and waking where there is no memory. But my subconscious chased me. Noises reverberated from the theater below as cast and crew called to one another, and excited voices drifted in from the window. I frowned, still clinging to the remnants of sleep.

The theater was rather noisy this morning.

I lurched upright. Soleil et Lune performed a matinee every Saturday. How could I have forgotten?

My face gave a particularly painful throb as I threw myself down on our bed. Oh, right—that's how. My nose had been smashed to bits, and I'd been forced to flee for my life.

The noise downstairs heightened as the overture began.

I groaned. Now I'd be stuck here until the performance was over, and I desperately needed to pee. Usually, it wasn't a problem to sneak downstairs to the toilet before the cast and crew arrived, but I'd overslept. Climbing to my feet, wincing at the dull pain in my back, I assessed the damage quickly. My nose was definitely broken, and my fingers had swollen to twice their size overnight. But I wore a fine enough dress to pass by the patrons unnoticed ... except for the bloodstains. I licked my good fingers and scrubbed at the stains furiously, but the fabric remained irrevocably red.

With an impatient sigh, I glanced between the racks of dusty costumes and the trunk beside the bed I shared with Coco. Wool pants, scarves, mittens, and shawls spilled out of it, along with a couple of moldy blankets we'd found in the garbage last week. I touched Coco's side of the bed gingerly.

I hoped she'd made it to her aunt safely.

Shaking my head, I turned back to the rack of costumes and picked out an outfit at random. Coco could take care of herself. Me, on the other hand ...

I gave up trying to undress after three excruciating attempts. My broken fingers refused to work properly, and my body simply couldn't contort itself to reach the buttons between my shoulders. I plucked a *bergère* hat and wire spectacles from a nearby bin and put them on instead. Last night's velvet ribbon still hid my scar, and my cloak covered up the worst of the bloodstains. They would have to do.

My bladder insisted on immediate relief, and I refused to pee in the corner like a dog.

Besides, I could always pop Angelica's Ring in my mouth if I needed to make a quick escape. I suspected the lobby would be too crowded to maneuver while invisible, or I would've forgone the disguise completely. Nothing roused suspicion like a specter stepping on one's toes.

Tilting my hat over my face, I crept down the staircase that led backstage. Most of the actors ignored me, except—

"You aren't supposed to be back here," a haughty, hook-nosed girl said. She had a round face and hair the color and texture of corn silk. When I turned toward her, she gasped. "Good lord, what happened to your face?"

"Nothing." I ducked my head hastily, but the damage was done.

Her haughtiness transformed into concern as she crept closer. "Has someone hurt you? Should I call the constabulary?"

"No, no." I flashed her an embarrassed smile. "Just lost my way to the toilet, that's all!"

"It's in the lobby." She narrowed her eyes at me. "Is that *blood* on your dress? Are you sure you're all right?"

"Perfect." I nodded like a maniac. "Thanks!"

I walked away a little too quickly to appear innocent. Though I kept my head down, I could feel other eyes on me as I passed. My face must've looked truly ghastly. Perhaps Angelica's Ring would've been wiser, after all.

The lobby was infinitely worse than backstage. Wealthy nobles and merchants who had yet to find their seats crowded around it. I kept to the outskirts of the room, angling toward the walls to avoid unwanted attention. Thankfully, the theatergoers were far too interested in each other to notice my skulking. Soleil et Lune was, after all, far more popular for its gossip than its plays.

I overheard one couple whispering that the Archbishop himself would be attending this matinee—another excellent reason to return to the attic as soon as possible.

As father of the Chasseurs, the Archbishop guided their spiritual warfare against Belterra's evil, proclaiming he'd been given a mandate from God to eradicate the occult. He'd burned dozens of witches—more than any other—yet still he didn't rest. I'd seen him only once, from afar, but I'd recognized the cruel light in his eye for what it was: obsession.

I ducked into the toilet before anyone else could notice me. After relieving myself, I tore the ridiculous hat from my head and stood in front of the mirror. It revealed at once why the crew had stared. My face was in shambles. Deep purple bruises had seeped beneath my eyes, and dried blood spattered my cheeks. I scrubbed at it with the cold water from the tap, rubbing my skin until it was pink and raw. It did little to improve the overall effect.

A polite knock sounded on the door.

"Sorry!" I called sheepishly. "Stomach trouble!"

The knocking ceased immediately. The woman's shocked, disapproving mutters drifted through the door as she shuffled away. Good. I needed to wait out the crowd, and a locked toilet was as good a place as any. Frowning at my reflection, I set to working the blood from my dress.

The voices outside gradually subsided as the music grew louder, signaling the start of the performance. Inching the door open, I peered into the lobby. Only three ushers remained. They nodded to me as I passed, oblivious to my bruised face in the dark.

My breathing came easier as I neared the door to backstage. I was only a few steps away when an auditorium door opened behind me.

"May I be of assistance, sir?" an usher asked.

Whoever it was murmured an answer, and the hair on my neck stood up. I should've proceeded to the attic. I should've run—every instinct screamed at me to flee, flee, *flee*—but I didn't. Instead, I peeked back at the man standing in the doorway. The very tall, copper-haired man in a blue coat.

"You," he said.

Before I could move, he pounced. His hands gripped my arms—vise-like—and he flung me around, positioning himself in front of the exit. I knew immediately that no amount of struggling would free me. He was simply too strong. Too *big.* There was only one way forward.

I smashed my knee straight into his groin.

He doubled over with a groan, grip loosening.

Tearing free—and throwing my hat at his face for good measure—I darted into the depths of the theater. There was another exit backstage. Crew members gaped as I sprinted past, knocking down crates and other props behind me as I went. When he caught the edge of my cloak, I ripped the fastening at my throat free, never faltering a step. It didn't matter. The Chasseur still pounded after me, his strides nearly thrice my own—

He latched on to my wrist as I spotted the hook-nosed girl from before. Though I thrashed away from him—my spectacles clattering to the floor as I struggled toward her—he only tightened his hold. Tears streamed down my ruined face. "Please, help me!"

The hook-nosed girl's eyes widened. "Let her go!"

The voices onstage faltered at her shout, and we all froze.

Shit. No, no, *no.*

Taking advantage of his hesitation, I twisted to break free, but his hand inadvertently met my breast. He loosened his grip, clearly appalled, but lunged as I pulled away, his fingers catching my neckline. Horrified, I watched in slow motion as the delicate fabric tore, as his feet tangled in my skirt. As we clutched one another, trying and failing to regain our balance.

As we tumbled through the curtain and onto the stage.

The audience gave a collective gasp—then fell silent. No one dared breathe. Not even me.

The Chasseur, who still held me atop him from our fall, stared up at me with wide eyes. I watched—numb—as dozens of emotions flitted across his face. Shock. Panic. Humiliation. Rage.

The hook-nosed girl skidded out after us, and the spell was broken. "You disgusting pig!"

The Chasseur flung me away like I'd bitten him, and I landed on my backside. Hard. Angry cries from the audience erupted as my dress gaped open. They took in my bruised face, my torn bodice, and made their own assumptions. But I didn't care. Staring out at the audience, horror seeped through me as I imagined who could be staring back. The blood left my face.

The hook-nosed girl wrapped her arms around me, gently helping me to my feet and leading me backstage. Two burly crew members appeared and seized the Chasseur as well. The crowd shouted their approval as they frog-marched him behind us. I glanced back, surprised he wasn't putting up a fight, but his face was as white as my own.

The girl grabbed a sheet from one of the crates and draped it around me. "Are you all right?"

I ignored her ridiculous question. Of course I wasn't all right. What had just *happened*?

"Hopefully they throw him in prison." She glared at the Chasseur, who stood amidst the crew in a daze. The audience still shouted their outrage.

"They won't," I said grimly. "He's a Chasseur."

"We'll all give our statements." She stuck her chin out and gestured to the crew. They hovered awkwardly, unsure of what to do. "We saw the whole thing. You're so lucky you were here." She glanced at my torn dress, eyes flashing. "Who knows what could have happened?"

I didn't correct her. I needed to leave. This whole fiasco had been a shoddy attempt at escape, and this was my last chance. The Chasseur couldn't stop me now, but the constabulary would arrive soon. They wouldn't care what the audience thought they'd seen. They'd cart me off to prison, regardless of my torn dress and bruises, and it would be all too easy for the Chasseurs to procure me once this mess had been sorted out.

I knew where that would lead. A stake and a match.

I'd just decided to throw caution to the winds and run for it—perhaps slip Angelica's Ring between my teeth once I reached the stairwell—when the door to stage right creaked open.

My heart stopped as the Archbishop stepped through.

He was shorter than I thought, though still taller than me, with salt-and-pepper hair and steely blue eyes. They flared briefly as he took me in—the bruised face, the ratted hair, the sheet draped around my shoulders—then narrowed at the devastation around me. His lip curled.

He jerked his head toward the exit. "Leave us."

The crew didn't need to be told twice—and neither did I. I nearly tripped over my feet in an effort to vacate the premises as quickly as possible. The Chasseur's hand snaked out and caught my arm.

"Not you," the Archbishop commanded.

The hook-nosed girl hesitated, her eyes darting between the three of us. One look from the Archbishop, however, had her scurrying out the door.

The Chasseur released me the second she disappeared and bowed to the Archbishop, covering his heart with his fist. "This is the woman from Tremblay's townhouse, Your Eminence."

The Archbishop nodded curtly, his eyes returning to mine. Again they searched my face, and again they hardened—as if my worth had been tallied and found lacking. He clasped stiff hands behind his back. "So you are our escaped thief."

I nodded, not daring to breathe. He'd said *thief.* Not witch.

"You have put us all in quite the predicament, my dear."

"I—"

"Silence."

My mouth snapped shut. I wasn't stupid enough to argue with the Archbishop. If anyone dwelled above the law, it was him.

He walked toward me slowly, hands still clasped behind his back. "You're a clever thief, aren't you? Quite talented in eluding capture. How did you escape the rooftop last night? Captain Diggory assures me the townhouse was surrounded."

I swallowed hard. There was that word again. Thief—not witch. Hope fluttered in my stomach. I glanced at the copper-haired Chasseur, but his face revealed nothing.

"My . . . my friend helped me," I lied.

He raised a brow. "Your friend, the witch."

Dread snaked down my spine. But Coco was miles away now—safe and hidden within La Forêt des Yeux. The Forest of Eyes. The Chasseurs would never be able to track her there. Even if they did, her coven would protect her.

I maintained careful eye contact, careful not to twitch or fidget or otherwise give myself away. "She is a witch, yes."

"How?"

"How is she a witch?" Though I knew I shouldn't bait him, I also couldn't help it. "I believe when a witch and a man love each other very much—"

He struck me across the face. The slap echoed in the silence of the empty auditorium. Somehow, the audience had been cleared away as quickly as the crew. Clutching my cheek, I glared at him in silent fury. The Chasseur shifted uncomfortably beside me.

"You disgusting child." The Archbishop's eyes bulged alarmingly. "How did it help you escape?"

"I will not betray her secrets."

"You dare to conceal information?"

A knock sounded from stage right, and a constable stepped forward. "Your Holiness, a crowd has formed outside. Several of the attendants and crew—they refuse to leave until they learn the fate of the girl and Captain Diggory. They are beginning to attract . . . attention."

"We will be along shortly." The Archbishop straightened and adjusted his choral robes, taking a deep breath. The constable bowed and ducked outside once more.

He returned his attention to me. A long moment of silence passed as we glared at each other. "What am I going to do with you?"

I dared not speak again. My face could only handle so much.

"You are a criminal who consorts with *demons*. You have publicly framed a Chasseur for assault, among . . . *other* things." His lip curled, and he regarded me with palpable disgust. I tried and failed to ignore the shame churning in my stomach. It'd been an accident. I hadn't framed him intentionally. And yet . . . if the audience's misapprehension helped me escape the stake . . .

I'd never claimed to be honorable.

"Captain Diggory's reputation will be ruined," the Archbishop continued. "I will be forced to relieve him of his duties, lest the Chasseurs' holiness be questioned. Lest *my* holiness be questioned." His eyes burned into mine. I arranged my features into a contrite expression, lest his fist get twitchy again. Appeased by my repentance, he began to pace. "What am I going to do with you? What am I going to *do?*"

Though I clearly repulsed him, his steely eyes kept drifting back to me. Like a moth drawn to flame. They roved my face as if searching for something, lingering on my eyes, my nose, my mouth. My throat.

To my dismay, I realized the ribbon had slipped during my scuffle with the Chasseur. I hastily tightened it. The Archbishop's mouth pursed, and he resumed staring at me.

It took all my willpower not to roll my eyes at his absurd inner struggle. I wasn't going to prison today, and I wasn't going to the stake, either. For whatever reason, the Archbishop and his pet had decided I wasn't a witch. I certainly wasn't going to question their oversight.

But the question remained . . . what *did* the Archbishop want? Because he definitely wanted *something.* The hunger in his eyes was unmistakable, and the sooner I figured it out, the sooner I could use it to my advantage. It took several seconds before I realized he'd continued his monologue.

". . . thanks to your little sleight of hand." He spun on his heel to face me, a peculiar sort of triumph in his expression. "Perhaps a mutually beneficial arrangement can be made."

He paused, looking between us expectantly.

"I'm listening," I muttered. The Chasseur nodded stiffly.

"Excellent. It's quite simple, really—marriage."

I stared at him, mouth falling open.

He chuckled, but the sound was without mirth. "As your wife, Reid, this distasteful creature would belong to you. You would've had every right to pursue her, to discipline her, especially after her indiscretions last night. It would have been expected. Necessary, even. There would have been no crime committed, no impurity to disparage. You would remain a Chasseur."

I laughed. It came out a strangled, desperate sound. "I'm not marrying anyone."

The Archbishop didn't share my laughter. "You will if you wish to avoid a public lashing and imprisonment. Though I'm not chief of the constabulary, he is a dear friend."

I gaped at him. "You can't blackmail me—"

He waved a hand as if swatting an irksome fly. "It is the sentence that awaits a thief. I would advise you to think very carefully about this, child."

I appealed to the Chasseur, determined to keep a level head despite the panic clawing up my throat. "You can't want this. Please, tell him to find another way."

"There is no other way," the Archbishop interjected.

The Chasseur stood very still indeed. He seemed to have stopped breathing.

"You are like a son to me, Reid." The Archbishop reached up to clasp the Chasseur's shoulder—a mouse comforting an elephant. Some disconnected part of my mind wanted to laugh. "Do not throw away your life—your promising career, your oath to *God*—for the sake of this heathen. Once she is your wife, you can lock her in the closet and never think of her again. You would have the legal right to do whatever you please with her." He shot him a meaningful look. "This arrangement would also solve . . . other matters."

Blood finally returned to the Chasseur's face—no, *flooded* his face. It raced up his throat and into his cheeks, burning hotter than even his eyes. His jaw clenched. "Sir, I—"

But I didn't hear him. Saliva coated my mouth, and my vision narrowed. Marriage. To a Chasseur. There had to be another way, *any* other way—

Bile rose in my throat, and before I could stop it, I heaved a spectacular arc of vomit onto the Archbishop's feet. He leapt away from me with a disgusted cry.

"How *dare* you—!" He raised a fist to strike me once more, but the Chasseur moved with lightning swiftness. His hand caught the Archbishop's wrist.

"*If* this woman is to be my wife," he said, swallowing hard, "you will not touch her again."

The Archbishop bared his teeth. "You agree, then?"

The Chasseur released his wrist and looked at me, a deeper blush creeping up his throat. "Only if she does."

His words reminded me of Coco.

Take care of yourself.

Only if you do.

Coco had said I needed to find protection. I stared up at the copper-haired Chasseur, at the Archbishop still rubbing his wrist. Perhaps protection had found me.

Andre, Grue, the constabulary, *her* . . . none of them could harm me if I had a Chasseur as a husband. Even the Chasseurs themselves would cease to be a threat—if I could keep up the act. If I could avoid doing magic near them. They'd never know I was a witch. I'd be hidden in plain sight.

But . . . I'd also have a husband.

I didn't want a husband. Didn't want to be shackled to anyone in marriage, especially someone as stiff and self-righteous as this Chasseur. But if marriage was my only alternative to spending life in prison, perhaps it was the most agreeable option. It certainly was the only option that would get me out of this theater unchained.

After all, I still had Angelica's Ring. I could always escape *after* the marriage certificate was signed.

Right. I straightened my shoulders and raised my chin. "I'll do it."

THE CEREMONY

Reid

Shouts escalated outside the theater, but I barely heard them. Blood roared in my ears. It drowned out every other sound: their cries for justice, the Archbishop's sympathy.

But not her footsteps. I heard every one of those.

Light. Lighter than mine. But more erratic. Less measured.

I focused on them, and the roaring in my ears gradually quieted. I could hear the theater manager and constabulary now, trying to calm the crowd.

I resisted the urge to unsheathe my Balisarda as the Archbishop opened the doors. My legs locked up, and my skin felt somehow hot and cold at the same time—and too small. Much too small. It itched and pricked as every eye on the street turned toward us. A small, warm hand rested on my arm.

Calloused palms. Slender fingers—two bandaged. I glanced down. Broken.

I didn't allow my eyes to follow her fingers up her arm. Because her arm would lead to her shoulder, and her shoulder would lead to her face. And I knew what I'd find there. Two bruised eyes, and a fresh welt forming on her cheek. A scar above her eyebrow. Another across her throat. It still peeked below the black ribbon, despite her attempt to hide it.

Célie's face rose in my mind. Unblemished and pure.

Oh, God. *Célie.*

The Archbishop stepped forward, and the crowd immediately quieted. With a frown, he pulled me in front of him. The woman—the *heathen*—didn't relinquish her grip. I still didn't look at her.

"Brothers!" The Archbishop's voice rang out across the now silent street, attracting even more attention. Every head turned in our direction, and she cringed into me. I glanced down at her then, frowning. Her eyes were wide, pupils dilated. Frightened.

I turned away.

You cannot give me your heart, Reid. I cannot have it on my conscience.

Célie, please—

Those monsters who murdered Pip are still out there. They must be punished. I will not distract you from your purpose. If you must give away your heart, give it to your brotherhood. Please, please, forget me.

I could never forget you.

Despair nearly knocked me to my knees. She would never forgive me.

"Your concern for this woman has been seen and is appreciated by God." The Archbishop spread his arms wide. Beseeching. "But do not be deceived. After attempting to rob an aristocrat such as yourselves last night, she had the ill grace to flee her husband as he attempted to discipline her this morning. Do not pity her, friends. *Pray* for her."

A woman at the front of the crowd glared at the Archbishop with unabashed loathing. Slim. Pale hair. Upturned nose. I tensed, recognizing the woman from backstage.

You disgusting pig!

As if she sensed my gaze, her eyes flicked to me and narrowed. I stared back at her, trying and failing to forget her whispered condemnation. *Hopefully they throw him in prison. Who knows what could have happened?*

I swallowed hard and looked away. Of course that was what it'd looked like. The little heathen knew her tricks, and I'd made it laughably easy. Fallen right into her trap. I cursed myself, longing to jerk my arm from her grasp. But that wouldn't do. Too many people watched us, and the Archbishop had been clear in his orders.

"We must confess our duplicity as soon as we return home," he'd said, frowning as he paced. "The people must believe you are already married." He'd turned toward her abruptly then. "Am I correct in assuming your soul is unsaved?" When she hadn't responded, he'd scowled. "As I thought. We shall remedy both situations immediately and journey straight to the Doleur for baptism. You must act as her husband until we formalize the union, Reid. Take that ring from her right hand and move it to her left. Walk beside her. The charade may end the second the crowd disperses. And—for goodness' sake, recover her cloak."

The heathen twisted the ring in question now. Shifted her feet. Reached up to touch a piece of hair by her face. She'd pinned the rest into a snarled knot at her nape, wild and untamed. Just like her. I loathed it.

"I implore you to see God's teaching in this woman." The Archbishop's voice rose. "Learn from her wickedness! Wives, *obey* your husbands. *Repent* your sinful natures. Only then can you be truly united with God!"

Several members of the crowd nodded, murmuring their agreement.

It's true. I've always said as much.

Womenfolk are as bad as witches these days.

What they all need is wood—the rod or the stake.

The pale-haired woman from backstage looked as if she'd like to inflict bodily harm on the Archbishop. She bared her teeth, fists clenched, before turning away.

The heathen tensed beside me, her grip tightening painfully on my arm. I glared down at her, but she didn't let go. That's when I smelled it—faint, subtle, almost too light to detect. But still there, lingering on the breeze. Magic.

The Archbishop groaned.

I turned just as he doubled over and clutched his stomach. "Sir, are you—"

I stopped abruptly as he broke shockingly loud wind. His eyes flew open, and his cheeks flamed red. Mutters broke out in the crowd. Shocked. Disgusted. He stood hastily, attempting to straighten his robes, but bent double again at the last second. Another bout wracked his system. I placed a hand on his back, uncertain.

"Sir—"

"Leave me," he snarled.

I backed away quickly and glared at the heathen, who shook with silent laughter. "Stop laughing."

"I couldn't even if I wanted to." She clutched a hand to her side, shaking, and a snort escaped her lips. I eyed her in growing distaste, bending down to inhale her scent. Cinnamon. Not magic. I leaned away quickly, and she laughed harder.

"This right here—this exact moment—it just might be worth marrying you, Chass. I'm going to cherish it forever."

The Archbishop insisted the heathen and I walk to the Doleur for her baptism. He rode in his carriage.

She scoffed as he disappeared down the street, kicking a rock at a nearby trash can. "That man's head is so far up his own ass, he could wear it as a hat."

My jaw clenched. *Don't rise. Remain calm.* "You will not disrespect him."

She grinned, tilting her head up to examine me. Then— incredibly—she rose to her toes and flicked me square on the nose. I staggered back, startled. My face flushed. She grinned wider and started walking. "I will do what I please, Chass."

"You're to be my wife." Catching up to her in two strides, I reached out to grab her arm, but stopped short of touching her. "That means you'll obey me."

"Does it?" She raised her brows, still grinning. "I suppose that means you'll honor and protect me, then? If we're adhering to the dusty old roles of your patriarchy?"

I shortened my pace to match hers. "Yes."

She clapped her hands together. "Excellent. At least this will be entertaining. I have many enemies."

I couldn't help it. I glanced at the deep bruises coloring her eyes. "Imagine that."

"I wouldn't, if I were you." Her tone was conversational. Light. As if we were discussing the weather. "You'll have nightmares for weeks."

Questions burned up my throat, but I refused to voice them. She seemed content in the silence. Her eyes moved everywhere at once. To the dresses and hats lining shop windows. To the apricots and hazelnuts filling merchants' carts. To the dirty windows of a small pub, the soot-stained faces of children chasing pigeons in the street. At every turn, a new emotion flitted across her face. Appreciation. Longing. Delight.

Watching her was strangely exhausting.

After a few minutes, I couldn't stand it any longer. I cleared my throat. "Did one of them give you those bruises?"

"Who?"

"Your enemies."

"Oh," she said brightly. "Yes. Well—two, actually."

Two? I stared at her, incredulous. Tried to imagine the tiny creature before me battling two people at once—then remembered her trapping me backstage, tricking the audience into believing I'd assaulted her. I scowled. She was more than capable.

The streets widened as we reached the outskirts of East End. The Doleur soon glinted in the bright afternoon sun ahead of us.

The Archbishop waited beside his carriage. To my surprise, so did Jean Luc.

Of course. He would be the witness.

The reality of the situation crashed over me like a bag of bricks upon seeing my friend. I was actually going to marry this woman. This—this *creature*. This heathen who scaled rooftops and robbed aristocrats, who brawled and dressed like a man and had a name to match.

She wasn't Célie. She was the furthest thing from Célie God could've possibly created. Célie was gentle and well mannered. Polite. Proper. Kind. She would've never embarrassed me, never presented herself as such a spectacle.

I glared at the woman who was to be my wife. Torn and blood-spattered dress. Bruised face and broken fingers. Scarred throat. And a smirk that left little doubt as to how she'd come to receive each injury.

She arched a brow. "See something you like?"

I looked away. Célie would be heartbroken when she learned what I'd done. She deserved better than this. Better than me.

"Come now." The Archbishop motioned us to the deserted riverbank. A dead fish was our only audience—and the flock of pigeons feasting on it. Its skeleton protruded through rotted flesh, and a single eye gaped up at the clear November sky. "Let us be done with this. The heathen must first be baptized at our Lord God's command. For ye shall not be unequally yoked. Light hath no communion with darkness."

My feet were leaden, each step an incredible effort in the sand

and mud. Jean Luc followed closely behind. I could feel his grin on my neck. I didn't want to imagine what he now thought of me—of this.

The Archbishop hesitated before striding into the gray water. He glanced back at the heathen, the first hint of uncertainty on his face. As if unsure she would follow. *Please change your mind*, I prayed. *Please forget this madness and send her to prison where she belongs.*

But then I would lose my Balisarda. My life. My vows. My purpose.

A small, ugly voice at the back of my mind scoffed. *He could pardon you, if he wanted. No one would question his judgment. You could remain a Chasseur without marrying a criminal.*

So why didn't he?

Chagrin washed through me at the very thought. Of course he couldn't pardon me. The people believed I'd accosted her. It didn't matter I hadn't. They *thought* I had. Even if the Archbishop explained—even if she confessed—people would still whisper. They would doubt. They would question the Chasseurs' integrity. Worse still—they might question the Archbishop himself. His motivations.

We'd already ensnared ourselves in the lie. The people believed she was my wife. If word spread otherwise, the Archbishop would be branded a liar. That couldn't happen.

Like it or not, this heathen would become my wife.

She stomped out after the Archbishop as if to reaffirm the fact. He scowled, wiping away the flecks of water she splashed on his face.

"What an interesting turn of events." Jean Luc's eyes danced with laughter as he watched the heathen. She appeared to be arguing with the Archbishop about something. Of course she was.

"She . . . tricked me." The confession stung.

When I didn't elaborate, he turned to look at me. The laughter in his eyes dimmed. "What about Célie?"

I forced the words out, hating myself for them. "Célie knew we wouldn't marry."

I hadn't told him about her rejection. I hadn't been able to stomach his ridicule. Or worse—his pity. He'd asked once, after Filippa's death, about my intentions with her. Shame burned in my gut. I'd lied through my teeth, telling him my vows meant too much. Telling him I'd never marry.

Yet here I was.

He pursed his lips, regarding me shrewdly. "Still, I'm . . . sorry." He stared out at the heathen, who had pointed a broken finger at the Archbishop's nose. "Marriage to such a creature will not be easy."

"Is marriage ever easy?"

"Perhaps not, but she seems particularly intolerable." He flashed me a halfhearted grin. "I suppose she has to move into the Tower, doesn't she?"

I couldn't bring myself to return his smile. "Yes."

He sighed. "Pity."

We watched in silence as the Archbishop's face grew steadily stonier. As he finally lost patience and jerked her toward him by the nape of her neck. As he threw her underwater and held her there a second too long.

I didn't blame him. Her soul would take longer to cleanse than a normal person's.

Two seconds too long.

The Archbishop appeared to be at war with himself. His body shook with the effort of keeping her under, and his eyes were wide—crazed. Surely he wasn't going to—?

Three seconds too long.

I plunged into the water. Jean Luc crashed after me. We threw ourselves forward, but our panic was unfounded. The Archbishop released her just as we reached them, and she sprang out of the water like an angry, hissing cat. Water cascaded down her hair and face and dress. I reached out to steady her, but she shoved me away. I yielded a step as she whirled, spluttering, toward the Archbishop.

"Fils de pute!" Before I could move to stop her, she dove at him. His eyes flew open as he lost his footing and tumbled backward into the water, limbs flailing. Jean Luc rushed to help him. I seized her, pinning her arms to her sides before she could tackle him back into the water.

She didn't seem to notice.

"Connard! Salaud!" She thrashed in my arms, kicking water everywhere. "I'm going to kill you! I'm going to rip those robes off your shoulders and strangle you with them, you misshapen, foul-smelling piece of *shit*—"

All three of us gaped at her—eyes wide, mouths open. The Archbishop recovered first. His face purpled and a strangled sound escaped his throat. "How *dare* you speak to me so?" He jerked away from Jean Luc, waving a finger in her face. I realized his mistake a split second before she lunged. Tightening my grip, I managed to haul her away before she could sink her teeth into his knuckle.

I was about to marry a wild animal.

"Let—me—*go*—" Her elbow sank deep into my stomach.

"No." More a gasp than a word. But still I held on.

She let out a frustrated noise then—something between a growl and a scream—and went mercifully still. I sent up a silent prayer of thanks before dragging her back to shore.

The Archbishop and Jean Luc joined us shortly thereafter. "Thank you, Reid." The Archbishop sniffed, wringing out his robes and readjusting the pectoral cross around his neck. Disdain dripped from his features when he finally addressed the hellcat. "Must we shackle you for the ceremony? Perhaps procure a muzzle?"

"You tried to *kill* me."

He looked down his nose at her. "Believe me, child, if I had wanted to kill you, you would be dead."

Her eyes blazed. "Likewise."

Jean Luc choked on a laugh.

The Archbishop stepped forward, his eyes narrowing to slits. "Release her, Reid. I should like to get this whole sordid affair behind us."

Gladly.

To my surprise—and disappointment—she didn't flee when I

let her go. She merely crossed her arms and planted her feet, staring at each of us in turn. Obstinately. Sullenly. A silent challenge.

We kept our distance.

"Make this quick," she grumbled.

The Archbishop inclined his head. "Step forward, both of you, and join hands."

We stared at each other. Neither moved. "Oh, hurry up." Jean Luc shoved me roughly from behind, and I surrendered a step. Watched in silent fury as she refused to bridge the remaining distance. Waited.

After several long seconds, she rolled her eyes and stepped forward. When I extended my hands, she stared at them as if they were spotted with leprosy.

One.

I forced myself to breathe. In through my nose. Out through my mouth.

Two.

Her brows furrowed. She watched me with a bemused expression—obviously questioning my mental capacity.

Three.

Four.

She took my hands. Grimaced as if in pain.

Five.

I realized a second too late she *was* in physical pain. I immediately loosened my grip on her broken fingers.

Six.

The Archbishop cleared his throat. "Let us begin." He turned to me. "Will thou, Reid Florin Diggory, have this woman to be thy wedded wife, to live together after God's ordinance in the holy estate of matrimony? Will thou love her, comfort her, honor and keep her, in sickness and in health, and, forsaking all others, keep thee only unto her, so long as you both shall live?"

My vision narrowed to a speck of white amidst the pigeons—a dove. My head spun. They all stared at me, waiting for me to speak, but my throat constricted. Choking me.

I couldn't marry this woman. I couldn't. Once acknowledged, the thought latched deep, sinking its claws into every fiber of my being. There had to be another way—*any* other way—

Small, warm fingers squeezed my own. My eyes darted up and met piercing blue-green. No—more blue than green now. Steely. Reflecting the iron water of the Doleur behind her. She swallowed and nodded almost imperceptibly.

In that brief movement, I understood. The doubt, the hesitation, the mourning of a future I'd never have—it belonged to her as well. Gone was the spitting hellcat. Now, there was only a woman. And she was small. And she was frightened. And she was strong.

And she was asking me to be the same.

I didn't know why I did it. She was a thief, a criminal, and I owed her nothing. She'd ruined my life when she dragged me on that stage. If I agreed, I was certain she'd do her best to continue doing so.

But I returned the pressure anyway. Felt the two small words rise to my lips, unbidden. "I will."

The Archbishop turned to her. I maintained the pressure between our hands, careful of her broken fingers. "What's your name?" he asked abruptly. "Your full name?"

"Louise Margaux Larue."

I frowned. *Larue.* It was a common enough surname among the criminals in East End, but usually a pseudonym. It literally meant *the streets.*

"Larue?" The Archbishop eyed her suspiciously, echoing my own doubts. "You should know if this name proves false, your marriage to Captain Diggory will be annulled. I need not remind you of your fate should this happen."

"I know the law."

"Fine." He waved a hand. "Will thou, Louise Margaux *Larue*, have this man to be thy wedded husband, to live together after God's ordinance in the holy estate of matrimony? Will thou obey him, and serve him, love, honor and keep him, in sickness and in health, and, forsaking all others, keep thee only unto him, so long as you both shall live?"

I could see the snort rising to her face, but she resisted, kicking a clump of sand at the birds instead. They scattered with cries of alarm. A lump rose in my throat as the dove took flight.

"I will."

The Archbishop continued without pausing. "By the power vested in me, I pronounce you husband and wife in the name of the Father, Son, and Holy Spirit." He paused, and every muscle in my body tensed, waiting for the next line. As if reading my thoughts, he cast me a scathing look. My cheeks flamed once more.

"For as the Lord God says"—he clasped his hands and bowed his head—"'two are better than one . . . For if they fall, the one will lift up his fellow. But woe to him who is alone when he falleth, for he hath not another to help him up. And if one prevail against him, two shall withstand him. A threefold cord is not quickly broken.'"

He straightened with a grim smile. "It is done. What therefore God hath joined together, let no man put asunder. We shall sign the certificate of marriage upon our return, and the matter shall be settled."

He moved toward the waiting carriage but stopped short, turning to scowl at me. "Of course, the marriage must be consummated to be legally binding."

She stiffened beside me, staring resolutely at the Archbishop— her mouth tight, her eyes tense. Heat washed over me. Hotter and fiercer than before. "Yes, Your Eminence."

He nodded, satisfied, and stepped into the carriage. Jean Luc climbed in after him, winking. If possible, my humiliation fanned and spread.

"Good." The Archbishop snapped the carriage door shut. "See that it's executed quickly. A witness shall visit your room later to confirm."

My stomach plummeted as he disappeared down the street.

PART II

Petit à petit, l'oiseau fait son nid.
Little by little, the bird makes its nest.
—French proverb

CONSUMMATION

Lou

Cathédral Saint-Cécile d'Cesarine rose up before me, a sinister specter of spires and towers and flying buttresses. Jewel-toned windows leered in the sunlight. Rosewood doors—carved and embedded in white stone—gaped open as we climbed the steps, and a handful of Chasseurs spilled out.

"Behave yourself," my new husband muttered. I smirked but said nothing.

A Chasseur stopped in front of me. "Identification."

"Er—"

My husband dipped his head stiffly. "This is my wife, Louise."

I stared at him, amazed the words had managed to escape through his clenched teeth. As usual, he ignored me.

The Chasseur in front of me blinked. Blinked again. "Your— your wife, Captain Diggory?"

He offered a barely perceptible nod, and I truly feared for his poor teeth. They'd surely chip if he kept gnashing them together. "Yes."

The Chasseur risked a glance at me. "This is . . . highly unusual. Is the Archbishop aware—"

"He's expecting us."

"Of course." The Chasseur turned to the pageboy who'd just appeared. "Inform the Archbishop that Captain Diggory and his . . . wife have arrived." He cast another furtive glance in my direction as the boy scurried away. I winked back at him. My husband made an impatient noise and seized my arm, steering me forcefully toward the door.

I tugged my arm away. "There's no need to cripple me."

"I told you to *behave*."

"Oh, please. I *winked*. It's not like I stripped and sang 'Big Titty Liddy'—"

A commotion rose behind us, and we turned as one. More Chasseurs marched up the street, carrying what looked like a body between them. Though they'd wrapped it in cloth for propriety's sake, there was no mistaking the hand that dangled below the sheet.

Or the vines that had grown between its fingers. Or the bark that dappled its skin.

I leaned closer—despite my husband yanking me back—and inhaled the familiar sweetness emanating from the body. Interesting.

One of the Chasseurs hastened to conceal the hand. "We found him just outside the city, Captain."

My husband jerked his head toward the alley beside the church without a word, and the Chasseurs hurried away.

Though my husband led me inside, I craned my neck to watch them go. "What was that about?"

"Never you mind."

"Where are they taking him?"

"I said never you—"

"Enough." The Archbishop strode into the foyer, eyeing the mud and water pooling at my feet in distaste. He'd already changed into fresh choral robes, of course, and washed the flecks of mud and sand from his face. I resisted the urge to fidget with my torn dress or finger-comb my matted hair. It didn't matter what I looked like. The Archbishop could piss off. "The marriage certificate is waiting in my study. From where should we retrieve your possessions?"

Feigning disinterest, I wrung out my soaking hair. "I have none."

"You . . . have none," he repeated slowly, looking me over with disapproval.

"That's what I said, yes—unless you and your cronies would like to ransack Soleil et Lune's attic. I've been borrowing costumes for years now."

He scowled. "I expected little else. We shall, however, endeavor to find you more presentable garments. I won't dishonor Reid by having his bride appear a heathen, even if she is one."

"How dare you?" I clutched the front of my ruined dress in mock affront. "I am a God-fearing Christian woman now—"

My husband hauled me away before I could utter another word.

I swore I heard one of his teeth crack.

After hastily signing the marriage certificate in the study, my husband steered me down a narrow, dusty corridor, clearly trying to avoid the crowded foyer. God forbid anyone saw his new wife. Rumors were probably already circulating the Tower about the scandal.

A spiral staircase tucked in the back of the corridor caught my attention. Unlike the archaic rosewood staircases nestled throughout the cathedral, this one was metal and clearly built after the original construction. And there was something there . . . in the air of the stairwell . . . I tugged on his arm and inhaled covertly. "Where does that staircase lead?"

He turned, following my gaze, before shaking his head curtly. "Nowhere you'll be visiting. Access beyond the dormitories is restricted. Only approved personnel are allowed on the upper floors."

Well, then. Count me in.

I said nothing more, however, allowing him to lead me up several different flights of stairs to a plain wooden door. He pushed it open without looking back at me. I paused outside, staring at the words inscribed above the doorway:

THOU SHALT NOT SUFFER A WITCH TO LIVE.

I shivered. So this was the infamous Chasseur Tower. Though no visible changes marked the corridor beyond, there was something . . . austere about the place. It lacked warmth, benevolence—the atmosphere as bleak and rigid as the men who resided within.

My husband poked his head back through the door a second later, glancing between the terrifying inscription and me. "What's wrong?"

"Nothing." I hurried after him, ignoring the cold trickle of dread down my spine as I crossed the threshold. There was no going back now. I was in the belly of the beast.

Soon to be in the *bed* of the beast.

Like hell.

He led me down the hall, careful not to touch me. "Through here." He gestured to one of the many doors lining the corridor, and I brushed past him into the room—and stopped short.

It was a matchbox. A painfully simple, miserably drab little matchbox with no defining characteristics whatsoever. The walls were white, the floorboards dark. Only a bed and desk filled the space. Worse, he had no personal effects whatsoever. No trinkets. No books. Not even a basket for dirty laundry. When I spotted the narrow window—too high on the wall to watch the sunset—I truly died a little inside.

My husband must've been the most insipid person ever born.

The door clicked shut behind me. It sounded final—like a jail cell clanging shut.

He moved in my periphery, and I whirled, but he only lifted his hands slowly, as if placating a feral cat. "I'm just taking off my jacket." He shrugged out of his sodden coat and draped it across the desk before starting to unbuckle his bandolier.

"You can stop right there," I said. "No—no more clothes coming off."

His jaw tightened. "I'm not going to force myself on you"—his nose wrinkled in disgust—"Louise."

"It's Lou." He twitched visibly at the name. "Is my name offensive to you?"

"Everything about you is offensive to me." He pulled the chair from the desk and sat down, heaving a great sigh. "You're a criminal."

"There's no need to sound so self-righteous, Chass. You're here because of *you*, not me."

He scowled. "This is your fault."

Shrugging, I moved to sit on his immaculately made bed. He cringed when my wet dress soiled the quilt. "You should've let me go at the theater."

"I didn't know you were going to—that you were going to *frame* me—"

"I'm a criminal," I reasoned, not bothering to correct him. It didn't matter now, anyway. "I behaved criminally. You should've known better."

He gestured angrily to my bruised face and broken fingers. "And how has behaving criminally treated you?"

"I'm alive, aren't I?"

"Are you?" He arched a copper brow. "You look like someone nearly killed you."

I waved a careless hand and smirked. "Hazard of the job."

"Not anymore."

"Excuse me?"

His eyes blazed. "You're my wife now, whether we like it or not. No man will ever touch you that way again."

Tension—taut and heavy—settled between us at his words.

I tilted my head and stalked toward him, a slow smile spreading across my face. He glared at me, but his breathing hitched when I leaned over him. His eyes flicked to my mouth. Even sitting, he was nearly taller than me.

"Good." I curled my hand around one of the knives in his bandolier. Flicking it to his throat before he could react, I dug the tip in hard enough to draw blood. His hand came down on my wrist—crushing it—but he didn't force me away. I leaned closer. Our lips were only a hair's breadth apart. "But you should know," I breathed, "that if a man touches me in *any* way without my permission, I'll cut him open." I paused for effect, dragging the knife from his throat to his navel and beyond. He swallowed hard. "Even if that man is my husband."

"We have to consummate the marriage." His voice was low, raw—angry. "Neither of us can afford an annulment."

I pushed away from him roughly, jerking up my sleeve to reveal the skin of my inner arm. Eyes never leaving his, I dug the tip of the knife in and sliced down. He moved to stop me, but it was too late. Blood welled. I ripped the blanket from his bed and let the blood drip on his bedsheets.

"There." I stalked to the bathing chamber, ignoring his shocked expression. "Marriage consummated."

I savored the pain in my arm. It felt real, unlike everything else in this wretched day. I cleaned it slowly, deliberately, before dressing it with a cloth from the cupboard in the corner.

Married.

If someone had told me this morning I'd be married by sunset, I would've laughed. Laughed, and then probably spat in their face.

The Chasseur pounded on the door. "Are you all right?"

"God, leave me alone."

The door cracked open. "Are you decent?"

"No," I lied.

"I'm coming in." He poked his head in first, eyes narrowing as he saw all the blood. "Was that necessary?"

"I'm nothing if not thorough."

He tugged the dressing down to examine the cut, forcing me to look squarely at his chest. He hadn't yet changed, and his shirt was still wet from the river. It clung to his chest in a particularly distracting way. I forced myself to stare at the tub instead, but my thoughts kept drifting back to him. He really was too tall. Abnormally tall. Entirely too big for this small of a space. I wondered if he had some sort of disease. My eyes cut back to his chest. Probably.

"They'll think I murdered you." He replaced the dressing and opened the small cupboard again, grabbing another cloth to mop up the floor and basin. I finished wrapping my arm and joined him.

"What do we do with the evidence?" I wiped my bloody hands on my hem.

"We burn it. There's a furnace downstairs."

My eyes lit up. "Yes! I set a warehouse on fire once. One match, and the whole thing went up like a smokestack."

He stared at me in horror. "You set a building on fire?"

These people obviously had hearing impairments. "That's what I just said, isn't it?"

He shook his head and knotted the towel. "Your dress," he said without looking at me. I glanced down at it.

"What about it?"

"It's covered in blood. It needs to go too."

"Right." I scoffed, rolling my eyes. "I don't have any other clothes."

"That's your problem. Hand it over."

I glared at him. He glared back. "I don't have any other clothes," I repeated slowly. Definite hearing impairment.

"You should've thought about that before you slashed open your arm." He thrust out his hand insistently.

Another second passed.

"Fine, then." A wild little laugh escaped my throat. "Just fine!" Two could play this game. I attempted to jerk my dress over my head, but my fingers—still stiff and painful—prevented me from succeeding. The wet fabric caught around my neck instead, strangling me, and I nearly broke the rest of my fingers in a desperate attempt to pry it away.

Strong hands soon reached forward to assist me. I leapt away on instinct, and my dress ripped as easily as it had done in the theater.

Flustered, I threw it in his face.

I wasn't naked. Soft, flexible undergarments covered my sensitive bits, but it was enough. When he extracted himself from my dress, his face was burning. He averted his eyes quickly.

"There's a shirt in there." He nodded to the cupboard before eyeing the wound on my arm. "I'll tell a maid to bring you a nightgown. Don't let her see your arm."

I rolled my eyes again as he left, slipping into one of his absurdly large shirts. It fell down past my knees.

When I was sure he'd gone, I crept back out to the bedroom. Golden light from the sunset shone through the lone window. I dragged the desk over to it, stacking the chair on top, before climbing up. Balancing my elbows on the ledge, I rested my chin in my hands and sighed.

The sun was still beautiful. And despite everything, it was still setting. I closed my eyes and basked in its warmth.

A maid soon entered to check the blood-specked sheets. Satisfied, she stripped them without a word. My stomach sank slowly to the floor as I watched her rigid back. She didn't look at me.

"Do you have a nightgown?" I asked hopefully, unable to stand the silence any longer.

She curtsied, prim and proper, but still avoided my eyes. "Market doesn't open until morning, *madame*."

She left without another word. I watched her go with a sense of foreboding. If I'd hoped for an ally in this wretched Tower, I'd been grossly optimistic. Even the staff had been brainwashed. But if they thought they could break me with silence—with isolation—they were in for a fun surprise.

Sliding down from my tower of furniture, I prowled the room for something I could use against my captor. Blackmail. A weapon. Anything. I wracked my brain, remembering the tricks I'd used on Andre and Grue over the years. After ripping open the desk drawer, I rummaged through its contents with all the courtesy my husband deserved. There wasn't much to inspect: a couple of quills, a pot of ink, a faded old Bible, and . . . a leather notebook. When I picked it up, flicking eagerly through the pages, several loose sheets fluttered to the ground. Letters. I bent closer, a slow smile spreading across my face.

Love letters.

A very confused, coppery-haired Chasseur poked me awake that night. I'd been curled in the tub—wrapped up in his ridiculous shirt—when he'd stormed in and impaled my rib with his finger.

"What?" I batted him away crossly, grimacing at the sudden light in my eyes.

"What are you doing?" He leaned back, still crouched on his knees, and set the candle on the floor. "When you weren't in bed, I thought maybe—maybe you'd—"

"Left?" I said shrewdly. "It's still on the agenda."

His face hardened. "That would be a mistake."

"'S all relative." I yawned, curling up once more.

"Why are you in the tub?"

"Well, I certainly wasn't going to sleep in your bed, was I? This seemed the best alternative."

There was a pause. "You don't . . . you don't have to sleep in here," he finally muttered. "Take the bed."

"No, thanks. It's not that I don't trust you, but—well, that's exactly what it is."

"And you think the tub can protect you?"

"Mmm, no." I sighed, eyelids fluttering. They were impossibly heavy. "I can lock the door—"

Wait.

I jolted awake then. "I *did* lock the door. How are you in here?"

He grinned, and I cursed my treacherous heart for stuttering slightly. The smile transformed his entire face, like—like the sun. I scowled, crossing my arms and nestling deeper into his shirt. I didn't want to invite *that* comparison, but now I couldn't get the image out of my head. His coppery hair—tousled, as if he too had fallen asleep somewhere he shouldn't—didn't help.

"Where have you been?" I snapped.

His grin faltered. "I fell asleep in the sanctuary. I . . . needed some space."

I frowned, and the silence between us lengthened. After a long moment, I asked, "How *did* you get in here?"

"You're not the only one who can pick a lock."

"Really?" I sat up, interest piqued. "Where would a holy Chasseur learn such a trick?"

"The Archbishop."

"Of course. He's such a hypocritical ass."

The fragile camaraderie between us crumbled instantly. He shoved to his feet. "Never disrespect him. Not in front of me.

He's the best man I've ever known. The bravest. When I was three, he—"

I tuned him out, rolling my eyes. It was quickly becoming a habit around him. "Look, Chass, you're my husband, so I feel I should be honest with you in saying I'll gladly murder the Archbishop at the first opportunity."

"He'd kill you before you even lifted a finger." A fanatical gleam shone in his eyes, and I raised a politely skeptical brow. "I'm serious. He's the most accomplished leader in Chasseur history. He's slain more witches than any other man alive. His skill is legend. *He* is legend—"

"He is *old*."

"You underestimate him."

"Seems to be a theme around here." I yawned and turned away from him, shifting to find a softer bit of tub. "Look, this has been fun, but it's time for my beauty sleep. I need to look my best for tomorrow."

"Tomorrow?"

"I'm going back to the theater," I murmured, eyes already closing. "What I caught of the performance this morning sounded fascinating."

There was another pause, much longer than before. I peeked at him over my shoulder. He fidgeted with the candle for a few seconds before taking a deep breath. "Now that you're my wife, it's best if you stay within Chasseur Tower."

I lurched upright, sleep instantly forgotten. "I don't think that's best at all."

"People saw your face at the theater"—anxiety flared in my stomach—"and now they know you're my wife. Everything you do will be monitored. Everything you say will reflect back on me—on the Chasseurs. The Archbishop doesn't trust you. He thinks it best you stay here until you can learn to behave yourself." He gave me a hard look. "I agree with him."

"That's unfortunate. I thought you had better sense than the Archbishop," I snapped. "You can't keep me locked in this *trou à merde*."

I might've laughed at his appalled expression if I hadn't been so angry. "Watch your mouth." His own mouth tightened, and his nostrils flared. "You're my wife—"

"Yes, you've mentioned that! Your *wife*. Not your slave, nor your *property*. I signed that stupid piece of paper to *avoid* imprisonment—"

"We can't trust you." His voice rose over mine. "You're a criminal. You're impulsive. God forbid you even *open* your mouth outside this room—"

"Shit! Damn! Fu—"

"Stop it!" Blood crept up his throat, and his chest rose and fell heavily as he struggled to control his breathing. "God, woman! How can you speak so? Have you no shame?"

"I won't stay here," I seethed.

"You'll do as you're told." The words were flat—final.

Like hell. I opened my mouth to tell him just that, but he'd already stormed out of the room, slamming the door shut with enough force to rattle my teeth.

THE INTERROGATION

Reid

I woke long before my wife. Stiff. Sore. Aching from a fitful night on the floor. Though I'd argued with myself—reasoned vehemently that she'd *chosen* to suffer in the tub—I hadn't been able to climb into bed. Not when she was injured. Not when she might wake in the night and change her mind.

No. I'd offered her the bed. The bed was hers.

I regretted my chivalry the moment I stepped into the training yard. Word of my new circumstance had obviously swept through the Tower. Man after man rose to meet me, each with a determined glint in his eye. Each waiting impatiently for his turn. Each attacking with uncharacteristic belligerence.

"Long night, huh, Captain?" my first partner sneered after clipping my shoulder.

The next managed to hit my ribs. He glared. "It isn't right. A criminal sleeping three rooms from me."

Jean Luc grinned. "I don't think they were doing much sleeping."

"She could cut our throats."

"She consorts with witches."

"It isn't right."

"It isn't fair."

"I heard she's a whore."

I bashed the handle of my sword into the last one's head, and he sprawled to the ground. Extending my arms, I turned in a slow circle. Challenging anyone who dared confront me. Blood ran from a cut on my forehead. "Does anyone else have a problem with my new circumstance?"

Jean Luc howled with laughter. He in particular seemed to enjoy my trial, judgment, and execution—until he entered the ring. "Give me your best, old man."

I was older than him by three months.

But even battered, even exhausted, even *old*, I would die before yielding to Jean Luc.

The fight lasted only a few minutes. Though he was quick and nimble, I was stronger. After a good hit, he too crumpled, clutching his ribs. I rubbed the blood from my freshly split lip before helping him up.

"We'll need to interrupt your conjugal bliss to interrogate her about Tremblay's, you know. Like it or not, the men are right." He touched a knot under his eye gingerly. "She does consort with witches. The Archbishop thinks she might be able to lead us to them."

I almost rolled my eyes. The Archbishop had already confided his hopes to me, but I didn't tell Jean Luc that. He enjoyed feeling superior. "I know."

Wooden swords still clacked, and bodies thudded together as our brothers continued around us. No others approached, but they shot me covert looks between rounds. Men who had once respected me. Men who had once laughed, joked, and called me friend. In only a few hours, I'd become the object of my wife's rejection and my brethren's scorn. Both stung more than I cared to admit.

Breakfast had been worse. My brethren hadn't allowed me to eat a bite. Half had been too eager to hear about my wedding night, and the others had studiously ignored me.

What was it like?

Did you enjoy it?

Don't tell the Archbishop, but . . . I tried it once. Her name was Babette.

Of course I hadn't actually *wanted* to consummate. With *her.* And my brothers—they would come around. Once they realized I wasn't going anywhere. Which I wasn't.

Crossing the yard, I threw my sword on the rack. The men parted for me in waves. Their whispers bit and snapped at my back. To my irritation, Jean Luc had no such scruples. He followed me like a plague of locusts.

"I must confess I'm anxious to see her again." He ensured his sword landed on top of mine. "After that performance on the beach, I think our brothers are in for a real treat."

I would've preferred the locusts.

"She isn't that," I disagreed in an undertone.

Jean Luc continued as if he hadn't heard me. "It's been a long time since a woman was in the Tower. Who was the last—Captain

Barre's wife? She wasn't anything to look at. Yours is much nicer—"

"I'll thank you not to speak of my wife." The whispers peaked behind us as we neared the Tower. Uninhibited laughter rang across the yard as we stepped inside. I gritted my teeth and pretended I couldn't hear them. "What she is or isn't is no concern of yours."

His eyebrows shot up. "What's this? Is that possessiveness I detect? Surely you haven't forgotten the love of your life so easily?"

Célie. Her name cut through me like a serrated knife. Last night, I'd written her a final letter. She deserved to hear what had happened from me. And now, we were . . . done. Truly done this time. I tried and failed to swallow the lump in my throat.

Please, please, forget me.

I could never forget you.

You must.

The letter had left with the post at first light.

"Have you told her yet?" Jean Luc kept hard on my heels, just tall enough to match my stride. "Did you go to her last night? One last rendezvous with your lady?"

I didn't answer.

"She won't be pleased, will she? I mean, you *chose* not to marry her—"

"Lay off, Jean Luc."

"—yet now you've married a filthy street rat who tricked you into a compromising position. Or did she?" His eyes flared, and he caught my arm. I tensed, longing to break his grip. Or his nose.

"One can't help but wonder . . . why did the Archbishop force you to marry a criminal if you're innocent?"

I jerked my arm away. Fought to control the anger threatening to explode. "I *am* innocent."

He touched the knot at his eye again, lip curling into a grin. "Of course."

"There you are!" The Archbishop's curt voice preceded him into the foyer. As one, we lifted our fists to our hearts and bowed. When we rose, the Archbishop's gaze fell on me. "Jean Luc has informed me you'll be interrogating your wife today about the witch at Tremblay's."

I nodded stiffly.

"You will, of course, communicate any developments to me directly." He clasped my shoulder with an easy camaraderie that probably drove Jean Luc mad. "We must keep a keen eye on her, Captain Diggory, lest she destroy herself—and you in the process. I would attend the interrogation myself, but . . ."

Though his voice trailed off, his meaning rang clear. *But I can't stand her.* I empathized.

"Yes, sir."

"Go and fetch her, then. I shall be in my study, preparing for evening Mass."

She wasn't in our room.

Or the washroom.

Or the Tower.

Or the entire cathedral.

I was going to strangle her.

I'd told her to stay. I'd presented the reasons—the perfectly rational, easily understandable reasons—and still she'd disobeyed. Still she'd left. And now who knew what foolish antics she was up to—foolish antics that would reflect back on me. A husband who couldn't control his own wife.

Furious, I sat at my desk and waited. Mentally recited every verse I could on patience.

"Be still before the Lord, and wait patiently for him; do not fret over those who prosper in their way, over those who carry out evil devices."

Of course she'd left. Why wouldn't she? She was a criminal. An oath meant nothing to her. My *reputation* meant nothing to her. I sat forward in my chair. Pressed my palms against my eyes to relieve the building pressure in my head.

"Refrain from anger, and forsake wrath. Do not fret—it leads only to evil. For the wicked shall be cut off, but those who wait for the Lord shall inherit the land."

But her face. Her bruises.

I have many enemies.

Surely being my wife couldn't be worse than *that*? She would be cared for here. Protected. Treated better than she deserved. And yet . . . a small, grim voice in the back of my mind whispered that perhaps it was good she had gone. Perhaps this solved a problem. Perhaps—

No. I had made a vow to this woman. To God. I would not forsake it. If she wasn't back in another hour, I'd go out and find her—ransack the city if I must. If I didn't have my honor,

I didn't have anything. She would not take that from me. I wouldn't allow it.

"Well, this is a fun surprise."

I jerked my head up at the familiar voice. Unexpected relief swept through me. Because there, leaning against the doorjamb and grinning, stood my wife. Her arms were crossed against her chest, and beneath her cloak, she wore—she wore—

"What are you wearing?" I shot up from my chair. Stared determinedly at her face and not . . . elsewhere.

She looked down at her thighs—her very visible, very shapely thighs—and parted her cloak farther with the brush of her hand. Casually. As if she didn't know what she was doing. "I believe they're called pants. Surely you've heard of them—"

"I—" Shaking my head, I forced myself to focus, to look *anywhere* but her legs. "Wait, what surprise?"

She strode farther into the room, trailing a finger down my arm as she passed. "You're my husband now, *dear*. What sort of wife would I be if I couldn't speak your language?"

"My language?"

"Silence. You're well versed in it." After tossing aside her cloak, she threw herself down on the bed and stuck a leg up in the air to examine it. I glared at the floor. "I'm a fast learner. I've only known you a few days, but I can already interpret the very angry, slightly doubtful, and frankly *worried* silence you've been fretting in all morning. I'm touched."

Refrain from anger. I unclenched my jaw and glared at the desk. "Where were you?"

"I went out to get a bun."

Forsake wrath. I gripped the back of the chair. Too hard. The wood bit into my fingertips, and my knuckles turned white. "A bun?"

"Yes, a bun." She shucked off her boots. They hit the floor with two dull thuds. "I overslept the matinee—probably because *someone* woke me up at the ass crack—"

"Watch your mouth—"

"—of dawn." She stretched leisurely and fell back against the pillows. Sharp pains shot up my fingers from my grip on the chair. I took a deep breath and let go. "A page boy brought me a rather unfortunate dress this morning—one of the maids', with a neckline up to my ears—to wear until someone could make it to market. No one had exactly made it a priority, so I charmed the kid into giving me the coin the Archbishop left for my wardrobe and took the liberty of purchasing it myself. The rest will be delivered this evening."

Dresses. To purchase *dresses*—not this unholy creation. This pair of trousers looked nothing like the grubby pair she'd worn before. She'd obviously had these tailored with the Archbishop's coin. They fit her like a second skin.

I cleared my throat. Maintained my visual of the desk. "And the guards—they let you—"

"Leave? Of course. We were under the impression this wasn't a prison sentence."

Refrain from anger. I turned slowly. "I told you to stay in the Tower."

I risked a glance at her then. Mistake. She'd propped her knees up, kicking one over the other. Flaunting every curve on her lower body. I swallowed hard and forced my gaze back to the floor.

She knew what she was doing, too. Devil.

"And you expected me to listen?" She laughed. No—chuckled. "Honestly, Chass, it was a little too easy to leave. The guards at the door almost begged me to go. You should've seen their faces when I actually came back—"

"Why did you?" The words came out before I could stop them. I cringed internally. It wasn't as if I *cared*. And it didn't matter, anyway. All that mattered was that she'd disobeyed me. As for my brothers . . . I would need to have a word with them. Clearly. No one abhorred the heathen's presence more than I, but the Archbishop had given orders.

She stayed. For richer or poorer. In sickness and in health.

"I told you, Chass." Her voice grew unusually quiet, and I risked another glance. She'd rolled to her side and now looked me square in the eye. Chin propped in her hand. Arm draped across her waist. "I have many enemies."

Her gaze didn't waver. Her face remained impassive. For the first time since I'd met her, emotion didn't radiate from her very being. She was . . . blank. Carefully, skillfully blank. She arched a brow at my appraisal. A silent question.

But there was no need to ask—to have her confirm what I already suspected. Stupid as it was to take a thief at her word, there wasn't a better explanation for why she'd returned. I didn't want to admit it, but she was clever. Masterful at the art of escape. Probably impossible to find once hidden.

Which meant she was here because she wanted to be. Because she needed to be. Whoever her enemies were, they must've been dangerous.

I broke our eye contact to stare at the bedpost. *Focus.* "You disobeyed me," I repeated. "I told you to stay in the Tower, and you didn't. You broke trust." She rolled her eyes, mask cracking. I tried to resurrect my previous anger, but it didn't burn quite as hot now. "The guards will be more vigilant, especially after the Archbishop hears of your indiscretions. He won't be pleased—"

"Unexpected bonus—"

"And you'll remain confined to the lower floors," I finished through clenched teeth. "The dormitories and commissary."

She sat up, curiosity flaring in her blue-green eyes. "What's on the top floors, again?"

"None of your business." I strode to the door without looking back at her, sighing in relief when a maid strode past. "Bridgette! Can my wife, er, borrow a gown? I'll return it first thing tomorrow morning." When she nodded, blushing, and hurried away, I turned back to Louise. "You'll need to change. We're going to the council room, and you can't wear those in front of my brothers."

She didn't move. "Your brothers? What could they possibly want with me?"

It must've been physically impossible for this woman to submit to her husband. "They want to ask you some questions about your witch friend."

Her answer came immediately. "I'm not interested."

"It wasn't a request. As soon as you're dressed appropriately, we leave."

"No."

I glared at her for a full second longer—waiting for her to concede, waiting for her to demonstrate the proper meekness befitting a woman—before realizing who this was.

Lou. A thief with a man's name. I turned on my heel. "Fine. Let's go."

I didn't wait for her to follow. Honestly, I didn't know what I'd do if she didn't. The memory of the Archbishop striking her reared in my mind, and the heat coursing through me burned hotter. That would never happen again. Even if she cursed— even if she refused to listen to a single word I ever said—I would never raise my fist to her.

Ever.

Which left me fervently hoping she followed.

After a few seconds, soft footsteps echoed behind me in the corridor. Thank God. I shortened my strides, so she could catch up. "Through here," I murmured, leading her down the staircase. Careful not to touch her. "To the dungeon."

She looked up at me in alarm. "The dungeon?"

I almost chuckled. Almost. "The council room is down there."

I ushered her through another corridor. Down a smaller, steeper flight of stairs. Terse voices drifted toward us as we descended. I pushed open the crude wooden door at the base of the stairs and motioned for her to step inside.

A dozen of my brethren stood arguing around an enormous circular table in the middle of the room. Bits of parchment littered it. Newspaper clippings. Charcoal sketches. Underneath it all stretched an enormous map of Belterra. Every mountain range—every bog, forest, and lake—had been inked with care and precision. Every city and landmark.

"Well, well, if it isn't the little thief." Jean Luc's eyes swept over her with keen interest. He sauntered around the table to examine her closer. "Come to grace us with her presence at last."

The others soon followed, ignoring me completely. My lips pressed together in unexpected irritation. I didn't know who bothered me most—my wife for wearing trousers, my brothers for staring, or myself for caring.

"Peace, Jean Luc." I stepped closer, towering behind her. "She's here to help."

"Is she? I thought street rats valued loyalty."

"We do," she said flatly.

He raised a brow. "You refuse to help us then?"

Behave, I pleaded silently. *Cooperate.*

She didn't, of course. Instead, she drifted toward the table, glancing at the bits of paper. I knew without looking who she saw. One face drawn a dozen times. A dozen ways. Mocking us.

La Dame des Sorcières. The Lady of the Witches.

Even the name rankled. She looked nothing like the hag at the parade. Nothing like the raven-haired mother, either. Her hair wasn't even black in her natural form, but a peculiar shade of blond. Almost white. Or silver.

Jean Luc followed her gaze. "You know of Morgane le Blanc?"

"Everyone knows of her." She lifted her chin and shot him a black look. "Even street rats."

"If you helped us get her to the stake, all would be forgiven," Jean Luc said.

"Forgiven?" She arched a brow and leaned forward, planting her bandaged fingers right across Morgane le Blanc's nose. "For what, exactly?"

"For publicly humiliating Reid." Jean Luc mirrored her gesture, his expression hardening. "For forcing him to disgrace his name, his *honor* as a Chasseur."

My brethren nodded their agreement, muttering under their breath.

"That's enough." To my horror, my hand came down on her shoulder. I stared at it—large and foreign on her slim frame. Blinked once. Twice. Then snatched it back and tried to ignore the peculiar look on Jean Luc's face as he watched us. I cleared my throat. "My wife is here to bear witness against the witch at Tremblay's. Nothing more."

Jean Luc raised his brows—politely skeptical, perhaps amused—before he extended a hand to her. "By all means, then, Madame Diggory, please enlighten us."

Madame Diggory.

I swallowed hard and stepped up to the table beside her. I hadn't yet heard the title aloud. Hearing the words . . . it felt strange. Real.

She scowled and knocked his hand away. "It's Lou."

And there she was again. I stared at the ceiling, trying and failing to ignore my brothers' indignant whispers.

"What do you know of the witches?" Jean Luc asked.

"Not much." She trailed her finger along the series of *X*s and circles marring the map's topography. Most were concentrated in La Fôret des Yeux. One circle for every tip we'd received about witches dwelling in the caves there. One *X* for every reconnaissance mission that had turned up nothing.

A grim smile tugged at Jean Luc's mouth. "It would be in your best interests to cooperate, *madame*. Indeed, it is only by the Archbishop's intervention that you are here, intact, rather than scattered across the kingdom as ash. Aiding and abetting a witch is *illegal*."

Tense silence descended as she looked from face to face, clearly deciding whether she agreed. I'd just opened my mouth to prod her in the right direction when she sighed. "What do you want to know?"

I blinked, shocked at her sudden prudence, but Jean Luc didn't pause to savor the moment. Instead, he pounced.

"Where are they located?"

"As if she would've told me."

"Who is *she*?"

She smirked. "A witch."

"Her *name*."

"Alexandra."

"Her surname?"

"I don't know. We operate with secrecy in East End, even amongst friends."

I recoiled at the word, disgust seeping through me. "You—you truly consider the witch a *friend*?"

"I do."

"What happened?" Jean Luc asked.

She glanced around, suddenly mutinous. "*You* did."

"Explain."

"When you busted us at Tremblay's, we all fled," she snapped at him. "I don't know where she went. I don't know if I'll ever see her again."

Jean Luc and I shared a look. If she was telling the truth, this was a dead end. From the little time I'd spent with her, however, I knew she *didn't* tell the truth. Probably wasn't even capable of it. But perhaps there was another way to procure the information we needed. I knew better than to ask about the man of their trio—the one who'd escaped, the one the constabulary searched for even now—but these enemies of hers . . .

If they knew my wife, they might also know the witch. And anyone who knew the witch was worth interrogating.

"Your enemies," I said carefully. "Are they her enemies too?"

"Maybe."

"Who are they?"

She glared down at the map. "They don't know she's a witch, if that's what you're thinking."

"I'd still have their names."

"Fine." She shrugged—immediately bored—and began ticking names off on her fingers. "There's Andre and Grue, Madame Labelle—"

"Madame Labelle?" I frowned, remembering the woman's familiarity with Tremblay the night of the robbery. She'd claimed her presence had been coincidental, but . . . I tensed in realization.

The seal on the Archbishop's tip—the letter he'd thrown in the fire—had been shaped like a rose. And Ansel's stammered description of the informant had been clear: *She had bright red hair and was very—very beautiful.*

Perhaps Madame Labelle's presence hadn't been coincidental after all. Perhaps she *had* known the witch would be there. And if so . . .

I shared a meaningful look with Jean Luc, who pursed his lips and nodded as he too drew the connection. We'd be speaking with Madame Labelle very soon.

"Yes." The heathen paused to scratch out Morgane le Blanc's eyes with a fingernail. I was surprised she didn't trace a mustache in the charcoal. "She tries to lure us into indentures with the Bellerose every few weeks. We keep refusing her. Drives her mad."

Jean Luc broke the shocked silence, sounding genuinely amused. "So you really are a whore."

Too far.

"*Don't,*" I growled, voice low, "call my wife a whore."

He held up his hands in apology. "Of course. How crass of me. Do continue the interrogation, Captain—unless you think we'll need the thumbscrews?"

She fixed him with a steely smile. "That won't be necessary."

I gave her a pointed look. "It won't?"

She reached up and patted my cheek. "I'll be more than happy to continue . . . as long as you say please."

If I hadn't known better, the gesture would've felt affectionate. But I did know better. And this wasn't affection. This was patronization. Even here, now—surrounded by my brethren— she dared to goad me. To humiliate me. My wife.

No—*Lou*. I could no longer deny the name suited her. A man's name. Short. Strong. Ridiculous.

I caught her hand and squeezed—a warning mitigated by my burning cheeks. "We'll dispatch men to interrogate these enemies, but first, we need to know everything that happened that night." I paused despite myself, ignoring my brothers' furious mutters. "Please."

A truly frightening grin split her face.

THE FORBIDDEN INFIRMARY

Lou

My tongue was thick and heavy from talking when my *darling* husband escorted me back to our room. I'd given them an abbreviated version of the tale—how Coco and I had eavesdropped on Tremblay and Madame Labelle, how we'd planned to rob him that night. How we'd stolen from his vault, but Bas—I hadn't bothered concealing his name, as the idiot hadn't bothered concealing mine—had pocketed everything when the Chasseurs arrived. How Andre and Grue had jumped me in that alley. How they'd almost *killed* me.

I'd really emphasized that point.

I *hadn't* mentioned Angelica's Ring. Or Madame Labelle's interest in it. Or Tremblay's trafficking. Or anything that might further connect me to the witches. I walked a thin line as it was, and I didn't need to give them another reason to tie me to the stake.

I knew Madame Labelle and Tremblay wouldn't risk incriminating themselves by mentioning the ring. I hoped Andre and

Grue were intelligent enough to follow suit. Even if they didn't—even if they stupidly revealed they'd known about Angelica's Ring without reporting it—it would be our word against theirs. The honor of Monsieur Tremblay, the king's *vicomte*, was surely worth more than the honor of a couple of criminals.

It also didn't hurt that my husband was in love with his daughter.

Either way—judging by the furious gleam in said husband's eyes—Andre and Grue were in for a thrashing.

You're my wife now, whether we like it or not. No man will ever touch you that way again.

I almost cackled. All in all, it hadn't been a bad afternoon. My husband was still the most pompous ass in an entire tower of pompous asses, but somehow, that had been easy to overlook in the dungeon. He'd actually . . . defended me. Or at least come as close as he was capable without his virtue imploding.

When we reached our room, I headed straight for the tub, craving time alone to think. To plan. "I'm taking a bath."

If my suspicions were correct—and they usually were—the tree man from yesterday had disappeared to the forbidden upper floors. Perhaps to an infirmary? A laboratory? A furnace?

No. The Chasseurs would never murder innocent people, though burning innocent women and children at the stake seemed like it *should* qualify. But I'd heard the Chasseurs' tired argument: there was a difference between murdering and killing. Murder was unjustified. What they did to the witches . . . well, we deserved it.

I turned on the tap and perched on the edge of the tub. Bigotry aside, I'd never considered where the witches' victims actually *went*, why there weren't bodies littering the streets after every attack. All those attacks. All those victims . . .

If such a place existed, it was surely *doused* in magic.

Just the sort of cover I needed.

"Wait." His heavy footsteps halted just behind me. "We have things to discuss."

Things. The word had never sounded so tedious. I didn't turn around. "Such as?"

"Your new arrangements."

"Arrangements?" Now I did turn, stomach sinking. "You mean my new warden."

He inclined his head. "If you'd like. You disobeyed me this morning. I told you not to leave the Tower."

Shit. Being watched . . . that didn't work for me. Didn't work for me at all. I had plans for this evening—namely, a little jaunt to the forbidden upper floors—and I'd be damned if another pompous ass would stand in my way. If I was right, if the Tower held magic, it was a visit I needed to make *alone*.

I took my time mulling over an answer, meticulously unlacing my boots and placing them beside the washroom door. Tying my hair on top of my head. Unwrapping the dressing on my arm.

He waited patiently for me to finish. Damn him. Exhausting all my options, I finally turned around. Perhaps I could . . . deter him. Surely he didn't *want* his new bride to spend ungodly amounts of time with another man? I labored under no delusions he liked me, but men of the Church tended to be possessive of their things.

"Go ahead, then." I smiled pleasantly. "Bring him in. For your sake, he'd better be handsome."

His eyes hardened, and he walked around me to turn off the tap. "Why would he need to be handsome?"

I strolled to the bed and fell back, rolling to my stomach and propping a pillow beneath my chin. I batted my lashes at him. "Well, we *are* going to be spending quite a bit of time together . . . unchaperoned."

He clenched his jaw so tight it looked likely to snap in two. "He *is* your chaperone."

"Right, right." I waved a hand. "Do continue."

"His name is Ansel. He's sixteen—"

"Oooh." I waggled my brows, grinning. "A bit young, isn't he?"

"He's perfectly capable—"

"I like them young, though." I ignored his flushing face and tapped my lip thoughtfully. "Easier to train that way."

"—and he shows great promise as a potential—"

"Perhaps I'll give him his first kiss," I mused. "No, I'll do him one better—I'll give him his first fuck."

My articulate husband choked on the rest of his words, eyes boggling. "Wh—*what* did you just say?"

Hearing impairment. It was getting alarming.

"Oh, don't be so priggish, Chass." I leapt up and crossed the room, flinging the desk drawer open and snatching the leather notebook I'd found—a journal, stuffed full of love letters from none other than Mademoiselle Célie Tremblay. I snorted at the irony. No wonder he loathed me. "'February twelfth—God took special care in forming Célie.'"

His eyes grew impossibly wider, and he lunged for the journal. I dodged—cackling—and ran into the washroom, locking the door behind me. His fists pounded against the wood. "Give me that!"

I grinned and continued reading. "'I long to look upon her face again. Surely there is nothing more beautiful in all the world than her smile—except, of course, her eyes. Or her laugh. Or her lips.' My, my, Chass. Surely thinking of a woman's mouth is impious? What would our dear Archbishop say?"

"Open—this—door." The wood strained as he pounded against it. "Right now!"

"'But I fear I'm being selfish. Célie has made it clear that my purpose is with my brotherhood.'"

"OPEN THIS DOOR—"

"'Though I admire her selflessness, I cannot bring myself to agree with her. Any solution that separates us is not a solution at all.'"

"I'M WARNING YOU—"

"You're *warning* me? What are you going to do? Break down the door?" I laughed harder. "Actually, do it. I dare you." Turning my attention back to his journal, I continued to read. 'I must confess, she still haunts my thoughts. Days and nights blur together as one, and I struggle to focus on anything but her memory. My training suffers. I cannot eat. I cannot sleep. There is only her.'

Good God, Chass, this is getting depressing. Romantic, of course, but still a little melodramatic for my taste—"

Something heavy crashed into the door, and the wood splintered. My livid husband's arm smashed through—again and again—until a sizeable hole revealed his brilliant crimson face. I laughed, chucking the journal through the splinters before he could reach my neck. It bounced off his nose and skidded across the floor.

If he hadn't been so obnoxiously virtuous, I think he would've sworn. After reaching an arm through to unlock the door, he scrambled inside to collect the journal.

"Take it." I nearly cracked a rib from trying not to laugh. "I've already read enough. Quite touching stuff, really. If possible, her letters were even worse."

He snarled and advanced on me. "You—you read my personal—my *private*—"

"How else could I get to know you?" I asked sweetly, dancing around the tub as he approached. His nostrils flared, and he looked closer to breathing fire than anyone I'd ever known. And I'd known quite a few dragonesque characters.

"You—you—"

Words seemed to be failing him. I braced myself, waiting for the inevitable.

"—you *devil*."

And there it was. The worst someone like my upstanding husband could invent. The *devil*. I failed to hide my grin.

"See? You've gotten to know me all by yourself." I winked at him as we circled the tub. "You're much cleverer than you look." I tilted my head, pursing my lips in consideration. "Though you were stupid enough to leave your most intimate correspondences lying around for anyone to read—*and* you keep a journal. Perhaps you aren't so clever after all."

He glared at me, chest heaving with each breath. After a few more seconds, his eyes closed. I watched in fascination as his lips subconsciously formed the words *one, two, three* . . .

Oh my god.

I couldn't help it. Truly, I couldn't. I burst out laughing.

His eyes snapped open, and he gripped the journal so hard he nearly tore it in half. Spinning on his heel, he stormed back into the bedroom. "Ansel will be here any moment. He'll fix the door."

"Wait—what?" My laughter ceased abruptly, and I hurried after him, careful of the splintered wood. "You still want to leave me with a guard? I'll corrupt him!"

He grabbed his coat and stuffed his arms inside. "I told you," he snarled. "You broke trust. I can't watch you all the time. Ansel will do it for me." Jerking open the door to the corridor, he shouted, "Ansel!"

Within seconds, a young Chasseur poked his head in. Wildly curly brown hair fell in his eyes, and his body had the appearance of being stretched somehow, like he'd grown too much in too little time. Beyond his gangly frame, however, he was actually quite handsome—almost androgynous with his smooth olive skin and long, curling eyelashes. Curiously, he wore a coat of pale blue rather than the deep royal blue typical of Chasseurs. "Yes, Captain?"

"You're on guard duty now." My *infuriating* husband's gaze was knifelike as he looked back at me. "Don't let her out of your sight."

Ansel's eyes turned pleading. "But what about the interrogations?"

"You're needed here." His words held no room for argument. I almost felt sorry for the boy—or I would have, if his presence hadn't foiled my entire evening. "I'll be back in a few hours. Don't listen to a word she says, and make sure she *stays put.*"

We watched him close the door in sullen silence.

Right. This was fine. I was nothing if not adaptable. Sinking back onto the bed, I groaned theatrically and muttered, "This should be fun."

At my words, Ansel straightened his shoulders. "Don't talk to me."

I snorted. "This is going to be quite boring if I'm not allowed to talk."

"Well, you're not, so . . . stop."

Charming.

Silence descended between us. I kicked my feet against the bed frame. He looked anywhere but at me. After a few long moments, I asked, "Is there anything to do here?"

His mouth thinned. "I said stop talking."

"Maybe a library?"

"Stop talking!"

"I'd love to go outside. Bit of fresh air, bit of sunshine." I motioned to his pretty skin. "You might want to wear a hat though."

"As if I'd take you outside," he sneered. "I'm not stupid, you know."

I sat up earnestly. "And neither am I. Look, I know I could never get past *you*. You're much too, er, tall. Great long legs like yours would run me down in an instant." He frowned, but I flashed him a winning smile. "If you don't want to take me outside, why don't you give me a tour of the Tower instead—"

But he was already shaking his head. "Reid told me you were tricky."

"Asking for a tour is hardly tricky, Ansel—"

"No," he said firmly. "We're not going anywhere. And you will address me as Initiate Diggory."

My grin vanished. "Are we long-lost cousins, then?"

His brows furrowed. "No."

"You just said your surname is Diggory. That's also my unfortunate husband's surname. Are the two of you related?"

"No." He looked away quickly to stare at his boots. "That's the surname all the unwanted children are given."

"Unwanted?" I asked, curious despite myself.

He scowled at me. "Orphans."

For some unfathomable reason, my chest constricted. "Oh." I paused in search of the right words, but found none—none except . . . "Would it help if I told you I don't have the best relationship with my own mother?"

His scowl only deepened. "At least you *have* a mother."

"I wish I didn't."

"You can't mean that."

"I do." Truer words had never been spoken. Every day of the last two years—every moment, every *second*—I'd wished her away. Wished I'd been born someone else. Anyone else. I offered him a small smile. "I'd trade places with you in an instant, Ansel—just the parentage, not the dreadful outfit. That shade of blue really isn't my color."

He straightened his coat defensively. "I told you to stop talking."

I fell back on the bed in resignation. Now that I'd heard his confession, the next part of my plan—the, uh, *guileful* part—left a sour taste in my mouth. But it didn't matter.

To Ansel's annoyance, I began to hum.

"No humming either."

I ignored him. "'Big Titty Liddy was not very pretty, but her bosom was big as a barn,'" I sang. "'Her creamery knockers drove men off their rockers, but she was blind to their charms—'"

"Stop!" His face burned so vivid a scarlet it rivaled my husband's. "What are you doing? That—that's indecent!"

"Of course it is. It's a pub song!"

"You've been in a pub?" he asked, flabbergasted. "But you're a *woman*."

It took every drop of my willpower not to roll my eyes. Whoever had taught these men about women had been *heinously* out of touch with reality. It was almost as if they'd never met a woman. A *real* woman—not a ludicrous pipe dream like Célie.

I had a duty to this poor boy.

"There are *lots* of women in pubs, Ansel. We aren't like you think. We can do anything you can do—and probably better. There's a whole *world* outside this church, you know. I could show you, if you wanted."

His expression hardened, though pink still bloomed in his cheeks. "No. No more talking. No more humming. No more singing. Just—just stop being you for a little while, eh?"

"I can't make any promises," I said seriously. "But if you gave me a tour..."

"Not happening."

Fine.

"'Big Willy Billy talked sort of silly,'" I bellowed, "'but his knob was long as his—'"

"Stop, STOP." Ansel waved his hands, cheeks flaming anew. "I'll take you on a tour—just, please, *please* stop singing about... that!"

I rose to my feet, clasping my hands together and beaming.

Voilà.

Unfortunately, Ansel started our tour with the vast halls of Saint-Cécile. More unfortunate—he knew an absurd amount about each architectural feature of the cathedral, as well as the history of each relic and effigy and stained-glass window. After listening to his intellectual prowess for the first fifteen minutes, I'd been mildly impressed. The boy was clearly intelligent. After listening to him for the next four hours, however, I'd longed to shatter the monstrance over his head. It'd been a reprieve when he'd concluded the tour for dinner, promising to continue tomorrow.

But he'd almost looked . . . hopeful. As if at some point during our tour, he'd started enjoying himself. As if he weren't used to having anyone's undivided attention, or perhaps having anyone listen to him at all. That hope in his doe-like eyes had quashed my urge to inflict bodily harm.

I couldn't, however, be distracted from my purpose.

When Ansel knocked on my door the next morning, my husband left us without a word, disappearing to wherever it was he went during the day. After the rest of my wardrobe had been delivered, we'd suffered a tense, silent evening together before I'd retired to the bathtub. His journal—and Célie's letters—had both mysteriously disappeared.

Ansel turned to me hesitantly. "Do you still want to finish your tour?"

"About that." I squared my shoulders, determined *not* to waste another day learning about a bone that might once have belonged to Saint Constantin. "As *thrilling* as our excursion was yesterday, I want to see the Tower."

"The Tower?" He blinked in confusion. "But there's nothing here you haven't already seen. The dormitories, dungeon, commissary—"

"Nonsense. I'm sure I haven't seen *everything*."

Ignoring his frown, I pushed him out the door before he could protest.

It took another hour—after feigning interest in the Tower's stables, training yard, and twenty-three cleaning closets—before I finally managed to drag Ansel back to the metal spiral staircase.

"What's up there?" I asked, planting my feet when he tried to lead me back to the dormitories.

"Nothing," he said swiftly.

"You're a terrible liar."

He tugged on my arm harder. "You're not allowed up there."

"Why?"

"Because you're not."

"Ansel." I stuck out my lip, wrapping my arms around his skinny bicep and batting my lashes. "I'll behave. I promise."

He glowered at me. "I don't believe you."

I dropped his arm and frowned. I had *not* just wasted the past hour waltzing about the Tower with a pubescent boy—however adorable he might be—to trip at the finish line. "Fine. Then you leave me no choice."

He eyed me warily. "What are you—"

He broke off as I turned and dashed up the staircase. Though he was taller, I'd guessed correctly: he wasn't yet used to his gangling height, and his limbs were a mess of awkwardness. He stumbled after me, but it wasn't much of a chase. I'd already raced up several flights before he'd worked out how to use his legs.

Skidding slightly at the top, I peered in dismay at the Chasseur sitting guard outside the door—no, *sleeping* outside the door. Propped up in a rickety chair, he snored softly, his chin drooping to his chest and drool dampening his pale blue coat. I darted around him to the door, heart leaping when the handle turned. More doors lined the walls of the corridor beyond at regular intervals, but they weren't what made me lurch to a halt.

No. It was the air. It swirled around me, tickling my nose. Sweet and familiar ... with just a hint of something darker lurking underneath. Something rotten.

You're here you're here you're here, it breathed.

I grinned. Magic.

But my grin quickly faltered. If I'd thought the dormitories were cold, I'd been wrong. This place was worse. Much worse. Almost ... forbidding. The sweetened air unnaturally still.

Two sets of clumsy footsteps broke the eerie silence.

"Stop!" Ansel tumbled through the door after me, lost his footing, and crashed into my back. The guard outside the door—finally awake, and much younger than I'd first assumed—followed suit. We fell in a whirl of curses and tangled bodies.

"Get *off,* Ansel—"

"I'm *trying*—"

"Who *are* you? You aren't supposed to be up here—"

"Excuse me!" We looked up as one toward the tinny voice. It belonged to a frail, teetering old man in white robes and thick spectacles. He held a Bible in one hand and a curious device in the other: small and metal, with a sharp quill at the end of a cylinder.

Shoving them both away and climbing to my feet, I searched frantically for something to say, for some reasonable explanation as to why we were wrestling in the middle of ... whatever this was, but the guard beat me to it.

"I'm sorry, Your Reverence." The boy shot us each a resentful look. His collar had creased his cheek during his nap, and a bit of drool had dried on his chin. "I have no idea who this girl is. *Ansel* let her in here."

"I did not!" Ansel colored indignantly, still out of breath. "*You* were asleep!"

"Oh, dear." The old man pushed his spectacles up the bridge of his nose to squint at us. "This won't do. This won't do at all."

Throwing caution to the winds, I opened my mouth to explain, but a smooth, familiar voice interrupted.

"They're here to see me, Father."

I froze, surprise jolting through me. I knew that voice. I knew it better than my own. But it shouldn't have been *here*—in the heart of Chasseur Tower—when it was supposed to be hundreds of miles away.

Dark, devious eyes settled on me. "Hello, Louise."

I grinned in response, shaking my head in disbelief. *Coco.*

"This is highly unusual, Mademoiselle Perrot," the priest wheezed, frowning. "Private citizens are not allowed in the infirmary without advance notice."

Coco motioned me forward. "But Louise isn't a private citizen, Father Orville. She's Captain Reid Diggory's wife."

She turned back to the guard, who stood gaping at her. Ansel wore a similar expression, his eyes comically wide and his jaw hanging open. Dumbfounded. I resisted the urge to stuff his tongue back in his mouth. It wasn't as if they could even see her figure beneath her enormous white robe. Indeed, the starched fabric of her neckline rose to just below her chin, and her sleeves draped almost to the tips of her fingers, where white gloves concealed the rest. An inconvenient uniform if I'd ever seen one—but a most convenient disguise.

"As you can see," she continued, skewering the guard with a pointed look, "your presence is no longer required. Might I suggest resuming your post? We wouldn't want the Chasseurs to learn about this horrible miscommunication, would we?"

The guard didn't need to be told twice. He hastened back out the door, stopping only when he'd crossed the threshold. "Just—just make sure she signs the register." Then he closed the door with a rather relieved *click*.

"Captain Reid Diggory, you say?" The priest stepped closer, tipping his head back to examine me through his spectacles. They magnified his eyes to an alarming size. "Oho, I've heard all about Reid Diggory and his new bride. You should be ashamed of yourself, *madame*. Tricking a holy man into matrimony! It's ungodly—"

"Father." Coco placed a hand on his arm and fixed him with a steely smile. "Louise is here to help me today . . . as penance."

"Penance?"

"Oh, yes," I added, catching on and nodding enthusiastically. Ansel stared between us with a bewildered expression. I stomped on his foot. Father Orville didn't even blink, the blind old bat. "You must allow me to atone for my sins, Father. I feel absolutely wretched about my behavior, and I've prayed long and hard about how best to punish myself."

I slipped the last of the Archbishop's coin from my pocket. Thank goodness Father Orville hadn't yet noticed my pants. He'd probably have had a fit and died. I stuffed the coin into his palm. "I pray you'll accept this indulgence to alleviate my sentence."

He harrumphed but slid it into his robes. "I suppose caring for the sick *is* a worthy pursuit—"

"Fantastic." Coco beamed and steered me away before he could change his mind. Ansel trailed behind as if unsure where he was supposed to go. "We'll read them Proverbs."

"Mind you follow protocol." Father Orville gestured to the washroom near the exit, where two pieces of parchment had been affixed to the wall. The first was clearly a register of names. I drifted closer to read the tiny script of the second.

INFIRMARY PROCEDURES—WESTERN ENTRANCE

As decreed by HIS EMINENCE, THE ARCHBISHOP OF BELTERRA,
all guests of the cathedral infirmary must present their name and identification to
the initiate on duty. Failure to do so will result in removal from the facilities and
lawful action.

Feuillemort Asylum representatives—
Please check in at Father Orville's office. Packages are distributed from the
Eastern Entrance.
Clergymen and healers—
Please utilize the register and inspection form located at the Eastern Entrance.

The following procedures must be observed at all times:

1. *The infirmary must remain clean and free of debris.*

2. *Irreverent language and behavior are not tolerated.*

3. *All guests must remain with a member of staff. Guests found unaccompanied will be escorted from the facilities. Lawful action may be taken.*

4. *All guests must wear appropriate garments. Upon entry, healers will distribute white robes to don over layperson garments. These robes must be returned to a member of staff before departure from the facilities. These robes aid odor control throughout Cathédral Saint-Cécile d'Cesarine and Chasseur Tower. They are required. Failure to don robes will result in permanent removal from the facilities.*

5. *All guests must wash thoroughly before departure from the facilities. The guest inspection form is located in the washroom near the Western Entrance. Failure to pass inspection will result in permanent removal from the facilities.*

Holy hell. This place was a prison.

"Of course, Father Orville." Coco grabbed my hand and steered me away from the sign. "We'll stay out of your hair. You won't even notice we're here. And you"—she glanced over her shoulder at Ansel—"run along and play. We don't require further assistance."

"But Reid—"

"Come now, Ansel." Father Orville made to clasp Ansel's shoulder and found his elbow instead. "Let the young ladies tend the sickbeds. You and I shall join in prayerful communion until they are done. I have accomplished all I can with the poor souls this morning. I regret two are heading for Feuillemort in the morning, as their souls are unresponsive to my healing hand. . . ."

His voice trailed off as he led Ansel down the corridor. Ansel threw a pleading look over his shoulder before disappearing around the bend.

"Feuillemort?" I asked curiously.

"Shh . . . not yet," Coco whispered.

She opened a door at random and pushed me through. At the sound of our entrance, the man's head twisted toward us—and kept twisting. We watched in horror, frozen, as he crept from the bed on inverted limbs, his joints bending and popping from their sockets unnaturally. An animalistic gleam lit his eyes, and he hissed, scuttling toward us like a spider.

"What in the—"

"Out, out, *out*!" Coco shoved me from the room and slammed the door shut. The man's body thudded against it, and he let out a strange wail. She took a deep breath, smoothing her healer's robes. "Okay, let's try that again."

I eyed the door apprehensively. "Must we?"

She cracked another door open and peered inside. "This one should be fine."

I peeked over her shoulder and saw a woman reading quietly. When she looked up at us, I jerked back, lifting a fist to my mouth. Her skin *moved*—like thousands of tiny insects crawled just beneath the surface.

"No." Shaking my head, I backed away quickly. "I can't do bugs."

The woman held up a pleading hand. "Stay, please—" A

swarm of locusts burst from her open mouth, choking her, and tears of blood streamed down her cheeks.

We slammed the door on her sobs.

"*I* choose the next door." Chest heaving inexplicably, I considered my options, but the doors were all identical. Who knew what fresh horrors lay beyond? Male voices drifted toward us from a door at the end of the corridor, joined by the gentle clinking of metal. Morbidly curious, I inched toward it, but Coco stilled me with a curt shake of her head. "What *is* this place, anyway?" I asked.

"Hell." She guided me up the corridor, casting a furtive look over her shoulder. "You don't want to go down there. It's where the priests . . . experiment."

"Experiment?"

"I stumbled in last night while they were dissecting the brain of a patient." She opened another door, surveying the room carefully before pushing it open wider. "They're trying to understand where magic comes from."

Inside, an elderly gentleman lay chained to an iron bedpost. He stared blankly at the ceiling.

Clink.

Pause.

Clink.

Pause.

Clink.

I looked closer and gasped. His fingers were tipped with black, his nails elongated and sharpened into points. He tapped his forearm with his pointer finger rhythmically. With each tap, a bead of inky blood welled—too dark to be natural. Poisonous. Hundreds of other marks already discolored his entire body—even his face. None had healed over. All wept black blood.

Metallic rot mingled with the sweet scent of magic in the air.

Clink.

Pause.

Clink.

Bile rose in my throat. He looked less a man now, and more a creature of nightmares and shadows.

Coco closed the door behind us, and his milky eyes found mine. The hair on my neck stood up.

"It's just Monsieur Bernard." Coco crossed the room and scooped up one of the manacles. "He must've slipped his chains again."

"Holy hell." I drifted closer as she gently clasped the manacle back around the man's free hand. He continued staring at me with those empty eyes. Unblinking. "What happened to him?"

"The same thing that happened to everyone else up here." She smoothed his limp hair from his face. "Witches."

I swallowed hard and walked to his bedside, where a Bible sat atop a lonely iron chair. Glancing at the door, I lowered my voice. "Perhaps we could help him."

Coco sighed. "It's no use. The Chasseurs brought him in early this morning. They found him wandering outside La Forêt des Yeux." She touched the blood on his hand and lifted it to her nose, inhaling. "His nails are poisoned. He'll be dead soon. That's why the priests have kept him here instead of sending him to the asylum."

Heaviness settled in my chest as I eyed the dying man. "And—and what was that torture device Father Orville was carrying?"

She grinned. "You mean the Bible?"

"Very funny. No—I meant the metal thing. It looked . . . sharp."

Her grin faded. "It is sharp. It's called a syringe. The priests use them for injections."

"Injections?"

Coco leaned back against the wall and crossed her arms. The white of her robes nearly blended into the pale stone, giving the illusion of a floating head staring at me across Monsieur Bernard's body. I shuddered again. This place gave me the creeps.

"That's what they're calling them." Her eyes darkened. "But I've seen what they can do. The priests have been tampering with poison. Hemlock, specifically. They've been testing it on the patients to perfect the dosage. I think they're creating a weapon to use against the witches."

Dread crept down my spine. "But the Church thinks only flame can truly kill a witch."

"Though they might call us demons, they know we're mortal. We bleed like humans. Feel pain like humans. But the injections aren't meant to kill us. They cause paralysis. The Chasseurs will just have to get close enough to inject us, and we're as good as dead."

A moment passed as I tried to grasp this disturbing development. I glanced down at Monsieur Bernard, a bitter taste coating my mouth. Remembered the insects crawling beneath a woman's skin only a few doors down, the bloody tears on her cheeks. Perhaps the priests weren't the only ones to blame.

Paralysis—or even the stake—was preferable to some fates.

"What are you doing here, *Mademoiselle Perrot?*" I finally asked. At least she hadn't used her real name. The Monvoisin family had a certain . . . notoriety. "You're supposed to be hiding with your aunt."

She actually had the gall to pout. "I could ask you the same question. How could you not invite me to your wedding?"

A bubble of laughter escaped my lips. It sounded eerie in the stillness. Monsieur Bernard's nail tapped against his manacle now.

Clink.

Clink.

Clink.

I ignored him. "Trust me, if I would've had any say in the guest list, you would've been there."

"Maid of honor?"

"Of course."

Slightly appeased, Coco sighed and shook her head. "Married to a Chasseur . . . When I heard the news, I didn't believe it." A small grin touched her lips. "You've got balls the size of boulders."

I laughed louder this time. "You are so *depraved*, Coco—"

"And what of your husband's balls?" She waggled her eyebrows fiendishly. "How do they compare to Bas's?"

"What do you know about Bas's balls?" My cheeks hurt from

smiling. I knew it was wrong—what with the cursed, dying Monsieur Bernard lying next to me—but the heaviness in my chest gradually eased as Coco and I fell back into our easy banter. It felt good to see a friendly face after wading through a sea of hostile ones for two straight days—and to know she was safe. For now.

She sighed dramatically and refolded the blanket atop Monsieur Bernard. He didn't stop clinking. "You talk in your sleep. I had to live vicariously." Her smile faded when she looked back at me. She nodded to my bruises. "Did your husband do that?"

"Courtesy of Andre, unfortunately."

"I wonder how Andre would fare without *his* balls. Perhaps I'll pay him a little visit."

"Don't bother. I set the Chasseurs on him—on both of them."

"What?" Her eyes widened in delight as I recounted the interrogation. "You fiendish little witch!" she crowed when I'd finished.

"Shhh!" I stole to the door and pressed my ear against the wood, listening for signs of movement outside. "Do you want them to catch us? Speaking of which . . ." I turned back to face her when I was sure no one hovered outside. "What are you doing here?"

"I came to rescue you, of course."

I rolled my eyes. "Of course."

"One of the healers resigned her post to get married last week. The Fathers needed a replacement."

I gave her a hard look. "And you know this how?"

"Easy." She sank onto the end of the bed. Monsieur Bernard

kept clinking away, though thankfully turned his disturbing stare to her now instead. "I waited for her replacement to show up early yesterday morning and convinced her I would be the better candidate."

"What? How?"

"I asked her nicely, of course." She fixed me with a pointed stare before rolling her eyes. "How do you think? I stole her letter of recommendation and bewitched her into forgetting her own name. The *real* Brie Perrot is currently vacationing in Amaris, and no one will ever know the difference."

"Coco! What a stupid risk—"

"I've been trying to find a way to speak with you all day, but the priests are relentless. I've been in *training*." She pursed her lips at the word before drawing a wrinkled piece of parchment from her robes. I didn't recognize the spiked handwriting, but I did recognize the dark stain of blood. The sharp scent of blood magic. "I sent a letter to my aunt, and she's agreed to protect you. You can come back with me. The coven is camped near the city, but they won't remain there long. They're heading north within the fortnight. We can sneak out of here before anyone knows you're gone."

My stomach sank. "Coco, I . . ." Sighing, I looked around the austere room for an explanation. I couldn't tell her I didn't trust her aunt—or anyone except for her, for that matter. Not really. "I think this might be the safest place for me right now. A Chasseur literally just took an *oath* to protect me."

"I don't like it." She shook her head fervently and rose to her feet. "You're playing with fire here, Lou. Sooner or later, you *will* get burnt."

I grinned halfheartedly. "Let's hope for later, then."

She glared at me. "This isn't funny. You're leaving your safety—your *life*—up to men who'll burn you if they discover what you are."

My grin faded. "No, I'm not." When she looked likely to argue, I spoke over her. "I'm not. I swear I'm not. It's why I came up here today—why I'll keep coming up here every day until she comes for me. Because she *will* come for me, Coco. I won't be able to hide forever."

I paused, taking a deep breath.

"And when she does, I'm going to be ready. No more depending on tricks and costumes. Or Babette's reconnaissance or Bas's lineage. Or you." I gave her an apologetic smile and twisted Angelica's Ring on my finger. "It's time I start being proactive. If this ring hadn't been in Tremblay's vault, I would've been in serious shit. I've let myself grow weak. The risk of discovery outside this corridor is too great, but here . . . here I can practice, and no one will ever know."

She smiled, slow and broad, and looped her arm through mine. "That's more like it. Except you're wrong about one thing. You'll absolutely keep depending on me, because I'm not going anywhere. We'll practice together."

I frowned, torn between begging her to stay and forcing her to go. But it wasn't my decision, and I already knew what she'd tell me if I tried to force her to do anything. I'd learned my favorite swear words from her, after all. "It'll be dangerous. Even with the smell disguising the magic, the Chasseurs could still discover us."

"In which case you'll *need* me here," she pointed out, "so I can drain all the blood from their bodies."

I stared at her. "Can you do that?"

"I'm not sure." She winked and bade goodbye to Monsieur Bernard. "Perhaps we should find out."

THE ESCAPE

Lou

Lavender-scented bubbles and warm water were lapping around my ribs when my husband returned later that afternoon. His voice echoed through the walls. "Is she in there?"

"Yes, but—"

The *tête carrée* didn't pause to listen or to question why Ansel stood in the corridor instead of in the bedroom. I grinned in anticipation. Though he was going to ruin my bath, the look on his face would make up for it.

Sure enough, he burst into the bedroom a second later. I watched as his eyes swept the room, searching for me.

Ansel had removed the washroom door in an attempt to patch the hole my husband had punched through it earlier, but I hadn't waited for him to finish. The frame now stood gloriously empty, a perfect showcase for my soapy, naked skin. And his humiliation. It didn't take long for him to find me. That same, wonderful choking noise burst from his throat, and his eyes widened.

I gave a cheery wave. "Hello there."

"I—what are you—Ansel!" He nearly collided with the door-frame in his effort to flee. "I asked you to fix the door!"

Ansel's voice rose hysterically. "There wasn't time—"

With a growl of impatience, my husband slammed the bedroom door shut.

I imagined a bubble as his face and flicked it. Then another. And another. "You're very rude to him, you know."

He didn't speak. Probably trying to control the blood rushing to his face. I could still see it, though. It crept up his neck and blended into his coppery hair. Leaning forward, I folded my arms over the edge of the tub. "Where have you been?"

His back stiffened, but he didn't turn. "We didn't catch them."

"Andre and Grue?"

He nodded.

"So what happens now?"

"We have Chasseurs monitoring East End. With any luck, we'll apprehend them soon, and they'll each spend several years in prison for assault."

"After they give you information on my friend."

"After they give me information on the witch."

I rolled my eyes, flinging water at the back of his head. It soaked his copper hair and cascaded down the collar of his shirt. He whirled indignantly, fists clenched—then stopped short, slamming his eyes shut.

"Can you put something on?" He waved a hand in my direction, the other firmly pressed against his eyes. "I can't talk to you when you're sitting there—sitting there—"

"Naked?"

His teeth clamped together with an audible *snap*. "Yes."

"Sorry, but no. I haven't finished washing my hair yet." I slid back beneath the bubbles with an irritated sigh. Water lapped against my collarbone. "But you can look now. All my fun bits are covered."

He cracked an eye open. Upon seeing me safely beneath the foam, he relaxed—or relaxed as much as someone like him was capable. He had a permanent stick up his ass, this husband of mine.

He moved closer cautiously and leaned against the empty doorframe. I ignored him, dumping more of the lavender soap in my palm. We were both silent as he watched me lather my hair.

"Where did you get those scars?" he asked.

I didn't pause. Though mine were nothing compared to Coco's and Babette's, I still had quite a few. A hazard of a life on the streets. "Which ones?"

"All of them."

I risked a glance at him then, and my heart plummeted when I realized he was staring at my throat. I directed him to my shoulder instead, pointing at the long, jagged line there. "Ran into the wrong end of a knife." I held up my elbow to show him another speckling of scars. "Tangled with a barbed-wire fence." Tapped beneath my collarbone. "Another knife. That one hurt like a bitch too."

He ignored my language, eyes inscrutable as he stared at me. "Who did it?"

"Andre." I dipped my hair back into the water, smiling when he averted his eyes. Hair clean, I wrapped my arms around my shins and rested my chin on my knees. "He got the jump on me when I first arrived in the city."

He sighed heavily, as if he were suddenly weary. "I'm sorry we didn't find them."

"You will."

"Oh?"

"They aren't the brightest. They'll probably show up here by morning, demanding to know why you're searching for them."

He chuckled and rubbed his neck, emphasizing the curve of his bicep. He'd rolled up his shirtsleeves since the interrogation, and I couldn't help but trace the long line of his forearm to his hand. To his callused fingers. To the fine, copper hair dusting his skin.

He cleared his throat and dropped his arm hastily. "I should go. We're interrogating Madame Labelle soon. Then the other one—the thief at Tremblay's. Bastien St. Pierre."

My heart stopped, and I pitched forward, sloshing bubbles and water in every direction. "Not Bas?" He nodded, eyes narrowing. "But—but he escaped!"

"We found him skulking outside a back entrance to Soleil et Lune." Disapproval radiated from him. "It's just as well. The constabulary would've arrested him sooner or later. He killed one of Tremblay's guards."

Holy hell. I sat back, chest tightening as panic clawed up my throat, and fought to control my breathing. "What will happen to him?"

His eyebrows drew together in surprise. "He'll hang."

Shit.

Shit, shit, *shit.*

Of *course* Bas had been arrested. Of *course* he'd murdered a guard instead of knocking him unconscious. Why had the idiot been at Soleil et Lune in the first place? He'd known they were looking for him. He'd *known.* Why hadn't he fled? Why hadn't he been halfway across the sea? Why hadn't he been, well, *Bas?*

Despite the warm bathwater, gooseflesh rose on my skin. Could he . . . could he have come back for me? Hope and despair warred in my chest, equally hideous, but panic soon conquered them both.

"You have to let me see him."

"That's out of the question."

"Please." I loathed the word, but if he refused—if pleading didn't work—I'd have only one option. Magic outside the infirmary was a huge risk, but it was one I'd have to take.

Because Bas knew about Coco, yes—but he also knew about me.

I wondered how much information on two witches was worth. His life? His prison sentence? A fair trade in the eyes of the Chasseurs, and one Bas was sure to make. Even if he *had* come back for me, he wouldn't hesitate with his life in the balance.

I cursed myself for confiding in him. I'd known his character. I'd known who he was, yet still I'd allowed myself to relax, to spill my deepest secrets. Well—one of them, anyway. And now I would pay the price, as would Coco.

Stupid. So, so *stupid.*

"Please," I repeated.

My husband blinked at the word, clearly stunned. But his shock soon gave way to suspicion. He scowled. "Why are you so concerned about him?"

"He's a friend." I didn't care that my voice sounded desperate. "A dear friend."

"Of course he is." At my pained expression, he glared at the ceiling and added, almost reluctantly, "He'll have a chance to save himself."

"How so?"

Though I already knew the answer, I held my breath, dreading his next words.

"The witch is still our priority," he confirmed. "If he gives us information that leads to its capture, his sentence will be reevaluated."

I clutched the edge of the tub for support, forcing myself to remain calm. My other hand rose to stroke the scar at my throat—an instinctive, agitated gesture.

After a long moment, his voice drifted toward me on a whisper. "Are you well? You look . . . pale."

When I didn't answer, he strode across the room and crouched beside the tub. I didn't care that the bubbles were thinning. Apparently, neither did he. He reached out and touched a strand of hair by my ear. Soap came away on his fingers. "You missed a spot."

I said nothing as he pooled water in his palm and let it trickle down my hair, but my breath caught when his fingers hovered above my throat. "How did you get this one?" he murmured.

Swallowing hard, I searched for a lie and found none. "That's a story for another day, Chass."

He leaned back on his heels, blue eyes searching my face.

I covered the scar instinctively and stared at my reflection in the soapy water. After everything I'd been through—after everything I'd endured—I would not burn for Bas. I was no one's sacrifice. Not then. Not now. Not ever.

There was only one thing to do.

I would have to save him.

My husband left me a few moments later to return to the council room. Vaulting from the tub, I hastened to find the candle I'd hidden within the linen cupboard. I'd nicked it from the sanctuary during Ansel's tour yesterday. With quick, practiced movements, I lit the wax and set it on the desk. Herbal smoke immediately overpowered the room, and I sighed in relief. The smell wasn't quite right, but it was close enough. By the time he returned, the magic would've faded. Hopefully.

After pacing the room frenetically for several long minutes, I forced myself to sit on the bed. Waited impatiently for Ansel to return.

He was young. Easily turned, perhaps. At least that's what I told myself.

After an eternity and a day, he knocked on the door.

"Come in!"

He walked into the room warily, eyes darting to the washroom. Clearly checking to make sure I was properly clothed.

I stood and took a deep breath, steeling myself for what was to come. I could only hope Ansel wasn't wearing his Balisarda.

Smiling coyly, I locked eyes with him as he stepped farther into the room. My skin tingled in anticipation. "I missed you."

He blinked at my strange voice, brows furrowing. Sauntering closer, I placed a hand on his forearm. He made to jerk away but paused at the last second. He blinked again.

I drew up against his chest and drank in his scent—his essence. My skin shone against the pale blue of his coat. We gazed at the glow together, lips parting. "So strong," I breathed. The words flowed deep and resonant from my lips. "So worthy. They have made a mistake in underestimating you."

A range of emotions flitted across his face at my words—at my touch.

Confusion. Panic. Desire.

I trailed a finger down his cheek. He didn't lean away from the contact. "I see the greatness in you, Ansel. You will kill many witches."

His eyelashes fluttered softly, and then—nothing. He was mine. I wrapped my arms around his narrow waist, glowing all the brighter. "Will you help me?" He nodded, eyes wide as he stared down at me. I kissed his palm and closed my eyes, breathing deeply. "Thank you, Ansel."

The rest was easy.

I allowed him to lead me to the dungeon. Instead of proceeding down the narrow stairwell to the council room, however, we veered right, to the cells where they held Bas. The Chasseurs—my husband included—still questioned Madame Labelle, and only two guards stood outside the cells. They wore pale blue coats like Ansel.

They turned to us in bewilderment as we approached, their hands immediately reaching for weapons—but not Balisardas. I smiled as shimmering, golden patterns materialized between us. They thought they were safe inside their Tower. So foolish. So careless.

Catching at a web of patterns, I clenched my fists and sighed as my affectionate memories of Bas—the love I'd once felt, the warmth he'd once brought me—slipped into oblivion. The guards crumpled to the floor, and the cords disappeared in a burst of shimmering dust. *Memory for memory,* the voice in my head crooned. *A worthy price. It is better this way.*

Bas's eyes shone triumphant as he beheld me. I drifted closer to the cell, tilting my head to the side as I examined him. They'd shaved his head and stubble in prison to prevent lice. It didn't suit him.

"Lou!" He clenched the bars and pressed his face between them. Panic flared in his eyes. "Thank god you're here. My cousin tried to bond me out, but they wouldn't listen. They're going to hang me, Lou, if I don't tell them about Coco—" He broke off, true fear distorting his features at the distant, otherworldly look on my face. My skin glowed brighter. Ansel dropped to his knees behind me.

"What are you doing?" Bas ground his palms against his eyes in an attempt to fight off the charm emanating from me. "Don't do this. I—I'm sorry I left you at Tremblay's. You know I'm not as brave, or as—as clever as you and Coco. It was wrong of me. I should've stayed—I should've h-helped . . ."

A shudder wracked his body as I drew closer, and I smiled, small and cold. "Lou, please!" he begged. Another shudder—stronger this time. "I wouldn't have told them anything about you. You know that! No—please, don't!"

His shoulders drooped, and when his hands fell to his sides once more, his face was blissfully blank.

"So clever, Bas. So cunning. You always had such pretty words." I cupped his face through the cell door. "I am going to give you something, Bas, and in return, you are going to give something to me. How does that sound?" He nodded and smiled. I leaned closer and kissed his lips. Tasted his breath. He sighed in contentment. "I am going to free you. All I ask for in return are your memories."

I tightened my fingers on his cheek—on the gold swirling around his handsome face. He didn't struggle as my fingernails bit into his skin, pricked the tiny silver scar on his jaw. I wondered briefly how he'd gotten it.

When I finished—when the golden mist had stolen every memory of my face and Coco's from his mind—Bas fell to the floor. His face bled due to my nails, but otherwise, he would recover. I bent to retrieve the keys from the guard's belt and dropped them beside him. Then I turned to Ansel.

"Your turn, precious." I knelt next to him and wrapped my

hands around his shoulders, brushing my lips against his cheek. "This might hurt a little."

Concentrating on the scene before us, I stole the memory from Ansel's mind. It took only a few seconds before he too fell to the floor.

I struggled to remain conscious, but black seeped into the edges of my vision as I repeated the process on the guards. I had to pay the price. I had taken, and now I must give. Nature demanded balance.

Swaying slightly, I toppled over Ansel and surrendered to the darkness.

I blinked awake a short time later. My head throbbed, but I ignored it, climbing hastily to my feet. The cell door was open, and Bas was gone. Ansel, however, showed no signs of stirring.

I bit my lip, deliberating. He'd be punished if found outside a prisoner's empty cell, especially with two guards unconscious at his feet. Worse, he'd have no memory of how he'd gotten there and no way to defend himself.

Scowling, I massaged my temples and tried to formulate a plan. I needed to hurry—needed to somehow wash the smell of magic from my skin before the Chasseurs caught up to me—but I couldn't just leave him. Seeing no other alternative, I hoisted him up beneath his armpits and dragged him away. We'd only made it a few paces when my knees began to buckle. He was heavier than he looked.

Angry voices reached me when I neared the staircase. Though Ansel was finally beginning to stir, I wasn't strong enough to haul him up each step. The voices grew louder. Cursing silently, I pushed him through the first door I saw and edged it shut behind us.

My breath left me in a relieved *whoosh* when I straightened and looked around. A library. We were in a library. Small and unadorned—like everything else in this wretched place—but still a library.

Footsteps stormed up and down the corridor, and more voices added to the cacophony.

"He's gone!"

"Search the Tower!"

But the library door remained—miraculously—closed. Praying it would remain that way, I heaved Ansel into one of the reading chairs. He blinked at me, his eyes struggling to focus, before slurring, "Where are we?"

"The library." I threw myself into the chair next to him and pulled a book at random from the shelf. *Twelve Treatises of Occult Extermination.* Of course. My hands shook with the effort not to rip the hideous pages from their binding. "We were just in the infirmary with Father Orville and Co— er, Mademoiselle Perrot. You brought me down here to—to—" I tossed *Twelve Treatises* on the nearest table and reached for the leather-bound Bible beside it. "To educate me. That's it."

"W-What?"

I groaned as the door burst open, and my husband and Jean Luc pounded in.

"It was you, wasn't it?" Jean Luc advanced toward me with murder in his eyes.

My husband stepped forward, but Ansel was already there. He

swayed slightly on his feet, but his eyes sharpened at Jean Luc's approach. "What are you talking about? What's happened?"

"The prisoner escaped," Jean Luc snarled. Beside him, my husband stilled, his nostrils flaring. Shit. The smell. It still clung to Ansel and me like a second skin, trailing from the empty cell straight to us. "His cell is empty. The guards were knocked unconscious."

I was doomed. Good and truly doomed this time. Gripping the Bible tighter to keep my hands from trembling, I met each of their gazes with forced calm. At least the Chasseurs would burn me. Not a drop of my blood would be spilled. I savored that small victory.

My husband watched me through narrowed eyes. "What . . . is that smell?"

More footsteps thudded outside, and Coco skidded into the room before I could answer. A fresh wave of sickly-sweet air washed over us at her arrival, and my heart lodged firmly in my throat.

"I overhead the priests talking about the prisoner's escape!" Her breath came out in short pants, and she clutched her side. When her eyes found mine, however, she nodded reassuringly and straightened, ensuring her white healer's robes still covered every inch of her skin. "I came to see if I could help."

Jean Luc's nose wrinkled in distaste at the reek emanating from her. "Who are you?"

"Brie Perrot." She swept into a curtsy, rapidly regaining her composure. "I'm the new healer in the infirmary."

He frowned, unconvinced. "Then you know healers aren't

allowed free rein of the Tower. You shouldn't be down here, especially with a prisoner roaming free."

Coco skewered him with a pointed look before appealing to my husband instead. "Captain Diggory, your wife accompanied me earlier while I read the patients Proverbs. Ansel escorted her. Isn't that right, Ansel?"

God, she was brilliant.

Ansel blinked at us, confusion clouding his eyes once more. "I—yes." He frowned and shook his head, obviously trying to account for the gap in his memories. "You took a bath, but we— we did go to the infirmary." His eyes narrowed in concentration. "I . . . I prayed with Father Orville."

I breathed a sigh of relief, hoping Ansel's memories stayed muddled.

"He can confirm?" my husband asked.

"Yes, sir."

"Charming. However, that doesn't explain why the cell reeked of magic." Clearly irritated by Coco's dismissal, Jean Luc glowered between the three of us. "*Or* the unconscious guards."

Coco fixed him with a razor-sharp smile. "Unfortunately, I was called away to attend a patient before I could instruct Madame Diggory in washing properly. She and Ansel left shortly after."

My husband's eyes nearly burned my face. "Naturally, you came here instead of returning to our room."

I willed myself to look repentant, returning the Bible to the table. With any luck, we might just be able to survive this mess.

"Ansel wanted to teach me some verses, and I . . . I went to see him in his cell. Bas." Fidgeting with a lock of hair, I looked up at him through lowered lashes. "You said he might be hanged, and I wanted to speak with him . . . before. One last time. I'm sorry."

He said nothing. Only glared at me.

"And the guards?" Jean Luc asked.

I rose and gestured to my small frame. "You really think I could knock two fully grown men unconscious?"

My husband's reply came instantaneously. "Yes."

Under different circumstances, I would've been flattered. Now, however, his unwavering faith in my abilities was damnably inconvenient.

"They were unconscious when I arrived," I lied. "And Bas was already gone."

"Why didn't you inform us at once? Why flee?" Jean Luc's pale eyes narrowed, and he stepped forward until I was forced to look up at him to maintain eye contact. I scowled.

Fine. If he wanted to intimidate, I could play along.

I broke our gaze and looked down at my hands, chin quivering. "I—I confess I'm sometimes inhibited by the weaknesses of my sex, *monsieur*. When I saw Bas had escaped, I panicked. I know it's no excuse."

"Good Lord." Rolling his eyes at my tears, Jean Luc shot an exasperated look at my husband. "You can explain this one to His Eminence, *Captain*. I'm sure he'll be delighted by another failure." He stalked toward the door, dismissing us. "Return to the infirmary, Mademoiselle Perrot, and take care to remember your place in the future. Healers are granted access only to contained locations—the infirmary, its dormitories, and the back stairwell. If you wish to visit any other area of the Tower, you're expected to wash and undergo inspection. As you're new to the Tower, I'll overlook your misstep this once, but I *will* be speaking to the priests. They'll ensure we don't repeat this little adventure."

If Coco could've exsanguinated someone, I was sure she would've done it just then. I hastened to intervene. "This is my fault. Not hers."

Jean Luc raised a dark brow, inclining his head. "How silly of me. You're right, of course. If you hadn't disobeyed Reid, all of this could've been avoided."

Though I'd asked for the blame, I still bristled at the reproach. Clearly, my husband *wasn't* the most pompous ass of all the asses; the title unequivocally belonged to Jean Luc. I'd just opened my mouth to tell him so when my inopportune husband interrupted.

"Come here, Ansel."

Ansel swallowed hard and stepped forward, clasping his quaking hands behind his back. Unease flitted through me.

"Why did you allow her in the infirmary?"

"I told you, I *invited*—" Coco started, but she stopped abruptly at the look on my husband's face.

Ansel's cheeks tinged pink, and he glanced to me, eyes pleading. "I—I only took Madame Diggory up there because— because—"

"Because we have an obligation to those poor souls. The healers are swamped—overworked and understaffed. They hardly have time to tend to the patients' basic needs, let alone nourish their spiritual welfare." When he remained unconvinced, I added, "Also, I was singing a bawdy song and refused to stop until he took me." I bared my teeth in an attempt at a smile. "Would you like to hear it? It's about a lovely woman called Big Titty—"

"Enough." Anger blazed in his eyes—true anger, this time. Not humiliation. Not irritation. Anger. He looked between the three of us slowly, deliberately. "If I find out any of you are lying, I'll show you no mercy. You'll all be punished to the full extent of the law."

"Sir, I swear—"

"I told you the infirmary was forbidden." His voice was hard and unforgiving as he looked at Ansel. "I expected my wife to disobey me. I didn't expect it from you. You're dismissed."

Ansel dropped his head. "Yes, sir."

Outrage washed over me as I watched him shuffle dejectedly to the door. I moved to follow him—yearning to hug him or otherwise console him somehow—but my pigheaded husband caught my arm. "Stay. I'd like a word with you."

I wrenched my arm away and fired up at once. "And I'd like a word with *you*. How dare you blame Ansel? As if any of this is his fault!"

Jean Luc heaved a long-suffering sigh. "I'll escort you to the infirmary, Mademoiselle Perrot." He extended his arm to her, clearly bored with the direction the conversation had taken. Her answering glare was withering. Scowling, he turned to leave without her, but Ansel had paused on the threshold, blocking the way. Tears clung to his lashes as he looked back at me, eyes wide—shocked that someone had spoken up for him. Jean Luc prodded his back impatiently, muttering something I couldn't hear. My blood boiled.

"He was charged with watching you." My husband's eyes blazed, oblivious to everyone but me. "He failed in his duty."

"Oh, *ta gueule*!" I crossed my arms to keep from wrapping my hands around his throat. "I'm a grown-ass woman, and I'm perfectly capable of making my own choices. This is no one's fault but mine. If you're going to bully *anyone*, it should be me, not Ansel. The poor kid can't catch a break with you—"

His face nearly purpled. "He isn't a child! He's training to become a Chasseur, and if that should happen, he must learn to take responsibility—"

"Ansel, move," Jean Luc said flatly, interrupting our tirade. He finally managed to push Ansel through the door. "As entertaining as this is, some of us have work to do, prisoners to find, witches to burn . . . those sorts of things. Mademoiselle Perrot, you're expected in the infirmary in ten minutes. I *will* be checking." He gave us both one last irritated look before stomping from the room. Coco rolled her eyes and moved to follow, but she hesitated on the threshold. Her eyes held a silent question.

"It's fine," I muttered.

She nodded once, shooting my husband an irritated look of her own, before closing the door behind her.

The silence between us was blistering. I half expected the books to catch fire. It would've been fitting, given every book in this hellish place was evil. I eyed *Twelve Treatises of Occult Extermination* with newfound interest, picking it up as golden patterns shimmered into existence around me. If I hadn't been so furious, I would've startled. It'd been a long time since unbidden patterns had appeared in my mind's eye. Already, I could feel my magic awakening, desperate for freedom after years of repression.

It would just take a spark, it coaxed. *Relinquish your anger. Set the page aflame.*

But I didn't want to relinquish my anger. I wanted to throttle my husband with it.

"You lied to us." His voice cut sharply through the silence. Though I continued staring at the book, I could clearly picture the vein in his throat, the taut muscles of his jaw. "Madame Labelle told us the witch's name is Cosette Monvoisin, not Alexandra."

Yes, and she's currently contemplating how to drain all the blood from your body. Perhaps I should help her. Instead, I chucked *Twelve Treatises of Occult Extermination* at his head. "You knew I was a snake when you picked me up."

He caught it before it could break his nose, throwing it back at me. I dodged, and it crumpled to the floor where it belonged. "This isn't a game!" he shouted. "We are charged with keeping this kingdom *safe*. You've seen the infirmary! Witches are *dangerous*—"

My hands curled into fists, and the patterns around me flickered wildly. "As if Chasseurs are any less so."

"We're trying to *protect* you!"

"Don't ask me to apologize, because I won't!" A ringing started in my ears as I stormed toward him—as I placed both hands on his chest and pushed. When he didn't budge, a snarl tore from my throat. "I will *always* protect those who are dear to me. Do you understand? *Always.*"

I pushed him again, harder this time, but his hands caught my own and trapped them against his chest. He leaned down, raising a copper brow. "Is that so?" His voice was soft again. Dangerous. "Is that why you helped your lover escape?"

Lover? Baffled, I lifted my chin to glare at him. "I don't know what you're talking about."

"So you deny it, then? That he's your lover?"

"I *said*," I repeated, staring pointedly at his hands around mine, "I don't know what you're talking about. Bas isn't my lover, and he never has been. Now let me *go.*"

To my surprise, he released me—hastily, as if startled he'd been touching me in the first place—and stepped back. "I can't protect you if you lie to me."

I charged to the door without looking at him. *"Va au diable."*
Go to hell.

LORD, HAVE MERCY

Lou

Hushed voices drifted toward us from the sanctuary, and fire-light cast shadows on the faces of the icons around us. Yawning, I stared at the one nearest me—a plain woman with a look of supreme boredom on her face. I sympathized.

"I still remember my first attempt. I hit the bull's-eye straight-away." The Archbishop chuckled, winding up as old men often do when reliving tales of the past. "Mind you, I was fresh off the street—just turned seven—with not a *couronne* in my pocket or any experience to my name. Hadn't even *held* a bow, let alone fired an arrow. The old bishop proclaimed it an act of God."

My husband's lips quirked in response. "I believe it."

I yawned again. The oratory was stifling, and the wool gown I wore—demure and drab and deliciously warm—didn't help matters. My eyelids drooped.

It would be an act of God if I made it through the service without snoring.

After the library fiasco, I'd thought it, ah, *prudent* to accept my husband's invitation to evening Mass. Though I didn't know if he believed Ansel's and my story about learning scripture, he'd latched on to the idea, and I'd spent the remainder of the day memorizing verses. The most diabolical of all punishments.

"'A continual dropping in a very rainy day and a contentious woman are alike,'" he'd recited, eyeing me irritably and waiting for me to repeat the verse. Still peeved from our earlier argument.

"Rain and men are both pains in the ass."

He'd scowled but continued. "'Whosoever hideth her hideth the wind, and the ointment of his right hand, which bewrayeth itself.'"

"Whosoever hideth her . . . something about ointment and a hand . . ." I'd waggled my eyebrows devilishly. "*Quel risque!* What sort of book is—"

He'd interrupted before I could further impugn his honor, voice hardening. "'Iron sharpeneth iron; so a man sharpeneth the countenance of his friend.'"

"Iron sharpeneth iron, so you're being an ass because I, too, am a piece of metal."

On and on and on it'd gone.

Honestly, the invitation to Mass had been a welcome reprieve.

The Archbishop clasped his shoulder with another hearty chuckle. "I missed the target entirely on my second attempt, of course."

"You still did better than me. I took a week to hit the target."

"Nonsense!" The Archbishop shook his head, still smiling at the memory. "I distinctly remember your natural talent. Indeed, you were quite a deal more skilled than the other initiates."

The clanging from the bell tower spared me from leaping into the fireplace.

"Ah." Seeming to remember himself, the Archbishop dropped his hand, straightening and rearranging the cloth at his neck. "The service is about to begin. If you'll excuse me, I must join the other attendants." He paused at the threshold, expression hardening as he turned. "And *do* remember what we discussed this afternoon, Captain Diggory. A closer eye is necessary."

My husband nodded, cheeks flushing. "Yes, sir."

I rounded on him as soon as the Archbishop left.

"A closer eye? What the hell does that mean?"

"Nothing." Clearing his throat hastily, he extended his arm. "Shall we?"

I strode past him into the sanctuary. "A closer eye, my ass."

Lit by hundreds of candles, the sanctuary of Saint-Cécile looked like something out of a dream—or a nightmare. Over half the city had gathered in the vast room to hear the Archbishop's sermon. Those wealthy enough to procure seats had dressed in jewel-toned finery: gowns and suits of rich burgundy, amethyst, and emerald with golden trim and lace sleeves, fur muffs and silk cravats. Pearls shone luminescent from their ears, and diamonds sparkled ostentatiously from their throats and wrists.

At the back of the sanctuary, the poorer sect of the congregation stood, faces solemn and dirty. Hands clasped. A number of blue-coated Chasseurs stood as well, including Jean Luc. He waved us over.

I cursed silently when my husband complied. "We *stand* for the entire service?"

He eyed me suspiciously. "Have you never attended Mass?"

"Of course I have," I lied, digging in my heels as he continued to steer me forward. I wished I'd worn a hood. There were more people here than I'd ever imagined. Presumably, none of them were witches, but one never knew . . . *I* was here, after all. "Once or twice."

At his incredulous expression, I gestured down the length of my body. "Criminal, remember? Forgive me for not memorizing every proverb and learning every rule."

Rolling his eyes, he pushed me the final few steps. "Chasseurs stand as an act of humility."

"But *I'm* not a Chasseur—"

"And praise God for that." Jean Luc stepped aside to make room for us, and my *domineering* husband forced me between them. They clasped forearms with tense smiles. "I didn't know if you'd be joining us, given the fiasco this afternoon. How did His Eminence handle the news?"

"He didn't blame us."

"Who did he blame, then?"

My husband's eyes flicked to me for the briefest of seconds before returning to Jean Luc's. "The initiates on duty. They've been relieved of their positions."

"Rightfully so."

I knew better than to correct him. Fortunately, their conversation ended when the congregation stood and began to chant. My husband and Jean Luc joined in seamlessly as the Archbishop and his attendants entered the sanctuary, proceeded up the aisle, and bowed to the altar. Bewildered—and unable to comprehend a word of their dreary ballad—I made up my own lyrics.

They may or may not have involved a barmaid named Liddy.

My husband scowled and elbowed me as silence descended once more. Though I couldn't be sure, Jean Luc's lips twitched as if he were trying not to laugh.

The Archbishop turned to greet the congregation. "May the Lord be with you."

"And also with you," they murmured in unison.

I watched in morbid fascination as the Archbishop lifted his arms wide. "Brethren, let us acknowledge our sins, and so prepare ourselves to celebrate the sacred mysteries."

A priest beside him lifted his voice. "Lord, have mercy!"

"You were sent to heal the contrite of heart," the Archbishop continued. "Lord, have mercy!"

The congregation joined in. "Lord, have mercy!"

"You came to gather the nations into the peace of God's kingdom. Lord, have mercy!"

The peace of God's kingdom? I scoffed, crossing my arms. My husband elbowed me again, mouthing, *Stop it.* His blue eyes bored into mine. *I'm serious.* Jean Luc definitely grinned now.

"Lord, have mercy!"

"You come in word and sacrament to strengthen us in holiness. Lord, have mercy!"

"Lord, have mercy!"

"You will come in glory with salvation for your people. Lord, have mercy!"

"Lord, have mercy!"

Unable to help myself, I muttered, "Hypocrite."

My husband looked likely to expire. His face had flushed red again, and a vein throbbed in his throat. The Chasseurs around us either glared or chuckled. Jean Luc's shoulders shook with silent laughter, but I didn't find the situation quite as funny as before. Where was my kin's salvation? Where was *our* mercy?

"May almighty God have mercy on us, forgive us our sins, and bring us to everlasting life."

"Amen."

The congregation immediately began another chant, but I stopped listening. Instead, I watched as the Archbishop lifted his arms to the heavens, closing his eyes and losing himself in the song. As Jean Luc grinned, nudging my husband when they both sang the wrong words. As my husband grudgingly laughed and pushed him away.

"You take away the sins of the world, have mercy on us," the boy in front of us sang. He clutched his father's hand, swaying to the cadence of their voices. "You take away the sins of the world, have mercy on us. You take away the sins of the world, receive our prayer."

Have mercy on us.

Receive our prayer.

At the end of my Proverbs torture session, there'd been a verse I hadn't understood.

As in water face answereth to face, so the heart of man to man.

"What does it mean?"

"It means . . . water is like a mirror," my husband had explained, frowning slightly. "It reflects our faces back to us. And our lives—the way we live, the things we do—" He'd looked at his hands, suddenly unable to meet my eyes. "They reflect our hearts."

It'd made perfect sense, explained like that. And yet... I looked around at the worshippers once more—the men and women who pleaded for mercy and cried for my blood on the same breath. How could both be in their hearts?

"Lou, I'm—" He'd cleared his throat and forced himself to look at me. Those blue eyes had shone with sincerity. With regret. "I shouldn't have shouted earlier. In the library. I'm . . . sorry."

Our lives reflect our hearts.

Yes, it'd made perfect sense, explained like that, but I still didn't understand. I didn't understand my husband. I didn't understand the Archbishop. Or the dancing boy. Or his father. Or Jean Luc or the Chasseurs or the witches or *her.* I didn't understand any of them.

Conscious of the Chasseurs' eyes on me, I forced a smirk and bumped my husband's hip, pretending that it'd all been a show. A laugh. That I'd just been goading him to get a reaction. That I wasn't a witch in Mass, standing amongst my enemies and worshiping someone else's god.

Our lives reflect our hearts.

They might've all been hypocrites, but I was the biggest one of all.

MADAME LABELLE

Reid

The next evening was the first snowfall of the year.

I sat up from the floor, brushing back my sweaty hair, and watched the flakes drift past the window. Only exercise worked the knots from my back. After stumbling upon me on the floor last night, Lou had claimed the bed. She hadn't invited me to join her.

I didn't complain. Though my back ached, the exercise kept my irritation in check. I'd quickly learned counting didn't work with Lou . . . namely, after she'd started counting right along with me.

She slammed the book she was reading down on the desk. "This is absolute drivel."

"What is it?"

"The only book I could find in that wretched library without the words *holy* or *extermination* in the title." She lifted it up for me to see. *Shepherd*. I almost chuckled. It'd been one of the first books the Archbishop had allowed me to read—a collection of pastoral poems about God's artistry in nature.

She flounced to my bed—*her* bed—with a disgruntled expression. "How anyone can write about grass for twelve pages is beyond me. That's the real sin."

I hoisted myself to my feet and approached. She eyed me warily. "What are you doing?"

"Showing you a secret."

"No, no, no." She scrambled backward. "I'm not interested in your *secret*—"

"Please." Scowling and shaking my head, I walked past her to my headboard. "Stop talking."

To my surprise, she complied, her narrowed eyes watching me scoot the bed frame from the wall. She leaned forward curiously when I revealed the small, rough-hewn hole behind it. My vault. At sixteen—when Jean Luc and I had shared this room, when we'd been closer than brothers—I'd gouged it into the mortar, desperate for a place of my own. A place to hide the parts of myself I'd rather him not find.

Perhaps we'd never been closer than brothers, after all.

Lou craned her neck to see inside, but I blocked her view, rifling through the items until my fingers grazed the familiar book. Though the spine had begun to split from use, the silver thread of the title remained pristine. Immaculate. I handed it to her. "Here."

She accepted it gingerly, holding it between two fingers as if expecting it to bite her. "Well, this is unexpected. *La Vie Éphémère . . .*" She looked up from the cover, lips pursed. "*The Fleeting Life.* What's it about?"

"It's . . . a love story."

Her brows shot up, and she examined the cover with new-found interest. "Oh?"

"Oh." I nodded, biting the inside of my cheek to keep from smiling. "It's tastefully done. The characters are from warring kingdoms, but they're forced to work together when they uncover a plot to destroy the world. They loathe each other initially, but in time, they're able to set aside their differences and—"

"It's a bodice-ripper, isn't it?" She waggled her eyebrows dev-ilishly, flitting through the pages to the end. "Usually the love scenes are toward the back—"

"What?" My urge to smile vanished, and I tugged it from her grasp. She tugged it back. "Of course it isn't," I snapped, grappling for it. "It's a story that examines the social construct of humanity, interprets the nuance of good versus evil, and explores the pas-sion of war, love, friendship, death—"

"Death?"

"Yes. The lovers die at the end." She recoiled, and I snatched the book away. My cheeks burned. I never should've shared it with her. Of course she wouldn't appreciate it. She didn't appreci-ate anything. "This was a mistake."

"How can you cherish a book that ends in death?"

"It doesn't end in death. The lovers die, yes, but the king-doms overcome their enmity and forge an alliance. It ends in hope."

She frowned, unconvinced. "There's nothing hopeful about death. Death is death."

I sighed and turned to place the book back in my vault. "Fine. Don't read it. I don't care."

"I never said I didn't want to read it." She held out a hand impatiently. "Just don't expect me to develop your weirdly evangelical zeal. The plot sounds dreary, but it can't be worse than *Shepherd*."

I clutched *La Vie Éphémère* with both hands, hesitating. "It doesn't describe grass."

"A decisive point in its favor."

Reluctantly, I handed it to her. This time, she accepted it carefully, examining the title with new eyes. Hope flickered in my chest. I cleared my throat and stared behind her at a dent in the headboard. "And . . . it does have a love scene."

She cackled, flipping through the pages eagerly.

I couldn't help it. I smiled too.

A knock sounded an hour later. I paused in the washroom, shirt halfway over my head. The tub half full. Lou made an exasperated noise from the bedroom. Pulling my shirt back down, I opened the newly repaired washroom door as she tossed *La Vie Éphémère* on the quilt and swung her legs from the bed. They barely reached the floor. "Who is it?"

"It's Ansel."

With a grumbled curse, she hopped down. I beat her to the door and pulled it open. "What is it?"

Lou glared at him. "I like you, Ansel, but this had better be something good. Emilie and Alexandre just had a *moment*, and I swear if they don't kiss soon, I will literally die."

At Ansel's confusion, I shook my head, fighting back a grin. "Ignore her."

He nodded, still bemused, before bowing hastily. "Madame Labelle is downstairs, Captain. She—she demands to speak with Madame Diggory."

Lou wriggled beneath my arm. I stepped aside before she could stomp on my toe. Or bite me. A learned experience from our time at the river. "What does she want?"

Lou crossed her arms and leaned against the doorframe. "Did you tell her to piss off?"

"Lou," I warned.

"She refuses to leave." Ansel shifted uncomfortably. "She says it's important."

"Well, then. I suppose Emilie and Alexandre will have to wait. Tragic." Lou elbowed past me to grab her cloak. Then she halted abruptly, nose wrinkling. "Also, Chass—you stink."

I blocked her path. Resisted the urge to rise. Or smell myself. "You're not going anywhere."

"Of course I am." She sidestepped me, scrunching her face and waving a hand in front of her nose. I bristled. Surely I didn't smell *that* bad. "Ansel just said she won't leave until she sees me."

Deliberately, I reached behind her, brushing my sweaty skin against her cheek, and grabbed my coat. She didn't move. Merely turned her head to glare at me, eyes narrowed. Our faces inches apart, I fought the urge to lean down and inhale. Not to smell me—but to smell *her*. When she hadn't been traipsing in the infirmary, she smelled . . . good. Like cinnamon.

Clearing my throat, I shoved my arms into my coat. My shirt, still damp with sweat, rolled and bunched up against my skin. Uncomfortable. "She shouldn't be here. We finished our interrogation yesterday."

And a lot of good it had done us. Madame Labelle was as slippery as Lou. After accidentally revealing the witch's true name, she'd remained tight-lipped and wary. Suspicious. The Archbishop had been furious. She was lucky he hadn't detained her for the stake—her and Lou.

"Perhaps she wants to extend another offer," Lou said, oblivious to the precariousness of her situation.

"Another offer?"

"To buy me for the Bellerose."

I frowned. "The purchase of human beings as property is illegal."

"She won't tell you she's purchasing *me*. She'll say she's purchasing an indenture—for training me, beautifying me, providing me room and board. It's how people like her slip through the cracks. East End runs on indentures." She paused, tilting her head. "But that's probably a moot point now that we're married. Unless you wouldn't mind sharing?"

I buttoned up my coat in tense silence. "She doesn't want to buy you."

She swept past me with a mischievous grin, wiping a bead of sweat from my brow. "Shall we find out?"

Madame Labelle waited in the foyer. Two of my brothers stood beside her. Expressions wary, they looked unsure whether she was welcome at this hour. The Tower—and kingdom—enforced strict curfews. She stood calmly between them, however. Chin held high. Her face—perhaps once exceptionally beautiful, but aged now, with fine lines around her eyes and mouth—broke into a wide smile upon seeing Lou.

"Louise!" She held her arms out as though expecting Lou to embrace her. I almost laughed. "How splendid to see you in such good health—though those bruises on your face look ghastly. I hope our gracious hosts aren't responsible?"

All inclination to laugh died in my throat. "We would never harm her."

Her eyes fell to me, and she clasped her hands together in feigned delight. "How wonderful to see you again, Captain Diggory! Of course, of course. I should've known better. You're far too noble, aren't you?" She smiled, revealing those unnaturally white teeth. "I do apologize for the lateness of the hour, but I need to speak with Louise immediately. I hope you won't mind me stealing her away for a moment."

Lou didn't move. "What do you want?"

"I'd rather hoped to discuss it in private, dear. The information is quite . . . sensitive. I attempted to speak with you yesterday after the interrogation, but my escort and I found you otherwise occupied in the library." She looked between the two of us with a knowing smile, leaning forward and whispering, "I never interrupt a lovers' quarrel. It's one of the few rules by which I live."

Lou's eyes boggled. "That *wasn't* a lovers' quarrel."

"No? Then perhaps you'd be amenable to reconsidering my offer?"

I resisted the urge to step between them. "You need to leave."

"Rest easy, Captain. I have no plans of whisking away your bride . . . yet." At my expression, she winked and laughed. "But I do insist on speaking privately. Is there a room that Madame Diggory and I could use? Somewhere less"—she gestured to the Chasseurs standing at attention around us—"congested?"

At that moment, however, the Archbishop stormed into the foyer in his nightcap. "What's all this commotion? Don't you all have duties to attend—" His eyes widened when he saw Madame Labelle. "Helene. What an unpleasant surprise."

She curtsied. "Likewise, Your Eminence."

I hastened to bow, fisting a hand over my heart. "Madame Labelle is here to speak with my wife, sir."

"Is she?" His gaze didn't waver. He stared at Madame Labelle with burning intensity, lips pressed into a hard line. "How unfortunate, then, that the church locks its doors in approximately"—he pulled a watch from his pocket—"three minutes."

Her answering smile was brittle. "Surely the church shouldn't lock its doors at all?"

"These are dangerous times, *madame*. We must do what we can to survive."

"Yes." Her eyes flicked to Lou. "We must."

Silence descended as we all glared at one another. Tense and awkward. Lou shifted uneasily, and I contemplated removing

Madame Labelle by force. Whatever she claimed otherwise, the woman had made her purpose perfectly clear, and I would burn the Bellerose to the ground before Lou became a courtesan. Like it or not, she'd made an oath to me first.

"Two minutes," the Archbishop said sharply.

Madame Labelle's face twisted. "I am not leaving."

The Archbishop jerked his head toward my brethren, and they inched closer. Brows furrowed. Torn between following orders and removing a woman from the premises. I suffered no such qualms. I too stepped forward, shielding Lou from view. "Yes, you are."

Something flickered in Madame Labelle's eyes as she looked at me. Her sneer faltered. Before I could throw her from the Tower, Lou touched my arm and murmured, "Let's go."

Then several things happened at once.

A crazed gleam entered Madame Labelle's eyes at Lou's words, and she lunged forward. Quicker than a snake's strike, she crushed Lou into her arms. Her lips moved rapidly at Lou's ear.

Furious, I wrenched Lou away at the same moment Ansel leapt to subdue Madame Labelle. My brethren joined him. They pinned her arms behind her back as she fought to return to Lou.

"Wait!" Lou thrashed in my arms, twisting toward her. Eyes wild. Face pale. "She was saying something—*wait!*"

But the room had descended into chaos. Madame Labelle shrieked as the Chasseurs attempted to drag her out of the building. The Archbishop motioned toward Lou before rushing forward. "Get her out of here."

I complied, tightening my grip around Lou's waist and hauling her backward. Away from the madwoman. Away from the panic and confusion of the room—of my thoughts.

"Stop!" Lou kicked and pounded against my arms, but I only tightened my grip. "I changed my mind! Let me speak to her! Let me *go*!"

But she'd made an oath.

And she wasn't going anywhere.

CHILL IN MY BONES

Lou

My throat is weeping.

Not tears. Something thicker, darker. Something that bathes my skin in scarlet, streams down my chest and soaks my hair, my dress, my hands. My hands. They scrabble at the source, fingers probing, searching, choking—desperate to stem the flow, desperate to make it stop, stop, *stop—*

Shouts are echoing around me through the pines. They disorient me. I can't think. But I need to think, to *flee*. And she's behind me, somewhere, stalking me. I can hear her voice, her laughter. She calls to me, and my name on her lips rings loudest of all.

Louise . . . I'm coming for you, darling.

Coming for you, darling

Coming for you, darling . . . darling . . . darling . . .

Blind terror. She can't find me here. I can't go back, or—or something terrible will happen. Gold still flickers. It lingers on the trees, the ground, the sky, scattering my thoughts like the blood on the pines. Warning me. *Leave, leave, leave. You can't come back here. Never again.*

I'm lunging into the river now, scrubbing my skin, washing away the trail of blood that follows me. Frantic. Feverish. The slash at my throat closes, the sharp pain receding the farther I run from home. The farther I run from my friends. My family. Her.

Never again never again never again

I can't see any of them ever again.

A life for a life.

Or I'll die.

I woke with a start, my eyes darting to the window. Flushed and agitated, I'd left it open last night. Snow coated the ledge in fine powder, and occasional gusts of wind blew snowflakes into our room. I watched them swirl through the air, trying to ignore the icy fear that had settled in the pit of my stomach. Blankets weren't enough to warm the chill in my bones. My teeth chattered.

Though I hadn't heard all of Madame Labelle's frantic words, her warning had been clear.

She is coming.

I sat up, rubbing my arms against the chill. Who was Madame Labelle, really? And how had she known about me? I'd been naive to think I could truly disappear. I'd lied to myself when I'd worn my disguises—when I married a Chasseur.

I'd never be safe.

My mother would find me.

Though I'd practiced again this morning, it wasn't enough. I needed to train harder. Every day. Twice a day. I needed to be stronger when she arrived—to be able to fight. A weapon wouldn't hurt either. In the morning, I would search for one. A knife, a sword. Anything.

Unable to stand my thoughts any longer, I swung from the bed and dropped to the floor beside my husband. He breathed, slow and rhythmic. Peaceful. Nightmares didn't plague *his* sleep. Slipping beneath the blankets, I pressed close to him. Rested my cheek against his back and savored his warmth as it seeped into my skin. My eyes fluttered shut, and my breathing slowed to match his.

In the morning. I would deal with everything in the morning.

His breathing faltered slightly as I drifted to sleep.

A CLEVER LITTLE WITCH

Lou

The small mirror above the basin was unkind the next morning. I scowled at my reflection. Pale cheeks, swollen eyes. Dry lips. I looked like death. I *felt* like death.

The bedroom door opened, but I continued staring at myself, lost in thought. Nightmares had always plagued my sleep, but last night—last night had been worse. I stroked the scar at the base of my throat softly, remembering.

It had been my sixteenth birthday. A witch entered woman-hood at sixteen. My fellow witchlings had been excited for theirs, anxious to receive their rites as Dames Blanches.

I'd been different. I'd always known my sixteenth birthday would be the day I died. I'd accepted it—welcomed it, even, when my sisters had showered me with love and praise. My purpose since birth had been to die. Only my death could save my people.

But as I'd laid on that altar, the blade pressing into my throat, something had changed.

I had changed.

"Lou?" My husband's voice echoed through the door. "Are you decent?"

I didn't answer him. Humiliation burned in my gut at last night's weakness. I clenched the basin, glaring at myself. I'd actually slept on the floor to be close to him. *Weak.*

"Lou?" When I still didn't respond, he cracked the door open. "I'm coming in."

Ansel hovered behind him, face drawn and concerned. I rolled my eyes at my reflection.

"What's wrong?" My husband's eyes searched my face. "Has something happened?"

I forced a smile. "I'm fine, thanks."

They exchanged glances, and my husband jerked his head to the door. I pretended not to notice as Ansel left, as an awkward silence descended.

"I've been thinking," he said finally.

"A dangerous pastime."

He ignored me, swallowing hard. He had the air of someone about to rip off a bandage—equal parts determined and terrified. "There's a show at Soleil et Lune tonight. Maybe we could go?"

"What show is it?"

"*La Vie Éphémère.*"

Of course it was. I chuckled without humor, staring at the shadows beneath my eyes. After Madame Labelle's visit, I'd stayed up late into the night finishing Emilie and Alexandre's story to distract myself. They'd lived and loved and died together—and for what?

It doesn't end in death. It ends in hope.

Hope.

A hope they would never see, would never feel, would never touch. As elusive as smoke. As flickering flames.

The story was more fitting than my husband would ever know. The universe—or God, or the Goddess, or *whoever*—seemed to be poking fun at me. And yet . . . I glanced around at the stone walls. My cage. It'd be nice to escape this wretched place, even for a little while.

"Fine."

I made to move past him into the bedroom, but he blocked the doorway. "Is something bothering you?"

"Nothing to concern yourself with."

"Well I am concerned with it. You aren't yourself."

I managed a sneer, but it was too difficult to maintain. I yawned instead. "Don't pretend to know me."

"I know if you aren't swearing or singing about well-endowed barmaids, something is wrong." His mouth quirked, and he tentatively touched my shoulder, blue eyes sparkling. Like the sun on the ocean. I shook the thought away irritably. "What is it? You can tell me."

No, I can't. I turned away from his touch. "I said I'm fine."

He dropped his hand, eyes shuttering. "Right. I'll leave you alone then."

I watched him leave with a twinge of what felt strangely like regret.

I poked my head out after a few moments, hoping he'd still be there, but he'd gone. My foul mood only worsened when I saw Ansel sitting at the desk. He watched me apprehensively, as if expecting me to sprout horns and spew fire—which, in this case, was exactly what I felt like doing.

I stormed toward him, and he leapt to his feet. A savage sort of satisfaction stole through me at his skittishness—then guilt. None of this was Ansel's fault, and yet . . . I couldn't force my spirits to lift. My dream still lingered. Unfortunately, so did Ansel.

"C-Can I help you with something?"

I ignored him, shouldering past his lanky form and yanking the desk drawer open. The journal and letters were still gone, leaving only a worn Bible inside. No knife. Damn it. I knew it'd been a long shot, but irritation—or perhaps fear—made me irrational. I turned and stomped toward the bed.

Ansel shadowed my footsteps, bewildered. "What are you doing?"

"Looking for a weapon." I scratched at the headboard, trying and failing to pry it from the wall.

"A weapon?" His voice hitched incredulously. "W-What do you need a weapon for?"

I threw my weight against the blasted thing, but it was too heavy. "In case Madame Labelle or—er, someone else comes back. Help me with this."

He didn't move. "Someone else?"

I bit back a growl of impatience. It didn't matter. He probably wouldn't have hidden a knife in his little hole anyway. Not after he'd shown it to me.

Dropping to my stomach, I wriggled under the bed frame. The floorboards were spotless. Practically clean enough to eat from. I wondered if it was the maids or my husband with the obsessive tendencies. Probably my husband. He seemed the type. Controlling. Freakishly neat.

Ansel repeated his question, closer this time, but I ignored him, probing the floor for a hidden seam or loose board. There was nothing. Undeterred, I began knocking at regular intervals, listening for a telltale hollow thud.

Ansel stuck his head beneath the bed. "There are no weapons under here."

"That's exactly what I'd expect you to say."

"Madame Diggory—"

"Lou."

He cringed in a perfect imitation of my husband. "Louise, then—"

"No." I whipped my head around to glare at him in the dark space, cracking my head against the frame and swearing violently. *"Not* Louise. Now move. I'm coming out."

He blinked in confusion at the reprimand but scrambled back regardless. I crawled out after him.

There was an awkward pause.

"I don't know why you're so frightened of Madame Labelle," he said finally, "but I assure you—"

Pffft. "I'm not frightened of Madame Labelle."

"The—the someone else, then?" His brows dipped together as he tried to make sense of my mood. My scowl softened, but only infinitesimally. Though Ansel had attempted to remain distant after our disaster in the library two days ago, his efforts had proved futile. Mostly because I wouldn't allow it. Beyond Coco, he was the only person in this wretched Tower I liked.

Liar.

Shut up.

"There is no one else," I lied. "But you can't be too careful. Not that I don't trust your *superior* fighting skills, Ansel, but I'd rather not leave my safety up to, well . . . you."

His confusion changed to hurt—then anger. "I can handle myself."

"Agree to disagree."

"You're not getting a weapon."

I hauled myself to my feet and brushed a nonexistent speck of dirt from my pants. "We'll see about that. Where did my unfortunate husband run off to? I need to speak with him."

"He won't give you one either. He's the one who hid them in the first place."

"Aha!" I threw a triumphant finger in the air, and his eyes widened as I advanced on him. "So he *did* hide them! Where are they, Ansel?" I jabbed his chest with my finger. "Tell me!"

He swatted at my hand and stumbled backward. "I don't know where he put them, so don't *poke* at me—" I poked him again, just for the hell of it. "Ouch!" He rubbed the spot angrily. "I said I don't know! Okay? I don't know!"

I dropped my finger, suddenly feeling much better. I chuckled despite myself. "Right. I believe you now. Let's go find my husband."

Without another word, I turned on my heel and marched out the door. Ansel sighed in resignation before following suit.

"Reid isn't going to like this," he grumbled. "Besides, I don't even know where he is."

"Well, what is it you all usually do during the day?" I made to pull open the door to the stairwell, but Ansel caught it and held it open for me. Okay, I didn't just like him—I *adored* him. "I assume it involves kicking puppies or stealing the souls of children."

Ansel looked around anxiously. "You can't *say* things like that. It's inappropriate. You're a Chasseur's wife now."

"Oh, please." I gave an exaggerated eye roll. "I thought I'd already made it clear I don't give a rat's ass about being *appropriate*. Shall I remind you? There are two more verses to 'Big Titty Liddy.'"

He paled. "Please don't."

I grinned in approval. "Then tell me where I can find my husband."

A short pause followed as Ansel considered whether I was serious about continuing my big-breasted ballad. He must've decided I was—wisely—because he soon shook his head and muttered, "He's probably in the council room."

"Excellent." I looped my arm through his and bumped his hip playfully. He tensed at the contact. "Lead the way."

To my frustration, my husband wasn't in the council room.

Instead, another Chasseur turned to greet me. His close-cropped black hair gleamed in the candlelight, and his pale green eyes—striking against his bronze face—narrowed when they found mine. I fought back a frown.

Jean Luc.

"Good morning, thief." He recovered his composure quickly, sweeping into a deep bow. "What can I do for you?"

Jean Luc wore his emotions as plainly as his beard, so it'd been easy to recognize his weakness. Though he masqueraded under pretense of friendship, I recognized jealousy when I saw it. Especially the festering kind.

Unfortunately, I had no time to play today.

"I'm looking for my husband," I said, already backing out of the room, "but I see he isn't here. If you'll excuse me—"

"Nonsense." He pushed away the papers he'd been examining and stretched leisurely. "Stay awhile. I need a break, anyway."

"And how exactly can I help with that?"

He leaned back against the table and crossed his arms. "What do you need from our dear captain?"

"A knife."

He chuckled, running a hand down his jaw. "Persuasive as you are, it's highly unlikely even *you* will be able to procure a weapon here. The Archbishop seems to think you're dangerous. Reid, as always, interprets His Eminence's opinion as the word of God."

Ansel moved farther into the room. His eyes narrowed. "You shouldn't speak that way about Captain Diggory."

Jean Luc inclined his head with a mocking smile. "I speak

only truth, Ansel. Reid is my closest friend. He's also the Archbishop's pet." He rolled his eyes, lip curling as if the word left a rancid taste in his mouth. "The nepotism is *staggering.*"

"Nepotism?" I arched a brow, looking between the two of them. "I thought my husband was orphaned."

"He was." Ansel glared daggers at Jean Luc. I hadn't realized he could look so . . . antagonistic. "The Archbishop found him in the—"

"Do save us the sob story, won't you? We all have one." Jean Luc dropped his hand and shoved away from the table abruptly. He glanced back at me before returning to his papers. "The Archbishop thinks he sees himself in Reid. They were both orphans, both hellions as children. But that's where the similarities end. The Archbishop created himself from nothing. His life work, his title, his influence—he fought for all of it. Bled for all of it." He sneered, crumpling one of his papers and chucking it at the bin. "And he plans to give it all to Reid for nothing."

"Jean Luc," I asked shrewdly, "are *you* an orphan?"

His gaze sharpened. "Why?"

"I— No reason. It doesn't matter."

And it didn't. Really. I didn't give a damn about Jean Luc's issues. But for someone to be so wholly *blind* to his own emotions . . . no wonder he was bitter. Cursing myself for my curiosity, I redirected my thoughts to my purpose. Procuring a weapon was more important—and frankly, more interesting—than those three's twisted love triangle.

"You're right, by the way." I shrugged as if bored, sauntering forward to trail my finger along the map. He eyed me suspiciously. "My husband doesn't deserve any of this. It's pathetic, really, the way he waits for the Archbishop's beck and call." Ansel shot me a bewildered look, but I ignored him, examining a bit of dust on my finger. "Like a good boy—begging for scraps."

Jean Luc smiled, small and grim. "Oh, you are devious, aren't you?" When I didn't respond, he chuckled. "While I empathize with you, Madame Diggory, I'm not so easily manipulated."

"You aren't?" I cocked my head at him. "Are you sure?"

He nodded and leaned forward on his elbows. "I'm sure. For all Reid's faults, he has good reason for hiding his weapons from you. You're a criminal."

"Right. Of course. It's just—I thought it might be beneficial to both of us."

Ansel touched my arm. "Lou—"

"I'm listening." Jean Luc's eyes gleamed with amusement now. "You want a knife. What's in it for me?"

I shrugged away from Ansel's hand and returned his smile. "It's simple. Giving me a knife would annoy the hell out of my husband."

He laughed then. Tossed his head back and slapped the table, scattering his papers. "Oh, you really are a clever little witch, aren't you?"

I stiffened, my smile slipping infinitesimally, before chuckling a second too late. Ansel didn't seem to notice, but Jean Luc, with his sharp eyes, stopped laughing abruptly. He tilted his head to consider me, like a hound scenting a rabbit's trail. Damn it. I forced a smile before turning to leave. "I've wasted enough of your time, Chasseur Toussaint. If you'll excuse me, I need to find my elusive husband."

"Reid isn't here." Jean Luc still watched me with unnerving focus. "He left earlier with the Archbishop. A lutin infestation was reported outside the city." Mistaking my frown for concern, he added, "He'll be back in a few hours. Lutins are hardly dangerous, but the constabulary aren't equipped to handle the supernatural."

I pictured the small hobgoblins I'd played with as a child. "They aren't dangerous at all." The words left my mouth before I could stop them. "I mean . . . what will he do to them?"

Jean Luc arched a brow. "He'll exterminate them, of course."

"Why?" I ignored Ansel's insistent tugs on my arm, heat rising to my face. I knew I should stop talking. I recognized the spark in Jean Luc's eyes for what it was—an inkling. An instinct. An idea that might soon turn into something more if I didn't keep my mouth shut. "They're harmless."

"They're nuisances to farmers, and they're unnatural. It's our job to eliminate them."

"I thought it was your job to protect the innocent?"

"And lutins are innocent?"

"They're harmless," I repeated.

"They shouldn't exist. They were born from reanimated clay and witchcraft."

"Wasn't Adam sculpted from the earth?"

He tilted his head slowly, considering me. "Yes . . . by the hand of God. Are you suggesting witches possess the same authority?"

I hesitated, finally realizing what I was saying—and where I was. Jean Luc and Ansel both stared at me, waiting for my response. "Of course not." I forced myself to meet Jean Luc's curious gaze, blood roaring in my ears. "That's not what I was saying at all."

"Good." His smile was small and unsettling as Ansel dragged me to the door. "Then we're in agreement."

Ansel kept shooting me anxious glances as we walked to the infirmary, but I ignored him. When he finally opened his mouth to question me, I did what I did best—deflected.

"I think Mademoiselle Perrot will be here this morning."

He brightened visibly. "Will she?"

I smiled and nudged his arm with my shoulder. He didn't tense this time. "There's a good chance."

"And—and will she let me visit the patients with you today?"

"Less of a chance."

He sulked the rest of the way up the stairs. I couldn't help but chuckle.

The familiar, soothing scent of magic greeted us as we stepped into the infirmary.

Come play come play come play

But I was hardly there to play. A fact Coco substantiated when she met us at the door. "Hello, Ansel," she said breezily, looping her arm through mine and steering me to Monsieur Bernard's room.

"Hello, Mademoiselle Perr—"

"Goodbye, Ansel." She shut the door in his besotted face.

I frowned at her. "He likes you, you know. You should be nicer to him."

She threw herself into the iron chair. "That's why I'm not encouraging him. That poor boy is far too good for me."

"Maybe you should let him decide that."

"Hmm . . ." She examined a particularly nasty scar on her wrist before tugging her sleeve back down. "Maybe I should."

I rolled my eyes and went to greet Monsieur Bernard.

Though it'd been two days, the poor man still hadn't died. He didn't sleep. He didn't eat. Father Orville and the healers had no idea how he stayed alive. Whatever the reason, I was glad. I'd grown rather fond of his eerie stare.

"I heard about Madame Labelle," Coco said. True to his word, Jean Luc had spoken with the priests, and true to *their* word, they'd kept a much closer eye on their newest healer after her interference in the library. She hadn't dared leave the infirmary again. "What did she want?"

I sank to the floor beside Bernie's bed and crossed my legs. His white, orb-like eyes followed me all the way down, his finger tapping against the chains.

Clink.

Clink.

Clink.

"To give me a warning. She said my mother is coming."

"She said that?" Coco's gaze sharpened, and I quickly related what had happened yesterday evening. By the time I'd finished, she was pacing. "It doesn't mean anything. We know she's after you. Of course she's coming. That doesn't mean she knows you're *here*—"

"You're right. It doesn't. But I still want to be ready."

"Of course." She nodded vigorously, curls bouncing. "Let's get started, then. Enchant the door. A pattern you haven't used before."

I stood and walked toward the door, rubbing my hands together against the chill in the room. Coco and I had decided to enchant it against eavesdroppers during our practice sessions. It wouldn't do for anyone to hear our whispered conversations about magic.

As I approached, I willed the familiar golden patterns to appear. They materialized at my call, hazy and ubiquitous. Against my skin. Inside my mind. I waded through them, searching for something fresh. Something different. After several fruitless minutes, I threw my hands up in frustration. "There's nothing new."

Coco came to stand beside me. As a Dame Rouge, she couldn't see the patterns I saw, but she tried nonetheless. "You're not thinking about it properly. Examine every possibility."

I closed my eyes, forcing myself to take a deep breath. Once, envisioning and manipulating patterns had come easily—as easily as breathing. But no longer. I'd been hiding for too long. Repressing my magic for too long. Too many dangers had lurked in the city: witches, Chasseurs, and even citizens all recognized the peculiar smell of magic. Though it was impossible to discern a witch from her appearance, unattended women always aroused suspicion. How long before someone had smelled me after an enchantment? How long before someone had seen me contorting my fingers and followed me home?

I'd used magic at Tremblay's, and look where it'd landed me.

No. It'd been safer to stop practicing magic altogether.

I explained to Coco that it was like exercising a muscle. When used routinely, the patterns came quickly, clearly, usually of their own volition. If left unattended, however, that part of my body—the part connected to my ancestors, to their ashes in the land—grew weak. And every second it took to untangle a pattern, a witch could strike.

Madame Labelle had been clear. My mother was in the city. Perhaps she knew where I was, or perhaps she didn't. Either way, I couldn't afford weakness.

As if listening to my thoughts, the golden dust seemed to shift closer, and the witches at the parade reared in my mind's eye. Their crazed smiles. The bodies floating helplessly above them. I repressed a shudder, and a wave of hopelessness crashed through me.

No matter how often I practiced—no matter how skilled I grew—I would never be as powerful as some. Because witches like those at the parade—witches willing to sacrifice everything for their cause—weren't merely powerful.

They were dangerous.

Though a witch couldn't see another's patterns, feats such as drowning or burning a person alive required enormous offerings to maintain balance: perhaps a specific emotion, perhaps a year's worth of memories. The color of their eyes. The ability to feel another's touch.

Such losses could . . . change a person. Twist her into something darker and stranger than she was before. I'd seen it happen once.

But that was a long time ago.

Even if I couldn't hope to grow more powerful than my mother, I refused to do *nothing*.

"If I hinder the healers' and priests' ability to hear us, I'm impairing them. I'm taking from them." I brushed aside the gold clinging to my skin, straightening my shoulders. "I have to impair myself as well, somehow. One of my senses . . . hearing is the obvious trade, but I've already done that. I *could* give another sense, like touch or sight or taste."

I paused and examined the patterns. "Taste isn't enough—the balance is still tipped in my favor. Sight is too much, as I'd be rendered ineffectual. So . . . it has to be touch. Or maybe smell?" I focused on my nose, but no new pattern emerged.

Clink.

Clink.

Clink.

I glared over at Bernie, my concentration slipping. The patterns vanished. "I love you, Bernie, but could you please shut up? You're making this difficult."

Clink.

Coco poked me in the cheek, directing my attention back to

the door. "Keep going. Try a different perspective."

I swatted her hand away. "That's easy for you to say." Gritting my teeth, I stared at the door so hard I feared my eyes might explode. Perhaps that would be *balance* enough. "Maybe . . . maybe I'm not taking from them. Maybe they're giving me something."

"Like secrecy?" Coco prompted.

"Yes. Which means—which means—"

"Maybe you could try telling a secret."

"Don't be stupid. It doesn't work like—"

A thin, golden cord snaked between my tongue and her ear. Shit.

That was the trouble with magic. It was subjective. For every possibility I considered, another witch would consider a hundred different ones. Just as no two minds worked the same, no two witches' magic worked the same. We all saw the world differently.

Still, I needn't tell Coco that.

She flashed a smug smile and raised a brow, as if reading my thoughts. "It sounds to me like there are no hard and fast rules to this magic of yours. It's intuitive." She tapped her chin thoughtfully. "To be honest, it reminds me of blood magic."

Footsteps echoed in the corridor outside, and we stilled. When they didn't pass—when they halted in front of the door—Coco retreated to the corner, and I slipped into the iron chair by Bernie's bed. I flipped the Bible open and began reading a verse at random.

Father Orville hobbled through the door.

"Oh!" He clutched his chest when he saw us, his eyes forming perfect circles behind his spectacles. "Dear me! You gave me a fright."

Smiling, I rose to my feet as Ansel hastened into the room. Bits of cookie sprinkled his lips. Obviously he'd invaded the healers' kitchen. "Is everything all right?"

"Yes, of course." I returned my attention to Father Orville. "My apologies, Father. I didn't mean to frighten you."

"Not at all, child, not at all. I'm just a bit overwrought this morning. We had a strange night. Our patients are unusually . . . agitated." He waved a hand, revealing a metal syringe, and joined me at Bernie's bedside. My smile froze in place. "I see you too are concerned for our Monsieur Bernard. Last night one of my healers found him attempting to jump out a window!"

"What?" I locked eyes with Bernie, frowning, but his mutilated face gave nothing away. Not even a flicker. He remained . . . blank. I shook my head. His pain must've been terrible.

Father Orville patted my shoulder. "Not to worry, child. It won't happen again." He lifted a feeble hand to show me the syringe. "We've perfected the dosage this time. I'm sure of it. This injection will soothe his agitation until he joins the Lord."

He pulled a thin dagger from his robes and cut a small incision on Bernie's arm. Coco stepped forward, eyes narrowed, as black blood oozed out. "He's gotten worse."

Father Orville fumbled with the syringe. I doubted he could even see Bernie's arm, but he finally managed to plunge the quill deep into the black cut. I cringed when he pushed the trigger, injecting the poison, but Bernie didn't move. He just kept staring at me.

"There now." Father Orville eased the quill out of his arm. "He should drift off to sleep momentarily. Might I suggest we leave him in peace?"

"Yes, Father," Coco said, bowing her head. She shot me a meaningful look. "C'mon, Lou. Let's go read some Proverbs."

LA VIE ÉPHÉMÈRE

Lou

A crowd lined the street outside Soleil et Lune. Aristocrats chatted outside the box office while their wives greeted each other with saccharine smiles. Fashionable carriages came and went. Ushers tried to shepherd the attendees to their seats, but this was the real entertainment of the evening. *This* was why the rich and affluent came to the theater . . . to preen and politicize in a complex social dance.

I'd always likened it to a peacock's mating ritual.

My husband and I certainly looked the part. Gone were my bloodstained dress and trousers. When he'd returned to our room earlier with a new evening gown—nearly bursting with pride and anticipation—I hadn't been able to refuse him. Burnished gold, it had a fitted bodice and tapered sleeves that had been embroidered with tiny, metallic blooms. They glimmered in the dying sunlight, transitioning smoothly into a train of champagne silk. I'd even magicked away a few of my bruises in the infirmary. Powder had covered the rest.

My husband wore his best coat. Though still Chasseur blue, gold filigree decorated the collar and cuffs. I resisted the urge to smile, envisioning the picture we made striding up the theater steps. He'd matched our outfits. I should've been appalled, but with his hand wrapped firmly around mine, I couldn't bring myself to feel anything but excitement.

I *had* insisted on wearing the hood of my cloak up, however. And a pretty lace ribbon to hide my scar. If my husband had noticed, he'd known better than to comment on either.

Perhaps he wasn't so bad.

The crowd drew away as we entered the foyer. I doubted anyone remembered us, but people tended to be uneasy—though others would call it *reverent*—around Chasseurs. No one wrecked a good party like a Chasseur. Especially if that Chasseur was as priggish as my husband.

He guided me to my seat. For once, I didn't resent his hand on my back. It actually felt . . . nice. Warm. Strong. Until he attempted to remove my cloak. When I tugged it out of his grasp, refusing to part with it, he frowned, clearing his throat in the ensuing awkwardness. "I never asked . . . did you enjoy the book?"

The gentleman in the seat beside me caught my hand before I could answer.

"Enchanté, mademoiselle," he crooned, kissing my fingers.

I couldn't help the giggle that escaped my lips. He was handsome in an oily way, with dark, slick hair and a thin mustache.

My husband flushed scarlet. "I'll *thank you* to take your hand from my wife, *monsieur.*"

The man's eyes boggled, and he looked to my empty ring finger. I laughed harder. I'd taken to wearing Angelica's Ring on my right hand, just to annoy my husband. "Your wife?" He dropped my hand as if it were a poisonous spider. "I didn't think Chasseurs were in the practice of marriage."

"This one is." He rose and jerked his head toward me. "Switch seats with me."

"I meant no offense, *monsieur*, of course." The oily man shot me a regretful glance as I sidled away from him. "Though you are a lucky man indeed."

My husband glowered, effectively silencing the man for the rest of the evening.

The lights dimmed, and I finally pushed back my hood. "You're a bit territorial, aren't you?" I whispered, grinning again. He was such a brute. A somewhat adorable, pompous-assed brute.

He wouldn't look at me. "Performance is starting."

The symphony began playing, and men and women flitted onto the stage. I recognized Hook-Nose immediately, chuckling at the memory of how she'd humiliated the Archbishop in front of his doting admirers. Ingenious. And to cast such an enchantment right under the noses of my husband and the Archbishop . . .

Hook-Nose was a fearless Dame Blanche.

Though she played only a minor role in the chorus, I eagerly watched her dance along with the actors playing Emilie and Alexandre.

My enthusiasm quickly dimmed, however, as the song progressed. There was something familiar about the way she held herself—something I hadn't noticed upon first meeting her. Unease gradually settled in my stomach as she twirled and danced, disappearing behind the curtain.

When the second song started, my husband leaned closer. His breath tickled the skin of my neck. "Jean Luc said you were looking for me this morning."

"It's rude to talk during a performance."

He narrowed his eyes, undeterred. "What did you want?"

I turned my attention back toward the stage. Hook-Nose had just swept back into view, her corn-silk hair rippling across her shoulders. The movement stirred a memory, but when I tried to grasp it fully, it slipped away again, like water between my fingers.

"Lou?" He tentatively touched my hand. His was warm, large, and calloused, and I couldn't bring myself to pull away.

"A knife," I admitted, eyes never leaving the stage.

He sucked in a breath. "What?"

"I wanted a knife."

"You can't be serious."

I glanced at him. "I'm deadly serious. You saw Madame Labelle yesterday. I need protection."

He gripped my hand tighter. "She won't touch you." The oily man beside us coughed pointedly, but we ignored him. "She won't be allowed inside Chasseur Tower again. The Archbishop gave his word."

I scowled. "Is that supposed to make me feel better?"

His expression hardened, and his jaw clenched tight. "It

should. The Archbishop is a powerful man, and he's vowed to protect you."

"His word means nothing to me."

"What of my word, then? I vowed to protect you as well."

It was laughable, really, his dedication to protecting a witch. He would've had kittens if he knew the truth.

I arched a wry brow. "Just as I promised to obey you?"

He skewered me with a black look, but the oily man wasn't the only one openly glaring now. I settled back in my seat with a smug toss of my hair. He was far too prim to argue in front of an audience.

"This conversation isn't over," he muttered, but he too sat back, staring moodily at the performers. To my surprise—and grudging delight—he kept my hand fixed beneath his. After several long moments, he casually brushed his thumb along my fingers. I wriggled in my seat. He ignored me, gazing steadily at the stage as the performance wore on. But his thumb continued moving, drawing small patterns on the back of my hand, circling my knuckles, tracing the tips of my nails.

I struggled to concentrate on the performance. Delicious tingles spread across my skin with each sweep of his thumb . . . until slowly, gradually, his touch trailed upward, and his fingers grazed the veins of my wrist, the inside my elbow. He stroked my scar there, and I shivered, pressing back in my seat and trying to focus on the performance. My cloak slipped down my shoulders.

The first act ended too soon, and intermission began. We

both remained seated, silently touching—hardly breathing—as the audience milled around us. When the candles dimmed again, I turned to look at him, heat rising from my belly to my cheeks.

"Reid," I breathed.

He stared back at me, his own flushed, panicked expression mirroring my own. I leaned closer, gaze falling to his parted lips. His tongue flicked out to moisten them, and my belly contracted.

"Yes?"

"I—"

In my periphery, Hook-Nose spun in a pirouette, her hair flying wild. Something clicked in my memory at the movement. A solstice celebration. Corn-silk hair braided with flowers. The maypole.

Shit.

Estelle. Her name was Estelle, and I'd known her once—in my childhood at Chateau le Blanc. She obviously hadn't recognized me before with my freshly smashed face, but if she saw me again, if she somehow remembered . . .

The heat in my belly froze to ice.

I had to get out of here.

"Lou?" Reid's voice echoed from afar, as if he called from the end of a tunnel and not from the seat next to me. "Are you all right?"

I inhaled deeply, willing my heart to calm. Surely he could hear it. It thundered through my entire body, condemning me with each treacherous beat. His hand stilled on my wrist. Shit. I pulled it away, twisting my fingers in my lap. "I'm fine."

He sat back in his seat, confusion and hurt flashing across his face. I cursed silently again.

The moment the final song ended, I leapt to my feet, pulling my cloak back on. Ensuring the hood covered my hair and shadowed my face. "Ready?"

Reid glanced around in bewilderment. The rest of the audience remained seated—some breathless, some weeping at Emilie and Alexandre's tragic deaths—as the curtain fell. The applause hadn't yet started. "Is something wrong?"

"No!" The word burst out too quick to be convincing. I cleared my throat, forcing a smile, and tried again. "Just tired is all."

I didn't wait for his answer. Tugging his hand, I led him past the aisles, past the patrons finally rising and applauding, and into the foyer—and skidded to a halt. The actors and actresses had already formed a line by the doors. Before I could change directions, Estelle's gaze found Reid. She scowled before glancing at my cloaked form beside him, eyes narrowing as she peered beneath my hood. Recognition lit. I tugged on Reid's hand, desperate to flee, but he didn't move as Estelle strode purposefully toward us.

"How are you?" Her eyes were kind, genuine, as she pushed back my hood to assess my various injuries. Rooted to the spot, I was helpless to stop her. She smiled. "It looks like you're healing nicely."

I swallowed the lump in my throat. "I'm fine, thanks. Perfect."

"Really?" She arched a brow in disbelief, and her kind eyes hardened as she looked to Reid, who seemed even less pleased to see her than she did him. Her lip curled. "And how are *you*? Still hiding behind that blue coat?"

She was very brave, taunting a Chasseur in public. Patrons tittered disapprovingly around us. Reid scowled and tightened his hold on my trembling fingers. "Let's go, Lou."

I flinched at the word, heart sinking miserably, but the damage was done.

"Lou?" Estelle's entire body tensed, and she tilted her head, eyes widening slowly as she reexamined my face. "As in . . . Louise?"

"Nice to see you again!" Before she could respond, I dragged Reid toward the exit. He followed without struggle, though I could feel his unspoken questions on my neck.

We fought our way through the crowd outside the theater. When I couldn't clear a path, he stepped in front of me. Whether it was his towering height or his royal blue coat, something about him made people step aside, tipping their hats. Our carriage waited several blocks down the queue—blocked by mingling patrons—so I pulled him in the opposite direction, rushing as far and as fast from the theater as my gown allowed.

When we finally cleared the crowd, he guided me down an empty side street.

"What was that about?"

I chuckled nervously, bouncing on the balls of my feet. We needed to keep moving. "It's nothing really. I just—" Something shifted behind him, and my stomach plummeted as Estelle melted from the shadows.

"I can't believe it's you." Her voice came out a breathless whisper, and she stared at me in awe. "I didn't recognize you before with the bruises. You look so . . . different."

It was true. Beyond my previous injuries, my hair was longer and lighter than when she'd known me, my skin darker and freckled from too many days in the sun.

"Do you two know each other?" Reid asked, frowning.

"Of course not," I said hastily. "Just—just from the theater. Let's go, Reid." I turned toward him, and he wrapped a reassuring arm around my waist, angling himself ever so slightly in front of me.

Estelle's eyes widened. "You can't leave! Not now that—"

"She can," Reid said firmly. While it was clear he had no idea what was going on, his desire to protect me seemed to override his confusion—and his intense dislike of Estelle. His hand was gentle on the small of my back as he led me away. "Good evening, *mademoiselle.*"

Estelle didn't even blink. She merely flicked her wrist as if swatting an irksome fly, and the shop sign above us ripped from its hinges and smashed into the back of his skull. The sharp tang of magic swept through the alley as he crashed to his knees. He reached feebly for his Balisarda.

"No!" I gripped his coat, attempting to pull him to his feet—to shield him with my body somehow—but Estelle wrung her fingers before either of us could counter.

When the sign bludgeoned him a second time, he flew backward. His head hit the alley wall with a sickening crack, and he crumpled to the ground and fell still.

A snarl tore from my throat, and I positioned myself between the two of them, lifting my hands.

"Don't make this difficult, Louise." She drifted closer, a fanatical gleam in her eyes, and panic constricted my thoughts. Though gold danced in my periphery, I couldn't focus on a pattern—couldn't focus on anything. It was as if the world had gone silent, waiting.

Except—

Reid stirred behind me.

"I won't go with you." I inched backward, lifting my hands higher to draw her eyes. "Please, stop this."

"Don't you understand? This is an *honor*—"

A blue streak launched past me.

Estelle couldn't react quickly enough, and Reid barreled into her outstretched arms. For a moment, it looked like a sick embrace. Then Reid wrenched her around so her back was to his chest—crushing her arms and hands between them—and flung an arm around her throat. I watched in horror as she struggled against him. Her face slowly purpled.

"Help—me—" She thrashed in terror, her wild eyes seeking mine. "Please—"

I didn't move.

It was over in less than a minute. With a final shudder, Estelle's body slumped in Reid's arms, and his grip slackened.

"Is she ... dead?" I whispered.

"No." His face was white, his hands shaking, as he let Estelle fall to the ground. When he finally looked at me, I stumbled under the ferocity of his stare. "What did it want with you?"

Unable to stand that look, I tore my gaze away—away from him, away from Estelle, away from the entire nightmarish scene—and looked instead to the stars. They were dim tonight, refusing to shine for me. Accusing.

After a long moment, I forced myself to answer him. Tears glistened on my cheeks. "She wanted me dead."

He watched me for another long moment before hauling Estelle's limp body over his shoulder.

"What are you going to do with her?" I asked fearfully.

"It's a witch." He started up the street without a backward glance, ignoring the alarmed looks of passersby. "It'll burn on earth, and then in Hell."

WITCH KILLER

Lou

Reid refused to speak to me on the way back to Chasseur Tower. I struggled to keep up, each step a knife in my heart.

Witch killer witch killer witch killer.

I couldn't look at Estelle, couldn't process the way her head lolled against Reid's back. The way her corn-silk hair rippled with each step.

Witch killer.

When Reid burst into the Tower, the guards hesitated for only a second, shocked, before leaping into action. I hated them. Hated that they'd prepared for this moment their entire lives. Eyes bright with anticipation, they handed Reid a metal syringe.

An injection.

My vision narrowed. Nausea rolled through my stomach.

"The Fathers have been anxious to test it on a witch." The Chasseur nearest Reid leaned forward eagerly. "Today is their lucky day."

Reid didn't hesitate. He swung Estelle forward, plunging the quill into her throat with brutal force. Blood trickled onto her shoulder and stained the white of her dress.

It might as well have been my soul.

She dropped from Reid's arms like a stone. No one bothered catching her, and she fell face-first upon the pavers. Unmoving. Her chest barely rose and fell. A second Chasseur chuckled, nudging her cheek with his boot. She still didn't move. "Guess that answers that question. The priests will be pleased."

The manacles came next—thicker and rusted with blood. They clapped them on her wrists and ankles before yanking her up by the hair and dragging her to the stairwell. The chains clinked on each step as she disappeared down, down, down—into the mouth of Hell.

Reid didn't look at me as he strode after them.

In that moment—left with only an empty syringe and Estelle's blood as reminders of what I'd done—I truly hated myself.

Witch killer.

I wept bitterly.

As if sensing my treachery, the sun didn't rise properly the next morning. It remained dark and ominous, the entire world cloaked in a thick blanket of black and gray. Thunder rumbled in the distance. I watched from my bedroom window, eyes red-rimmed and glassy.

The Archbishop wasted no time in throwing open the church doors to shout Estelle's sins to the heavens. He brought her out in chains and threw her to the ground at his feet. The crowd shouted obscenities, hurling bits of mud and rock at her. Frantically, she whipped her head back and forth in search of someone.

In search of me.

As if drawn to my gaze, her head snapped up, and pale blue eyes met my own. I didn't need to hear the words to see the shape her lips formed—to see the venom that poured from her very soul.

Witch killer.

It was the ultimate dishonor.

Reid stood at the front of the crowd, his hair blowing wildly in the wind. A raised platform had been built overnight. The crude wooden stake atop it pierced the sky, spilling forth the first icy drops of rain.

To this stake, they tied my sister. She still wore her chorus costume—a simple white gown that brushed her ankles—though it was bloody and soiled from whatever horrors the Chasseurs had inflicted on her in the dungeon. Just last night, she'd been singing and dancing at Soleil et Lune. Now, she faced her death.

It was all my fault.

I'd been a coward, too afraid to face death myself to save Estelle. To save my people. Hundreds of witches—dead. I clamped a hand around my throat—right over my scar—and bit down on a sob.

Ansel shifted uncomfortably behind me. "It's hard to see the first time," he said in a strained voice. "You don't have to watch."

"Yes, I do." My breathing hitched as he came to stand beside my tower of furniture. Tears flowed freely down my cheeks, forming a pool on the sill. "This is my fault."

"It's a witch," Ansel said softly.

"*No one* deserves to die like this."

He startled at my vehemence. "Witches do."

"Tell me, Ansel." I turned toward him, suddenly urgent, desperate for him to understand. "Have you ever met a witch?"

"Of course not."

"Yes, you have. They're everywhere, all over the city. The woman who patched your coat last week might've been one, or the maid downstairs who blushes every time you look at her. Your own *mother* could've been one, and you never would've known." Ansel shook his head, eyes widening. "They aren't all evil, Ansel. Some are kind and caring and good."

"No," he insisted. "They're wicked."

"Aren't we all? Isn't that what your own god teaches?"

His face fell. "It's different. They're . . . unnatural."

Unnatural. I dug my palms into my eyes to stem the tears. "You're right." I gestured below, where the crowd's shouts escalated. A dun-haired woman at the back of the crowd sobbed. "Behold, the natural way of things."

Ansel frowned as Reid handed the Archbishop a torch.

Estelle trembled. She kept her eyes trained on the sky as the Archbishop brought the torch down in a sweeping arc, igniting the bits of hay below her. The crowd roared its approval.

I remembered a knife coming down on my own throat. I felt the kiss of the blade on my skin.

I knew the terror in Estelle's heart.

The fire spread quickly. Though tears clouded my vision, I forced myself to watch the flames lick up Estelle's dress. I forced myself to hear her screams. Each one wracked my very soul, and soon I clutched the window ledge for support.

I couldn't stand it anymore. I wanted to die. I *deserved* to die—to writhe and burn in an endless lake of black fire.

I knew what I had to do.

Without thinking—without stopping to consider the consequences—I clenched my fists.

The world was on fire.

I screamed, toppling to the floor. Ansel scrambled toward me, but his hands couldn't hold my thrashing body. I convulsed, biting my tongue to stop the shrieking as the fire ripped through me, as it blistered my skin and peeled muscle from bone. I couldn't breathe. I couldn't think. There was only agony.

Below, Estelle's screams stopped abruptly. Her body relaxed into the flames, and a blissful smile crossed her face as she drifted peacefully into the afterlife.

SOUL ACHE

Lou

I woke with a cool cloth on my forehead. Blinking reluctantly, I allowed my eyes to acclimate to the semidarkness. Moonlight bathed the room in silver, illuminating a hunched figure in the chair beside my bed. Though the moon bleached his coppery hair, there was no mistaking him.

Reid.

His forehead rested against the edge of the mattress, not quite touching my hip. His fingers lay inches from my own. My heart contracted painfully. He must've been holding my hand before he'd fallen asleep.

I didn't know how I felt about that.

Touching his hair tentatively, I fought the despair in my chest. He'd burned Estelle. No—*I* had burned Estelle. I'd known what he would do if I waited for him to wake in that alley. I'd known he would kill her.

That's what I'd wanted.

I withdrew my hand, disgusted with myself. Disgusted with

Reid. For just a moment, I'd forgotten why I was here. Who I was. Who *he* was.

A witch and a witch hunter bound in holy matrimony. There was only one way such a story could end—a stake and a match. I cursed myself for being so stupid—for allowing myself to get too close.

A hand touched my arm. I turned to find Reid staring at me. Stubble shadowed his jaw, and dark circles colored his eyes, as if he hadn't slept in a long time.

"You're awake," he breathed.

"Yes."

He sighed in relief and closed his eyes, squeezing my hand. "Thank God."

After a second of hesitation, I returned the pressure. "What happened?"

"You collapsed." He swallowed hard and opened his eyes. They were pained. "Ansel went running for Mademoiselle Perrot. He didn't know what to do. He said—he said you were screaming. He couldn't get you to stop. Mademoiselle Perrot couldn't calm you either." He stroked my palm absently, staring at it without truly seeing it.

"When I arrived, you were . . . sick. Really sick. You screamed when they touched you. You only stopped when I—" He cleared his throat and looked away, throat bobbing. "Then you—you went still. We thought you might be dead. But you weren't."

I stared at his hand in mine. "No, I'm not."

"I've been feeding you ice chips, and maids have been

changing the bedsheets hourly to keep you comfortable."

At his words, I noticed the dampness of my nightgown and sheets. My skin, too, felt sticky with sweat. I must've looked like hell. "How long was I out?"

"Three days."

I groaned and sat up, rubbing my clammy face. "Shit."

"Has this ever happened before?" He searched my face as I threw off the blankets and shivered from the cold night air.

"Of course not." Though I tried to remain civil, the words came out sharp, and his expression hardened.

"Ansel thinks the burning did it. He said he told you not to watch."

The burning. That's all it was to Reid. His world hadn't gone up in flames at that stake. He hadn't betrayed his people. Anger rekindled in my belly. He probably didn't even know Estelle's name.

I headed to the washroom, refusing to meet his eyes. "I rarely do what I'm told."

My anger burned hotter when Reid followed. "Why? Why watch when it upset you so?"

I turned the tap and watched the steaming water fill the tub. "Because we killed her. It was the least we could do to watch it happen. She deserved as much."

"Ansel said you were crying."

"I was."

"It was a *witch*, Lou."

"*She*," I snarled, whirling on him. "*She* was a witch—and a *person.* Her name was Estelle, and we burned her."

"Witches aren't *people*," he said impatiently. "That's a child's fantasy. They aren't little fairy creatures who wear flowers and dance under the full moon, either. They're demons. You've seen the infirmary. They're malevolent. They'll *hurt* you if given the chance." He raked an agitated hand through his hair, glaring at me. "They deserve the stake."

I clenched my hands on the tub to prevent myself from doing something I'd regret. I wanted—no, *needed*—to rage at him. I needed to wrap my hands around his throat and shake him—to make him see sense. I was half tempted to slit my arm open again, so he could see the blood that flowed there. The blood that was the same color as his own.

"What if I were a witch, Reid?" I asked softly. "Would the stake be what I deserve?"

I turned off the tap, and absolute silence filled the chamber. I could feel his eyes on my back . . . wary, assessing. "Yes," he said carefully. "If you were a witch."

The unspoken question hung in the air between us. I met his eyes over my shoulder, daring him to ask it. Praying he wouldn't. Praying he would. Unsure of how I would answer if he did.

A long second passed as we stared at each other. Finally, when it became clear he wouldn't ask—or perhaps *couldn't*—I turned back to the water and whispered, "We both deserve the stake for what we did to her."

He cleared his throat, obviously uncomfortable with the new direction of the conversation. "Lou—"

"Just leave me alone. I need time."

He didn't argue, and I didn't watch him leave. When the door closed, I inched into the hot water. It steamed, nearly boiling, but was still a cool caress compared to the stake. I slipped beneath the surface, remembering the agony of the flames on my skin.

I'd spent years hiding from La Dame des Sorcières. My mother. I'd done terrible things to protect myself, to ensure my survival. Because above all else, *that* is what I did: I survived.

But at what cost?

I'd reacted instinctively with Estelle. It'd been her life or mine. The way forward had seemed clear. There had been only one choice. But . . . Estelle had been one of my own. A witch. She hadn't wanted me dead—only to be free of the persecution plaguing our people.

Unfortunately, those two were mutually exclusive now.

I thought of her body, of the wind carrying away her ashes— and all the other ashes that had been carried away over the years.

I thought of Monsieur Bernard, rotting away on a bed upstairs—and all the others who had waited to die in torment.

Witches and people alike. One and the same. All innocent. All guilty.

All dead.

But not me.

When I was sixteen, my mother had tried to sacrifice me— her only child. Even before my conception, Morgane had seen a pattern no other Dame des Sorcières had seen before, had been willing to *do* what none of her predecessors had ever dreamed: kill her lineage. With my death, the king's line also would've died.

All his heirs, legitimate and bastard, would've ceased breathing with me. One life to end a hundred years' worth of persecution. One life to end the Lyons' reign of tyranny.

But my mother didn't just want to kill the king. She wanted to *hurt* him. To *destroy* him. I could still imagine her pattern at the altar, shimmering around my heart and branching out into the darkness. Toward his children. The witches planned to strike amidst his grief. They planned to eviscerate what remained of the royal family . . . and everyone who followed them.

I broke through the surface of the water, gasping for breath.

All these years, I've been lying to myself, convinced I'd fled the altar because I couldn't take the lives of innocents. Yet here I was with innocent blood on my hands.

I was a coward.

The pain of the realization went beyond my sensitive skin, beyond the agony of the flames. This time, I'd damaged something important. Something irrevocable. It ached deep inside me. *Witch killer.*

For the first time in my life, I wondered if I'd made the right choice.

Coco checked on me later that day, her face drawn as she sat beside me on the bed. Ansel became inordinately interested in his coat buttons.

"How are you feeling?" She lifted a hand to stroke my hair. At her touch, all my wretched emotions flooded back to the surface. A tear escaped down my cheek. I wiped it away, scowling.

"Like hell."

"We thought you were a goner."

"I wish."

Her hand stilled. "Don't say that. You've just got a soul ache, that's all. Nothing a few sticky buns can't fix."

My eyes snapped open. "A soul ache?"

"Sort of like a headache or stomachache, but much worse. I used to get them all the time when I lived with my aunt." She smoothed my hair away from my face and leaned down, brushing another tear from my cheek. "It wasn't your fault, Lou. You did what you had to."

I stared at my hands for a long moment. "Why do I feel like such shit about it, then?"

"Because you're a good person. I know it's never pretty to take a life, but Estelle forced your hand. No one can blame you for what you did."

"I'm sure Estelle would feel differently."

"Estelle made her choice when she put her faith in your mother. She chose wrong. The only thing you can do now is move forward. Isn't that right?" She nodded to Ansel, who blushed scarlet in the corner. I looked hastily away.

He knew now, of course. He would've smelled the magic. Yet here I was . . . alive. More tears pooled in my eyes. *Stop it,* I chided. *Of course he didn't tell on you. He's the only decent man in this entire tower. Shame on you for thinking otherwise.*

Throat constricting, I toyed with Angelica's Ring, unable to meet anyone's eyes.

"I have to warn you," Coco continued, "the kingdom is praising

Reid as a hero. This is the first burning in months, and with the current climate, well . . . it's been a celebration. King Auguste invited Reid to dine with him yesterday, but Reid refused." At my questioning look, she pursed her lips in disapproval. "He didn't want to leave you."

Suddenly much too warm, I kicked my blankets away. "There was nothing *heroic* about what he did."

She and Ansel exchanged a glance. "As his wife," she said carefully, "you're expected to think otherwise."

I stared at her.

"Listen, Lou." She sat back, heaving an impatient sigh. "I'm just looking out for you. People heard your screams during the execution. Many are *very* interested in why a witch burning sent you into hysterics—including the king. Reid finally accepted his dinner invitation this evening to placate him. You need to be careful. Everyone will be watching you extra closely now." Her gaze flicked to Ansel. "And you know the stake isn't just for witches. Witch sympathizers can meet a similar fate."

My heart sank as I looked between them. "Oh, god. The two of you—"

"The three of us," Ansel murmured. "You're forgetting Reid. He'll burn too."

"He murdered Estelle."

Ansel stared down at his boots, swallowing hard. "He believes Estelle was a demon. They all do. He . . . he was trying to protect you, Lou."

I shook my head, furious tears threatening to spill once more.

"But he's wrong. Not all witches are evil."

"I know you believe that," Ansel said softly, "but you can't force Reid to believe it." He finally looked up, and his brown eyes held profound sadness—sadness someone his age never should've known. "There are some things that can't be changed with words. Some things have to be seen. They have to be felt."

He walked to the door but hesitated, looking over his shoulder at me. "I hope you can find your way forward together. He's a good person, and . . . so are you."

I watched him go in silence, desperate to ask how—*how* could a witch and witch hunter find their way forward together? How could I ever trust a man who would have me burned? How could I ever love him?

Ansel had been right about one thing, however. I couldn't hold Reid fully accountable for what had happened to Estelle. He truly believed witches were evil. It was a part of him as much as his copper hair or towering height.

No, Estelle's death wasn't on Reid's hands.

It was on mine.

Before Reid returned that evening, I crawled out of bed and dragged myself to his desk. My skin itched and burned as I healed—a constant reminder of the flames—but my limbs were a different story. My muscles and bones felt stiffer, heavier, as if they would pull me through the floor if they could. Each step to the desk was a struggle. Sweat beaded along my forehead, matted the hair on my neck.

Coco had said my fever would linger. I hoped it'd break soon.

Collapsing into the chair, I pulled the desk drawer open with the last of my energy. Reid's faded old Bible still lay inside. With trembling fingers, I opened it and began to read—or tried to read, at least. His cramped handwriting filled every inch of the narrow margins. Though I brought the silk-thin pages clear to my nose, I couldn't focus on the scripture without my vision swimming.

I tossed it back in the drawer with a disgruntled sigh.

Proving witches weren't inherently evil might be harder than I anticipated.

Still, I'd formed a plan after Coco and Ansel had left this afternoon. If Ansel could be convinced we weren't evil, perhaps Reid could too. In order to do that, I needed to understand his ideology. I needed to understand *him*. Cursing quietly, I rose to my feet once more, steeling myself for the descent into hell.

I'd have to visit the library.

Nearly a half hour later, I pushed open the dungeon door. A welcome draft of cold air swept across my sticky skin, and I sighed in relief. The corridor was quiet. Most of the Chasseurs had retired for the evening, and the rest were busy doing . . . whatever it was they did. Guarding the royal family. Protecting the guilty. Burning the innocent.

When I reached the library, however, the council room door swung open, and the Archbishop strolled out, licking what appeared to be icing from his fingers. In his other hand, he held a half-eaten sticky bun.

Shit. Before I could shove Angelica's Ring in my mouth to

disappear, he turned and spotted me. We both froze with our hands halfway to our mouth—equally absurd—but he recovered first, hiding the sticky bun hastily behind his back. A bit of icing remained on the tip of his nose.

"Louise! What—what are you doing down here?" He shook his head at my bewildered expression, clearing his throat, before rising to his full, inconsiderable height. "This is a restricted area. I must ask you to leave at once."

"Sorry, I—" With a shake of my own head, I averted my gaze, looking anywhere but his nose. "I wanted to borrow a Bible."

He stared at me as if I'd sprouted horns—ironic, given my request. "A what?"

"Is that a . . . bun?" I inhaled the cinnamon and vanilla deeply, brushing a strand of sweaty hair from my forehead. Despite the fever, saliva pooled in my mouth. I'd know that smell anywhere. That was *my* smell. What the hell was he doing with it? It didn't belong in this dark, dismal place.

"Enough impertinent questions." He scowled and wiped his fingers on the back of his robes surreptitiously. "If you truly seek to procure a Bible—which I doubt—I shall of course provide you with one, so long as you return to your room directly." Reluctantly, his eyes assessed my face: the pale skin, the sweaty brow, the shadowed eyes. His expression softened. "You should be in bed, Louise. Your body needs time to—" He shook his head once more, catching himself, as if not quite sure what had gotten into him. I empathized. "Do not move from this spot."

He pushed past me into the library, returning a moment later.

"Here." He thrust an ancient, dusty tome into my hands. Icing smeared the spine and cover. "Ensure you take care of it properly. This is the word of God."

I ran my hand over the leather binding, tracing lines through the dust and icing. "Thank you. I'll return it when I'm finished."

"No need." He cleared his throat again, frowning and clasping his hands behind his back. He looked as uncomfortable as I felt. "It is yours. A gift, if you will."

A gift. The words sent a bolt of displeasure through me, and I was struck by the oddity of this situation. The Archbishop, hiding the icing on his fingers. Me, clutching a Bible to my chest. "Right. Well, I'm going to go—"

"Of course. I, too, must retire—"

We parted ways with equally awkward nods.

Reid opened the bedroom door quietly that night. I shoved the Bible beneath his bed and greeted him with a guilty "Hello!"

"Lou!" He nearly leapt out of his skin. I might've even heard him curse. Eyes wide, he tossed his coat on the desk and approached warily. "It's late. What are you doing awake?"

"Couldn't sleep." My teeth chattered, and I burrowed deeper into the blanket in which I'd cocooned myself.

He touched a hand to my forehead. "You're burning up. Have you visited the infirmary?"

"Brie said the fever would last a few days."

When he moved to sit beside me on the bed, I clambered to my feet, abandoning my blanket. My muscles protested the sudden movement, and I winced, shivering. He sighed and stood as well. "I'm sorry. Please, sit. You need to rest."

"No, I *need* to get this hair off my neck. It's driving me mad." Inexplicably furious, I yanked the offending strands away from my sensitive skin. "But my arms, they're so . . . heavy . . ." A yawn eclipsed the rest of my words, and my arms drooped. I sank back onto the bed. "I can't seem to hold them up."

He chuckled. "Is there something I can do to help?"

"You can braid it."

The chuckle died abruptly. "You want me to—to what?"

"Braid it. Please." He stared at me. I stared back. "I can teach you. It's easy."

"I highly doubt that."

"Please. I can't sleep with it touching my skin."

It was true. Between the scripture, the fever, and the lack of sleep, my mind whirled deliriously. Every brush of hair against my skin was agony—somewhere between cold and pain, tingle and ache.

He swallowed hard and stepped around me. A welcome shiver swept down my back at his presence, his proximity. His heat. He expelled a resigned breath. "Tell me what to do."

I resisted the urge to lean into him. "Divide it into three sections."

He hesitated before gently wrapping his hands around my hair. Fresh gooseflesh rose on my arms as he threaded his fingers through the strands. "Now what?"

"Now take an outside section and cross it over the middle section."

"What?"

"Must I repeat everything?"

"This is impossible," he muttered, trying and failing to keep the strands separated. He gave up after a few seconds and started over. "Your hair is thicker than a horse's tail."

"Hmm." I yawned again. "Is that a compliment, Chass?"

After several more attempts, he successfully managed the first step. "What's next?"

"Now do the other side. Cross it over into the middle. Make sure it's tight."

He growled low in his throat, and a different sort of chill swept through me. "This looks terrible."

I let my head fall forward, relishing the feel of his fingers on my neck. My skin didn't protest as it had earlier. Instead, it seemed to warm under his touch. To melt. My eyes fluttered closed. "Talk to me."

"About what?"

"How did you become captain?"

He didn't answer for a long moment. "Are you sure you want to know?"

"Yes."

"A few months after I joined the Chasseurs, I found a pack of loup garou outside the city. We killed them."

Though no witch could ever claim friendliness with a were-wolf, my heart contracted painfully at his pragmatism. His tone held no remorse, no emotion whatsoever—a simple statement of fact. As cold, barren, and improbable as a frozen seascape. Jean Luc would've called it truth.

Unable to muster the energy to continue the conversation, I

sighed heavily, and we lapsed into silence. He braided steadily down my back, his movements quickening as he gained confidence. His fingers were nimble. Skilled. He seemed to sense the tension in my shoulders, however, because his voice was much softer when he asked, "How do I finish it?"

"There's a leather cord on the nightstand."

He wrapped the cord around the braid several times before tying it into a neat knot. At least, I assumed it was neat. Every aspect of Reid was precise, certain, every color in its proper place. Undiluted by indecision, he saw the world in black and white, suffering none of the messy, charcoal colors in between. The colors of ash and smoke. Of fear and doubt.

The colors of me.

"Lou, I . . ." He ran his fingers down my braid, and fresh chills washed over my skin. When I finally turned to look at him, he dropped his hand and stepped back, refusing to meet my eyes. "You asked."

"I know."

Without another word, he strode into the washroom and closed the door.

A TIME FOR MOVING ON

Reid

"Let's go somewhere," Lou announced.

I looked up from my Bible. She'd visited the infirmary again this morning. Since returning from the foul place, she'd done nothing but sit on the bed and stare at empty air. But her eyes hadn't been idle. No, they flicked back and forth as if watching something, her lips moving imperceptibly. Her fingers twitching.

Though I didn't say anything, I feared the patients were beginning to rub off on her. One patient in particular, a Monsieur Bernard, worried me. A few days ago, Father Orville had pulled me aside to inform me the man was kept under constant sedation— and chained—to prevent suicide. Father Orville seemed to think Lou would suffer a shock when the inevitable happened.

Perhaps time away would do us both good.

I set aside my Bible. "Where do you want to go?"

"I want a sticky bun. Do you remember the patisserie where we first met? The one in East End? I used to go there all the time before, well . . . all of this." She waved a hand between us.

I eyed her warily. "Do you promise to behave yourself?"

"Of course not. That would ruin the fun." She hopped down from the bed. Fetched her cloak from the rack. "Are you coming or not?"

A sparkle lit her eyes that I hadn't seen since the theater. Before the burning. Before, well . . . all of this. I eyed her carefully, searching for any sign of the woman I'd known the past week. Though her fever had abated quickly, her spirits hadn't. It'd been like she was balancing on the tip of a knife—one wrong move, and she'd impale someone. Likely me.

Or herself.

But today she seemed different. Perhaps she'd turned a corner. "Are you . . . feeling better?" I asked, hesitant.

She stilled in tying her cloak. "Maybe."

Against my better judgment, I nodded and reached for my own coat—only to have her snatch it out of reach.

"No." She wagged a finger in front of my nose. "I'd like to spend the day with Reid, not the Chasseur."

Reid.

I still hadn't grown used to her saying my name. Every time she did, an absurd little thrill shot through me. This time was no different. I cleared my throat and crossed my arms, trying and failing to remain impassive. "They're the same person."

She grimaced and held the door open for me. "We'll see about *that*. Shall we?"

It was a blustery day. Icy. Unforgiving. Bits of the last snowfall clung to the edge of the streets, where footsteps had turned it slushy and brown. I stuffed my hands into my trouser pockets. Blinked irritably into the brilliant afternoon sunshine. "It's freezing out here."

Lou turned her face into the wind with a grin. Closed her eyes and extended her arms, the tip of her nose already red. "The cold stifles the reek of fish. It's wonderful."

"That's easy for you to stay. *You* have a cloak."

She turned to me, grin widening. Pieces of her hair tore free of her hood and danced around her face. "I can swipe you one, if you'd like. There's a clothier next door to the patisserie—"

"Don't even think about it."

"Fine." She burrowed deeper into the folds of her cloak. Charcoal. Stained. Fraying at the hem. "Suit yourself."

Scowling, I trudged down the street after her. Every muscle in my body seized with cold, but I didn't allow myself to shiver. To give Lou the satisfaction of—

"Oh, good lord," she said, laughing. "This is painful to watch. Here."

She threw one side of her cloak around me. It barely covered my shoulders, but I didn't complain—especially when she nestled beneath my arm, drawing it tighter around us. I wrapped my arm around her shoulders in surprise. She laughed harder. "We look ridiculous."

I glanced down at us, lips quirking. It was true. I was simply too big for the fabric, and we were forced to shuffle awkwardly in order to stay covered. We tried to synchronize our steps, but I soon stepped wrong—and we ended up in a tangled heap in the snow. A spectacle. Passersby eyed us in disapproval, but for the first time in as long as I could remember, I didn't care.

I laughed too.

By the time we burst into the patisserie, our cheeks and noses were red. Our throats ached from laughter. I stared at her as she swept the cloak from my shoulders. She smiled with her whole face. I'd never seen such a transformation. It was . . . infectious.

"Pan!" Lou flung her arms open. I followed her gaze to the familiar man behind the counter. Short. Heavyset. Bright, beady eyes that lit with excitement upon seeing Lou.

"Lucida! My darling child, where have you been?" He waddled around the counter as fast as his legs would carry him. "I was beginning to think you had forgotten your friend Pan! And"—his eyes widened comically, and his voice dropped to a whisper—"what have you done to your *hair*?"

Lou's smile slipped, and her hand shot to her hair. Oblivious, Pan swept her into his arms, holding her a second longer than appropriate. Lou gave a reluctant chuckle. "I—I needed a change. Something darker for winter. Do you like it?"

"Of course, of course. But you're much too thin, child, much too thin. Here, let us fatten you up with a bun." He turned back toward the counter, but halted when he finally noticed me. He raised his brows. "And who is this?"

Lou grinned, devious. I braced myself for whatever scheme she'd concocted—praying it wasn't something illegal. Knowing it probably was.

"Pan." She took my arm and tugged me forward. "I'd like you to meet . . . Bas."

Bas? I looked down at her in surprise.

"*The* Bas?" Pan's eyes nearly popped out of his head.

She winked at me. "The one and only."

Pan scowled. Then—incredibly—he rose to his toes and poked a finger in my chest. I frowned, bewildered, and made to step back, but the man followed. Poking me all the way.

"Now you listen to me, young man—yes, I've heard all about you! You don't know how lucky you are to have this *cherie* on your arm. She is a pearl, and you will treat her as such from this point on, do you understand? If I hear differently, you will answer to me, and you do not want Pan as an enemy, oh no!"

I glared at Lou, indignant, but she only shook with silent laughter. Useless. I took a quick step backward. Too quick for the man to follow. "I— Yes, sir."

"Very good." He still eyed me shrewdly as he fetched two sticky buns from behind the counter. After handing one to Lou, he promptly threw the other in my face. I hastened to stop it from sliding down my shirt. "Here you are, my dear. *You* have to pay," he added, glaring at me.

I wiped icing from my nose incredulously. The man was a lunatic. As was my wife.

When Pan retreated back behind the counter, I rounded on her. "Who is Lucida? And *why* did you tell him my name is—is—*that*?"

It took her several seconds to answer—to chew through the enormous glob of sticky bun in her mouth. Her cheeks bulged with it. To her credit, she managed to keep her mouth closed. To my credit, I did too.

She finally swallowed. Licked her fingers with a reverence that belonged in Mass. No—with a reverence that most definitely did *not* belong in Mass. I looked anywhere but at her tongue. "Mmm . . . so territorial, Chass."

"Well?" I asked, unable to conceal my jealousy. "Why would you tell him I'm the thief?"

She grinned at me and continued licking her thumb. "If you must know, I use him to guilt Pan into giving me sweets. Just last month, the wicked, *wicked* Bas tricked me into elopement, only to leave me at the dock. Pan gave me free buns for a week."

I forced myself to meet her eyes. "You're deplorable."

Her eyes glittered. She knew exactly what she was doing. "Yes, I am. Are you going to eat that?" She motioned to my plate. I shoved it toward her, and she bit into my bun with a soft sigh. "Like manna from Heaven."

Surprise jolted through me. "I didn't realize you were familiar with the Bible."

"You probably don't realize a lot of things about me, Chass." She shrugged, stuffing half the bun into her mouth. "Besides, it's the only book in the entire Tower except *La Vie Éphémère*, *Shepherd*, and *Twelve Treatises of Occult Extermination*—which is rubbish, by the way. I don't recommend."

I hardly heard a word she said. "Don't call me that. My name is Reid."

She arched a brow. "I thought they were the same person?"

I leaned back, studying her as she finished my bun. A bit of icing covered her lip. Her nose was still red from the cold, her hair wild and windblown. My little heathen. "You dislike the Chasseurs."

She fixed me with a pointed stare. "And I tried so hard to hide it."

I ignored her. "Why?"

"I don't think you're ready to hear that answer, Chass."

"Fine. Why did you want to come out today?"

"Because it was time."

I suppressed a sigh of frustration. "Meaning . . . ?"

"Meaning there's a time for mourning, and there's a time for moving on."

It was always the same with her. She always hedged. As if sensing my thoughts, she crossed her arms, leaning onto the table. Expression inscrutable. "All right, then. Maybe you *are* ready to hear some answers. Let's make a game of it, shall we? A game of questions to get to know each other."

I leaned forward too. Returning the challenge. "Let's."

"Fine. What's your favorite color?"

"Blue."

She rolled her eyes. "Boring. Mine's gold—or turquoise. Or emerald."

"Why doesn't that surprise me?"

"Because you aren't as stupid as you look." I didn't know whether to be insulted or flattered. She didn't give me time to decide. "What's the most embarrassing thing you've ever done?"

"I—" Blood crept up my throat at the memory. I coughed and stared at her empty plate. "The Archbishop once caught me in a—er, compromising position. With a girl."

"Oh my god!" She smacked her palms against the table, eyes widening. "You got caught having sex with Célie?"

The people at the next table swiveled to stare at us. I ducked my head, thankful—for the first time ever—I wasn't wearing my uniform. I glared at her. "Shhh! Of course not. She kissed me, okay? It was just kissing!"

Lou frowned. "Just kissing? That's no fun at all. Hardly something to be embarrassed about."

But it had been something to be embarrassed about. The look on the Archbishop's face—I forced the memory away quickly. "What's yours, then? Did you strip naked and dance the *bourrée*?"

She snorted. "You wish. No—I sang at a festival when I was a child. Missed every note. Everyone laughed. I'm a shit singer."

Our neighbors tsked in disapproval. I grimaced. "Yes, I know."

"Right. Biggest pet peeve?"

"Swearing."

"Killjoys." She grinned. "Favorite food?"

"Venison."

She pointed to her empty plate. "Sticky buns. Best friend?"

"Jean Luc. You?"

"Really?" Her grin faded, and she stared at me with what looked like—like *pity*. But that couldn't be right. "That's . . . unfortunate. Mine is Brie."

Ignoring the jab—the *look*—I interrupted before she could ask another question. "Fatal flaw?"

She hesitated, dropping her gaze to the tabletop. Tracing a knot in the wood with her finger. "Selfishness."

"Wrath. Greatest fear?"

This time she didn't hesitate. "Death."

I frowned and reached across the table to grasp her hand. "There's nothing to fear in death, Lou."

She looked up at me, blue-green eyes inscrutable. "There isn't?"

"No. Not if you know where you're going."

She gave a grim laugh and dropped my hand. "That's the problem, isn't it?"

"Lou—"

She stood and thrust a finger against my mouth to silence me. I blinked rapidly, trying not to fixate on the sweetness of her skin.

"Let's not talk about this anymore." She dropped her finger. "Let's go see the Yule tree. I saw them putting it up earlier."

"The Christmas tree," I corrected automatically.

She continued as if she hadn't heard me. "We really ought to get you a coat first, though. Are you sure you don't want me to steal one? It would be easy. I'll even let you pick the color."

"I'm not going to let you steal anything. I'll *buy* a coat." I accepted the bit of cloak she offered me, pulling it around us once more. "And I can buy you a new cloak as well."

"Bas bought this for me!"

"Exactly." I steered her down the street toward the clothier's shop. "All the more reason to throw it in the trash where it belongs."

An hour later, we emerged from the shop in our new garments. A navy wool coat with silver fastenings for me. A white cloak of crushed velvet for Lou. She'd protested when she saw the price, but I'd insisted. The white looked striking against her golden skin, and she'd left her hood down for once. Her dark hair blew loose in the breeze. Beautiful.

I hadn't mentioned that last bit, though.

A dove cooed above us as we made our way to the village center, and snowflakes fell thick and fast. They caught in Lou's hair, in her eyelashes. She winked at me, catching one on her tongue. Then another. And another. Soon she twirled in a circle trying to catch them all at once. People stared, but she didn't care. I watched her with reluctant amusement.

"C'mon, Chass! Taste them! They're divine!"

I shook my head, a grin tugging at my lips. The more people who muttered around us, the louder her voice became. The wilder her movements. The broader her smile. She reveled in their disapproval.

I shook my head, grin fading. "I can't."

She spun toward me and grabbed my hands. Her fingers were freezing—like ten tiny icicles. "It won't kill you to live a little, you know."

"I'm a Chasseur, Lou." I spun her away from me once more with a pang of regret. "We don't . . . frolic."

Even if we wanted to.

"Have you ever tried it?"

"Of course not."

"Maybe you should."

"It's getting late. Do you want to see the Christmas tree or not?"

She stuck her tongue out at me. "You're no fun, Chass. A frolic in the snow might be just what you and the rest of those Chasseurs need. It's a good way to get the stick out of your ass, I'm told."

I glanced around nervously. Two passing shoppers skewered me with disapproving glares. I caught Lou's hand as she spun back toward me. "*Please* behave."

"*Fine.*" She reached up to brush the snowflakes from my hair, smoothing the furrow between my brows as she went. "I will refrain from using the word *ass*. Happy?"

"Lou!"

She cackled and grinned up at me. "You, sir, are too easy. Let's go see this Yule tree."

"Christmas tree."

"Nuance. Shall we?" Though we no longer shared a cloak, she wrapped her arms around my waist. Pulling her closer with an exasperated shake of my head, I couldn't stop the small smile that touched my lips.

Mademoiselle Perrot greeted us in the church foyer that evening, her face pinched. Troubled. She ignored me—as per usual—and walked straight to Lou.

"What is it?" Lou frowned and took her gloved hands. "What's happened?"

"It's Bernie," Mademoiselle Perrot said quietly. Lou's brows dipped as she scanned Mademoiselle Perrot's face.

I clasped Lou's shoulder. "Who's Bernie?"

Mademoiselle Perrot didn't even glance at me. But Lou did. "Monsieur Bernard." Ah. The suicidal patient. She turned her attention back to Mademoiselle Perrot. "Is he—is he dead?"

Mademoiselle Perrot's eyes gleamed too bright in the candlelight of the foyer. Too wet. Lined with unshed tears. I braced myself for the inevitable. "We don't know. He's gone."

This caught my attention. I stepped forward. "What do you mean *gone*?"

She exhaled sharply through her nose, finally deigning to look at me. "Gone as in *gone*, Captain Diggory. Bed empty. Chains torn free. No sign of a body."

"No sign of a body?" Lou's eyes widened. "So—so that means he didn't die by suicide!"

Mademoiselle Perrot shook her head. Grim. "It doesn't mean anything. He could've dragged himself off somewhere and done it. Until we find the body, we don't know."

I had to agree with her. "Have my brethren been alerted?"

She pursed her lips. "Yes. They're searching the church and Tower now. A unit has been deployed to scour the city as well."

Good. The last thing we needed was someone stumbling upon a corpse riddled with magic. The people would panic. I nodded and squeezed Lou's shoulder. "They'll find him, Lou. One way or the other. You needn't worry."

Her face remained rigid. "But what if he's dead?"

I spun her around to face me—much to Mademoiselle Perrot's

irritation. "Then he's no longer in pain." I leaned down to her ear, away from Mademoiselle Perrot's keen eyes. Her hair tickled my lips. "He knew where he was going, Lou. He had nothing to fear."

She leaned back to look at me. "I thought suicide was a mortal sin."

I reached out, brushing a strand of hair behind her ear. "Only God can judge us. Only God can read the depths of our soul. And I think he understands the power of circumstance—of fear." I dropped my hand and cleared my throat. Forced the words out before I could change my mind. "I think there are few absolutes in this world. Just because the Church believes Monsieur Bernard will suffer eternally for his mental illness . . . doesn't mean he will."

Something swelled in Lou's eyes at my words. I didn't recognize it at first. Didn't recognize it until several hours later, as I drifted to sleep on my bedroom floor.

Hope. It had been hope.

THE GUEST OF HONOR

Lou

King Auguste scheduled a ball on the eve of Saint Nicolas Day to commence a weekend of celebration. And to honor Reid. Apparently, the king felt indebted to Reid for saving his family's skin when the witches had attacked. Though I hadn't stuck around to watch the chaos unfold, I had no doubt my husband had acted . . . *heroic*.

Still, it felt odd celebrating Reid's victory when his failure would've solved my predicament. If the king and his children were already dead, there would be no reason for me to die too. Indeed, my throat would've very much appreciated his failure.

Reid shook his head in exasperation as Coco burst into the room without knocking, a filmy white gown draped across her arm. Slinging his best Chasseur coat over his shoulder and sighing, he bent to tuck a piece of my hair behind my ear in farewell.

"I need to meet the Archbishop." He paused at the door, the corner of his mouth quirking in a lopsided smile. Excitement danced in his sea-blue eyes. Despite my reservations, I couldn't help myself; I smiled back. "I'll return shortly."

Coco lifted the gown for my appraisal after he left. "You're going to look divine in this."

"I look divine in everything."

She grinned and winked at me. "That's the spirit." Tossing the gown on the bed, she forced me into the desk chair, raking her fingers through my hair. I shivered at the memory of Reid's fingers. "The priests agreed to let me attend the ball since I'm such a *close* personal friend of you and your husband." She pulled a brush from her robes with a determined glint in her eyes. "Now, it's time to brush your hair."

I scowled at her and leaned away. "I don't think so."

I never brushed my hair. It was one of the few rules I lived by, and I certainly didn't see a need to start breaking it now. Besides, Reid liked my hair. Since I'd asked him to braid it, he seemed to think he could continue touching it at every opportunity.

I didn't correct him because . . . well, I just didn't.

"Oh, but I do." She pushed me back down in my seat, attacking my hair as if it'd personally offended her. When I tried to wriggle away, she whacked me on top of the head with her brush. "Be still! These rats have to come out!"

Nearly two hours later, I stared at myself in the mirror. The front of the gown—crafted of thin white silk—skimmed my torso before billowing artfully at the knees, soft and simple. Delicate petals and silver crystals dusted the sheer fabric of the back, and Coco had pinned my hair at my nape to showcase the elaborate appliqué. She'd also insisted I heal the remainder of my bruises.

Another velvet ribbon covered my scar.

Overall, I looked . . . good.

She stood behind me now, preening at her own reflection over my shoulder. A fitted black gown accentuated her every curve—the high neckline and tight sleeves adding to her allure—and she'd pinned her wayward curls into an elegant chignon at her crown. I eyed her with a familiar pang of jealousy. I didn't fill out my own dress quite so well.

She smoothed the rouge on her lips with a finger and smacked her lips. "We look straight out of the Bellerose. Babette would be proud."

"Is that supposed to be an insult?" I reached into my gown to lift each breast, squeezing my shoulders together and frowning at the results. "Those courtesans are so beautiful people *pay* to be with them."

Ansel entered the bedroom a moment later. He'd trimmed his mop of curls and smoothed them away from his face, emphasizing his high cheekbones and flawless skin. The new style made him look . . . older. I eyed the long lines of his body—the sharp cut of his jaw, the full curve of his mouth—with newfound appreciation.

His eyes boggled at the sight of Coco. I didn't blame him. Her gown was a far cry from the oversized healing robes she normally wore. "Mademoiselle Perrot! You look—er, you look very—very good." Her brows rose in wry amusement. "I mean—er—" He shook his head quickly and tried again. "Reid—er, Captain Diggory—he wanted me to tell you—I mean, not *you*, but Lou—that, ah—"

"Good lord, Ansel." I grinned as he tore his gaze from her. He blinked rapidly, dazed, as if someone had clubbed him in the head. "I feel a little insulted."

But he clearly wasn't listening. His eyes had already gravitated back to Coco, who stalked toward him with a catlike grin. She tilted her head as if surveying a particularly juicy mouse. He swallowed hard.

"You look very good as well." She circled him appreciatively, trailing a finger across his chest. He went rigid. "I had no idea you were so handsome under all that hair."

"Was there something you needed, Ansel?" I gestured to the room at large, sweeping an arm past Coco's impressive bosom. "Or are you just here to admire the general decor?"

He cleared his throat, eyes gleaming determinedly as he opened his mouth once more. "Captain Diggory requested I escort you to the castle. The Archbishop insisted he go on with him. I can also escort you, Mademoiselle Perrot."

"I think I'd like that." Coco slid an arm around his, and I burst out laughing at the alarmed look on his face. Every single muscle in his body tensed—even his eyelids. It was extraordinary. "And please—call me Brie."

He took great care to touch as little of Coco as possible as we walked down the stairwell, but Coco went out of her way to make the endeavor difficult. The Chasseurs who had been forced to stay behind stared unabashedly as we passed. Coco winked at them.

"Might as well give them a show," I whispered.

Coco grinned wickedly and pinched Ansel's backside in response. He yelped and leapt forward, whirling mutinously as the guards snickered behind us. "That *wasn't funny.*"

I disagreed.

Ancient and unadorned, the castle of Cesarine was a fortress befitting its city. It boasted no intricate buttresses or spires, no windows or arches. It loomed over us as we joined the throng of carriages already in the receiving line, the setting sun tinging the stone with bloody red light. The evergreens in the courtyard— tall and narrow, like two spears piercing the sky—only added to the grim picture.

We waited for what seemed like hours before a footman in Lyon livery approached our carriage. Ansel stepped out to greet him, whispering something in his ear, and the man's eyes widened. He hastily took my hand. "Madame Diggory! Captain Diggory has been anxiously awaiting your arrival."

"As he should be." Coco didn't wait for the footman to help her down. Ansel scrambled to catch her elbow, but she brushed him off too. "I'm anxious to see if this Chasseur of yours is as doting in public as he is in private."

The footman looked startled but said nothing. Ansel groaned under his breath.

"Please, *mesdames*, make your way to the antechamber," the footman said. "The herald will ensure you are properly announced."

I lurched to a halt. "Properly announced? But I have no title."

"Yes, *madame*, but your husband is the guest of honor. The king insists on treating him as royalty tonight."

"Potentially problematic," Coco murmured as Ansel tugged the two of us forward.

Definitely problematic. And not the fun kind.

I had no intention of being announced to a room full of strangers. There was no telling who could be in there watching. I'd learned my lesson with Estelle. There was no need for a repeat performance.

I took in my surroundings, seeking a discreet entrance. At a ball held in my husband's honor, however, I had no idea how I might *remain* discreet—especially in such a ridiculously sheer dress. I cursed inwardly as every eye turned toward us as we passed. Coco's sinful figure didn't help matters.

Richly dressed aristocrats milled about the antechamber, which was as dark and dismal as the exterior. Like a prison. A prison with candles flickering in gold candelabras and wreaths of evergreen and holly draped across the doorways. I think I even spotted mistletoe.

Ansel craned his neck to find the herald. "There he is." He pointed to a short, squat man with a wig and scroll who stood beside a large archway. Music and laughter poured from the room beyond. Another servant appeared to take our cloaks. Though I held on to mine for a second too long, the servant succeeded in tugging it from my hands. Feeling naked, I watched it disappear with a sense of helplessness.

When Ansel pulled me toward the herald, however, I dug in

my heels. "I'm not being announced."

"But the footman said—"

I jerked out of his grasp. "I don't care what the footman said!"

"Lou, the king insisted—"

"Darlings." Coco smiled wide, looping her arms through ours. "Let's not make a scene, hmm?"

Taking a deep breath, I forced myself to smile and nod at the eavesdropping aristocrats. "I'll be entering from over *there*," I informed Ansel through clenched teeth, gesturing across the antechamber to where servants were coming and going from a smaller, secondary set of doors.

"Lou," he began, but I was already halfway to the doors. Coco hurried to follow, leaving Ansel behind.

The ballroom was much larger and grander than the antechamber. Iron chandeliers hung from the beamed ceiling, and the wooden floor gleamed in the candlelight. Musicians played a festive tune in the corner next to an enormous evergreen. Some guests already danced, though most preferred to stroll around the perimeter of the room, drinking champagne and wheedling the royal family. Judging from the loud, slurred voices of the aristocrats nearest me, they'd been hitting the bubbly for hours.

"Yes, Ye Olde Sisters, that's what I heard—"

"They've traveled all the way from Amandine to perform! My cousin says they're quite brilliant."

"Sunday, you said?"

"After Mass. Such a fitting way to end the weekend. The Archbishop deserves the honor—"

Scoffing, I marched past them into the room. Any person who chose to string together the words *the Archbishop deserves the honor* wasn't worth my attention. I scanned the sea of blue coats and sparkling gowns for Reid, spotting his coppery hair at the far end of the ballroom. A group of admirers surrounded him, though the young woman clinging to his arm drew my particular attention. My heart plummeted.

Anxiously awaiting, my ass.

Even from a distance, I could tell the woman was beautiful: delicate and feminine; her porcelain skin and raven hair shone in the candlelight. She shook with genuine laughter at something Reid had just said. Uneasiness flitted through me.

This could only be one person.

One boring, docile, wretchedly inconvenient pipe dream.

Coco followed my gaze, wrinkling her nose in distaste when she too spotted Reid and the raven-haired beauty. "Please tell me that's not who I think it is."

"I'll come find you later." My eyes never left Reid's face. Coco knew better than to follow this time.

I'd just descended into the ballroom when another man stepped in my path. Though I'd never encountered him this close, I recognized his tawny complexion and hooded eyes at once. Black hair styled to perfection, he wore more diamonds on his crown than were in Tremblay's entire vault.

Beauregard Lyon.

Damn it. I didn't have time for this shit. Even now, that stupid cow was probably sinking her claws deeper into my husband—reminding him of her *beautiful* lips, and smile, and eyes, and laugh—

"That is quite the dress." His gaze swept up my body lazily, and he smirked, arching a brow.

"Your Highness." I dropped into a curtsy, clamping down on a slew of more appropriate honorifics. He eyed my breasts appreciatively as I leaned down, and I straightened at once. Bloody pervert.

"Your name." It wasn't a question.

"Madame Diggory, Your Highness."

His grin widened in delight. "Madame Diggory? As in— Madame *Reid* Diggory?"

"The very same."

He actually threw his head back and laughed. The aristocrats nearest us paused, eyeing me with renewed interest. "Oh, I've heard all about you." His golden eyes sparkled with glee. "Tell me, how exactly did you trick our dear captain into marrying you? I've heard the rumors, of course, but everyone has their own theories."

I would've gladly broken a finger to break one of his other appendages.

"No tricks, Your Highness," I said sweetly. "We're in love."

His grin faded, and his lip curled slightly. "How wretched."

At that moment, the crowd shifted, revealing Reid and his many admirers. The raven-haired woman reached up to brush something from Reid's hair. My blood boiled.

The prince's brows rose as he followed my gaze. "Love, huh?"

He leaned closer, his breath warm against my ear. "Should we make him jealous?"

"No, thank you," I snapped. "*Your Highness.*"

"Call me Beau." His grin turned wicked as he stepped aside. I stormed past him, but he caught my hand and brushed a kiss against my palm at the last second. I resisted the urge to snap his fingers. "Come find me if you change your mind. We would have fun together, you and I."

With one last, lingering look, he sauntered off, winking at one of the women who hovered nearby. I scowled after him for a moment before turning back to Reid.

But he and Célie were gone.

A DANGEROUS GAME

Lou

It didn't take long for me to spot them, as Reid towered over everyone in the crowd. *Connasse* that she was, Célie still clutched his arm as they headed toward a door partially hidden by two evergreens.

I trailed after them. To my annoyance, and perhaps trepidation, they remained completely absorbed in each other, walking through the door without a backward glance. I made to slip through after them, but a hand caught my arm.

I whirled around to face the Archbishop.

"I wouldn't." He dropped my arm as if worried he'd catch something. "Envy is a mortal sin, child."

"So is adultery."

He ignored me, his gaze falling on the door. His face was paler than usual, drawn, and he looked like he'd lost weight since I last saw him. "We stole a future from him, you and I. Célie is everything a woman should be. Reid would have been happy." He looked back at me, and his mouth tightened. "Now he pays for both our sins."

"What are you talking about?"

"I don't blame you for your hedonistic upbringing, Louise, but you *are* a heathen." His eyes shone fervid with conviction. "Perhaps if someone had been there—if someone had intervened—all of this could have been avoided."

I stood motionless, rooted to the spot like the evergreens beside us, as he began to pace. "Now it's too late. Let Reid enjoy this small pleasure away from your corruption."

My bewilderment hardened into something glittering and cold at the words. As if *I* were the one who had done the corrupting. As if *I* were the one who should be ashamed.

I lifted my chin, stepping forward until I was offensively close to his pale face. "I don't know what the hell you're talking about, but you need to look in the mirror. There's a special circle in Hell for liars and hypocrites, Your Eminence. Perhaps I'll see you there."

He gaped at me, but when I turned on my heel, he made no move to follow. The savage satisfaction coursing through me quickly dissipated as I entered what could only be a kitchen.

It was empty.

An icy breeze soon bit at my skin, however, and I realized the opposite door had been left ajar. The wind whistled through the narrow crack. I inched it open farther to see Reid and Célie standing in a dead herbal garden. Snow coated the brown bits of sage and rosemary.

I leaned forward, barely able to discern their voices over the wind.

"I'm sorry, Célie." Reid cradled the woman's hands in his own.

She held her shoulders stiff—angry.

You shouldn't be here, the small, disapproving voice at the back of my head warned. *This is wrong. Private. You're breaking trust.*

He's *the one breaking trust.*

"There has to be something we can do," Célie said bitterly. "It isn't right. The Archbishop *knows* you're innocent. We could go to him—ask him for an annulment. He loves you as if you're his own son. Surely he wouldn't keep you trapped in a loveless marriage."

My stomach dropped to somewhere below my ankles.

Reid stroked her fingers with his thumb. "The Archbishop is the one who suggested it."

"The king, then. My father is the *vicomte.* I'm sure I could arrange a meeting—"

"Célie," he said softly.

She sniffled, and I knew instinctively it wasn't because of the cold. "I *hate* her."

"Célie, you . . . you didn't want me."

My chest constricted at the emotion in his voice. At the pain.

"I *always* wanted you," she said fiercely. "This wasn't supposed to happen. I was angry, heartbroken, and I just—I needed time. I wanted to be *selfless* for her. For Pip." She wrapped her arms around his neck, and I saw her face clearly for the first time. She had lovely high cheekbones, with wide, doe-like eyes and full lips. "But I don't care anymore, Reid. I don't care if it's selfish. I want to be with you."

Surely there is nothing more beautiful in all the world than your smile—except, of course, your eyes. Or your laugh. Or your lips.

I watched her press those lips to Reid's cheek and felt sick. Suddenly, I didn't find their love letters funny anymore.

He pulled away before she could move to his mouth. "Célie, don't. Please. Don't make this any harder."

She paused, lower lip trembling. Her next words were a direct blow to my chest. "I love you, Reid." She clung to him, pleading. "I'm so sorry I pushed you away, but we can still be together. We can fix this. You haven't consummated the marriage. Speak to the Archbishop, ask for an annulment. He'll send that whore to prison where she belongs, and—"

"She isn't a whore."

I leaned forward as Célie pulled back, frowning at something she saw in his face. "She was a thief, Reid, and she *framed* you. She—she doesn't deserve you."

Reid gently disentangled himself from her arms. "Célie, this can't continue." His voice was low, resigned. "Whether or not you like her, I made a vow. I will honor it."

"Do *you* like her?" Célie demanded, eyes narrowing.

"It doesn't matter."

"It matters to me!"

And me.

"What do you want me to say, Célie? She's my wife. Of course I like her."

Célie rocked back as if he'd slapped her. "What's happened to you, Reid?"

"Nothing—"

"The Reid I know would abhor that woman. She is *everything* you stand against—"

"You don't know her."

"I obviously don't know you either!"

"Célie, please—"

"Do you love her?"

I held my breath, fingers biting into the doorjamb. There was a heavy pause. Then—

"No." He exhaled heavily, looking down. "But I think—I think maybe I could—"

"But you said you loved *me*." She backed away slowly, eyes wide with shock and hurt. Tears slid down her cheeks. "You asked to marry me! *Me*—not her!"

"I— Célie, I did. But Lou . . ." He sighed and shook his head. "I won't hurt her."

"You won't hurt *her*?" She cried in earnest now, patches of color rising to her pale cheeks. "What about *me*, Reid? We've known each other since we were children!" Her tears soaked her bodice, ruining the black silk. "What about *Pip*? What about your *oath*?"

Reid's hands hung limp at his sides. "I'm sorry. I never meant for this to happen."

"I'm sorry too, Reid," she sobbed. "I'm sorry I ever met you."

I inched away from the door, numbness creeping down my limbs. I shouldn't have been here. This moment hadn't been meant for my eyes.

Back in the ballroom, I stood apart from the crowd, my mind still reeling.

Reid had loved her.

I shook my head, disgusted with myself. Of course he had. He'd said as much in his stupid journal—which I *never* should've read—and even if he hadn't, he was a young, attractive man. He would've had his choice amongst any number of women if he hadn't devoted his life to the Chasseurs. The thought rankled more than it should've. As did the thought of Célie's lips—of *any-one's* lips—pressed to his cheek.

Célie reemerged several moments later, wiping her face as inconspicuously as possible. She ducked her head before anyone could question her, heading straight for the antechamber. I swallowed the lump in my throat as Reid too reappeared. Watching as he searched for me, I debated following Célie.

How could I face him after what I'd heard? After learning what he'd given up?

Do you love her?

No. But I think—I think maybe I could—

Could what? Love me? Panic clawed up my throat at the word. Just as I'd lifted my skirts to flee toward the carriage, however, Reid spotted me in the crowd. I waved awkwardly, cursing my sudden insecurity, as his blue eyes met mine and widened. He started forward, politely excusing himself from the many aristocrats who tried to stop and congratulate him along the way.

I shifted my feet—intensely and horribly aware of my thunderous heartbeat, my tingling limbs, my flushed skin—when he finally reached me.

He took my hand. "You look beautiful."

I flushed further under his gaze. Unlike the prince's haughty appreciation, Reid was almost . . . reverent. No one had ever looked at me like that before.

"Thank you." My breath caught, and he tilted his head, eyes searching mine in silent question. I looked away, embarrassed, but Coco chose that moment to swoop down on us.

She didn't bother with pleasantries. She never did with Reid. "Tell me, Chasseur Diggory, who was that lovely woman you were with earlier? Your sister, perhaps?"

I glared at her pointedly, but she ignored me. Subtlety had never been Coco's forte.

"Oh—er, no," Reid said. "That was the *vicomte*'s daughter, Mademoiselle Tremblay."

"Close personal friend?" Coco pressed. "Her-dad-is-friends-with-your-dad type of thing?"

"I've never met my father," Reid answered woodenly.

But Coco didn't bat an eye. "How do you know one another then?"

"Brie." I forced a smile and reached for her hand, squeezing it mercilessly. "I think I'd like a little time alone with my husband. Where's Ansel?"

She waved her other hand behind us dispassionately. "Probably beating his chest and challenging that other Chasseur to a duel."

I looked back to where she waved. "What other Chasseur?"

"The pompous one. The asshat." She pursed her lips in concentration, but she needn't have bothered. I knew exactly to whom she referred. "Jean Luc."

"What happened?"

"Oh, the usual male condition. Ansel didn't want Jean Luc playing with his new toy." She rolled her eyes. "I swear, my female paramours are never so much trouble."

My grin was genuine now. Poor Ansel. He didn't stand a chance against Jean Luc—or Coco. "Perhaps you should go referee."

Coco studied my hand clasped around Reid's, and the feverish complexion of my cheeks. The way he stood close. Much too close. Her eyes narrowed. "Perhaps I should."

She stepped forward to embrace me, but Reid wouldn't let go of my hand. Shooting him a glare, she hugged me regardless—awkward, but fierce. "I'll see you later," she murmured in my ear. "Let me know if I need to exsanguinate him."

Reid watched her leave with an inscrutable expression. "We need to talk," he said finally. "Somewhere private."

I followed him in silent apprehension to the same herb garden of Célie's heartbreak. This time, I made sure to shut the kitchen door firmly behind us. Whatever he wanted to confess—and I had an inkling it would hurt like a bitch—I didn't need an audience.

He dragged a hand through his coppery hair in agitation. "Lou, the woman you and Mademoiselle Perrot saw me with, that was—"

"Don't." I wrapped my arms around my waist to keep from shivering. I couldn't take it. I couldn't relive the wretched conversation again. Hearing it once had been enough. "You don't have to explain anything. I understand."

"I do need to explain," he disagreed. "Look, I know we were married under less than ideal circumstances. But, Lou, I—I want this to work. I want to be your husband. I know I can't force you to want the same, but—"

"I do want the same," I whispered.

His eyes widened, and he took a tentative step closer. "You do?"

"Yes."

He smiled, then—truly smiled—before faltering slightly. "Then there can't be any secrets between us." He hesitated, as if searching for the right words. "The woman you saw was Célie. You read my letters, so you know I loved her. But—but nothing happened. I promise. She found me when I arrived with the Archbishop, and she . . . she refused to leave my side. I brought her out here just a few moments ago to explain the new parameters of our relationship. I told her I didn't—"

"I know."

I took a deep breath, preparing myself for the unpleasantness to come. He frowned. "How can you know that?"

Because I'm a shit person. Because I didn't trust you. Because she is everything you deserve, and I am your enemy.

"I followed the two of you out here," I admitted quietly. "I . . . I heard everything."

"You spied on us?" Disbelief colored his voice.

I trembled. Whether from the cold or shame, I didn't know. "Old habits die hard."

His brows pinched together, and he drew back slightly. "That's not how I would've chosen for you to find out."

I shrugged, attempting a bit of my old swagger, but it fell flat. "Easier this way though."

He stared at me for a long moment—so long I didn't know whether he would speak at all. I recoiled from his intensity. "No more secrets, Lou," he said finally. "No more lies."

I cursed myself for not being able to give him the answer he wanted. The answer *I* wanted. Because there it was—leering at me.

I didn't want to lie to him anymore.

"I . . . I'll try," I whispered.

It was the best I could give him.

He nodded, slow and understanding. "Let's go back inside. You're shivering."

"Wait." I grabbed his hand before he could turn, my heart lodged firmly in my throat. "I—I want to—"

Make a complete and total fool of myself. I shook my head, cursing silently. I was no good at this. Honesty, sincerity—both were too troublesome to bother with usually. But now . . . with Reid . . . I owed him both.

"I want to thank you—for everything." I squeezed his fingers, my own stiff and aching from the cold. "Célie was right. I don't deserve you. I made a real mess of your life when I came into it."

His other hand came down on top of mine. Warm and steady. To my surprise, he smiled. "I'm glad you did."

Blood crept into my frozen cheeks, and I suddenly found it

difficult to look at him. "Right, well, then . . . let's go back inside. I'm freezing my ass off out here."

The celebration still raged when we returned to the ballroom. I grabbed a flute of champagne from a passing servant and downed it in one swallow.

Reid eyed me incredulously. "You drink like a man."

"Maybe men can learn a thing or two from women." I waved the servant back and grabbed two more flutes, passing one to Reid. He didn't take it. "Relax, Chass. Indulge. This is the best champagne money can buy. It's an insult to His Majesty not to drink it." I scanned the crowd with feigned boredom. "Where is King Auguste, anyway? He's supposed to be here, isn't he?"

"He is. He introduced me earlier."

"What was he like?"

"About as you'd expect."

"So a smarmy bastard like his son?" I waved the flute of champagne under his nose, but he merely shook his head. I shrugged, downing his glass too and chuckling at his expression.

After a few moments, delicious warmth spread through my body. The music—previously a slow, insipid waltz—sounded much better now. Livelier. I downed the third glass. "Dance with me," I said abruptly.

Reid looked at me in bewilderment. "What?"

"Dance with me!" I stood on my tiptoes and threw my arms around his neck. He tensed, glancing around, but I tugged him down determinedly. He complied, stooping slightly, and wrapped his arms around my waist. I laughed.

We looked ridiculous, all bent and straining to fit together, but I refused to let him go.

"This—this isn't the proper way to dance."

I lifted my chin and looked him directly in the eyes. "Of course it is. You're the guest of honor. You can dance any way you want."

"I—I don't usually do this—"

"Reid, if you don't dance with me, I'll go and find someone who will."

His grip tightened on my hips. "No, you won't."

"Then the way forward is clear. We dance."

He blew out a breath and closed his eyes. "Fine."

As nervous as he'd been to dance, he proved himself capable within moments, moving with unnatural grace for someone so tall. I myself stumbled more than once. I would've blamed the train of my stupid dress, but really, it was just me. I couldn't concentrate. His hands were strong on my waist, and I couldn't help but imagine them . . . elsewhere. My blood heated at the thought.

The song ended far too soon.

"We should go," he said, voice rough. "It's getting late."

I nodded and stepped away from him, not trusting myself to speak.

It didn't take much time to find Coco. She leaned against the wall near the antechamber, chatting with none other than Beauregard Lyon. He had an arm braced against the wall above her head. Even from a distance, I could see they were flirting shamelessly.

Both their gazes flicked to me as Reid and I approached.

"Well, well, well . . . if it isn't Madame Diggory." The prince's eyes glittered with amusement. "I see your husband made the right choice."

I ignored him, though Reid bristled at his words. "Brie, we're ready to go. Are you coming?"

Coco looked to the prince, who smirked. "This lovely creature will not be leaving my side for the remainder of the evening. Sorry, darling," he whispered to me conspiratorially. "I'll need to postpone that offer . . . unless you or your husband would care to join?"

I glared at him. Ass.

Reid's eyes narrowed. "What offer?"

I tugged on his arm. "Let's go find Ansel."

"He already left." Coco wrapped her arms around the prince's waist. A wicked gleam lit her dark eyes. "Just the two of you on the ride home. I hope you don't mind."

I bared my teeth in an attempt at a smile. "Can I talk to you in private for a moment, Brie?"

Surprise flashed across her features, but she quickly recovered. "Of course."

Smile slipping, I dragged her into the antechamber. "What are you doing?"

She shimmied her hips. "Trying to get you some alone time with your husband. The dance floor didn't look like it was cutting it."

"I meant with the *prince*."

"Oh." She arched a brow and grinned. "Probably the same

thing you'll be doing with Reid."

"Are you *insane?* He'll see your scars!"

She raised a shoulder in indifference, tugging at her tight black sleeve. "So I'll tell him I was in an accident. Why would he suspect anything else? It's not like Dames Rouges are common knowledge, and everyone here thinks I'm Brie Perrot, a healer and close friend of Captain Reid Diggory. Besides, aren't you being a bit hypocritical? Beau and I are just sex, but you and Reid . . . I won't claim to know what the hell is going on with you two, but *something* is going on."

I scoffed, but my face flushed treacherously. "You really are insane."

"Am I?" Coco took my hands, eyes searching my face. "I don't want to tell you your business, Lou, but please . . . be careful. You're playing a dangerous game. Reid is still a Chasseur, and you're still a witch. You know you'll have to part ways eventually. I don't want to see you get hurt."

My anger evaporated at her concern, and I squeezed her hands in reassurance. "I know what I'm doing, Coco."

But even I knew that was a lie. I had no idea what I was doing when it came to Reid.

She dropped my hands, frowning. "Right. I'll just leave you alone then, and the two of you can continue this stupidity together."

My stomach sank inexplicably as I watched her go. I didn't like fighting with Coco, but there was nothing I could do to fix it this time.

Reid reappeared by my side a moment later, taking my arm and leading me to the carriage—the carriage that was suddenly too small, too warm, with Reid sitting beside me. His fingers brushed my thigh in a seemingly innocent gesture, and I couldn't help but remember the feel of them on my waist. I shuddered and closed my eyes.

When I opened them a moment later, Reid was staring at me. I swallowed, and his gaze fell to my lips. I willed him to lean forward—to bridge the distance between us—but his eyes shuttered at the last second, and he pulled away.

Disappointment crashed through me, replaced quickly by the sharp sting of humiliation.

It's for the best. I glared out the window. Coco had been right: Reid was still a Chasseur, and I was still a witch. No matter what happened between us, no matter what changed, this one, insurmountable obstacle would remain. And yet . . . I studied his rigid profile, the way his eyes kept gravitating back to me.

It would be stupid to start down this path. There was only one way it could end. That knowledge did nothing to stop my heart from racing at his proximity, however, nor dim my spark of hope. Hope that, perhaps, our story could end a different way.

But . . . Coco had been right.

I *was* playing a dangerous game.

A QUESTION OF PRIDE

Reid

The tension in our room that night was physically painful.

Lou lay in my bed. I heard her shift in the darkness, her breathing loud and then quiet. She shifted again. Rolled slowly to her side. Her back. Her side. Her back. Trying to stay silent. Inconspicuous.

But she was neither, and I heard her. Over and over and *over* again.

The woman was driving me mad.

Finally, she leaned over the side of the bed, blue-green eyes meeting mine in the darkness. Her hair spilled to the floor.

I sat up on my elbows too quickly, and her eyes dropped to where my nightshirt gaped open across my chest. Heat rushed to my stomach. "What is it?"

"This is stupid." She scowled, but I was at a loss for why *she* was irritated. "You don't have to sleep on the floor."

I eyed her suspiciously. "Are you sure?"

"Okay, first of all, *stop* looking at me like that. It's not a big deal." She rolled her eyes before scooting to make room for me. "Besides, it's freezing in here. I need your big-ass body heat to keep warm." When I still didn't move, she patted the spot beside her coaxingly. "Oh, c'mon, Chass. I don't bite . . . much."

I swallowed hard, violently blocking out the image of her mouth on my skin. With slow, cautious movements—giving her every chance to change her mind—I climbed onto the bed. Several seconds of awkward silence passed.

"Relax," she finally whispered, though she too lay stiff as a board. "Quit being awkward."

I almost laughed. Almost. As if I could've possibly relaxed with her so . . . so close. The bed, standard issue in the dormitories, hadn't been built for two. Half of my body jutted out into empty space. The other half pressed into her.

I didn't complain.

After another moment of torturous silence, she turned toward me, her breasts brushing my arm. My pulse spiked, and I gritted my teeth, reining in my rampant thoughts.

"Tell me about your parents."

Just like that, all thoughts of intimacy fled. "There's nothing to tell."

"There's always something to tell."

I stared resolutely at the ceiling. Silence descended once more, but she continued to watch me. I couldn't resist glancing over at her. At her eager, wide-eyed expression. I shook my head and sighed. "I was abandoned. A maid found me in the garbage when I was a baby."

She stared at me, horrified.

"The Archbishop took me in. I was a pageboy for a long time. Then I hit a growth spurt." The side of my mouth quirked up of its own volition. "He began training me for the Chasseurs not long after. I claimed my spot when I was sixteen. It's all I've ever known."

She rested her head on my shoulder. "Claimed your spot?"

Closing my eyes, I rested my chin on top of her head and inhaled. Deeply. "There are only one hundred Balisardas— one drop of St. Constantin's relic in each. It limits the positions available. Most serve for life. When a Chasseur retires or dies, a tournament is held. Only the winner may join our ranks."

"Wait." She sat up, and my eyes snapped open. She grinned down at me, her hair tickling my chest. "Are you telling me *Ansel* beat out all the other contenders?"

"Ansel isn't a Chasseur."

Her grin faltered. "He's not?"

"No. He's training to be, though. He'll compete in the next tournament, along with the other initiates."

"Oh." She frowned now, twirling a lock of hair around her finger. "Well, that explains a lot."

"It does?"

She nestled back into me with a sigh. "Ansel is different than everyone else here. He's . . . tolerant. Open-minded."

I bristled at the insinuation. "It's not a crime to have principles, Lou."

She ignored me. Her fingers traced the collar of my shirt.

"Tell me about your tournament."

I cleared my throat, struggling to ignore the gentle movement. But her fingers were very warm. And my shirt was very thin. "I was probably Ansel's age." I chuckled at the memory—at how my knees had trembled, how I'd vomited down my coat minutes before the first round. The Archbishop had been forced to procure me another. Though it'd only been a few years ago, the memory felt very far away. A different time. A different life. When I'd lived and breathed to secure a future within my patriarch's world. "Everyone else was bigger than me. Stronger too. I don't know how I did it."

"Yes, you do."

"You're right." Another laugh rose to my throat, unbidden. "I do. They weren't *that* much bigger, and I practiced every day to grow stronger. The Archbishop trained me himself. Nothing mattered but becoming a Chasseur." My smile faded as the memories resurfaced, one after another, with painful clarity. The crowd. The shouts. The clang of steel and tang of sweat in the air. And—and Célie. Her cheers. "I battled Jean Luc in the championship."

"And you beat him."

"Yes."

"He resents you for it."

"I know. It made beating him even sweeter."

She poked me in the stomach. "You're an ass."

"Probably. But he's worse. Things . . . changed between us that year. He was still an initiate when the Archbishop promoted me to captain. He had to wait until the next tournament to win his spot. I don't think he ever forgave me."

She didn't speak again for several moments. When she finally did, I wished she hadn't. "And . . . and Célie? Did you continue seeing her after your vows?"

All remnants of humor withered and died on my tongue. I stared at the ceiling once more. Though she said nothing, her fingers resumed tracing my collar. Coaxing. Waiting. I sighed again. "You saw the letters. We . . . maintained our courtship."

"Why?"

I stiffened, immediately wary. "What do you mean *why*?"

"Why continue your courtship after you swore yourself to the Chasseurs? I've never heard of a Chasseur marrying before you. There are no other wives in the Tower."

I would've given my Balisarda to end this conversation. How much had she heard of my conversation with Célie? Did she—I swallowed hard—did she know Célie had rejected me? "It's not unheard of. Just a few years ago, Captain Barre married."

I didn't mention that he'd left our brotherhood a year later.

She sat up, fixing me with those unnerving eyes. "You were going to marry Célie."

"Yes." I tore my gaze away, back toward the ceiling. A snowflake drifted in from the window. "Growing up . . . Célie and I were sweethearts. Her kindness appealed to me. I was an angry child. She tempered me. Begged me not to throw rocks at the constabulary. Forced me to confess when I stole the communion wine." A grin tugged at my lips at the memory. "I had a chip on my shoulder. The Archbishop had to beat it out."

Her eyes narrowed at my words, but she wisely said nothing. Lowering herself back against my chest, she brushed her finger against my bare collarbone. Heat erupted across my skin—and everywhere else—in its wake. I shifted my hips away, cursing silently.

"How many witches have you killed?"

I groaned and turned my head into the pillow. The woman could freeze Hell over. "Three."

"Really?"

The judgment in her voice rankled. I nodded, trying not to seem affronted. "Though it's difficult to catch a witch, they're vulnerable without their magic. Still, the witch at the theater was cleverer than most. It didn't attack me with magic. It used magic to attack me. There's a difference."

She trailed her finger down my arm. Idly. I resisted a shudder. "Do you know about magic, then?"

Clearing my throat, I forced myself to focus on the conversation. On her words. Not her touch. "We know what the Archbishop taught us in training."

"Which is what?"

I looked away, jaw tight. I didn't understand Lou's infatuation with the occult. She'd made it clear countless times she didn't agree with our ideology. But she kept bringing it up, like she *wanted* to fight. Like she *wanted* me to lose my temper.

I heaved a sigh. "That witches channel their magic from Hell."

She snorted. "That's ridiculous. Of course they don't channel their magic from Hell. They channel their magic from their *ancestors.*"

I eyed her incredulously. "How could you possibly know that?"

"My friend told me."

Of course. The witch from Tremblay's. The witch we *still* hadn't found. I resisted the urge to snap at her. No amount of pestering had convinced her to give us more information. I was surprised the Archbishop hadn't threatened to tie her to the stake instead.

But I'd never heard anything like this before. "Their ancestors?"

Her finger continued down my arm. Grazed the hair on my knuckles. "Mmm hmm."

I waited for her to continue, but she seemed lost in thought. "So . . . a witch, it can—"

"*She.*" Her head snapped up abruptly. "A witch is always a *she*, Reid. Not an *it.*"

I sighed, half tempted to end the argument there. But I couldn't. Witch friend or no, Lou couldn't spout such blasphemy around the Tower, or she *would* end up on the stake. And there wouldn't be anything I could do to stop it.

I had to end this infatuation now. Before it got out of hand. "I know you think that—"

"I *know* that—"

"—but just because a witch looks and acts like a woman—"

"If it looks like a duck and quacks like a duck—"

"—doesn't mean it's a duck. I mean, er, a woman."

"Witches can give birth, Reid." She flicked my nose. I blinked, lips quirking up in surprise. "That makes them female."

"But they only give birth to females." Grinning, I thrust my face toward hers in response. She jerked back and nearly toppled off the bed. I arched a brow in wry amusement. "Sounds like asexual reproduction to me."

She scowled, and a furious blush stole across her cheeks. If I didn't know better, I would've thought she was uncomfortable. I grinned wider, wondering what could've caused the sudden change. My physical nearness? The word *reproduction*? Both?

"Don't be stupid." She punched her pillow into shape and threw herself back down. Careful not to touch me this time. "Of course witches have sons."

My smile vanished. "We've never encountered a male witch."

"That's because there are none. Magic passes only to females. The males are sent away after they're born."

"Why?"

She shrugged. "Because they don't have magic. My friend said males are only allowed at the Chateau as consorts, and even then they aren't allowed to stay."

"She told you all this?"

"Of course." She lifted her chin and looked down her nose at me, as if daring me to contradict her. "You should really educate yourself, Chass. A common street thief knows more about your enemies than you do. How embarrassing."

Chagrin washed through me. Lou burrowed deeper in the blankets as the wind picked up outside.

"Are you cold?"

"A little."

I inched closer, lifting my arm. "Will you accept an olive branch?"

She swallowed hard and nodded.

I pulled her against my chest, locking my hands at the small of her back. She returned to being a piece of wood. Small. Tense. Unyielding. Stripped of her prying questions and insulting banter, it was almost as if she were . . . nervous.

"Relax," I murmured against her hair. "I don't bite . . . much." Quiet laughter rumbled through my chest. If possible, she stiffened even more. She needn't have worried. Surely she heard the thundering of my heart and realized her advantage.

"Was that a joke, Chass?"

My arms tightened around her. "Maybe." When she said nothing in return, I pulled back to look at her. Another smile tugged at my lips.

And, suddenly, I recalled our first night together.

"You don't have to be nervous, Lou." I stroked her back, forcing myself to remain still as she wriggled against me. "I'm not going to try anything."

A noise of protest escaped her. "Why not?"

"I seem to remember you threatening to cut me open if I touched you without permission." I tilted her chin up, cursing and congratulating myself in equal measure when her eyes fluttered shut. When her breath hitched. I leaned closer, my lips nearly brushing hers. "I won't touch you until you ask."

Her eyes flew open, and she pushed me away with a snarl. "You can't be serious."

"Oh, I am." I smirked again and settled back against the pillow. "It's late. We should sleep."

Her eyes sparked with anger. With understanding.

With grudging admiration.

Triumphant, I watched her sift through her thoughts—watched each emotion play out on her freckled face. She scowled at me. "It appears I underestimated you."

I raised my brows. "Just say the words. Ask me."

"You're an ass."

I shrugged. "Have it your way." In one fluid motion, I lifted the hem of my shirt up and over my head. Her eyes flew open incredulously.

"What are you doing?" She grabbed my shirt and threw it back at me.

I caught it. Tossed it to the floor. "I'm hot."

"You—you— Get out of my bed! Get out!" She shoved me, probably with all her strength, but I didn't budge. I only grinned.

"This is my bed."

"No, this is where *I* sleep. *You* sleep on the—"

"Bed." I clasped my hands behind my head. She gaped at me, eyes flicking to my arms—my chest. I grinned wider and resisted the urge to flex. "I've had a knot in my back for two weeks. I'm done sleeping on the floor. This is my bed, and I'm sleeping in it from now on. You're welcome to join me, otherwise the tub is still free."

She opened her mouth angrily. Closed it again. "I— This is— I am *not* sleeping in the—" Her eyes darted around the bed, clearly searching for something to impale me with. They landed on a pillow.

Whack.

I caught it before she could hit me again, trapping it against my chest. Clamping my lips together to keep from laughing. "Lou—lie down. Go to sleep. Nothing has changed. Unless you want to ask me something?"

"Don't hold your breath." She yanked the pillow from me. "Actually—do."

I chuckled before turning away. "Good night, Lou."

She fell asleep long before I did.

BLOOD, WATER, AND SMOKE

Lou

I woke the next morning with my face buried against Reid's chest. His arms draped across my ribs, and his hands rested on my lower back. I arched into him sleepily, savoring the sensation of his skin against my own—then froze. My nightgown had pooled around my waist in the night, and my legs and belly were bare against him.

Shit, shit, *shit.*

I scrambled to pull down my nightgown, but he jerked awake at the movement. Instantly alert, he swept his eyes from my panicked expression to the empty room. The corner of his lips quirked, and a blush crept up his throat. "Good morning."

"Is it?" I shoved away from him, my own cheeks treacherously warm. He grinned wider and grabbed his shirt from the floor before heading to the washroom. "Where are you going?" I asked.

"To train."

"But—but it's Saint Nicolas Day. We have to celebrate."

He poked his head back out with a bemused expression. "Oh?"

"Oh," I affirmed, sliding out of bed to join him. He stepped aside as I passed, though his hand snaked out to catch a strand of my hair. "We're going to the festival."

"We are?"

"Yes. The food is *amazing*. There are these ginger macarons—" I broke off, mouth already watering, and shook my head. "I can't describe them properly. They must be experienced. Plus I need to buy you a present."

He dropped my hair reluctantly and moved to the cabinet. "You don't need to buy me anything, Lou."

"Nonsense. I love buying presents almost as much as I love receiving them."

An hour later, we strolled arm in arm through East End.

Though I'd attended the festival last year, I hadn't been interested in decorating the evergreen trees with fruit and candy, or adding a log to the bonfire in the village center. No, I'd been much more invested in the dice games and stalls of cheap trinkets—and the food, of course.

The spice of cinnamon treats wafted through the air now, mingling with the ever-present stench of fish and smoke. I eyed the cart of cookies closest to us longingly. Sables, madeleines, and palmiers stared back at me. When I reached out to lift one—or three—Reid rolled his eyes and tugged me onward. My stomach gave an indignant growl.

"How can you still be hungry?" he asked, incredulous. "You ate three helpings at breakfast this morning."

I made a face. "That was *tuna*. I have a second stomach for dessert."

The streets bustled with revelers bundled in coats and scarves, and a light coating of snow dusted everything—the shops, the stalls, the carriages, the street. Wreaths with red bows hung from nearly every door. The wind caught at the ribbons and made the tails dance.

For Cesarine, it was beautiful.

The gauche flyers tacked to every building, however, were not:

YE OLDE SISTERS
TRAVELING COMPANY

invites you to honor our patriarch
HIS EMINENCE, FLORIN CARDINAL CLÉMENT,
ARCHBISHOP OF BELTERRA

by attending the performance of the century tomorrow morning,
the seventh day of December
at Cathédral Saint-Cécile d'Cesarine.

Joyeux Noël!

I thrust a flyer under Reid's nose, laughing. "Florin? What a *terrible* name! No wonder he never uses it."

He frowned at me. "Florin is my middle name."

I crumpled it up and tossed it in a bin. "A true tragedy." When he tried to lead me away, I slipped my arm from his, raising the hood of my cloak. "All right, time to split up."

Still frowning, he scanned the crowded square. "I don't think that's a good idea."

I rolled my eyes. "You can trust me. I won't run away. Besides, presents are supposed to be a *surprise*."

"Lou—"

"We'll meet up at Pan's in an hour. *Do* get me something good."

Ignoring his protests, I turned and wove through the shoppers toward the smithy at the end of the street. The blacksmith there, Abe, had always been friendly with East End's underbelly. I'd purchased many knives from him—and stolen one or two more. Before Tremblay's, Abe had shown me a beautiful copper-handled dagger. It matched Reid's hair perfectly. I hoped he hadn't sold it.

Pushing back my hood and mustering up a touch of my old swagger, I strode into the smithy. Embers smoldered in the forge, but beyond a barrel of water and bag of sand, there was nothing else in the earthen room. No swords. No knives. No customers. I frowned. The blacksmith was nowhere to be seen. "Abe? Are you here?"

A thickset, bearded man stepped through the side entrance, and I grinned. "There you are, old man! I thought you'd gone negligent for a moment." My smile faltered at his furious scowl, and I glanced around. "Business booming?"

"You've got a lot of nerve coming back here, Lou."

"What are you talking about?"

"Rumor has it you sold out Andre and Grue. East End is crawling with constables thanks to you." He took a step forward, fists clenched. "They've been here twice, asking questions they shouldn't have known to ask. My customers are leery. No one wants to do business with the constabulary sniffing around."

Yikes. Perhaps I shouldn't have told the Chasseurs everything, after all.

I withdrew a pouch from my cloak with a flourish. "Ah, but I've brought an olive branch. See?" I shook the bag, and the coins inside clinked together in a jaunty tune. His dark eyes remained suspicious.

"How much?"

I tossed the pouch in the air with deliberate nonchalance. "Enough to purchase a beautiful copper dagger. A present for my husband."

He spat on the floor in disgust. "Marrying a blue pig. I didn't think even *you* could stoop that low."

Anger pricked in my chest, but this wasn't the time or the place to pick a fight over my husband's honor. "I did what I had to. I don't expect you to understand."

"That's where you're wrong. I do understand."

"Oh?"

"We all do what we have to." He eyed the pouch in my hand with a hungry expression. "I remember the copper dagger. I'd rather saw off my fingers than see it with a huntsman, but gold is gold. Stay here. I'll go and fetch it."

I shifted uneasily in the silence that followed, running my fingers over the money pouch.

Marrying a blue pig. I didn't think even you *could stoop that low.*

I wanted to tell Abe he could piss off, but a part of me remembered what it felt like to hate the Chasseurs. To hate Reid. I remembered fleeing to the shadows when they passed, ducking every time I caught a glimpse of blue.

The fear was still there, but to my surprise . . . the hatred had gone.

I nearly jumped out of my skin at a small noise against the door. Probably a mouse. Mentally shaking myself, I straightened my shoulders. I didn't hate the Chasseurs any longer, but they *had* made me complacent. And that was inexcusable.

Standing in my old haunt and jumping at nothing, I realized just how far my edge had slipped. And where the hell was Abe?

Inexplicably furious—at Abe, at Reid, at the Archbishop and every other godforsaken man who'd ever stood in my way—I whirled and stomped toward the side door Abe had disappeared through.

Fifteen minutes was long enough. Abe could take my *couronnes* and shove them up his ass for all I cared. I made to wrench the door open, determined to tell him just that, but stopped short when my hand touched the knob. My stomach sank.

The door was locked.

Shit.

I took a deep breath. Then another. Perhaps Abe hadn't wanted me to follow him into his inner chambers. Perhaps he'd locked the door to prevent me from sneaking in and pocketing something valuable. I'd done it before. Perhaps he was just being cautious.

Still, a shiver swept down my spine as I turned to try the main door. Though I couldn't see through the soot and grime of the window, I knew few revelers ventured this far down the street. I twisted the knob.

Locked.

Backing away, I tried to assess my options. The window. I could break it, climb out before—

The side door clicked open, and for a single, glorious second, I fooled myself into believing it was Abe's hulking form in the door.

"Hello, Lou Lou." Grue stepped forward, cracking his knuckles. "You're a tricky little bitch to catch."

Panic spiked through me as Andre appeared behind him, pulling a knife from his cloak. Abe's dark eyes appeared over their shoulders. "You were right, Lou." His lip curled. "We all do what we have to." Then he turned and disappeared into the neighboring room, slamming the door behind him.

"Hello again, Grue. Andre, your eye healed nicely." Forcing nonchalance despite my rising hysteria, I searched my peripheral vision for something I could use as a weapon: the barrel of water, the bag of sand, the rusted tongs by the forge. Or—or I could—

Gold flickered wildly in my periphery. My gaze flicked to the water, the bellows attached to the forge. We were in an enclosed space. No one would see me do it. No one would know I was here. I'd be gone long before Abe returned, and the chances of him alerting the constabulary or Chasseurs of my involvement were slim. He'd have to risk incriminating himself. He'd have to explain how two men were murdered in his smithy.

Because I *would* kill them if they touched me. One way or the other.

"You betrayed us," Andre snarled. I inched toward the forge, turning my attention back to his knife. "We can't hide anywhere. Those bastards know every one of our haunts. They almost *killed* us yesterday. Now we're gonna kill you."

A crazed gleam lit his eyes, and I knew better than to speak. Sweat coated my palms. One wrong move—one misstep, one mistake—and I'd be dead. The gold flared brighter, more urgent, snaking toward the hot coals in the forge.

Flame for flame. You know this pain. You know it fades. Burn him, the voice whispered.

I cringed away from it instinctively, remembering the agony of Estelle's flames, and groped at another pattern. This one glittered innocently in the sand, hovered near Andre's eyes—and my own. Blinding me.

An eye for an eye.

But I couldn't surrender my vision for Andre's. Not when there were two of them.

Think. Think, think, *think.*

I continued inching backward, patterns appearing and disappearing quicker than I could follow. Angelica's Ring burned hot as I neared the forge. *Of course.* Cursing myself for not remembering it sooner, I slowly inched the band down my finger. Andre caught the movement, and his eyes narrowed when he saw the money pouch still clutched in my hand. Greedy bastard.

With a careful push of my thumb, I eased Angelica's Ring over my knuckle—but it slid too quickly over the damp skin and clattered to the floor.

Once.

Twice.

Three times.

I watched in horror as Grue's foot came down on it. Eyes gleaming, he bent to retrieve it, a nasty smile splitting his face. My mouth went dry.

"So this is your magic ring. All this trouble for a speck of gold." He pocketed the ring with a sneer, stalking closer. Andre shadowed his movements. "I never liked you, Lou. You've always thought you're better than us, smarter than us, but you're not. And you've crossed us too many times."

He lunged, but I moved quicker. Seizing the tongs—ignoring the blistering heat on my palms—I smashed them across his face. The sickening smell of cooked flesh filled the room, and Grue staggered back. Andre charged forward, but I thrust the tongs at him next. He lurched to a halt just in time, rage contorting his features.

"Stay back!" I jabbed the tongs at him again for good measure. "Don't come any closer!"

"I'm going to cut you into fucking pieces." Grue dove at me again, but I dodged, swinging the tongs wildly. Andre's knife slashed past my face. I jerked backward, but Grue was already there. His hand caught the end of the tongs, and he ripped them from my grasp with brutal force.

I flung my hand toward the sand bag, desperately guiding the pattern to his eyes—and *away* from mine.

Andre screamed as the sand rose in a wave and pelted toward him. He stumbled back, hands flying to his face, tearing at his skin, attempting to scrub away the tiny knives in his eyes. I watched in wild fascination—my own eyes perfectly intact—until Grue moved beside me. A blur. I spun, lifting my hands in self-defense, but my mind turned sluggish and slow. He lifted his fist. I stared at it. Unable to comprehend what he meant to do with it. Unable to anticipate his next move. Then he struck.

Your vision for his.

Pain burst from my nose, and I staggered backward. He grinned, wrapping his hand around my throat and lifting me off my feet. I gasped and clawed at his hand, drawing blood, but his grip didn't loosen.

"I've never killed a witch before. I should've known. You've always been a *freak*." He leaned closer, his breath hot and foul against my cheek. "After I cut you up, I'm going to send you back to your blue pig, piece by fucking piece."

I struggled harder, lights popping in my vision.

"Don't kill her too quickly." Tears and blood streamed from Andre's ruined eyes. The sand had fallen now, mingling with the golden dust at his feet. The gold winked once more before vanishing. He bent to retrieve his knife. "I want to enjoy this."

Grue's grip loosened. I coughed and spluttered as his hand fisted in my hair instead, yanking my head back and exposing my throat.

Andre's knife found the scar there. "Looks like somebody beat us to it."

White dotted my vision, and I thrashed against them.

"Ah, ah, ah." Grue jerked my hair, and pain radiated across my scalp. "Not again, Lou Lou." He jerked his head toward the knife at my throat. "Not there. Too quick. Start on her face. Cut off an ear—no, wait." He grinned down at me, eyes burning with true hatred. "Let's carve out her heart instead. That'll be the first piece we send to the pig."

Andre dragged the knife down my throat to my chest. I focused on his revolting face, willing another pattern to emerge. *Any* pattern.

And there it came, glowing brighter than before. Taunting me.

I didn't hesitate. Clenching my fingers, I jerked the cord sharply, and the coals in the forge careened toward us. I braced for the pain, elbowing Grue in the stomach and twisting away. When the coals struck their faces, my own skin burned. But I knew this pain. I could endure it. I *had* endured it.

Gritting my teeth, I seized Andre's knife and plunged it into his throat, slashing through skin and tendon and bone. His scream ended in a gurgle. Grue lunged toward me blindly, bellowing with fury, but I used his momentum to drive the blade into his chest—and his stomach, and his shoulder, and his throat. His blood sprayed across my cheek.

When their bodies thudded to the floor, I collapsed right along with them, pawing at Grue's corpse for Angelica's Ring. I thrust it back on my finger as a knock sounded on the door.

"Is everything okay in there?"

I froze at the unfamiliar voice, panting and shaking. The doorknob rattled, and a new voice joined the first. "The key is broken off."

"I heard shouting." Another knock, louder this time. "Is anyone in there?"

The doorknob rattled again. "Hello? Can someone hear me?"

"What's going on here?"

That voice I knew. Strong. Confident. Damnably inconvenient.

Leaping to my feet, I staggered to the water barrel, praying the door would hold against Reid's strength. I cursed quietly. *Of course* Reid was here, now, with magic lingering in the air and two corpses burning on the floor. I slid a little in their blood as I tipped the barrel. The water cascaded over them, diluting the worst of the smell. The embers hissed at the contact, smoking slightly, and a sickening, charred scent swathed the room. I tilted the barrel and doused myself too.

The voices outside paused as the barrel slipped from my fingers and crashed to the floor. Then—

"Someone is in there." Without waiting for confirmation, Reid kicked the door. It bowed under his weight. When he kicked again, the wood gave an ominous crack. I lunged toward the forge and pumped the bellows feverishly. Coal smoke poured into the room, thick and black. The door splintered, but I kept pumping.

Kept pumping until my eyes watered and my throat burned. Until I couldn't smell the magic. Until I couldn't smell anything.

I dropped the bellows just as the door exploded.

Sunlight streamed in, illuminating Reid's silhouette in the whorls of smoke. Massive. Tense. Waiting. He'd drawn his Balisarda, and the sapphire glinted through the shifting smoke. Two concerned citizens stood behind him. As the smoke cleared, I better saw his face. His eyes swept across the scene quickly, narrowing at the blood and bodies—and landing on me. He blanched. "Lou?"

I nodded, not trusting myself to speak. My knees gave way.

He moved forward quickly—ignoring the blood, water, and smoke—and dropped to his knees before me. "Are you all right?" He gripped my shoulders, forcing me to look at him. Pushed my wet hair from my face, tipped my chin, touched the marks on my throat. His fingers stilled on the thin scar there. The cold mask of fury cracked, leaving only the frantic man beneath. "Did they— did they hurt you?"

I winced and caught his hands, halting his assessment. My hands shook. "I'm fine, Reid."

"What happened?"

Quickly, I recounted the nightmarish experience, omitting any mention of magic. The water and smoke had done their job— and the charred flesh. With each word, his face grew stonier, and by the time I finished, he trembled with rage. Exhaling heavily, he rested his forehead against our knotted hands. "I want to kill them for touching you."

"Too late," I said weakly.

"Lou, I— If they'd hurt you—" He lifted his gaze to mine, and once again, the vulnerability there pierced my chest.

"H-How did you know I was here?"

"I didn't. I came to buy one of your Christmas gifts." He paused, jerking his head to send the two citizens away. Terrified, they scuttled out the door without another word. "A knife."

I stared at him. Perhaps it was the adrenaline still pounding through my body. Or his disobedience to the Archbishop. Or my own wretched realization that I was afraid. Truly afraid, this time.

And I needed help.

No. I needed *him*.

Whatever the reason, I didn't care.

One second, we knelt together on that bloody floor, and the next, I flung my arms around his neck and kissed him. He pulled away for a fraction of a second, startled, but then he fisted the fabric at the back of my cloak and crushed me to him, mouth hard and unrelenting.

Control deserted me. As close as Reid held me, I wanted to be closer. I wanted to feel every inch of him. Tightening my hold, I molded my body to the hard shape of him—to the broad expanse of his chest, his stomach, his legs.

With a low groan, he snaked his hands under my thighs and hitched me up against him. I wrapped my legs around his waist, and he bore me to the floor, deepening the kiss.

Something warm seeped through the back of my dress, and

I broke away abruptly, stiffening. I glanced over to Andre and Grue.

Blood.

I was lying in their blood.

Reid realized it the same second I did, and he vaulted to his feet, pulling me up with him. Spots of color rose on his cheeks, and his breathing sounded uneven. "We should go."

I blinked, deflating slightly as the heat between us cooled and icy reality set in. I'd killed. Again. Sagging against his chest, I looked back to where Andre and Grue lay. Forced myself to stare into their cold, dead eyes. They gaped at the ceiling, unseeing. Blood still seeped from their wounds.

Revulsion coiled in my stomach.

Vaguely aware of Reid disentangling himself from my arms, I stared down at my cloak. The white velvet was ruined now—stained irrevocably red.

Two more deaths. Two more bodies left in my wake. Just how many would join them before all was said and done?

"Here." Reid thrust something into my limp hand, and I wrapped my fingers around it instinctively. "An early Christmas present."

It was Andre's knife, still slick with its master's blood.

OF MY HOME

Lou

The sun was setting by the time we made our way back to Chasseur Tower. Reid had insisted on reporting the whole messy affair to the constabulary. Question after question they'd asked, until I'd finally snapped.

"Do you see my throat?" I'd jerked my collar down to show them my bruises for the hundredth time. "Do you think I gave them to myself?"

Reid had been quite keen to leave after that.

I supposed I should've been grateful for his reputation as a Chasseur. Otherwise, I had little doubt the constabulary would've seized the opportunity to throw me in prison for murder.

Outside, I turned my face to the dying sun, breathing deeply and trying to collect myself. Andre and Grue were dead. The Chasseurs still hadn't found Monsieur Bernard, which meant he probably was too. I hadn't seen or spoken to Coco since our disagreement at the ball, and Reid and I—we'd just—

He halted beside me without a word, slipping his fingers

through mine. Closing my eyes, I savored the callouses on his palm, the roughness of his skin. Even the bite of the wind on my cheeks wasn't unbearable with him near. It swirled around us and filled me with his scent—vaguely woodsy, like fresh air and mountain pines, with a hint of something richer, deeper, that was entirely Reid.

"I want to show you something, Reid."

His lips quirked up in my favorite lopsided grin. "What's that?"

"A secret."

I tugged his hand to lead him away, but he dug his feet in, suddenly suspicious. "It's not something illegal, is it?"

"Of course not." I tugged harder, but Reid didn't budge. Trying to move him was like trying to move a mountain. He raised his eyebrows at my futile attempts, clearly amused. I finally gave up, slapping his chest. "God, you're a huge ass! It's not illegal, all right? Now move, or I swear to God, I will strip naked right here and dance the *bourrée*!"

I thrust my hands on my hips and looked at him expectantly.

He didn't even glance at the people around us. He didn't get flustered. And Reid always got flustered.

Instead, he kept his eyes trained on mine, a slow smirk spreading across his face.

"Do it."

I narrowed my eyes and straightened my shoulders, drawing myself up to my full—if not inconsiderable—height. "I will. Don't think I won't. I'll do it right now."

He raised his brows, still smirking. "I'm waiting."

I glared at him, hands jerking up to the silver fastening of my cloak. I forced myself not to glance at the lingering shoppers around us, though they certainly glanced at us. A bloody white cloak was hardly inconspicuous. "I'm not afraid to cause a scene. I thought you knew that."

He shrugged and shoved his hands into his pockets. "The first time worked out pretty well for me." My cloak fell to the ground, and he eyed it appreciatively. "I'm thinking this time might too."

My stomach—traitorous thing it was—swooped at his words, at the way his eyes tracked my every movement. "You're a pig."

"You're the one who volunteered." He nodded his head toward Pan's patisserie as I began untying the laces of my dress. "But you should know, we have an audience."

Sure enough, Pan stood at the window of his shop, watching us closely. He startled slightly when I turned and waved a little too quickly to be natural. My fingers stilled on my lacings.

"You got lucky." I snatched my cloak from the ground, throwing it back around my shoulders inside out to hide the worst of the blood. Unable to help it this time, I glanced around, but the shoppers had lost interest. Relief washed over me.

"Agree to disagree."

"You really are a pig!" I whirled to storm back toward Chasseur Tower, but he caught my hand.

"Stop, please." He raised his other hand placatingly, but the arrogant smile still played at the corner of his lips. "I want to see your secret. Show me."

"Too bad. I changed my mind. I don't want to show you after all."

He turned me around to face him, wrapping his hands around my arms. "Lou. Show me. I know you want to."

"You don't know me at all."

"I know stripping in public is too much, even for you." He laughed. It was a lovely, rare sound. "I know you'll never admit you wouldn't have done it."

The amusement in his eyes slowly darkened as he held me, and I became painfully aware this was the closest we'd been since our kiss that morning. He stared at his thumb as it brushed my bottom lip.

"I know you have a filthy mouth." He pressed down hard on my lip for emphasis. I shivered. "And you're used to getting your way. I know you're vulgar and dishonest and manipulative—"

I recoiled, nose wrinkling, but he only gripped me tighter.

"—but you're also compassionate and free-spirited and brave." He tucked my hair behind my ear. "I've never met anyone like you, Lou."

Based on his frown, the thought made him uneasy. I didn't care to examine my emotions too closely either.

Marrying a blue pig. I didn't think even you *could stoop that low.*

Whatever Reid was, he wasn't a blue pig. But he *was* still a Chasseur. He believed what he believed. I wasn't foolish enough to think I could change that. He would look at me differently if he knew who I truly was. His hands—touching me so gently now—would touch me differently, too.

Estelle's face flashed in my mind. Reid's hands wrapped around her throat. *My* throat.

No. I stumbled away from him, eyes wide. His brows dipped in confusion.

Awkward silence descended, and I chuckled nervously, wiping my palms on my skirt. "I changed my mind again. I want to show you a secret after all."

Soleil et Lune soon came into view.

"The theater?" Reid peered at the empty steps in bewilderment. "That's a bit tame for you, isn't it? I was expecting an underground bootlegging operation—"

"Don't be ridiculous, Chass." I paused by the backstage door, hiking my skirt and climbing atop the trash bin. "I'd never be caught underground."

He inhaled sharply as he realized my intent. "This is trespassing, Lou!"

I grinned at him over my shoulder. "It's only trespassing if we get caught." Then I hoisted myself over the gutters, winked, and slipped out of sight.

He hissed my name in the gathering shadows, but I ignored him, wiping the slime off my boots and waiting.

Hands appeared a moment later as he hauled himself up after me.

I couldn't help but laugh at his scowl. "Took you long enough. We'll be here all night at this pace."

"I'm a Chasseur, Lou. This is totally inappropriate!"

"Always with that stick up your ass—"

"Lou!" His eyes darted to the rooftop. "I am *not* climbing this building."

"Oh, *Chass.*" My own eyes widened as understanding swept through me, and I snorted in an undignified way. "*Please* tell me you aren't afraid of heights."

"Of course I'm not." He gripped the stone tightly. "It's a matter of principle. I won't break the law."

"I see." I nodded in mock agreement, forcing back a smile. I could let him have this one. I could resist the urge to rile him, just this once. "Well, fortunately, I don't give a damn about the law. I'm going up regardless. Feel free to sic the constabulary on me."

"Lou!" He tried to grab my ankle, but I was already several feet above him. "Get down!"

"Come get me instead! And for heaven's sake, Chass, stop trying to look up my skirt!"

"I am *not* trying to look up your skirt!"

I chuckled to myself and kept climbing, savoring the bite of cold air on my face. After the nightmarish incident at the smithy, it felt good to simply . . . let go. To laugh. I wished Reid would do the same. I rather enjoyed his laugh.

Glancing back at him, I allowed myself to ogle his powerful shoulders in action for only a second before pushing myself to climb faster. It wouldn't do for him to beat me inside.

He gasped when I slipped through the broken window of the attic, hissing my name with increasing alarm. The next moment, he hauled himself in after me. "This is breaking and entering, Lou!"

Shrugging, I moved to the pile of costumes that had once been my bed. "You can't break and enter into your own home."

A beat of silence passed.

"This—this is where you lived?"

I nodded, inhaling deeply. It smelled exactly like I remembered: the perfume of old costumes mingled with cedar, dust, and just a hint of smoke from the oil lamps. Trailing my fingers along the trunk Coco and I had shared, I finally looked at him. "For two years."

Stoic as ever, he said nothing. But I knew where to look to hear him—in the tension of his shoulders, the tautness of his jaw, the tightness of his mouth. He disapproved. Of course he did.

"Well," I said, sweeping my arms open wide, "this is the secret. It's no epic romance, but . . . welcome to my humble abode."

"This isn't your home anymore."

I dropped to my bed, tucking my knees to my chin. "This attic will always be my home. It's the first place I ever felt safe." The words slipped out before I realized I'd said them, and I cursed silently.

His gaze sharpened on me. "What happened two years ago?"

Glaring at the blue velvet cloak I'd used as a pillow, I swallowed hard. "I don't want to talk about it."

He sank to a crouch beside me, lifting my chin gently. His eyes held mine with unexpected intensity. "I do."

Never had two words sounded more odious. Or foreboding. Crushing the velvet in my fist, I forced a chuckle and wracked my brain for a deflection—any deflection. "I ran into the wrong end of another knife, that's all. A bigger one."

He sighed heavily and dropped my chin, but he didn't move

away. "You make it impossible to know you."

"Ah, but you already know me so well." I flashed what I hoped was a winning smile, still deflecting. "Foul-mouthed, manipulative, *fantastic* kisser—"

"I don't know anything about your past. Your childhood. Why you became a thief. Who you were before . . . all of this."

My smile slipped, but I forced my voice to remain light. "There's nothing to know."

"There's always something to know."

Damn him for using my own words against me. The conversation stalled as he stared at me expectantly, and I stared at the blue velvet. A moth had riddled the sumptuous fabric with holes, and I picked at them in feigned boredom.

Finally, he turned me to face him. "Well?"

"I don't want to talk about it."

"Lou, please. I just want to know more about you. Is that so terrible?"

"Yes, it is." The words came out sharper than I would've liked, and I winced internally at the flicker of hurt on his face. If I had to bite and snap to discourage him from this wretched conversation, however, so be it. "That shit is in my past for a reason, and I said I don't want to talk about it—not with anyone, especially you. Isn't it enough I showed you my home? My secret?"

He recoiled, expelling a sharp breath. "I told you I was found in the garbage. Do you think that was easy to talk about?"

"So why did you?" I tore through a hole in the velvet viciously. "I didn't force you."

He tugged my chin up once more, eyes livid. "Because you asked. Because you're my wife, and if anyone deserves to know the worst parts of me, it's you."

I jerked away from him. "Oh, don't worry, I know them all right—"

"Likewise."

"You asked me not to lie to you." I set my jaw and lurched to my feet, folding my arms across my chest. "Don't ask about my past, and I won't have to."

He slowly followed suit, towering over me with a black expression. His jaw clenched, unclenched, as he glanced to my throat. "What are you hiding, Lou?"

I stared at him, my heartbeat pounding suddenly violent in my ears. I couldn't tell him. He couldn't ask me. It would ruin everything.

And yet . . . I would have to tell him eventually. This game couldn't last forever. Swallowing hard, I lifted my chin. Perhaps after everything we'd been through, he would be able to see past it. Perhaps he could change—for me. For us. Perhaps I could too.

"I'm not hiding anything, Reid. Ask me whatever you want."

He sighed heavily at the tremble in my voice, pulling me close and lifting a hand to stroke my hair. "I won't force you. If you aren't comfortable enough to tell me, it's my fault, not yours."

Of course he would think that. Of course he would think the worst of himself instead of seeing the truth—that the worst was in me. I buried my face in his chest. Even in his frustration, Reid was kinder to me than anyone I'd ever known. I didn't deserve it.

"It's not you." I clutched him closer in the gathering shadows, breathing in his scent. It melded perfectly with the comforting smells of the attic. Of my home. "It's me. But I—I can try. I can try to tell you."

"No. We don't have to talk about this now."

I shook my head determinedly. "Please . . . ask me."

His hand stilled on my hair, and the world stilled with it—not unlike the eerie calm before magic. Even the breeze through the window seemed to pause, lingering in my hair, between his fingers. Waiting. I forgot how to breathe.

But the question never came.

"Are you from Cesarine?" His hand trailed down my hair to the small of my back, and the wind swept on, dissatisfied. I focused on the gentle movement, disappointment and hideous relief warring in my heart.

"No. I grew up in a small community north of Amandine." I smiled wistfully against his chest at the half-truth. "Surrounded by mountains and sea."

"And your parents?"

The words flowed easier now, the tightness in my chest easing as the immediate danger passed. "I never knew my father. My mother and I are . . . estranged."

His hand halted again. "She's alive, then?"

"Yes. Very."

"What happened between the two of you?" He pulled back, searching my face with renewed interest. "Is she here in Cesarine?"

"I sincerely hope not. But I'd rather not talk about what happened. Not yet."

Still a coward.

"Fair enough."

Still a gentleman.

His gaze fell to my scar, and he bent down slowly, brushing a kiss against it. Goosebumps erupted across my skin. "How did you get this?"

"My mother."

He jerked back as if the silver line had bitten him, horror clouding his eyes. "What?"

"Next question."

"I— Lou, that's—"

"Next question. Please."

Though his brows still furrowed in concern, he pulled me to him once more. "Why did you become a thief?" His voice grew rougher, graver, than before. I wrapped my arms around his waist and squeezed him tight.

"To get away from her."

He tensed against me. "You're not going to elaborate, are you?"

I rested my cheek against his chest and sighed. "No."

"You had a cruel childhood."

I almost laughed. "Not at all. My mother pampered me, actually. Gave me everything a little girl could ever want."

His voice dripped with disbelief. "But she tried to kill you." When I didn't answer, he shook his head, sighing and stepping away. My arms fell heavy to my sides. "It must be one hell of a story. I'd like to hear it someday."

"Reid!" I swatted his arm, all thoughts of blood rituals and altars falling away, and an incredulous grin split my face. He looked suddenly sheepish. "Did you just *curse?*"

"*Hell* isn't a curse word." He refused to meet my eyes, staring instead at the racks of costumes behind me. "It's a place."

"Of course it is." I inched back to the window, the beginning of a smile tugging on my lips. "Speaking of fun places . . . I want to show you another secret."

WHERE YOU GO

Lou

He collapsed on the rooftop a few moments later, white-faced and panting, his eyes shut tight against the open sky. I poked him in the ribs. "You're missing the view."

He clenched his jaw and swallowed as if about to be sick. "Give me a minute."

"You do realize how ironic this is, right? The tallest man in Cesarine is afraid of heights!"

"I'm glad you're enjoying it."

I lifted one of his eyelids and grinned at him. "Just open your eyes. I promise you won't regret it."

His mouth tightened, but he opened his eyes grudgingly. They widened when he saw the sweeping expanse of stars before us.

I hugged my knees to my chest and gazed up at them with longing. "Aren't they beautiful?"

Soleil et Lune was the tallest building in Cesarine, and it offered the only unimpeded view of the sky in the entire city. Above the smoke. Above the smell. The whole of the heavens stretched out in one great panorama of obsidian and diamond. Infinite. Eternal.

There was only one other place with a view like this . . . and I would never visit the Chateau again.

"They are," Reid agreed quietly.

I sighed and held myself tighter against the chill. "I like to think God paints the sky just for me on nights like this."

He tore his gaze from the stars in disbelief. "You believe in God?"

What a complicated question.

I propped my chin on my knees, still peering upward. "I think so."

He sat up. "But you rarely attend Mass. You—you celebrate Yule, not Noël."

I shrugged and picked at a bit of dead leaf in the snow. It crinkled beneath my fingers. "I never said it was *your* god. Your god hates women. We were an afterthought."

"That isn't true."

I finally turned to face him. "Isn't it? I read your Bible. As your wife, am I not considered your property? Do you not have the legal right to do whatever you please with me?" I grimaced, the memory of the Archbishop's words leaving a bitter taste in my mouth. "To lock me in the closet and never think of me again?"

"I've *never* considered you my property."

"The Archbishop does."

"The Archbishop is . . . mistaken."

My brows shot up. "Doth mine ears deceive me, or did you

just speak ill of your precious patriarch?"

Reid raked a hand through his coppery hair in frustration. "Just—don't, Lou. Please. Despite what you think, he's given me everything. He gave me a life, a purpose." He hesitated, eyes meeting mine with a sincerity that made my heart stutter. "He gave me you."

I brushed the broken leaf aside and turned to look at him. To *really* look at him.

Reid truly believed his purpose was to kill witches. He believed the Archbishop had given him a gift, that the Archbishop was good. I reached for his hand. "The Archbishop didn't give me to you, Reid." I looked up to the sky with a small smile. "*He* did—or she."

There was a heavy pause as we stared at one another.

"I have a present for you." He leaned closer, blue eyes boring into my very soul. I held my breath, willing him to close the distance between our lips.

"Another one? But it's not Yule yet."

"I know." He looked down at our hands, sweeping a thumb across my ring finger. "It's . . . it's a wedding ring."

I gasped as he withdrew it from his coat pocket. Thin, beaten gold made up the band, and an oval mother-of-pearl stone sat at the center. It was clearly very old. It was also the most beautiful thing I'd ever seen. My heart pounded wildly as he held it out to me.

"May I?"

I nodded, and he slid Angelica's Ring off my finger and slipped his on instead. We both stared at it for a moment. He swallowed hard.

"It was my mother's . . . or at least, I think it was. It was clenched in my fist when they found me." He hesitated, eyes meeting mine. "It reminds me of the sea . . . of you. I've wanted to give it to you for days now."

I opened my mouth to say something—to tell him how lovely it was or how honored I'd be to wear something so meaningful, to carry that little piece of him with me always—but the words caught in my throat. He watched me raptly.

"Thank you." My throat bobbed as an unfamiliar emotion threatened to choke me. "I . . . love it."

And I did. I did love it.

But not as much as I loved him.

He wrapped his arms around my waist, and I leaned back into his chest, trembling at the realization.

I loved him.

Shit. I *loved* him.

My breathing grew more painful the longer I sat there—each breath jarring and stoking all at once. Hyperventilating. That's what I was doing. I needed to get it together. I needed to collect my thoughts—

Reid gently pulled my hair aside, and the small touch nearly undid me. His lips brushed the curve of my neck. Blood roared in my ears.

"'Do not urge me to leave you or turn back from you.'" He trailed his fingers down my arm in slow, torturous strokes. My head fell back on his shoulder, my eyes fluttering closed, as his lips continued to move against my neck. "'Where you go, I will go. Where you stay, I will stay.'"

A low, breathless sound escaped the back of my throat—so at odds with the reverent words he'd spoken. His fingers stilled instantly, and his gaze honed in on my rapidly moving chest.

"Don't stop," I breathed. Pleaded.

His body tensed, and his hands clamped down on my arms in an unyielding grip. "Ask me, Lou." His voice turned low, urgent. Raw. Heat pooled directly in my belly at the sound of it.

My mouth opened. The time for games was done. He was my husband, and I was his wife. It was foolish to pretend I no longer wanted the relationship. To pretend I didn't crave his attention, his laughter, his . . . touch.

I wanted him to touch me. I wanted him to become my husband in every sense of the word. I wanted him—

I wanted *him*.

All of him. We could make it work. We could write our own ending, witch and witch hunter be damned. We could be happy.

"Touch me, Reid." To my surprise, the words came out steady despite my breathlessness. "Please. Touch me."

He grinned—slow and triumphant—against my neck. "That's not a question, Lou."

My eyes snapped open, and I turned to scowl at him. He raised a brow in question, pressing his lips to my skin. His eyes locked with mine. Lips parting, he trailed warm, open-mouthed kisses down the side of my throat and onto my shoulder.

His tongue moved slowly, worshiping me with each stroke, and I practically combusted.

"Fine." My traitorous neck extended under his mouth, but my pride refused to succumb so easily. If he wanted to play one more game, I would oblige him—and I would win. "Would you, oh brave and virtuous Chasseur, stick your tongue down my throat and your hands up my skirt? My ass needs grabbing."

He spluttered and reared back incredulously. I arched against him, grinning despite myself. "Too much?"

When he didn't respond, disappointment trickled through the fire in my blood. I turned to face him fully. His eyes were wide, and—to my chagrin—his face was pale. He didn't look like he wanted to ravish me, after all. Perhaps I'd overplayed my hand.

"I'm sorry." I extended a tentative hand to his face. "I didn't mean to upset you."

There was something in his gaze as he looked at me— something hesitant, something almost *self-conscious*—that made me pause. His hands trembled slightly where they clutched me, and his chest rose and fell in rapid succession. He was nervous. No—terrified.

It took only a second for understanding to rush in: Reid really *was* a virtuous Chasseur. A *holy* Chasseur.

Reid had never had sex.

He was a virgin.

For all his earlier arrogance, he'd merely been posturing. He hadn't ever touched a woman—not in the way that counted, at least. I tried not to gape at him, but I knew he could easily read my thoughts by the way his expression fell.

I searched his face. How could Célie have abandoned him in this? What else was first love good for but bumbling hands and breathless discovery?

At least she'd taught him to kiss properly. I supposed I should be grateful for that. My throat and shoulder still tingled from his tongue. But there was so much more than just kissing.

Slowly, purposefully, I shifted in his lap, taking his face in both my hands. "Let me show you."

His eyes darkened as I straddled him. My skirt slid up at the movement—the wind tickling my bare legs—but I didn't feel the cold. There was only Reid.

I watched his throat bob, heard his breath hitch. His eyes darted to mine in a question when I pulled his hands to the lacings on my dress. I nodded, and he carefully pulled.

Despite the chill, his fingers were competent. They moved steadily until the front of my dress fell open, revealing the thin chemise beneath. Neither of us breathed as he reached a hand up and skimmed the bare skin of my upper breast.

I leaned into his palm, and he inhaled sharply.

Faster than I could blink, he swept aside the shoulders of my chemise, sending the fabric to pool around my waist. His eyes roved my naked torso hungrily.

I couldn't help but grin. Perhaps he wouldn't need much teaching after all.

Not to be outdone, I tugged the hem of his shirt from his pants. He pulled it up over his head, mussing his coppery hair, before his lips came down hard against mine, and we were pressed together, skin to skin.

It was short work after that.

He lifted me easily, and I tossed my dress away.

His eyes burned—pupils dilating, the blue around them hardly visible—as they took in my stomach, my breasts, my thighs. His fingers tightened on my hips possessively, but not tight enough. I wanted—no, *needed*—him to press me tighter, hold me closer.

"You're so beautiful," he breathed.

"Shut up, Chass." My own voice came out a gasp. Locking my arms behind his neck, I rolled my hips against him. His own hips bucked up to meet mine in response, and he groaned. I gripped his shoulders to still him. "Like this." Leaning back, I motioned to where our bodies met. We watched in unison as I rocked against him—slowly, deliberately, rubbing up and down at an agonizing pace.

He tried to increase my speed—his hands desperate, insistent—but I resisted, pressing myself flush against his chest and biting the sensitive spot where his neck met his shoulder. He jerked, and another low groan escaped his lips.

"This is how you touch a woman." I pressed into him harder for emphasis, grabbing his hand and bringing it between my legs. "This is how you touch *me*."

"Lou," he said in a strangled voice.

"Right there." I directed his fingers, my breath turning ragged at his touch. My chest heaving as he continued the movement I'd shown him. He bent forward abruptly and took my breast in his mouth, and I gasped. His tongue was hot, demanding. A deep, delicious ache built too quickly in my belly. "God, Reid—"

At the sound of his name, he bit down lightly.

I shattered completely, lost in the pleasure and pain. His arms tightened around me as I came, his lips crashing down upon mine as if to devour my cries.

It wasn't enough.

"Your pants." I fumbled at his laces, crushing my lips against his between breaths. "Take them off. Now."

Reid was only too happy to oblige, lifting me awkwardly to strip them down his legs. Tossing them aside, he watched me anxiously, face still pale, as I straddled him once more. I grinned in response, tracing a salacious finger down the length of him, savoring the feel of him pressed against me. He trembled at the contact, eyes shining with need.

"Another time," I said, pushing him gently against the rooftop, "I'll show you just how foul my mouth can be."

"Lou," he repeated, pleading.

In a single, fluid movement, I sank down, burying him inside me.

His eyes screwed shut, and his entire body jerked upward as he plunged himself deeper, right to the hilt. I would've cried out—it was too deep—but I didn't. I couldn't. There was pain, but—as he receded and thrust again—the pain intensified into something else, something sharp and deep and aching. Something needy. He filled me completely, and the way he moved . . . I threw my head back and lost myself in the sensation. In him.

The ache spiraled upward, and I couldn't stop from kissing him, from tangling my fingers in his hair, from raking my nails down his arms. It hurt, this throbbing, yearning feeling in my chest. It consumed and obliterated and overwhelmed everything I'd ever known.

His arm snaked around my waist, and he spun, pinning me beneath him. I arched upward—desperate to be closer, desperate to relieve the building ache—and hooked my legs around his sweat-slicked back. His hand came down between us as he increased his pace, and my legs began to stiffen. He touched me exactly the way I'd shown him, stroking me determinedly, relentlessly. A low growl escaped his throat.

"Lou—"

Everything inside me tightened, and I clung to him as he pushed me over the edge. With one final, shuddering thrust, he collapsed on top of me, unable to catch his breath.

We lay like that for several moments, oblivious to the cold. Staring helplessly at each other. For the first time in my life, I had no words. The heady ache in my chest was still there—stronger now, more painful than ever before—but I found myself defenseless against it. Utterly and completely defenseless.

And yet . . . I'd never felt more safe.

When Reid finally withdrew, I winced despite myself.

He didn't miss the movement. His hand shot to my chin, lifting it, and his eyes grew wide and anxious. "Did I hurt you?"

I attempted to shimmy out from beneath him, but he was too heavy. Realizing what I wanted, he pushed up on his elbows to accommodate me before rolling to his back. He dragged me on top of him as he went.

"There's a fine line between pleasure and pain." Trailing kisses down his chest, I grazed my teeth against his skin—then bit down abruptly. A hiss escaped his lips, and his arms clenched around me. When I leaned back to meet his gaze, however, it wasn't pain in his eyes, but longing. My own chest throbbed in response. "It's a good hurt." I smiled and flicked his nose. "Well done, you."

MONSIEUR BERNARD

Lou

The Saint Nicolas Festival bustled around me and Reid as we left Pan's the next morning. He'd bought me yet another new cloak—red this time instead of white. Appropriate. But I refused to let the events at the smithy poison my good mood today. Grinning, I glanced up at him and remembered the feel of snow on my bare skin. Of icy wind in my hair.

The rest of the evening had proved just as memorable. At my request, he'd agreed to stay with me in the attic, and I'd made the most of my last night there. I wouldn't be returning to Soleil et Lune again.

I'd found a new home.

And the way he was currently licking the icing off his fingers . . . My stomach contracted deliciously.

His eyes cut to mine, the corner of his mouth quirking. "Why are you looking at me like that?"

Crooking an eyebrow, I brought his pointer finger to my mouth and licked the rest of the icing off with slow, deliberate strokes. I'd expected his eyes to boggle and dart around us, his cheeks to flush and his jaw to clench, but again, he remained unfazed. This time he actually had the gall to chuckle.

"You are insatiable, Madame Diggory."

Delighted, I stood on tiptoe to press a kiss to his nose—then flicked it for good measure. "You don't know the half of it. I still have *lots* to teach you, Chass."

He grinned at the endearment, pressing my fingers to his lips before tucking my arm firmly beneath his. "You really are a heathen."

"A *what?*"

His cheeks flamed, and he looked away sheepishly. "I used to call you that. In my head."

I laughed out loud, oblivious to passersby. "Why does that not surprise me? *Of course* you wouldn't have called me by, you know, my *name*—"

"You didn't call me by my name!"

"That's because you're a prig!" The breeze kicked up a muddy Ye Olde Sisters flyer before sending it spiraling back to the snow. I stomped it beneath my boot, still laughing. "Come on. We need to hurry if we want to catch the Archbishop's special performan—" His eyes sharpened on something behind me, and the word died in my throat. Turning, I followed his gaze and saw Madame Labelle striding purposefully toward us.

"Shit."

He shot me an aggrieved look. "Don't."

"I sincerely doubt curse words will offend her. She's a madam.

Believe me, she's seen and heard much worse."

She wore another gown that set off the magnificent blue of her eyes, and her fiery red hair had been swept back with a pearl comb. A small, nagging sensation buzzed at the back of my skull at the sight of her. Like an itch I couldn't scratch.

"Louise, darling! How marvelous it is to see you again." She clasped my free hand in both of her own. "I *had* hoped we might run into one another—"

She stopped short, eyes falling on the mother-of-pearl ring on my finger. I tightened my grip on Reid's arm. The movement didn't go unnoticed.

She stared at the ring—then between the two of us—her eyes widening and mouth parting as she took in Reid's face. He shifted under her scrutiny, clearly uncomfortable. "May we help you, *madame?*"

"Captain Reid Diggory." She said the words slowly, as if tasting them for the first time. Her blue eyes were still alight with astonishment. "I don't believe we've been formally introduced. My name is Madame Helene Labelle."

He scowled at her. "I remember you, *madame.* You attempted to purchase my wife for your brothel."

She stared at him raptly, not seeming to notice his hostility. "Your surname means 'lost one,' yes?"

I glanced between them, the buzzing at the back of my head growing louder. More insistent. It was an odd, unexpected question. Reid didn't seem sure how to answer it.

"I believe so," he finally muttered.

"What do you want, *madame?*" I asked suspiciously. Everything

I knew about this woman warned me she wasn't here for polite conversation.

Her eyes grew almost desperate as they bored into mine—and held a startlingly familiar intensity. "Is he a good man, Lou? A kind one?"

Reid stiffened at the offensively personal question, but the buzzing in my head began to take shape. I looked between the two of them again, noting the identical shade of their blue eyes.

Holy hell.

My heart sank to somewhere below my ankles. I'd stared into Reid's eyes long enough now to recognize them in another's face.

Madame Labelle was Reid's mother.

"He is." My whisper was barely audible over the chatter of the market—over my own thumping heart.

She expelled a breath, and her telltale blue eyes fluttered shut in relief. Then they snapped open again, suddenly and alarmingly sharp. "But does he know you, Lou? *Truly* know you?"

My blood turned to ice. If Madame Labelle wasn't careful, the two of us would soon be having a very different conversation. I carefully maintained her gaze, articulating an unspoken warning. "I don't know what you're talking about."

Her eyes narrowed. "I see."

Unable to help it, I glanced at Reid. His face had quickly transformed from puzzled to irritated. Based on the taut line of his jaw, he didn't appreciate us talking about him as if he wasn't there. He opened his mouth—probably to ask what the hell was going on—but I cut him off.

"Let's go, Reid." I shot Madame Labelle one last, disparaging look before turning away, but her hand snaked out and grabbed my own—the one bearing Angelica's Ring.

"Wear it always, Lou, but don't let her see." I moved to pull away, alarmed, but the woman's grip was like iron. "She's here, in the city."

Reid stepped forward, fists clenched. "Let go, *madame*."

She only clutched me tighter. Faster than she could react, Reid pried away her fingers forcibly. She flinched in pain, but continued on, undeterred, as Reid pulled me down the street. "Don't take it off!" The panic in her eyes shone clear even from afar, even as her voice began to fade. "Whatever you do, don't let her see!"

"*What*," Reid snarled, his grip on my arm tighter than strictly necessary, "the hell was that about?"

I didn't answer him. Couldn't. My mind still reeled from Madame Labelle's onslaught, but a sudden burst of clarity sliced through the haze of my thoughts. Madame Labelle was a witch. She had to be. Her interest in Angelica's Ring, her knowledge of its powers, of my mother, of *me*—there was no other explanation.

But the revelation brought more questions than answers. I couldn't focus on them—couldn't focus on anything but the raw, debilitating fear that clawed up my throat, the clammy sweat that seeped across my skin. My gaze darted around us, and an involuntary shiver swept through me. Reid was saying something, but I didn't hear him. A dull roar had started in my ears.

My mother was in the city.

The Saint Nicolas Festival lost its charm on our return to Chasseur Tower. The evergreens stood less beautiful. The bonfire burned less bright. Even the food lost its allure, the overpowering smell of fish returning to choke me.

Reid assaulted me with questions the whole way. When he realized I had no answers to give, he fell silent. I couldn't bring myself to apologize. It was all I could do to hide my trembling fingers, but I knew he saw them anyway.

She hasn't found you.

She won't find you.

I repeated the mantra over and over, but it did little to convince me.

Saint-Cécile soon rose up before us, and I breathed a sigh of relief. The sigh instantly turned to a shriek when something moved unexpectedly in the alley beside us.

Reid jerked me to him, but his face relaxed the next second. He expelled an exasperated breath. "It's fine. Just a beggar."

But it wasn't just a beggar. Numbness crept through my limbs as I looked closer . . . and recognized the face that turned, the milky eyes that stared at me from the shadows.

Monsieur Bernard.

He crouched over a trash bin with bits of what looked like dead animal dangling from his mouth. His skin—once wet with his own blood—had deepened to pitch black, the lines of his body hazy somehow. Blurred. As if he'd become a living, breathing shadow.

"Oh my god," I breathed.

Reid's eyes widened. He pushed me behind him, drawing his Balisarda from the bandolier beneath his coat. "Stay back—"

"No!" I ducked under his arm and threw myself in front of his knife. "Leave him alone! He's not hurting anyone!"

"*Look* at him, Lou—"

"He's harmless!" I grappled with his arm. "Don't touch him!"

"We can't just leave him here—"

"Let me talk to him," I pleaded. "Maybe he'll come back to the Tower with me. I—I always visited him in the infirmary. Maybe he'll listen to me."

Reid looked between the two of us anxiously. After a long second, his face hardened. "Stay close. If he moves to harm you, get behind me. Do you understand?"

I would've rolled my eyes had I not been so terrified. "I can handle myself, Reid."

He grabbed my hand and crushed it to his chest. *"I have a blade that cuts through magic. Do you understand?"*

I swallowed hard and nodded.

Bernie watched us approach with utterly empty eyes. "Bernie?" I smiled encouragingly, keenly aware of Andre's knife in my boot. "Bernie, do you remember me?"

Nothing.

I reached out to him, and something flickered behind his vacant eyes when my fingers brushed his skin. Without warning, he lunged over the trash bin toward me. I yelped and stumbled backward, but he held my hand in a vise-like grip. A terrifying leer split his face. "I'm coming for you, darling."

Pure, unadulterated fear snaked down my spine. Paralyzing me.

I'm coming for you, darling . . . darling . . . darling . . .

Reid pulled me backward with a snarl, twisting Bernie's wrist with brutal force. His blackened fingers splayed, and I managed to snatch my hand away. As soon as our contact ceased, Bernie fell limp once more—like a marionette with cut strings.

Reid stabbed him anyway.

When the Balisarda pierced his chest, the shadows enveloping his skin melted away into nothingness, revealing the true Monsieur Bernard for the first time.

Bile rose in my throat as I took in his paper-thin skin, the white of his hair, the laugh lines around his mouth. Only his milky eyes remained the same. Blind. He gasped and spluttered as blood—red this time, clean and untainted—bloomed from his chest. I fell to my knees beside him, taking his hands in my own. Tears ran freely down my face. "I'm so sorry, Bernie."

His eyes turned to me one last time. Then closed.

The covered wagons of Ye Olde Sisters gathered outside the church, but I hardly saw them. Moving as if in another's body, I floated silently above the crowd.

Bernie was dead. Worse—he'd been enchanted by my mother.

I'm coming for you, darling.

The words echoed in my thoughts. Over and over and over again. Unmistakable.

I shivered, recalling the way Bernie had reanimated at my touch. The way he'd watched me so closely in the infirmary. I'd foolishly thought he'd wanted to end his pain when he'd tried to jump from the infirmary window. But his escape . . . Madame Labelle's warning . . .

The timing couldn't have been coincidence. He'd been trying to go to my mother.

Reid said nothing as we walked to our room. Bernie's death seemed to have similarly shaken him. His golden skin had turned ashen, and his hands shook slightly as he pushed open our bedroom door. Death. It followed wherever I went, touching everyone and everything dear to me. It seemed I couldn't outrun it. Couldn't hide. This nightmare would never end.

When he closed the door firmly behind us, I tore off my new cloak and bloody dress, flinging Andre's knife into the desk. Desperate to scrub away all memory of blood on my skin. The knife wouldn't protect me, anyway. Not from her. Pulling a fresh dress over my head, I tried and failed to hide my trembling fingers. Reid's mouth pressed into a thin line as he watched me, and I knew from the tense silence stretching between us that he'd give me no respite.

"What?" I sank onto the bed, weariness beating out all vestiges of pride.

His gaze didn't soften. Not this time. "You're hiding something from me."

But I didn't have the strength for this conversation now. Not after Madame Labelle and Bernie. Not after the crippling realization my mother knew where I was.

I fell back against my pillow, eyelids heavy. "Of course I am. I told you as much in Soleil et Lune's attic."

"What did Madame Labelle mean when she asked if I knew the *true* you?"

"Who could know?" I sat up, offering him a weak grin. "She's stark raving mad."

His eyes narrowed, and he gestured to Angelica's Ring on my finger. "She was talking about your ring. Did she give it to you?"

"I don't know," I whispered.

He tore a hand through his hair, clearly growing more agitated by the second. "*Who* is coming for you?"

"Reid, please—"

"Are you in danger?"

"I don't want to talk abou—"

He pounded the desk with his fist, and one of the legs splintered. "Tell me, Lou!"

I flinched away from him instinctively. His fury fractured at the small movement, and he dropped to his knees before me, eyes burning with unspoken emotion—with fear. He caught at my hands like they were a lifeline.

"I can't protect you if you won't let me," he pleaded. "Whatever it is, whatever has you so frightened, you can tell me. Is it your mother? Is she looking for you?"

I couldn't stop fresh tears from spilling down my cheeks. A greater fear than any I'd ever known gripped me as I stared at him. I had to tell him the truth. Here. Now.

It was time.

If my mother knew where I was, Reid was in danger too.

Morgane wouldn't hesitate to kill a Chasseur, especially if he stood between her and her prize. He couldn't be blindsided. He had to be prepared.

Slowly . . . I nodded.

His face darkened at the confession. He cupped my cheeks, brushing aside my tears with a tenderness at odds with the ferocity of his gaze. "I won't let her hurt you again, Lou. I'll protect you. Everything will be all right."

I shook my head. The tears fell faster now. "I need to tell you something." My throat constricted, as if my very body rebelled against what I was about to do. As if it knew the fate that awaited it if the words escaped. I swallowed hard, forcing them out before I could change my mind. "The truth is—"

The door burst open, and to my shock, the Archbishop strode in.

Reid rose and bowed at once, his face registering the same surprise—and wariness. "Sir?"

The Archbishop's eyes cut between us, fierce and determined. "We just received word from the royal guard, Reid. Dozens of women have collected outside the castle, and King Auguste is nervous. Make haste to disband them. Secure every Chasseur you can."

Reid hesitated. "Has someone confirmed magic, sir?"

The Archbishop's nostrils flared. "Would you suggest we wait to find out?"

Reid glanced back at me, torn, but I swallowed hard and nodded. The words I hadn't spoken congealed at the back of my throat, choking me. "Go."

He bent to give my hand a quick squeeze. "I'm sorry. I'll send Ansel to you until I get back—"

"No need," the Archbishop said curtly. "I'll stay with her myself."

We turned as one to gape at him. "You—you, sir?"

"I have an urgent matter to discuss with her."

Reid's hand lingered on my trembling knee. "Sir, if I might ask—could you postpone this conversation? She's had a very difficult day, and she's still recovering from—"

The Archbishop skewered him with a glare. "No, I cannot. And while you kneel there arguing with me, people could be dying. Your *king* could be dying."

Reid's expression hardened. "Yes, sir." Jaw taut, he released my hand and brushed a kiss against my forehead. "We *will* talk later. I promise."

With a sense of foreboding, I watched him walk toward the door. He paused at the threshold and turned back to me. "I love you, Lou."

Then he was gone.

YE OLDE SISTERS

Lou

I stared into the corridor for a full moment before his words sank in.

I love you, Lou.

Warmth spread from the tips of my fingers to my toes, chasing away the numbing fear that plagued me. He loved me. He *loved* me.

This changed everything. If he loved me, it wouldn't matter that I was a witch. He would love me anyway. He would understand. He really *would* protect me.

If he loved me.

I'd almost forgotten the Archbishop until he spoke. "You have deceived him."

I turned toward him in a daze. "You can leave." The words came without the bite I'd intended. A few tears still leaked down my face, but I brushed them away impatiently. I wanted nothing more than to bask in the heady warmth overwhelming me. "You really don't have to stay. The performance should be starting soon."

He didn't move, continuing as if he hadn't heard me. "You are a very good actress. Of course, I should have expected it—but I shan't shame myself by being fooled twice."

My bubble of happiness punctured slightly. "What are you talking about?"

He ignored me once more. "It's almost as if you truly care for him." Striding toward the door, he pushed it shut with an ominous *snap*. I hastened to my feet, eyeing the desk drawer where I'd stored Andre's knife. His lip curled. "But we both know that isn't possible."

I inched closer to the desk. Though Reid trusted his patriarch implicitly, I knew better. That furtive gleam still shone in his eyes, and I sure as hell wasn't going to be trapped on a bed.

As if reading my mind, he halted—shifted so he was directly in front of the desk drawer. My mouth went dry. "I *do* care for him. He's my husband."

"'And the great dragon was thrown down, the serpent of old who is called the devil and Satan, who deceives the whole world.'" His eyes flashed. "*You* are that serpent, Louise. A viper. And I will not allow you to destroy Reid for another moment. I can no longer stand idly by—"

A knock sounded on the door. Brows knitting together angrily, he whirled in a storm of crimson and yellow. "Come in!"

A page boy poked his head inside. "Begging your pardon, Your Eminence, but everyone is waiting for you outside."

"I am *aware*," the Archbishop snapped, "and I will be along to witness the hedonism momentarily. I have business to attend to here first."

Oblivious to the reprimand, the boy bounced on the balls of his feet in barely contained anticipation. His eyes gleamed with excitement. "But the performance is about to start, sir. They— they told me to come fetch you. The crowd is getting restless."

An agitated muscle worked in the Archbishop's jaw. When his steely eyes finally settled on me, I motioned pointedly toward the door, sending up a silent prayer of thanks. "You don't want to keep them waiting."

He bared his teeth in a smile. "You shall accompany me, of course."

"I don't think that's necessary—"

"Nonsense." He actually reached out and grabbed my arm, tucking it firmly beneath his. I flinched away from the contact instinctively, but it was no use. Within seconds, he'd dragged me out into the corridor. "I promised Reid I would stay with you, and stay with you I shall."

The crowd milled around the wagons eating treats and clutching brown paper packages, noses red from a day of shopping in the cold. The Archbishop waved when he saw them—then stopped short when he noticed the eclectic band of performers on the cathedral steps.

He wasn't the only one. Those not feasting on macarons and hazelnuts whispered behind their hands in disapproval. One word rose above the rest, a soft hiss repeated over and over in the wind.

Women.

The actors in this troupe were all women.

And not just any women: though they ranged in age from crones to maidens, all held themselves with the telltale grace of artists. Proud and erect, but also fluid. They watched the crowd murmur with impish smiles. Already performing before the show began. The youngest couldn't have been older than thirteen, and she winked at a man twice her age. He nearly choked on his popcorn.

I don't know what these idiots had expected. The troupe's name was Ye Olde *Sisters*.

"Abominable." The Archbishop halted at the top of the steps, lip curling. "A woman should never debase herself with such a disreputable profession."

I smirked and withdrew my arm from his. He didn't stop me. "I've heard they're very talented."

At my words, the youngest caught sight of us. Her eyes met mine, and she flashed a mischievous grin. With an imperious toss of her wheat-colored hair, she lifted her hands to the crowd. "*Joyeux Noël à tous!* Our guest of honor has arrived! Quiet, now, so we might begin our special performance!"

The crowd instantly quieted, and eyes everywhere turned to her in anticipation. She paused, arms still spread wide, to bask in their attention. For someone so young, she held an uncommon amount of confidence. Even the Archbishop stood transfixed. At her nod, the other actors darted into one of the wagons.

"We all know the story of Saint Nicolas, bringer of gifts and protector of children." She spun in a slow circle, arms still wide. "We know the evil butcher, Père Fouettard, lured the foolish brothers into his meat shop and *cut* them into little pieces." She sliced her hand through the air to mimic a knife. Those near her drew back with disapproving looks. "We know Saint Nicolas arrived and defeated Père Fouettard. We know he resurrected the children and returned them safe and whole to their parents." She inclined her head. "We know this story. We cherish it. It is why we gather every year to celebrate Saint Nicolas.

"But today—today we bring you a different story." She paused, another naughty smile touching her lips. "Lesser known and darker in nature, but still the tale of a holy man. We shall call him an archbishop."

The Archbishop stiffened beside me as a woman strode out of the wagon wearing choral robes uncannily similar to his own. Even the shades of crimson and gold matched. She trained her face into a severe expression. Brows furrowed, mouth tight.

"Once upon a time in a faraway place," the young narrator began, her voice turning musical, "or not so far, as is truly the case, lived an orphan boy, bitter and ignored, who found his call in the work of the Lord."

With each word, the woman portraying the Archbishop stepped closer, lifting her chin to glare down her nose at us. The real Archbishop remained still as stone. I risked a glance at him. His gaze was locked on the young narrator, his face noticeably paler than a few moments ago. I frowned.

The pretend Archbishop lit a match and held it before his eyes, watching it smoke and burn with unsettling fervency. The narrator dropped her voice to a dramatic whisper. "With faith and fire in his heart, he hunted the wicked and set them apart to burn at the stake for evil committed . . . for the Lord's word no magic permitted."

My sense of foreboding returned tenfold. Something was wrong here.

A commotion down the street distracted the audience, and the Chasseurs appeared. Reid rode in front, with Jean Luc following closely behind. Their identical expressions of alarm became clear as they drew closer, but the troupe's wagons—and the audience—blocked the street. They hurried to dismount. I started toward them, but the Archbishop caught my arm. "Stay."

"Excuse me?"

He shook his head, eyes still fixed on the narrator's face. "Stay close to me." The urgency in his voice stilled my feet, and my unease deepened. He didn't release my arm, his skin clammy and cold on mine. "Whatever happens, do not leave my side. Do you understand?"

Something was *very* wrong here.

The pretend Archbishop raised a fist. "Thou shalt not suffer a witch to live!"

The narrator leaned forward with a wicked gleam in her eyes and brought a hand to her mouth, as if revealing a secret. "But he failed to remember God's plea to forgive. So Fate, a cruel, cunning mistress, did plan another end for this blood-thirsty man."

A tall, elegant woman with deep brown skin swept from the wagon next. Her black robes billowed as she circled the pretend

Archbishop, but he didn't see her. The real Archbishop's grip on me tightened.

"A beautiful witch, cloaked in guise of damsel, soon lured the man down the path to Hell." A third woman fell from the wagon, clothed in dazzling white robes. She cried out, and the pretend Archbishop raced forward.

"What is going on?" I hissed, but he ignored me.

The pretend Archbishop and the woman in white moved in a sensual circle around one another. She trailed her hand down his cheek, and he drew her into his arms. Fate looked on with a sinister smile. The crowd muttered, gazes shifting between the actors and the Archbishop. Reid stopped trying to push through the crowd. He stood rooted to the spot, watching the performance through narrowed eyes. A ringing started in my ears.

"To bed did he take her, forsaking his oath, revering her body—the curve of her throat." At this, the narrator glanced up at the Archbishop and winked. The blood left my face, and my vision narrowed to her ivory skin, to the youthful radiance emanating from her. To her eerily familiar green eyes. Like emeralds.

The ringing grew louder, and my mind emptied of coherent thought. My knees buckled.

The pretend Archbishop and the woman in white embraced, and the crowd gasped, scandalized. The narrator cackled. "She waited until the height of his sin to reveal herself and the magic within. Then she leapt from his bed and into the night. How he cursed her moonbeam hair and skin white!"

The woman in white cackled and twisted out of the pretend

Archbishop's hold. He fell to his knees, fists raised, as she fled back to the wagon.

Moonbeam hair. Skin white.

I turned slowly, my heart beating a violent rhythm in my ears, to stare at the Archbishop. His grip on my hand turned painful. "Listen to me, Louise—"

I jerked away with a snarl. "Don't *touch* me."

The narrator's voice rose. "From that night forward, he strove to forget, but alas! Fate had not tired of him yet."

The woman in white reappeared, her stomach swollen with child. She pirouetted gracefully, her gown fanning out around her, and from the folds of her skirt, she pulled forth a baby. No more than a year old, the child cooed and giggled, her blue eyes crinkling with delight. Already, a constellation of freckles sprinkled her nose. The pretend Archbishop fell to his knees when he saw her, tearing at his face and robes. His body heaved with silent shrieks. The crowd waited with bated breath.

The narrator bent beside him and stroked his back, crooning softly in his ear. "A visit soon came from the witch he reviled with the worst news of all"—she paused and looked up at the crowd, grinning salaciously—"she'd borne his child."

Reid broke through the crowd as their muttering grew louder, as they turned to stare at the Archbishop, the disbelief in their eyes shifting into suspicion. The Chasseurs followed, hands tight on their Balisardas. Someone shouted something, but the words were lost in the tumult.

The narrator rose slowly—young face serene amidst the

descending chaos—and turned toward us. Toward *me*.

The face of my nightmares.

The face of death.

"And with not just any a child did he share." She smiled and extended her hands to me, face aging, hair lightening to brilliant silver. Screams erupted behind her. Reid was sprinting now, shouting something indiscernible. "But with *the* Witch, the Queen . . . La Dame des Sorcières."

PART III

C'est cela l'amour, tout donner, tout sacrifier sans espoir de retour.
That is love, to give away everything, to sacrifice everything,
without the slightest desire to get anything in return.
—Albert Camus

SECRETS REVEALED

Lou

Screams rent the air, and the crowd scattered in panic and confusion. I lost sight of Reid. I lost sight of everyone but my mother. She stood still in the swarming crowd—a beacon of white in the impending shadows. Smiling. Hands extended in supplication.

The Archbishop pulled me behind him as the witches converged. I cringed away, unable to process the emotions pounding through me—the wild disbelief, the debilitating fear, the violent *rage*. The witch in black, Fate, reached us first, but the Archbishop tore his Balisarda from his robes and sliced it deep across her breast. She staggered down the steps into her sister's arms. Another shrieked and charged forward.

Blue flashed, and a knife split her chest from behind. She gasped, clutching helplessly at the wound, before a hand pushed her forward. She slid off the blade slowly and crumpled.

There stood Reid.

His Balisarda dripped with her blood, and his eyes burned with primal hatred. Jean Luc and Ansel fought behind him.

With a quick jerk of his head, he motioned me forward. I didn't hesitate, abandoning the Archbishop and rushing into his outstretched arms.

But the witches kept coming. More and more seemed to appear from thin air. Worse—I'd lost sight of my mother.

An enchanted man with vacant eyes lumbered forward to meet the Archbishop. A witch stood closely behind, wringing her fingers with a ferocious snarl. Magic exploded in the air. "Get her inside!" the Archbishop cried. "Barricade yourselves in the Tower!"

"No!" I shoved away from Reid. "Give me a weapon! I can fight!"

Three sets of hands seized me, all dragging me back into the church. Other Chasseurs broke through the crowd now. I watched in horror as they drew silver syringes from their coats.

Reid shoved the church doors closed as fresh screams started.

Moving quickly, he began to lift the enormous wooden beam across the doors. Jean Luc hurried to help, while Ansel hovered by my side, face white. "Was it all true—what the witches said? D-Does the Archbishop have—does he have a child with Morgane le Blanc?"

"Perhaps." Jean Luc's shoulders strained under the weight of the beam. "But perhaps it was—all a—diversion." With one last heave, they set the beam into place. He looked me up and down, breathing heavily. "Like the witches at the castle. They'd almost breached its walls when we arrived. Then they vanished."

Glass shattered, and we looked up to see a witch scuttling through the rose window hundreds of feet above us. "Oh my

God," Ansel breathed, face twisting in horror.

Jean Luc shoved me forward. "Take her upstairs! I'll handle the witch!"

Reid grabbed my hand, and together we sprinted for the staircase. Ansel pounded along behind.

When we reached our bedroom, Reid slammed the door shut and thrust his Balisarda through the handle. In the next moment, he strode across the room to peer out the window, hand darting into his coat to retrieve a small pouch. Salt. He dumped the white crystals along the window ledge frantically.

"That won't help." My voice came out low and fervent—guilty.

Reid's hands stilled, and he turned slowly to face me. "Why are the witches after you, Lou?"

I opened my mouth, searching desperately for a reasonable explanation, but found none. He grabbed my hand and leaned down, lowering his voice. "The truth now. I can't protect you without it."

I took a deep breath, bracing myself. Every laugh, every look, every touch—it all came down to this moment.

Ansel made a strangled noise behind us. "Look out!"

We turned as one to see a witch hovering outside the window, her dun-colored hair whipping around her in a violent wind. My heart stopped. She stepped onto the sill, right through the line of salt.

Reid and I moved in front of each other at the same instant. His foot crushed mine, and I crashed to my knees. The witch cocked her head as he dove after me—after *me*, not his Balisarda.

Ansel didn't make the same mistake. He lunged toward the

knife, but the witch was faster. At a curt flick of her wrist, the sharp tang of magic scorched my nose, and Ansel flew into the wall. Before I could stop him—before I could do anything but shout a warning—Reid launched himself at her.

With another flick, his body flew upward, and his head smashed into the ceiling. The entire room trembled. Another, and he collapsed to the ground at my feet, alarmingly still.

"No!" Heart leaping to my throat, I rolled him over with frantic fingers. His eyes fluttered. Alive. My head snapped toward the dun-haired witch. "You *bitch*."

Her face twisted into a feral snarl. "You burned my sister."

A memory surfaced—a dun-haired woman at the back of the crowd, sobbing as Estelle burned. I pushed it away.

"She would've taken me." Lifting my hands warily, I wracked my brain for a pattern. Bits of gold flickered rapidly all around her. I willed them to solidify as she floated down from the sill.

Deep circles lined her bloodshot eyes, and her hands trembled with rage. "You dishonor your mother. You dishonor the Dames Blanches."

"The Dames Blanches can burn in Hell."

"You aren't worthy of the honor Morgane bestows upon you. You never have been."

Golden cords snaked between her body and mine. I caught one at random and followed it, but it branched into hundreds of others, wrapping around our bones. I recoiled from them, the cost—and risk—too great.

She bared her teeth and lifted her hands in response, eyes alight with hatred. I braced myself for the blow, but it never came.

Though she thrust her hand toward me again and again, each blast washed over my skin and dissipated.

Angelica's Ring burned hot on my finger—dispelling her patterns.

She stared at it incredulously. I lifted my hands higher with a smile, eyes lighting on a promising pattern. Backing away, she glanced at the Balisarda, but I clenched my fists before she could reach it.

She collided with the ceiling in an identical arc to Reid's, and bits of wood and mortar rained down on my head. My heartbeat slowed in response, my vision spinning, as she toppled to the floor. I lifted my hands—groping for a second pattern, something to steal her consciousness—but she tackled me around the waist into the desk.

The desk.

I jerked the drawer open, hand closing around my knife, but she caught my wrist and twisted sharply. With a feral cry, she smashed her head into my nose. I staggered sideways—blood pouring down my chin—as she wrenched the knife from my grasp.

Reid's Balisarda glinted from the doorway. I lunged for it, but she slashed my knife in front of my nose, blocking my path. Gold flared briefly, but I couldn't concentrate, couldn't think. I thrust my elbow into her ribs instead. When she broke away, doubled over and gasping, I finally saw my opportunity.

My knee connected with her face, and she dropped my knife. I swooped it up triumphantly.

"Go ahead." She clutched her side, blood dripping from her

nose to the floor. "Kill me like you killed Estelle. *Witch killer.*"

The words were more weapon than the knife ever could be.

"I—I did what I had to—"

"You murdered your kin. You married a huntsman. *You* are the only Dame Blanche who will burn in Hell, Louise le Blanc." She straightened, spitting a mouthful of blood on the floor and wiping her chin. "Come with me now—accept your birthright—and the Goddess may still spare your soul."

Tendrils of doubt snaked around my heart at her words.

Perhaps I would burn in Hell for what I'd done to survive. I'd lied and stolen and killed without hesitation in my relentless quest to *live*. But when had such a life become worth living? When had I become so ruthless, so accustomed to the blood on my hands?

When had I become one of *them*—but worse than both? At least the Dames Blanches and Chasseurs had chosen a side. Each stood for *something*, yet I stood for nothing. A coward.

All I'd wanted was to feel the sun on my face one last time. I hadn't wanted to die on that altar. If that made me a coward . . . so be it.

"With your sacrifice, we'll reclaim our homeland." She stepped closer as if sensing my hesitation, wringing her bloody hands. "Don't you understand? We'll *rule* Belterra again—"

"No," I objected, "*you* will rule Belterra. *I* will be dead."

Her chest heaved with passion. "Think of the witchlife you'll save by your sacrifice!"

"I can't allow you to slaughter innocent people." My voice quieted with resolve. "There *has* to be another way—"

My words faltered as Reid rose to his knees in my periphery. The witch's face wasn't wholly human as she turned to look at him—as she lifted her hand. I felt the unnatural energy shimmering between them, sensed the death blow before she struck.

I flung a hand toward him desperately. "No!"

Reid flew aside—eyes widening as my magic lifted him—and the witch's black energy blasted through the wall instead. But my relief was short-lived. Before I could reach him, she'd darted to his side and pressed the knife to his throat, reaching into his coat to withdraw something small. Something silver.

I stared at it in horror. A vicious smile split her face as he struggled. "Come here, or I'll slit his throat."

My feet moved toward her without hesitation. Instinctive. Though leaden, though suddenly clumsy and stiff, they knew where I had to go. Where I'd always been destined to go. Since birth. Since conception. If it meant Reid would live, I would gladly die.

Chest heaving, Reid stared resolutely at the floor as I approached. He didn't flee when the witch released him, didn't move to stop her when she stabbed the quill into my throat.

I felt it pierce my skin as if I were in another's body—the pain disconnected, somehow, as the thick liquid congealed in my veins. It was cold. The icy fingers crept steadily down my spine—paralyzing my body—but it was nothing compared to the ice in Reid's gaze as he finally looked at me.

That was the ice that pierced my heart.

I slumped forward, eyes never leaving his face. *Please,* I silently begged. *Understand.*

But there was no understanding in his eyes as he watched my body fall to the floor, as my limbs began to spasm and twitch. There was only shock, anger, and . . . disgust. Gone was the man who had knelt before me and gently wiped my tears away. Gone was the man who had held me on the rooftop, who had laughed at my jokes and defended my honor and kissed me under the stars.

Gone was the man who had claimed to love me.

Now, there was only the Chasseur.

And he hated me.

Tears tracked through the blood on my face to the floor. It was the only outward sign that my heart had cleaved in two. Still Reid did not move.

The witch lifted my chin, piercing my skin with her fingernails. Black hovered at the edges of my vision, and I struggled to remain conscious. The drug swirled in my mind, tempting me with oblivion. She bent down to my ear. "You thought he would protect you, but he'd tie you to the stake himself. Look at him, Louise. Look at his hatred."

With enormous effort, I raised my head. Her fingers loosened in surprise.

I looked directly into Reid's eyes. "I love you."

Then I blacked out.

OBLIVION

Lou

When I woke, I was vaguely aware of the floor moving beneath me—and a long, lean pair of arms. They wrapped around my waist, holding me close. Then came the throbbing pain of my throat. I clasped a hand to it, feeling fresh blood.

"Lou," a familiar voice said anxiously. "Can you hear me?"

Ansel.

"Wake up, Lou." The floor still shifted. Something crashed nearby, followed by a thunderous *boom*. A woman cackled. "Please wake up!"

My eyes fluttered open.

I was sprawled on the floor behind the bed with my head in Ansel's lap, a syringe discarded beside us.

"It's the antidote," he whispered frantically. "There wasn't enough for a full dose. He's losing, Lou. The witch—she blasted the door. His Balisarda flew into the corridor. You have to help him. Please!"

He's losing.

Reid.

Adrenaline spiked through me, and I sat up quickly, coughing on the dust pervading the air. The world spun around me. Reid and the witch had decimated the room; holes had been blasted through the floor and walls, and the desk and headboard lay in splinters. Ansel dragged me out of the way as a chunk of mortar crashed to the floor where my legs had been.

Reid and the witch circled one another in the center of the room, but Reid appeared to be having difficulty moving. He gritted his teeth, forcing his muscles to obey as he swung my knife at the witch. She darted easily out of reach before flicking her fingers once more. Reid inhaled sharply as if she'd struck him.

I struggled to my feet. Darkness still swirled in my vision, and my limbs were as clumsy and heavy as Reid's. But it didn't matter. I had to stop this.

Neither acknowledged me. The witch thrust her hand forward, and Reid dove out of the way. The blast leveled the wall instead. A sadistic smile played on her lips. She was toying with him. Toying with the man who'd burned her sister.

Ansel tracked the witch's every movement. "Everyone is still outside."

I swayed, vision blurring as I raised my hands. But there was nothing. I couldn't concentrate. The room tilted and spun.

The witch's gaze snapped toward us. Reid moved to strike, but she flicked her wrist, throwing him against the wall once more. I started forward as he crumpled.

"You are a fool," the witch said. "You've seen his hatred, yet still you rush to his aid—"

A cord sprang into existence, plunging to her voice box. I clenched my fist, and the words died in her throat. My blood flowed thicker from the syringe punctures while she struggled to breathe. I swayed again, breaking concentration, but Ansel caught me before I could fall. The witch gasped and clutched her throat as her breath returned.

I was too weak to continue fighting. I could barely stand, let alone fight a witch and hope to win. I had no physical strength left to give, and my mind was too drug-saturated to distinguish patterns.

"You two deserve each other." The witch blasted me from Ansel's arms, and I flew through the air and collided with Reid's chest. He staggered back at the impact, but his arms wrapped around me, softening the blow. Stars danced in my vision.

Ansel's battle cry revived me, but it too was cut short. Another thud sounded behind us, and he skidded into our knees.

"I can't . . . beat her." Though my bleeding had stopped, I still felt faint. Light-headed. I couldn't keep my eyes open. "Too . . . weak . . ."

Darkness beckoned, and my head lolled.

But Reid's grip on me turned almost painful. My eyes snapped open to see him staring down at me determinedly.

"Use me."

I shook my head with as much force as I could muster. Stars dotted my vision.

"It could work." Ansel nodded frantically, and Reid released me. I swayed on my feet. "The witches use other people all the time!"

I opened my mouth to tell them *no*—that I wouldn't hurt him, wouldn't wield his body like other witches did—but a hand tore me backward by my hair. I landed in the dun-haired witch's embrace, back pressed against her chest.

"I grow weary of this, and your mother is waiting. Will you kill them, or will I?"

I couldn't bring myself to answer. Every last bit of my focus centered on the thin, deadly rope that had emerged in the air between the witch and Reid.

A pattern.

I was weak, but Reid . . . he was still strong. And, despite everything, I loved him. Loved him enough that nature had acknowledged him a worthy trade. He wasn't just another body. Another shield of flesh. He was . . . me.

This could work.

With a ragged breath, I clenched my fist. The pattern vanished in a burst of gold.

Reid's eyes widened as his neck went taut, and his back bowed off the wall. His spine strained to remain intact as the magic pulled him upward as if he were caught in a noose. The witch shrieked, dropping me, and I knew without looking she was in a similar position. Before she could counter, I flicked my wrist, and Reid's arms snapped to his sides, pinned, his fingers adhering together. His head tilted back unnaturally, extending his throat. Exposing it.

Ansel dove into the corridor as the witch's shrieks turned strangled—desperate.

"Ansel," I said sharply. "A sword."

He raced forward, handing me Reid's Balisarda. The witch struggled harder against the enchantment binding her—fear finally breaking loose in those hateful eyes—but I held strong.

Lifting the knife to her throat, I took a deep breath. Her eyes darted wildly.

"I'll see you in Hell," I whispered.

I flexed my hand, and the witch's and Reid's bodies collapsed in unison, the pattern dissolving. The blade severed her throat as she fell, and her lifeblood coursed, warm and thick, down my arm. Her body slumped to the floor. It stopped twitching within seconds.

Witch killer.

The silence in the room was deafening.

I stared down at her body—Balisarda dangling limply at my side—and watched her blood pool at my feet. It coated my boots and stained the hem of my dress. The sounds of the battle outside had faded. I didn't know who had won. I didn't care.

"Ansel," Reid said with deadly calm. I flinched at the sound of his voice. *Please. If you can hear me, God, let him understand.* But Ansel's eyes widened at whatever he saw on Reid's face, and I didn't dare turn around. "Get out."

Ansel's gaze flicked back to me, and I pleaded wordlessly with him not to leave. He nodded, straightening and stepping toward Reid. "I think I should stay."

"Get. Out."

"Reid—"

"GET OUT!"

I whirled, tears streaming down my cheeks. "Don't talk to him like that!"

His eyes sparked with fury, and his hands curled into fists. "You seem to have forgotten who I am, Louise. I'm a captain of the Chasseurs. I will speak to him as I wish."

Ansel backed hastily into the corridor. "I'll be right outside, Lou. I promise."

A wave of hopelessness swept through me as he left. I felt Reid's eyes burning into my skin, but I couldn't bring myself to look at him again. Couldn't bring myself to acknowledge the hatred I would find there . . . because once I acknowledged it, it became real. And it couldn't be real. It couldn't be.

He loved me.

Silence stretched between us. Unable to stand it any longer, I glanced up. His blue eyes—once so beautiful, like the sea—were living flames.

"Please say something," I whispered.

His jaw clenched. "I have nothing to say to you."

"I'm still *me*, Reid—"

He jerked his head in swift dismissal. "No, you're not. You're a witch."

More tears leaked down my face as I struggled to collect my thoughts. There was so much I wanted to say—so much I *needed* to tell him—but I couldn't concentrate on anything but the loathing in his eyes, the way his lip curled as if I were something repulsive and strange. I closed my eyes against the image, chin quivering once more.

"I wanted to tell you," I began softly.

"Then why didn't you?"

"Because I . . . I didn't want to lose you." Eyes still closed, I extended his Balisarda tentatively. An offering. "I love you, Reid."

He scoffed and jerked the handle from my grip. "*Love* me. As if someone like you is even *capable* of love. The Archbishop told us witches were clever. He told us they were cruel. But I fell for the tricks, same as him." An angry, unnatural sound tore from his throat. "The witch said your mother was waiting for you. It's her, isn't it? Morgane le Blanc. You—you're the daughter of La Dame des Sorcières. Which means—" An anguished noise this time, raw with disbelief, as if he'd been stabbed through the heart without warning. I didn't open my eyes to watch the realization dawn. Couldn't bear to see the final piece click into place. "The witches' story was true, wasn't it? Their performance. The Archbishop—"

He broke off abruptly, and silence descended once more. I felt his gaze on my face like a brand, but I didn't open my eyes.

"I don't know how I didn't see it before." His voice was colder now. Chilling. "His unnatural interest in your welfare, his refusal to punish your defiance. The way he *forced* me to marry you. It all makes sense. You even *look* alike."

I didn't want it to be true. I wished it away with every fragment of my fractured heart. My tears fell thicker and faster, a torrent of sorrow Reid ignored.

"And here I was—pouring my foolish heart out to you." His

voice grew louder and louder with each word. "I fell right into your trap. That's all this was, wasn't it? You needed a place to hide. You thought the Chasseurs would protect you. You thought *I* would protect you. You—" His breathing turned ragged. "You used me."

The truth of his words was a knife to my own heart. My eyes snapped open. For a split second, I saw the flicker of misery and hurt beneath his fury, but then it was gone, buried beneath a lifetime of hatred.

A hatred proving stronger than love.

"That's not true," I whispered. "At first—maybe—but something *changed*, Reid. Please, you have to believe me—"

"What am I supposed to *do*, Lou?" He wrung his hands in the air, voice escalating to a roar. "I'm a Chasseur! I took an oath to hunt witches—to hunt *you*! How could you do this to me?"

I flinched again and stepped back until my legs pressed against the bed frame. "You—Reid, you also made an oath to *me*. You're my husband, and I'm your wife."

His hands dropped to his sides. Defeated. A spark of hope flared in my chest. But then he closed his eyes—seeming to collapse in on himself—and when he opened them again, they were void of all emotion. Empty. Dead.

"You are not my wife."

What was left of my heart shattered completely.

I pressed a hand to my mouth in an effort to stem my sobs. Tears blurred my vision. Reid didn't move as I fled past him, didn't reach out to catch me as I tripped over the threshold. I crashed to my hands and knees outside the door.

Ansel's arms wrapped around me. "Are you hurt?"

I pushed away from him wildly, scrambling to my feet. "I'm sorry, Ansel. I'm so sorry."

Then I was running—running as hard and fast as my broken body would allow. Ansel called after me, but I ignored him, hurtling down the stairs. Desperate to put as much distance between myself and Reid as possible.

Do not urge me to leave you or turn back from you. His words stabbed through me with each step. *Where you go, I will go. Where you stay, I will stay.*

I won't let her hurt you again, Lou. I'll protect you. Everything will be all right.

I love you, Lou.

You are not my wife.

I turned into the foyer, chest heaving. Past the shattered rose window. Past the witches' corpses. Past the milling Chasseurs.

God—if he was there, if he was watching—took pity on me when none moved to block my path. The Archbishop was nowhere in sight.

You are not my wife.

You are not my wife.

You are not my wife.

Fleeing through the open doors, I lurched blindly into the street. The sunset shone too bright on my stinging eyes. I stumbled down the church steps, peering around blearily, before starting down the street for Soleil et Lune.

I could make it. I could seek shelter there one last time.

A pale hand snaked out from behind me and wrapped around my neck. I tried to turn, but a third quill stabbed my throat. I struggled weakly—pathetically—against my captor, but the familiar cold was already creeping down my spine. Darkness fell swiftly. My eyelids fluttered as I collapsed forward, but pale, slender arms held me upright.

"Hello, darling," a familiar voice crooned in my ear. White, moonbeam hair fell across my shoulder. Gold shimmered in my vision, and the scar at my throat puckered in a burst of pain. The beginning of the end. The life pattern reversing.

Never again never again never again.

"It's time to come home."

This time, I welcomed oblivion.

BEATING A DEAD WITCH

Reid

"What have you done?"

Ansel's voice echoed too loudly in the silence of the room—or what was left of it. Holes riddled the walls, and the stench of magic lingered on my furniture. My sheets. My skin. A pool of blood spread from the witch's throat. I stared at the corpse, hating it. Longing for a match to set it aflame. To burn it—and this room, and this moment—from my memory forever.

I turned away, unwilling to look in its dull eyes. Its lifeless eyes. It looked nothing like the graceful actresses we would burn in the furnace tonight. Nothing like the beautiful, white-haired Morgane le Blanc.

Nothing like her daughter.

I stopped the thought before it took a dangerous direction.

Lou was a witch. A viper. And I was a fool.

"What have you done?" Ansel repeated, voice louder.

"I let her leave." Legs wooden, uncooperative, I shoved my Balisarda in my bandolier and knelt beside the corpse. Though my body still ached from Lou's attack, the witch needed to be burned, lest it reanimate. I paused at the edge of blood. Reluctant to touch it. Reluctant to draw near to this thing that had tried to kill Lou.

For as much as I hated to admit it—as much as I *cursed* her name—a world without Lou was wrong, somehow. Empty.

When I lifted the corpse, its head lolled back grotesquely, throat gaping where Lou had slit it. Blood soaked through the blue wool of my coat.

I'd never hated the color more.

"Why?" Ansel demanded. I ignored him, focusing on the dead weight in my arms. Again, my traitorous mind wandered to Lou. To last night when I'd held her briefly under the stars. She'd been so light. And vulnerable. And funny and beautiful and warm—

Stop.

"She was drugged and obviously injured," he insisted. I hoisted the corpse higher, ignoring him, and kicked open the splintered door. Exhaustion crashed through me in waves. But he refused to give up. "Why did you let her go?"

Because I couldn't kill her.

I glared at him. He'd defended her even after she'd revealed her true nature. Even after she'd proved herself a liar and a snake—a Judas. And that meant Ansel had no place among the Chasseurs.

"It doesn't matter."

"It *does* matter. Lou's mother is *Morgane le Blanc*. Didn't you hear what the witch said about reclaiming their homeland?"

With your sacrifice, we'll reclaim our homeland. We'll rule Belterra again.

I can't allow you to slaughter innocent people.

Yes. I'd heard it.

"Lou can take care of herself."

Ansel pushed past me and planted his feet in the middle of the corridor. "Morgane is out in the city tonight, and so is Lou. This—this is bigger than us. She needs our help—" I shouldered past him, but he stepped in front of me again and shoved my chest. "Listen to me! Even if you don't care for Lou anymore— even if you hate her—the witches are planning something, and it involves Lou. I think— Reid, I think they're going to kill her."

I pushed his hands away, refusing to hear his words. Refusing to acknowledge the way they made my mind spin, my chest tighten. "No, *you* listen, Ansel. I'll only say this once." I lowered my face slowly, deliberately, until our eyes were level. "*Witches. Lie.* We can't believe anything we heard tonight. We can't trust this witch spoke truth."

He scowled. "I know what my gut tells me, and it says Lou is in trouble. We have to find her."

My own gut twisted, but I ignored it. My emotions had betrayed me once. Not this time. Not ever again. I needed to focus on the present—on what I *knew*—and that was disposing of the witch. The furnace in the dungeon. My brethren downstairs.

I forced one foot in front of the other. "Lou is no longer our responsibility."

"I thought Chasseurs were bound to *protect* the innocent and helpless?"

My fingers tightened on the corpse. "Lou is hardly innocent *or* helpless."

"She's not herself right now!" He chased me down the stairwell, nearly tripping and sending us both crashing to the floor. "She's drugged, and she's weak!"

I scoffed. Even drugged, even wounded, Lou had impaled the witch like Jael had Sisera.

"You saw her, Reid." His voice fell to a rough whisper. "She won't stand a chance if Morgane shows up."

I cursed Ansel and his bleeding heart.

Because I *had* seen her. That was the problem. I was doing my best to *un*-see her, but the memory had been seared into my eyelids. Blood had covered her beautiful face. It'd stained her throat. Her hands. Her dress. Bruises had already formed from the witch's assault . . . but that wasn't what haunted me. That wasn't what cut through the haze of my fury.

No—it had been her eyes.

The light in them had gone out.

The drug, I reassured myself. *The drug dimmed them.*

But deep down, I knew better. Lou had broken in that moment. My wild-hearted, foul-mouthed, steel-willed heathen had broken. *I* had broken her.

You are not my wife.

I hated myself for what I'd done to her. I hated myself more for what I still felt for her. She was a witch. A bride of Lucifer. So what did that make me?

"You're a coward," Ansel spat.

I lurched to a halt, and he stumbled into me. His anger flickered out at my expression—at the rage coursing through my blood, heating my face.

"By all means, *go*," I snarled. "Go after her. Protect her from Morgane le Blanc. Perhaps the witches will let you live with them at the Chateau. You can burn with them too."

He reared back, stunned. Hurt.

Good. I turned savagely and continued into the foyer. Ansel walked a dangerous line. If the others found out he empathized with a witch . . .

Jean Luc strode through the open doors, carrying a witch over his shoulder. Blood dribbled down the demon's neck from an injection. Behind him, a dove lay amongst the dead on the cathedral steps. Feathers bloodstained and rumpled. Eyes empty. Unseeing.

I looked away, ignoring the stinging pressure behind my own eyes.

My brethren moved purposefully around us. Some carried in corpses from the street. Though most of the witches had escaped, a handful joined the pile of bodies in the foyer—separate from the others. Untouchable. Theirs wouldn't be a public execution. Not after Ye Olde Sisters. Not after that performance. Even if the Archbishop controlled the damage, word would spread. Even if he denied the accusation—even if some believed him—the seed had been planted.

The Archbishop had conceived a child with La Dame des Sor-cières.

Though he was nowhere to be seen, his name filled the hall. My brothers kept their voices low, but I still heard them. Still saw their sidelong glances. Their suspicion. Their doubt.

Jean Luc elbowed Ansel aside to stand before me. "If you're

looking for your wife, she's gone. I watched her dash through here not a quarter hour ago . . . crying."

Crying.

"What happened upstairs, Reid?" He tilted his head to consider me, arching a brow. "Why would she flee? If she fears the witches, surely the Tower is the safest place for her." He paused, and a truly frightening smile split his face. "Unless, of course, she now fears us more?"

I dropped my corpse on top of the pile of witches. Ignored the trepidation settling in my stomach like lead.

"I think your wife has a secret, Reid. And I think you know what it is." Jean Luc inched closer, watching me with too-sharp eyes. "I think *I* know what it is."

My trepidation dropped to outright panic, but I forced my face to remain calm. Blank. Void of all emotion. I wouldn't tell them about Lou. They would hunt her. And the thought of their hands on her—touching her, *hurting* her, tying her body to the stake—I wouldn't allow it.

I looked Jean Luc directly in the eyes. "I don't know what you're talking about."

"Where is she then?" He raised his voice and gestured around us, drawing the eyes of our brethren. My fingers curled into fists. "Why did the little witch flee?"

Red crept steadily into my vision, blurring those closest to us—those who had stilled, heads turning, at Jean Luc's accusation. "Take care what you say next, Chasseur Toussaint."

His smile faltered. "So it's true, then." He scrubbed a hand down his face and sighed heavily. "I didn't want to believe it—but look at you. You would defend her still, even though you *know* she's a—"

I lunged at him with a snarl. He attempted to dodge, but he wasn't quick enough. My fist struck his jaw with an audible crack, breaking the bone. Ansel leapt forward before I could strike again. Despite him tugging on my arms, I barreled past him, barely feeling his weight. Jean Luc scrambled backward, screaming in pain and outrage, as I drew my fist once more.

"Enough," the Archbishop said sharply from behind us.

I froze, fist cocked midair.

A few of my brethren bowed, fists to hearts, but most remained standing. Resolute. Wary. The Archbishop eyed them with growing fury, and a few more dropped their heads. Ansel released my arms and followed suit. To my surprise, so did Jean Luc—though his left hand remained pressed to his swelling jaw. He glared at the floor with murder in his eyes.

A tense second passed as they waited for me, their captain, to honor our forefather.

I didn't.

The Archbishop's eyes flashed at my insolence, but he hastened forward anyway. "Where is Louise?"

"Gone."

Disbelief contorted his face. "What do you mean *gone*?"

I didn't answer, and Ansel stepped forward in my stead. "She—she fled, Your Eminence. After this witch attacked her." He gestured to the corpse on top of the pile of witches.

The Archbishop moved closer to inspect it. "You killed this witch, Captain Diggory?"

"No." My fist throbbed from striking Jean Luc's jaw. I welcomed the pain. "Lou did."

He clasped my shoulder in a show of camaraderie for my brethren, but I heard the unspoken plea. Saw the vulnerability in his eyes. In that second, I knew. Any doubts I'd had vanished, replaced by a disgust deeper than any I'd ever known. This man—the man I'd looked to as a father—was a liar. A fraud. "We must find her, Reid."

I stiffened and shrugged away. "No."

His expression hardened, and he motioned one of my brothers forward. A mutilated corpse hung over his shoulder. Angry red burns riddled its face and neck, disappearing down the collar of its dress.

"I've had the pleasure of speaking with this creature for the past half hour. With a bit of persuasion, it became a plethora of information." The Archbishop took the corpse and dumped it atop the pile. The bodies shifted, and blood seeped onto my boots. Bile rose in my throat. "You don't know what the witches have planned for the kingdom, Captain Diggory. We cannot allow them to succeed."

Jean Luc straightened, instantly alert. "What do they have planned?"

"Revolution." The Archbishop's eyes remained fixed on mine. "Death."

Silence settled over the hall at his ominous pronouncement.

Feet shifted. Eyes darted. No one dared ask what he meant—not even Jean Luc. Just as no one dared ask the one other question that mattered. The one other question on which our entire creed hinged.

I glanced at my brothers, watching as they stared between the Archbishop and the tortured, mutilated witch. As the conviction returned to their faces. As their suspicion shifted to excuses, bridging the way back to the comfortable world we'd once known. The comfortable lies.

It was all a diversion.

Yes—a diversion.

The witches are cunning.

Of course they would frame him.

Except Jean Luc. His sharp eyes were not so easily fooled. Worse—a garish grin stretched across his face. Warped by his swelling jaw.

"We must find Louise before the witches do," the Archbishop urged. Pleaded. "She is the key, Reid. With her death, the king and his posterity will die. We *all* will die. You must put aside your quarrel with her and protect this kingdom. Honor your vows."

My vows. True fury coursed through me at the words. Surely, this man who had lain with La Dame des Sorcières—this man who had *deceived* and *betrayed* and *broken* his vows at every turn—couldn't be speaking to me about *honor*. I exhaled slowly through my nose. My hands still shook with anger and adrenaline. "Let's go, Ansel."

The Archbishop bared his teeth at my dismissal—and turned

unexpectedly to Jean Luc. "Chasseur Toussaint, assemble a team of men. I want you on the street within the hour. Alert the constabulary. She *will* be found by morning. Do you understand?"

Jean Luc bowed, flashing me a triumphant smile. I glared back at him, searching his face for any flicker of hesitation, of regret, but there was none. His time had finally come. "Yes, Your Eminence. I will not disappoint you."

Ansel followed hurriedly as I departed. We ascended the stairs three at a time. "What are we going to do?"

"*We* are going to do nothing. I don't want you caught up in this."

"Lou is my friend!"

His friend.

At those two small words, my patience—already stretched too thin—snapped completely. Swiftly, before the boy could so much as gasp, I grabbed his arm and shoved him into the wall. "She's a *witch*, Ansel. You must understand this. She is not your friend. She is not my wife."

His cheeks flushed with anger, and he shoved me in the chest. "Keep telling yourself that. Your pride is going to get her killed. She's in trouble—" He shoved me again for emphasis, but I caught his arm and twisted it behind his back, slamming his chest into the wall. He didn't even flinch. "Who cares if the Archbishop lied? You're better than him, better than this."

I snarled, quickly approaching my breaking point.

Lou, Ansel, Morgane le Blanc, the Archbishop . . . it was all too much. Too sudden. My mind couldn't rationalize the emotions flooding through me—each too quick to name, each more painful than the last—but the time to choose rapidly approached.

I was a huntsman.

I was a man.

But I couldn't be both. Not anymore.

I let go of Ansel and backed away, breathing ragged. "No, I'm not."

"I don't believe that."

I balled my hands into fists, resisting the urge to smash them through the wall—or Ansel's face. "All she's ever done is lie to me, Ansel! She looked me in the eyes and told me she loved me! How do I know that wasn't a lie too?"

"It wasn't a lie. You know it wasn't." He paused, lifting his chin in a gesture so like Lou I nearly wept. "You . . . you called her *she*. Not *it*."

Now I did strike the wall. Pain exploded from my knuckles. I welcomed it—welcomed anything to distract me from the agony ripping my chest in two, the tears burning my eyes. I leaned my forehead against the wall and gasped for breath. No, Lou wasn't an *it*. But she'd still lied to me. Betrayed me.

"What should she have done instead?" Ansel asked. "Told you she was a witch and tied herself to the stake?"

My voice broke. "She should've trusted me."

He touched my back, voice softening. "She'll die, Reid. You heard the Archbishop. If you do nothing, she'll die."

And just like that, the rage left me. My hands fell to my sides.

Limp. My shoulders slumped . . . defeated.

There had never been a choice. Not for me. From the first moment I'd seen her at the parade—dressed in that ridiculous suit and mustache—my fate had been sealed.

I loved her. Despite everything. Despite the lies, the betrayal, the hurt. Despite the Archbishop and Morgane le Blanc. Despite my own brothers. I didn't know if she returned that love, and I didn't care.

If she was destined to burn in Hell, I would burn with her.

"No." Deadly purpose pounded through my veins as I pushed from the wall. "Lou isn't going to die, Ansel. We're going to find her."

HELL HATH NO FURY

Reid

A few initiates lingered outside my destroyed room when Ansel and I returned. They ducked their heads and scattered upon seeing me. Glowering at them, I stepped inside to think. To plan.

Lou had spent the last two years as a thief, so she was better than most at disappearing. She could've been anywhere. I wasn't foolish enough to think I knew all her haunts, but I did have a better chance of finding her than Jean Luc. Still, the Chasseurs swarming the city complicated things.

Closing my eyes, I forced myself to breathe deeply and *think*. Where would she go? Where could she hide? But the magic in the air scorched my throat, distracting me. It lingered on the bedsheets, the splintered desk. The bloody pages of my Bible. On my skin, my hair. My eyes snapped open, and I resisted the urge to roar in frustration. I didn't have time for this. I needed to find her. Quickly. Each passing moment could be her last.

She'll die, Reid. If you do nothing, she'll die.

No. That couldn't happen. *Think.*

The theater seemed her most likely hiding place. But would she return there after she'd shared it with me? Probably not. Perhaps we could stake out Pan's instead. It would be only a matter of time before she visited the patisserie—unless she'd left Cesarine altogether. My heart sank.

Ansel moved to the window and peered out to watch my brethren march past. He knew better than to suggest we join them. Though we shared a common purpose in finding Lou, the Archbishop had lied to me—had broken trust, broken faith. More important, I didn't know what they planned for Lou when they found her. Though the Archbishop might try to protect her, Jean Luc knew she was a witch. How long would it take before he told the others? How long before someone suggested killing her?

I had to find her first. Before them. Before the witches.

Ansel cleared his throat.

"What?" I snapped.

"I—I think we should visit Mademoiselle Perrot. The two are . . . close. She might know something."

Mademoiselle Perrot. Of course.

Before we could move, however, what was left of my door crashed open. Standing in the threshold—panting and glaring—stood Mademoiselle Perrot in the flesh.

"Where is she?" She advanced on me with threat of violence in her eyes. She'd abandoned her white healer's robes for leather trousers and a blood-speckled shirt. "Where's Lou?"

I frowned at the lattice of scars on her exposed collarbone and forearms.

Startled, Ansel stumbled forward to explain, but I shook my head curtly, stepping in front of him. Forcing the words out before I could swallow them back. "She's gone."

"What do you mean *gone?* You have thirty seconds to tell me what happened before I spill blood, *Chasseur.*" She hurled the last word at me—like she meant it as an insult. I scowled. Forced a deep breath. Then another.

Wait—spill blood?

"Tick tock," she snarled.

Though I loathed the thought of telling her what had transpired between me and Lou, it was no good lying. Not if I wanted her help. If she didn't know where Lou was, I had little else to go on. Little chance of ever finding her. That couldn't happen.

"The witches attacked the castle as a diversion and came here—"

"I *know.*" She swiped an impatient hand. "I was at the castle with Beau when they vanished. I meant what happened with *Lou.*"

"She ran off," I repeated through clenched teeth. "A witch— she followed us up here and attacked. Lou saved my life." I broke off, chest tight, and considered how to break the news. She needed to know. "Mademoiselle Perrot . . . Lou is a witch."

To my surprise, she didn't even blink. A slight tightening of her mouth was the only indication she'd heard me at all. "Of course she is."

"What?" Disbelief colored my voice. "You—you *knew?*"

She gave me a scathing look. "You'd have to be a total idiot not to see it."

Like you. Her unspoken words echoed around the room. I ignored them, the sharp sting of yet another betrayal rendering me momentarily speechless. "Did . . . did she tell you?"

She snorted, rolling her eyes toward the ceiling. "There's no need to look so wounded. No, she didn't tell me. She didn't tell Ansel here either, yet he knew too."

Ansel's eyes flicked between the two of us rapidly. He swallowed hard. "I—I didn't *know* anything—"

"Oh, please." She scowled at him. "You're insulting everyone by lying."

His shoulders slumped, and he stared at the floor. Refusing to look at me. "Yes. I knew."

All the air left me in a whoosh. Three words. Three perfect punches.

Bitter anger returned with my breath. "Why didn't you say anything?"

If Ansel had told me—if Ansel had been a *real* Chasseur— none of this would've happened. I wouldn't have been blindsided. I could have *dealt* with this before—before I—

"I told you." Ansel still stared at his boots, nudging a piece of fallen mortar with his toe. "Lou is my friend."

"When?" I deadpanned. "When did you know?"

"During the witch burning. When—when Lou had her fit. She was crying, and the witch was screaming—then they switched. Everyone thought Lou was seizing, but I saw her. I smelled the magic." He looked up, throat bobbing. Eyes shining. "She was burning, Reid. I don't know how, but she took away that witch's pain. She gave it to herself." He exhaled heavily. "That's why I didn't tell you. Because even though I knew Lou was a witch, I knew she wasn't evil. She burned at the stake once. She doesn't deserve to do it twice."

Silence met his pronouncement. I stared between the two of them, eyes stinging. "I never would've hurt her."

As the words left my mouth, I realized their truth. Even if Ansel *had* told me, it wouldn't have changed anything. I wouldn't have been able to tie her to a stake. I dropped my face in my hands. Defeated.

"Enough," Mademoiselle Perrot said sharply. "How long has she been gone?"

"About an hour."

Ansel shifted in obvious discomfort before murmuring, "The witch mentioned Morgane."

My hands fell as genuine fear twisted Mademoiselle Perrot's face. Her eyes—once hateful, once accusing—met mine with sudden, unsettling urgency. "We need to leave." Throwing the door open, she rushed into the corridor. "We can't talk about this here."

Trepidation knotted my stomach. "Where can we go?"

"To the Bellerose." She didn't bother looking back. Seeing no other choice, Ansel and I hurried after her. "I told Beau I'd meet him—and there's someone there who might know where Lou is."

The inside of the Bellerose was dimly lit. I'd never been inside a brothel, but I assumed the marble floors and the gold leaf on the walls marked this a more glamorous whorehouse than others. A harpist sat in one corner. She strummed her instrument and crooned a mournful ballad. Women clad in sheer white clothes danced slowly. A handful of drunken men watched them with hungry eyes. A fountain bubbled in the center of the room.

It was the most ostentatious thing I'd ever seen. It suited Madame Labelle perfectly.

"We're wasting time. We should be out there searching for Lou—" I started angrily, but Mademoiselle Perrot shot me a withering glare over her shoulder before striding toward a partially concealed table in the back.

Beauregard Lyon rose as we approached, eyes narrowing. "What the hell are they doing here?"

She threw herself into a chair with a heavy sigh, waving a hand between the three of us. "Look, Beau, I have more pressing matters to handle this evening than you and your pissing contest."

He dropped into another chair, crossing his arms and sulking. "What could possibly be more pressing than me?"

She jerked her head toward me. "This idiot lost Lou, and I need to perform a locator spell to find her."

Locator spell?

I watched in confusion as she drew a small vial from her cloak. Uncorking it, she spilled the dark powder on the table. Beau looked on as if bored, tipping back in his chair. I glanced at Ansel—seeking confirmation the woman before us had gone mad—but he wouldn't look at me. When she pulled out a knife and lifted her opposite hand, my stomach dropped with realization.

Tremblay's townhouse. Three poisoned dogs. Blood running from their maws. The stench of magic piercing the air—black and biting, more acrid than the magic in the infirmary. Different.

Her eyes met mine as she slashed her palm open, letting the blood drip onto the table. "I should probably tell you, Chass, my name isn't Brie Perrot. It's Cosette, but my friends call me Coco."

Cosette Monvoisin. She'd been hiding in the Tower all along. Right under our noses.

I reached for my Balisarda instinctively, but Ansel's hand came down on my arm. "Reid, don't. She's helping us find Lou."

I wrenched away from him—horrified, furious—but my hand stilled. She winked at me before returning her attention to the tabletop. The dark powder congealed under her blood— then began moving. Bile rose in my throat, and my nose burned. "What is that?"

"Dried blood of a hound." She watched raptly as strange symbols formed. "It'll tell us where Lou is."

Beau tipped forward, propping his chin in his elbow against the table. "And just where do you think she might be?"

A small furrow appeared between Coco's eyes. "With Morgane le Blanc."

"Morgane le Blanc?" He straightened and looked at us incredulously, as if expecting one of us to laugh. "Why would the bitch witch queen be interested in Lou?"

"Because she's her mother." The shapes stilled suddenly, and

Coco's eyes snapped to mine. Wide. Panicked. "Lou's trail disappears north into La Forêt des Yeux. I can't see past it." I stared at her, and she nodded imperceptibly at my unspoken question. Her chin trembled. "If Morgane has Lou, she's as good as dead."

"No." I shook my head vehemently, unable to accept it. "We just need to find the Chateau. You're a witch. You can lead us to it—"

Angry tears sprang to her eyes. "I don't know where the Chateau *is*. Only a *Dame Blanche* can find it, and you've lost the only Dame Blanche I know!"

"You—you're not a Dame Blanche?"

She flung her bloody palm under my nose as if it should mean something. "Of course not! Are Chasseurs really this ignorant?"

I stared at the blood pooling there with rising hysteria. The same acrid smell from before assaulted me. "I don't understand."

"I'm a Dame Rouge, you idiot. A Red Lady. A *blood witch*." She slapped her hand on the table, splattering the black shapes. "I can't find the Chateau because I've never *been* there."

A ringing started in my ears. "No." I shook my head. "That can't be true. There has to be another way."

"There isn't." Tears spilled down her cheeks as she shoved to her feet, but she wiped them away quickly. The scent around us sharpened. "Unless you know another Dame Blanche—another Dame Blanche willing to betray her sisters and lead a *Chasseur* into their home—Lou is *gone*."

No.

"Do you know a witch like that, Chass?" She stuck a finger

in my chest, tears still streaming. They hissed and smoked when they dripped on her shirt. Beau rose, placing an uncertain hand on her back. "Do you know a witch willing to sacrifice *everything* for you the way Lou did? *Do you?*"

No.

"Actually," a cool, familiar voice replied, "he does."

We turned as one to look upon my savior. I nearly choked at her fiery red hair.

God, no.

Madame Labelle waved a hand toward the eavesdropping men nearest us. "This is a private conversation, dears. I hope you understand."

Magic—the normal, cloying kind—burst through the air, and their bloodshot eyes glazed over. They turned their attention back to the dancing girls, who now wore equally vacant expressions.

Coco leapt forward, pointing at her in accusation. "You knew about Morgane. You warned Lou. You're a witch."

Madame Labelle winked.

I looked between them in confusion, nostrils burning. Mind reeling. Witch? But Madame Labelle wasn't a—

Realization rushed in, and hot blood rose to my face.

Fuck.

I was so stupid. So *blind*. My fists clenched as I pushed to my feet. Madame Labelle's taunting smile faltered, and even Coco shrank back at the fury in my eyes.

Of course Madame Labelle was a witch.

And Mademoiselle Perrot was Coco.

And Coco was a witch. But not just any witch—a Dame Rouge. An entirely new species of witch, who practiced in *blood*.

And my wife—the fucking *love of my life*—was the daughter of La Dame des Sorcières. The heiress of Chateau le Blanc. The goddamned *princess* of the witches.

And everyone had known. Everyone except me. Even fucking Ansel.

It was too much.

Something snapped inside me. Something permanent. In that second, I was no longer the Chasseur—if I'd ever been a Chasseur in the first place.

Unsheathing my Balisarda, I watched with vindictive pleasure as the others eyed me. Wary. Afraid. The harpist in the corner stopped playing. She stared blankly at the floor, her mouth gaping open. The silence grew eerie—waiting.

"Sit," I said softly, flicking my gaze to Madame Labelle and Coco. When neither of them moved, I took a step closer. Beau's hand closed around Coco's wrist. He tugged her down beside him.

But Madame Labelle remained standing. I turned my dagger to her. "Lou is gone." I moved the blade—slowly, pointedly—from her face to the empty chair. "Morgane le Blanc took her. Why?"

Her eyes narrowed, flicking to the misshapen black symbols on the table. "If Morgane has indeed taken her—"

"Why?"

I inched the blade closer to her nose, and she frowned. "Please, Captain, this is no way to behave. I will tell you anything you wish to know."

Reluctantly, I lowered the knife as she dropped to a chair. My blood grew hotter with each tic of my jaw.

"Such an unfortunate turn of events." She glared up at me, smoothing her skirt in agitation. "I assume the witches revealed your wife's true identity. Louise le Blanc. The only child of La Dame des Sorcières."

I nodded stiffly.

Ansel cleared his throat before Madame Labelle could continue. "Begging your pardon, *madame*, but why have we never heard of Louise le Blanc before now?"

She cast him an appraising look. "Dear boy, Louise was Morgane's most jealously guarded secret. Even some of the witches didn't know of her existence."

"Then how did you?" Coco countered.

"I have many spies at the Chateau."

"You aren't welcome there yourself?"

"I'm as welcome there as you are, my dear."

"Why?" I asked.

She ignored me. Her gaze fell instead to Beau. "What do you know of your father, Your Highness?"

He leaned back and arched a dark brow. Thus far, he'd observed the proceedings with cool detachment, but Madame Labelle's question seemed to catch him by surprise. "The same as everyone else, I suppose."

"Which is?"

He shrugged. Rolled his eyes. "He's a notorious whoremonger. Despises his wife. Funds the toe-rag Archbishop's crusade against these magnificent creatures." He stroked Coco's spine appreciatively. "He's devilishly handsome, shit at politics, and a piss poor father. Should I go on . . . ? I fail to see how any of this is relevant."

"You would do well not to speak of him so." Her lips pursed angrily. "He's your father—and a good man."

Beau snorted. "You're certainly the first to think so."

She sniffed and smoothed her skirts again. Obviously still displeased. "It hardly matters. This is bigger than your father— though it will certainly end with him, if Morgane has her way."

"Explain," I growled.

She shot me an irritated look, but continued anyway. "This war is hundreds of years in the making. It's older than all of you. Older than me. Older than even Morgane. It started with a witch named Angelica and a holy man named Constantin."

A holy man named Constantin. She couldn't mean the man who'd forged the Sword of Balisarda. The saint.

"Lou told me this story!" Coco leaned forward, her eyes bright. "Angelica fell in love with him, but he died, and her tears made L'Eau Mélancolique."

"Half right, I'm afraid. Shall I tell you the true tale?" She paused, glancing up at me. Expectant. "I assure you we have time."

With a growl of impatience, I sat. "You have two minutes."

Madame Labelle nodded approvingly. "It's not a very pretty

story. Angelica did indeed fall in love with Constantin—a knight from a neighboring land—but she dared not tell him what she was. Her people lived in harmony with his, and she did not wish to upset the delicate balance between kingdoms. As so often happens, however, she soon longed for him to know her entirely. She told him of her people's magic, of their connection with the land, and at first, Constantin and his kingdom accepted her. They cherished her and her people—Les Dames Blanches, they called them. The White Ladies. Pure and bright. And as the purest and brightest of all, Angelica became the first Dame des Sorcières."

Her eyes darkened. "But as time passed, Constantin came to resent his lover's magic. He grew jealous and fitful with rage that he too did not possess it. He tried to take it from her. When he couldn't, he took the land instead. His soldiers marched on Belterra and slaughtered her people. But the magic didn't work for him and his brethren. Try as they might, they could not possess it—not as the witches did. Driven mad with desire, he eventually died by his own hand."

Her gaze found Coco's, and she smiled, small and grim. "Angelica wept her sea of tears and followed him into the afterlife. But his brethren lived on. They drove the witches into hiding and claimed the land—and its magic—for their own.

"You know the rest of the story. The blood feud rages to this day. Each side bitter—each side vindicated. Constantin's descendants continue to control this land, despite renouncing magic for religion years ago. With each new Dame des Sorcières, the witches attempt to marshal their forces, and with each attempt, the witches fail. Aside from being woefully outnumbered, my sisters cannot hope to defeat both the monarchy and the Church in combat—not with your Balisardas. But Morgane is different than those before her. She is more clever. Cunning."

"Sounds like Lou," Coco mused.

"Lou is *nothing* like that woman," I snarled.

Beau sat forward and glared around the table. "Forgive me, all, but I don't give a shit about Lou—or Morgane or Angelica or Constantin. Tell me about my father."

My knuckles turned white on my dagger.

Sighing, Madame Labelle patted my arm in silent warning. When I jerked away from her touch, she rolled her eyes. "I'm getting to him. Anyway—yes, Morgane is different. As a child, she recognized this kingdom's twofold power." She glanced to Beau. "When your father was crowned king, an idea took shape—a way to strike at both the crown and the Church. She watched as he married a foreign princess—your mother—and gave birth to you. She rejoiced as he left bastard after bastard in his wake."

She paused, deflating slightly. Even I watched with rapt attention as her eyes turned inward. "She learned their names, their faces—even those of which Auguste himself had no knowledge." Her faraway eyes met mine then, and my stomach contracted inexplicably. "With each child, her joyousness—her *obsession*—only grew, though she waited to reveal her purpose to us."

"How many?" Beau interrupted, voice sharp. "How many children?"

She hesitated before answering. "No one quite knows. I believe the last count was around twenty-six."

"Twenty-six?"

She hurried on before he could continue. "Shortly after your birth, Your Highness, Morgane announced to our sisters that she was with child. And not just any child—the Archbishop's child."

"Lou," I said, feeling vaguely sick.

"Yes. Morgane spoke of a pattern to free the witches from persecution, of a baby to end the Lyons' tyranny. Auguste Lyon would die . . . and so would all his descendants. The child in her womb was the price—a *gift*, she said—sent by the Goddess. The final strike against the kingdom and the Church."

"Why did Morgane wait to kill Lou?" I asked bitterly. "Why didn't she just kill her when she was born?"

"A witch receives her rites on her sixteenth birthday. It is the day she becomes a woman. Though the witches craved deliverance, most were uncomfortable with the thought of slaughtering a child. Morgane was content to wait."

"So Morgane . . . she only conceived Lou for vengeance." My heart twisted. I'd once felt sorry for my own miserable entrance into the world, but Lou—hers was a fate much worse. She'd literally been born to die.

"Nature demands balance," Coco whispered, tracing the cut on her palm. Lost in thought. "In order to end the king's line, Morgane must also end her own."

Madame Labelle nodded wearily.

"Jesus," Beau said. "Hell hath no fury."

"But . . ." I frowned. "It doesn't make sense. One life for twenty-six? That's not balanced."

Madame Labelle's brows knitted together. "Perception is a powerful thing. By killing Louise, Morgane will end the line of le Blanc forever. The magic of La Dame des Sorcières will pass on to another line when Morgane dies. Surely ending her own legacy is a worthy sacrifice to end another's?"

My frown only deepened. "But the numbers still don't add up."

"Your perception is too literal, Reid. Magic is nuanced. All of her children will die. All of his children will die." She picked at a nonexistent speck on her skirt. "Of course, this speculation doesn't matter. No one else can see the pattern, so we must use Morgane's interpretation."

Coco looked up suddenly, eyes narrowed. "What's your role in all this, *madame*? You tried to *buy* Lou."

"To protect her." Madame Labelle waved an impatient hand. I frowned at the movement. Gold bands covered her every finger, but there—on her left ring finger—

A mother-of-pearl ring. Nearly identical to the one I'd given Lou.

"I knew Morgane would find her eventually, but I did everything in my power to prevent that from happening. So, yes, I did attempt to *buy* Lou—as you so crassly phrased it—but only for her protection. Though not ideal, I could've watched her at the Bellerose. I could've kept her safe until other arrangements were made. Again and again she rebuffed my proposal, however."

She lifted her chin, meeting Coco's eyes. "Last year, my spies informed me Angelica's Ring had been stolen. I approached every known trafficker in the city—all of whom had family recently murdered by the witches."

I sat forward at this new information. Filippa. *Filippa* had been murdered by the witches. Which meant . . .

"When I learned Monsieur Tremblay had procured the ring, I finally saw my opportunity."

I closed my eyes. Shook my head in disbelief. In sorrow. Monsieur Tremblay. All these months, I'd focused on avenging their family, on punishing the witches who'd harmed them. But the witches had been avenging themselves.

My would-be father-in-law. A trafficker of magical objects. *He* had been the real cause of Filippa's death—of Célie's pain. But I forced myself to return to the present. To open my eyes.

There's a time for mourning, and there's a time for moving on.

"I knew Lou desperately sought it," Madame Labelle continued. "I instructed Babette to contact her, to assist her in eavesdropping on me and Tremblay. For her benefit, I even asked him where he had hidden it. And then—when Babette confirmed the two of you planned to steal it—I alerted the Archbishop where his daughter would be that night."

"You *what?*" Coco exclaimed.

She shrugged delicately. "It was rumored he'd been searching for her for years—many witches believed she was the reason he became so possessed with hunting us. He wanted to find her. I prefer to think he slaughtered us as some sort of macabre penance for his sin, but it matters not. I took a calculated risk he wouldn't harm her. He is her father, after all, and he could hardly deny it after seeing her. They're practically identical. And what better place to hide her than within Chasseur Tower?"

Coco shook her head, incredulous. "A little honesty would've gone a long way!"

Madame Labelle knitted her hands together on her knee, smiling in satisfaction. "When she escaped Tremblay's, I thought all was lost, but the scene at the theater forced the Archbishop's hand in a permanent way. Not only did she receive *his* protection, but she also received a husband's. And not just any husband—a captain of the Chasseurs." Her smile widened as she gestured to me. "It really worked out better than I could have ever—"

"Why?" I stared at the mother-of-pearl ring on her finger. "Why go to all the trouble? Why do you care if Auguste Lyon dies? You're a witch. You would only benefit from his death."

My gaze rose slowly to her face. Her red hair. Her widening blue eyes.

A memory resurfaced. Lou's voice echoed in my head.

Don't be ridiculous. Of course witches have sons.

Realization trickled in.

Her smile vanished. "I—I could never stand by and watch innocent people die—"

"The king is hardly innocent."

"The king will not be the only one affected. *Dozens* of people will die—"

"Like his children?"

"Yes. His children." She hesitated, glancing between me and

the prince. Damning herself. "There will be no surviving heirs. The aristocracy will divide itself fighting for succession. The Archbishop's credibility has already suffered—and his authority, if your presence here is any indication. I would be surprised if the king hasn't already demanded an audience. The Chasseurs will soon be leaderless. In the ensuing chaos, Morgane will strike."

I barely heard her words. The trickling realization became a flood. It coursed through me, further igniting the fury in my veins. "You fell in love with him, didn't you?"

Her voice shot up an octave. "Well—dear, it's a bit more complicated than—" My fist slammed on the tabletop, and she flinched. Shame mingled with my fury as her face fell in defeat. "Yes, I did."

Silence fell around the table. Her words washed over me. Through me. Beau's brows flattened in disbelief.

"You didn't tell him you were a witch." My words were hard, sharp, but I did nothing to soften them. This woman did not deserve my sympathy.

"No." She stared at her hands, lips pursing. "I didn't. I never told him what I was. I—I didn't want to lose him."

"Good Lord," Beau said under his breath.

"And Morgane . . . did she find you together?" Coco asked.

"No," Madame Labelle said softly. "But . . . I soon became pregnant, and I—I made the mistake of confiding in her. We were friends, once. Best friends. Closer than sisters. I thought she would understand." She swallowed and closed her eyes. Her chin quivered. "I was a fool. She tore him from my arms when he was born—my beautiful baby boy. I never told Auguste."

Beau's face contorted with disgust. "You birthed a sibling of mine?"

Coco elbowed him sharply. "What happened to him?"

Madame Labelle's eyes remained shut. As if she couldn't bear to look at us—at me. "I never knew. Most male babies are placed within caring homes—or orphanages, if the child is unlucky—but I knew Morgane would never bestow such a kindness on my son. I knew she would punish him for what I'd done—for what Auguste had done." She exhaled shakily. When her eyes fluttered open, she looked directly at me. "I searched for him for years, but he was lost to me."

Lost. My face twisted. That was one way of putting it.

Another would be: *stuffed in the garbage and left to die.*

She winced at the loathing on my face. "Perhaps he will always be lost to me."

"Yes." Hatred burned through my very core. "He will."

I shoved to my feet, ignoring the others' curious looks. "We've wasted too much time here. Lou could already be half-way to Chateau le Blanc. You"—I pointed my dagger at Madame Labelle—"will take me there."

"*Us* there," Ansel said. "I'm coming too."

Coco stood. "As am I."

Beau grimaced as he too rose from his seat. "I suppose that means I'm coming as well. If Lou dies, *I* die, apparently."

"Fine," I snapped. "But we leave now. Lou is miles ahead of

us already. We have to make up time, or she'll be dead before we reach the Chateau."

"She won't be." Madame Labelle stood also, wiping the tears from her cheeks. Squaring her shoulders. "Morgane will wait to perform the sacrifice. At least a fortnight."

"Why?" Though I wanted nothing more than to never speak to this woman again, she was my only path to Lou. A necessary evil. "How do you know this?"

"I know Morgane. Her pride suffered terribly when Lou escaped the first time, so she will ensure as many witches as possible are present to witness her triumph. To the witches, Christmas Eve is Modraniht. Already, witches from all over the kingdom are traveling to the Chateau for the celebration." She skewered me with a pointed look. "Modraniht is a night to honor their mothers. Morgane will delight in the irony."

"How fortunate I don't have one." Ignoring her wounded expression, I turned on my heel and walked past the empty-eyed dancers and drunken men to the exit. "We reconvene here in an hour. Make sure you aren't followed."

THE SOUL REMEMBERS

Lou

The wooden floor beneath me pitched abruptly, and I fell into someone's lap. Soft arms enveloped me, along with the cool, crisp scent of eucalyptus. I froze. The smell had haunted my nightmares for the past two years.

My eyes burst open as I attempted to jerk away, but—to my horror—my body didn't respond. Paralyzed, I had no choice but to stare into my mother's vivid green eyes. She smiled and brushed a kiss against my forehead. My skin crawled.

"I've missed you, darling."

"What have you done to me?"

She paused, laughing softly. "Extraordinary, those little injections. When Monsieur Bernard brought one to me, I perfected the medicine. I like to think my version is more humane. Only your body is affected, not your mind." Her smile widened. "I thought you'd enjoy a little taste of your friends' medicine. They worked so hard to create it for you."

The floor lurched again, and I glanced around, finally

registering my surroundings. The covered troupe wagon. No light filtered through the thick canvas, so I couldn't discern how long we'd been traveling. I strained my ears, but the steady *clip-clops* of horse hooves were the only sounds. We'd left the city.

It didn't matter. No help would be coming. Reid had made that much clear.

Grief swept through me in a debilitating wave as I remembered his parting words. Though I tried to hide it, a solitary tear still escaped down my cheek. Morgane's finger wiped it away, bringing it to her mouth to taste it. "My beautiful, darling girl. I'll never allow him to hurt you again. It would be fitting to watch him burn for what he's done to you, yes? Perhaps I can arrange for you to light his pyre yourself. Would that make you happy?"

The blood drained from my face. "Don't touch him."

She arched a white brow. "You have forgotten he is your enemy, Louise. But fret not . . . all will be forgiven at Modraniht. We'll arrange your husband's burning before our little celebration." She paused, giving me the chance to bite and snap at the mention of Reid. I refused. I wouldn't give her the satisfaction.

"You remember the holiday, don't you? I thought we would make it special this year."

A tendril of fear crept through me. Yes, I remembered Modraniht.

Mothers' Night. Dames Blanches from all over Belterra would gather at the Chateau to feast and honor their female ancestors with sacrifices. I had little doubt what my role would be this year.

As if reading my thoughts, she touched my throat affectionately. I gasped, remembering the burst of pain in my scar before I'd collapsed. She chuckled. "Do not worry yourself. I've healed your wound. I couldn't waste any of that precious blood before we reached the Chateau." Her hair tickled my face as she leaned closer, right next to my ear. "It was a clever bit of magic, and difficult to deconstruct, but even it won't save you this time. We're almost home."

"That place is not my home."

"You've always been so dramatic." Still chuckling, she reached forward to flick my nose, and my heart stopped at the sight of the golden ring on her finger. She followed my gaze with a knowing smile. "Ah, yes. And naughty, too."

"How did you—" Choking on the words, I struggled against the injection binding me, but my limbs remained cruelly unresponsive.

Morgane couldn't have Angelica's Ring. She *couldn't*. I needed it to dispel her enchantment. If I wore it when she drained my blood, the blood would be useless. The magic would be broken. I would die, yes, but the Lyons would live. Those *innocent children* would live.

I struggled harder, the veins in my throat nearly bursting from the strain. But the more I fought, the more difficult it became to speak—to breathe—around the heaviness of my body. My limbs felt as if they would soon fall through the wagon floor. Panicked, I focused on bringing a pattern forth—*any* pattern— but the gold winked in and out of focus, blurred and disjointed from the drug.

I cursed bitterly, my resolve quickly crumbling into hopelessness.

"Did you really think I wouldn't recognize my own ring?" Morgane smiled tenderly and brushed a lock of hair behind my ear. "You must tell me, though, however did you find it? Or was it *you* who stole it in the first place?" When I didn't answer, she sighed heavily. "How you disappoint me, darling. The running, the hiding, the ring—surely you realize it's all folly."

Her smile vanished as she lifted my chin, and her eyes burned into mine with sudden, predatory focus. "For every seed you've scattered, Louise, I've scattered a thousand more. You are my daughter. I know you better than you know yourself. You cannot outsmart me, you cannot escape me, and you cannot hope to triumph against me."

She paused as if waiting for a reply, but I didn't indulge her. With every ounce of my concentration, I focused on moving my hand, on shifting my wrist, on lifting even a finger. Darkness swam in my vision from the effort. She watched me struggle for several minutes—the intensity in her eyes dulling to a strange sort of wistfulness—before she resumed stroking my hair. "We must all die eventually, Louise. I urge you to make peace with it. On Modraniht, your life will fulfill its purpose at last, and your death will liberate our people. You should be proud. Not many receive such a glorious fate."

With one last, desperate heave, I attempted to lash out at her—to strike her, to *hurt* her, to tear the ring from her finger somehow—but my body remained cold and lifeless.

Already dead.

My days passed in torment. Though the drug paralyzed my body, it did nothing to dull the ache in my bones. My face and wrist continued to throb from the witch's attack, and a hard knot had formed at my throat from being stabbed by so many quills.

To think, Andre and Grue had once been the worst of my problems.

Morgane's pale fingers traced the knot, circling to the finger-shaped bruises beneath my ear. "Friends of yours, darling?"

I scowled and focused on the burning sensation in my hands and feet—the first indicator of the drug waning. If I were quick, I could snatch Angelica's Ring and roll from the wagon, disappearing before Morgane reacted. "Once."

"And now?"

I tried to wiggle my fingers. They remained limp. "Dead."

As if sensing my thoughts, Morgane withdrew the familiar steel syringe from her bag. I closed my eyes, trying and failing to prevent my chin from quivering. "Your sisters will heal your body when we reach the Chateau. These ghastly bruises must be gone before Modraniht. You will be wholesome and pure again." She massaged the knot on my throat, preparing it for the quill. "Fair as the Maiden."

My eyes snapped open. "I'm hardly a maiden."

Her saccharine smile faltered. "You didn't actually *lie* with that filthy huntsman?" Sniffing delicately, she wrinkled her nose in disgust. "Oh, Louise. How disappointing. I can smell him all over you." Her eyes flicked to my abdomen, and she cocked her head, inhaling deeper. "I *do* hope you took precautions, darling.

The Mother is alluring, but her path is not yours."

My fingers twitched in agitation. "Don't pretend you're above slaughtering a grandchild."

She sank the quill deep into my throat in response. I bit my cheek to keep from screaming as my fingers grew heavy once more.

"Thy blood is the price." She caressed my throat longingly. "Your womb is empty, Louise. *You* are the last of my line. It's almost a shame . . ." She bent down, brushing her lips against my scar. Déjà vu swooped sickeningly through my stomach as I remembered Reid kissing the same spot only days ago. "I think I would've enjoyed killing the huntsman's baby."

"Wake up, darling."

I blinked awake to Morgane's whisper in my ear. Though I had no way of knowing how much time had passed—whether minutes, hours, or days—the wagon's cover had finally been discarded, and night had fallen. I didn't bother trying to sit up.

Morgane pointed to something in the distance anyway. "We're almost home."

I could see only the stars above me, but the familiar, crashing sound of waves on rock told me enough. The very *air* here told me enough. It was different than the fishy air I'd suffered in Cesarine: crisp and sharp, infused with pine needles and salt and earth . . . and just a hint of magic. I inhaled deeply, closing my eyes. Despite everything, my stomach still flipped at being this close. At finally returning home.

Within minutes, the wheels of the wagon clicked against the wooden slats of a bridge.

The bridge.

The legendary entrance to Chateau le Blanc.

I listened harder. Soft, nearly indiscernible laughter soon echoed around us, and the wind picked up, swirling snow into the cold night air. It would've been eerie had I not known it was all an elaborate production. Morgane had a flair for the dramatic.

She needn't have bothered. Only a witch could find the Chateau. An ancient and powerful magic surrounded the castle—a magic to which each Dame des Sorcières had contributed for thousands of years. I would've been expected to strengthen the enchantment myself someday if things had been different.

I glanced up at Morgane, who smiled and waved to the white-clad women now running barefoot alongside the wagon. They left no footprints in the snow. Silent specters.

"Sisters," she greeted warmly.

I scowled. These were the infamous guardians of the bridge. Actors in Morgane's production—though they *did* enjoy luring the occasional man to the bridge at night.

And drowning him in the murky waters below.

"Darling, look." Morgane propped me up in her arms. "It's Manon. You remember her, don't you? You were inseparable as witchlings."

My cheeks burned as my head lolled onto my shoulder. Worse, Manon was indeed there to witness my humiliation, her dark eyes bright with excitement as she ran. As she smiled joyously and showered the wagon with winter jasmine.

Jasmine. A symbol of love.

Tears burned behind my eyes. I wanted to cry—to cry and rage and burn the Chateau and all its inhabitants to the ground. They'd claimed to love me, once. But then . . . so had Reid.

Love.

I cursed the word.

Manon reached for the wagon and pulled herself up. A garland of holly rested atop her head; the red berries looked like drops of blood against her black hair and skin. "Louise! You've finally returned!" She threw her arms around my neck, and my limp body fell against hers. "I feared I'd never see you again."

"Manon has volunteered to accompany you at the Chateau," Morgane said. "Isn't that lovely? You'll have such fun together."

"I sincerely doubt that," I muttered.

Manon's ebony face fell. "Did you not miss me? We were sisters once."

"Do you often try to murder your sisters?" I snapped.

Manon had the decency to flinch, but Morgane only pinched my cheek. "Louise, stop being naughty. It's dreadfully dull." She lifted her hand to Manon, who hesitated, glancing at me, before hurrying to kiss it. "Now run along, child, and prepare a bath in Louise's room. We must rid her of this blood and stench."

"Of course, my Lady." Manon kissed my limp hands, transferred me back to Morgane's lap, and leapt from the wagon. I waited until she'd melted into the night before speaking.

"Drop the pretense. I don't want company—her or anyone else. Just post guards at my door, and be done with it."

Morgane picked the jasmine blooms from the wagon floor and wove them through my hair. "How incredibly rude. She's your sister, Louise, and desires to spend time with you. What a poor way to repay her love."

There was that word again.

"So, according to you, *love* made her watch as I was chained to an altar?"

"You resent her. How interesting." Her fingers raked through my tangled hair, braiding it away from my face. "Perhaps if it had instead been the stake, you would've married her."

My stomach twisted. "Reid never hurt me."

For all his faults, for all his prejudice, he hadn't lifted a finger against me after the witch attacked. He could've, but he hadn't. I wondered now what might've happened if I'd stayed. *Would* he have tied me to the stake? Perhaps he would've been kinder and driven a blade through my heart instead.

But he'd already done that.

"Love makes fools of us all, darling."

Though I knew she was goading me, I couldn't keep my mouth shut. "What do you know about love? Have you ever loved anyone but yourself?"

"Careful," she said silkily, fingers stilling in my hair. "Do not forget to whom you are speaking."

But I wasn't feeling careful. No, as the great white silhouette of the Chateau took shape above me—and Angelica's Ring glinted on her finger—I was feeling precisely the *opposite* of careful.

"I'm your daughter," I said angrily, recklessly. "And you would sacrifice me like some prized cow—"

She wrenched my head back. "A very loud, disrespectful cow."

"I know you think this is the only way." My voice grew desperate now, choked with emotions I didn't care to examine. Emotions I'd locked away tight when I'd grown old enough to realize my mother's plan for me. "But it's not. I've lived with the Chasseurs. They're capable of change—of tolerance. I've seen it. We can show them another way. We can show them we aren't what they believe us to be—"

"You have been corrupted, *daughter.*" She enunciated the last word with a sharp tug to my hair. Pain radiated across my scalp, but I didn't care. Morgane had to see. She had to *understand.* "I feared this would happen. They've poisoned your mind as they've poisoned our homeland." She jerked my chin up. "Look at them, Louise—look at your people."

I had no choice but to gaze at the witches still dancing around us. Some faces I recognized. Others I didn't. All regarded me with unadulterated joy. Morgane pointed to a set of sisters with brown skin and braided hair. "Rosemund and Sacha—their mother burned after delivering an aristocrat's breech baby. They were six and four."

She pointed to a small, olive-skinned woman with silver marks disfiguring half her face. "Viera Beauchêne escaped after they tried to burn her and her wife—acid this time instead of flame. An experiment." She gestured to another. "Genevieve left our homeland with her three daughters to marry a clergyman, severing their connection to our ancestors. Her middle daughter soon sickened. When she begged her husband to return here to heal her, he refused. Her daughter died. Her eldest and youngest despise her now."

Her fingers gripped my chin hard enough to bruise. "Tell me again about their tolerance, Louise. Tell me again about the monsters you call friends. Tell me about your time with them—about how you spit on your sisters' suffering."

"*Maman*, please." Tears leaked down my face. "I know they've wronged us—and I know you hate them—and I *understand*. But you cannot do this. We can't change the past, but we *can* move forward and heal—together. We can share this land. No one else needs to die."

She only gripped my chin harder, leaning down next to my ear. "You are *weak*, Louise, but do not fear. I will not falter. I will not hesitate. I will make them suffer as we have suffered."

Releasing me, she straightened with a deep breath, and I toppled to the wagon floor. "The Lyons will rue the day they stole this land. Their people will writhe and thrash on the stake, and the king and his children will choke on your blood. Your *husband* will choke on your blood."

Confusion flared briefly before hideous despair consumed me, obliterating all rational thought. This was my mother—my *mother*—and these were her people. That was my husband, and those were his. Each side despicable—a twisted perversion of what should've been. Each side suffering. Each side capable of great evil.

And then there was me.

The salt of my tears mingled with the jasmine in my hair, two sides of the same wretched coin. "And what of me, *Maman*? Did you ever love me?"

She frowned, her eyes more black than green in the darkness. "It matters not."

"It matters to me!"

"Then you are a fool," she said coldly. "Love is a nothing but a disease. This desperation you have to be loved—it is a sickness. I can see in your eyes how it consumes you, weakens you. Already it has corrupted your spirit. You long for his love as you long for mine, but you will have neither. You've chosen your path." Her lip curled. "Of course I do not love you, Louise. You are the daughter of my enemy. You were conceived for a higher purpose, and I will not poison that purpose with *love*. With your birth, I struck the Church. With your death, I strike the crown. Both will soon fall."

"*Maman*—"

"*Enough*." The word was quiet, deadly. A warning. "We will reach the Chateau soon."

Unable to endure the cruel indifference on my mother's face, I closed my eyes in defeat. I soon wished I hadn't. Another face lingered behind my eyelids, taunting me.

You are not my wife.

If this agony was love, perhaps Morgane was right. Perhaps I was better off without it.

Chateau le Blanc stood atop a cliff overlooking the sea. True to its name, the castle had been built of white stone that shone in the moonlight like a beacon. I gazed at it longingly, eyes tracing the narrow, tapering towers that mingled with the stars. There—on

the tallest western turret, overlooking the rocky beach below—
was my childhood room. My heart lurched into my mouth.

When the wagon creaked to the gatehouse, I lowered my
gaze. The le Blanc family signet had been carved into the ancient
doors: a crow with three eyes. One for the Maiden, one for the
Mother, and one for the Crone.

I'd always hated that dirty old bird.

Dread crept through me as the doors closed behind us with
ringing finality. Silence cloaked the snowy courtyard, but I knew
witches lingered just out of sight. I could feel their eyes on me—
probing, assessing. The very air tingled with their presence.

"Manon will accompany you day and night until Modraniht.
Should you attempt to flee," Morgane warned, eyes cold and
cruel, "I will butcher your huntsman and feed you his heart. Do
you understand?"

Fear froze the scathing reply on my tongue.

She nodded with a sleek smile. "Your silence is golden, darling. I cherish it in our conversations." Turning her attention to
an alcove out of my sight, she shouted something. Within seconds, two hunched women I vaguely recognized emerged. My
old nursemaids. "Accompany her to her room, please, and assist
Manon while she sees to her wounds."

They both nodded fervently. One stepped forward and cupped
my face in her withered palms. "At last you have returned, *maî-
tresse*. We have waited so long."

"Only three days remain," the other crooned, kissing my hand,
"until you may join the Goddess in the Summerland."

"Three?" I glanced to Morgane in alarm.

"Yes, darling. Three. Soon, you will fulfill your destiny. Our sisters will feast and dance in your honor forevermore."

Destiny. Honor.

It sounded so lovely, phrased like that, as if I were receiving a fabulous prize with a shiny red bow. A hysterical giggle burst from my lips. The blood would be red, at least.

One of the nursemaids tilted her head in concern. "Are you quite all right?"

I had just enough self-awareness left to know I was most certainly *not* all right.

Three days. That was all I had left. I laughed harder.

"Louise." Morgane snapped her fingers in front of my nose. "Is something funny?"

I blinked, my laughter dying as abruptly as it'd started. In three days, I'd be dead. *Dead*. The steady pounding of my heartbeat, the cold night air on my face—it would all cease to exist. *I* would cease to exist—at least, in the way I was now. With freckled skin and blue-green eyes and this terrible ache in my belly.

"No." My eyes rose to the clear night sky above us, where the stars stretched on for eternity. To think, I'd once thought this view better than Soleil et Lune's. "Nothing is funny."

I'd never laugh with Coco again. Or tease Ansel. Or eat sticky buns at Pan's or scale Soleil et Lune to watch the sunrise. Were there sunrises in the afterlife? Would I have eyes to see them if there were?

I didn't know, and it frightened me. I tore my gaze from the stars, tears clinging to my lashes.

In three days, I would be parted from Reid forever. The

moment my soul left my body, we would be permanently separated . . . for where I was going, I was certain Reid couldn't follow. This was what frightened me most.

Where you go, I will go. Where you stay, I will stay.

But there was no place for a huntsman in the Summerland, and there was no place for a witch in Heaven. If either place even existed.

Would my soul remember him? A small part of me prayed I wouldn't, but the rest knew better. I loved him. Deeply. Such a love was not something of just the heart and mind. It wasn't something to be felt and eventually forgotten, to be touched without it in return touching you. No . . . this love was something else. Something irrevocable. It was something of the soul.

I knew I would remember him. I would feel his absence even after death, would ache for him to be near me in a way he could never be again. *This* was my destiny—eternal torment. As much as it hurt to think of him, I would bear the pain gladly to keep even a small part of him with me. The pain meant we'd been real.

Death couldn't take him away from me. He *was* me. Our souls were bound. Even if he didn't want me, even if I cursed his name, we were one.

I became vaguely aware of two sets of arms around me, carrying me away. Where they took me, I didn't care. Reid wouldn't be there.

And yet . . . he would be.

HARBINGER

Reid

"I'm freezing," Beau moaned bitterly.

We'd camped within a grove of ancient, gnarled pines in La Forêt des Yeux. Clouds obscured whatever light the moon and stars may have provided. Fog clung to our coats and blankets. Heavy. Unnatural.

The snow on the ground had soaked through my pants. I shivered, glancing around the company. They too were feeling the effects of the cold: Beau's teeth chattered violently, Ansel's lips slowly turned blue, and Coco's mouth was stained with rabbit blood. I tried not to stare at the dead carcass at her feet. And failed miserably.

Noticing my stare, she shrugged and said, "Their blood runs hotter than ours."

Unable to keep quiet, Ansel scooted toward her. "Do you—do you always use animal blood for magic?"

She scrutinized him a moment before answering. "Not always. Different enchantments require different additives. Just like each Dame Blanche senses unique patterns, each Dame Rouge senses unique additives. Lavender petals might induce sleep, but so might bat blood or tart cherries or a million other things. It depends on the witch."

"So—" Ansel blinked in confusion, his face scrunching as he glanced at the rabbit carcass. "So you just *eat* the tart cherries? Or . . . ?"

Coco laughed, lifting her sleeve to show him the scars crisscrossing her skin. "My magic lives inside my blood, Ansel. Tart cherries are just tart cherries without it." She frowned then, as if worried she'd said too much. Ansel wasn't the only one listening intently. Both Madame Labelle and Beau had been hanging on her every word, and—to my shame—I too had inched closer. "Why the sudden interest?"

Ansel looked away, cheeks coloring. "I just wanted to know more about you." Unable to resist, his gaze returned to her face seconds later. "Do—do all the blood witches look like you?"

She arched a brow in wry amusement. "Are they all breathtakingly beautiful, you mean?" He nodded, eyes wide and earnest, and she chuckled. "Of course not. We come in all shapes and colors, just like the Dames Blanches—and Chasseurs."

Her eyes flicked to mine then, and I looked away hastily.

Beau moaned again. "I can't feel my toes."

"Yes, you've mentioned that," Madame Labelle snapped, scooting her log closer to me. To my great irritation, she'd affixed herself to my side for the journey. She seemed intent on making me as uncomfortable as possible. "Several times, in fact, but we're *all* cold. Grousing about it hardly helps."

"A fire would," he grumbled.

"No," she repeated firmly. "No fires."

As loath as I was to admit it, I agreed. Fires brought unwanted attention. All sorts of malevolent creatures roamed these woods. Already a misshapen black cat had started following us—a harbinger of misfortune. Though it kept a wide distance, it had crept into our packs the first night and eaten nearly all our food.

As if in response, Ansel's stomach gave a mighty gurgle. Resigned, I pulled the last hunk of cheese from my pack and tossed it to him. He opened his mouth to protest, but I cut him short. "Just eat it."

A morose silence fell over the company as he complied. Though it was very late, no one slept. It was too cold. Coco moved closer to Ansel, offering some of her blanket to him. He buried his hands in it with a groan. Beau scowled.

"We're very close now," Madame Labelle said to no one in particular. "Only a few more days."

"Modraniht is in three," Beau pointed out. "If we don't starve or freeze to death first."

"Our arrival will be close," Madame Labelle admitted.

"We're wasting time," I said. "We should continue on. No one is sleeping anyway."

Only a few hours into our journey, Madame Labelle had uncovered two witches tailing us. Scouts. Coco and I had dispatched them easily, but Madame Labelle had insisted we chart a new course.

"The road is being watched," she'd said darkly. "Morgane wants no surprises."

Seeing no alternative that didn't involve slaughtering Lou's kin, I'd been forced to agree.

Madame Labelle glanced to where the black cat had reappeared. It wove between the pine branches nearest her. "No. We remain here. It is unwise to travel these woods at night."

Beau followed our gazes. His eyes narrowed, and he lurched to his feet. "I'm going to kill that cat."

"I wouldn't," Madame Labelle warned. He hesitated, scowl deepening. "Things are not always as they appear in this forest, Your Highness."

He dropped back to the ground in a huff. "Stop calling me that. I'm freezing my ass off out here, same as you. Nothing *high* about it—"

He stopped abruptly as Coco's head snapped up. Her eyes locked on something behind me.

"What is it?" Ansel whispered.

She ignored him, pushing off her blanket and moving to my side. She glanced at me in silent warning.

I rose slowly to my feet.

The forest was still. Too still. Tendrils of fog curled around us in the silence . . . watching, waiting. Every nerve in my body tingled. Warned me we were no longer alone. A twig snapped somewhere ahead of us, and I sank into a crouch, creeping closer and brushing aside a pine branch to peer into the darkness. Coco shadowed my movements.

There—a stone's throw away from us—marched a squadron of twenty Chasseurs. They moved silently through the fog, Balisardas drawn. Eyes sharp. Muscles tense. Recognition razed through me at the short, dark hair of the man leading them.

Jean Luc.

The bastard.

As if sensing our gaze, his eyes flicked toward us, and we shrank back hastily. "Stop," he murmured, his voice carrying to my brethren in the eerie silence. They halted immediately, and he drifted closer, pointing his Balisarda in our direction. "There's something there."

Three Chasseurs moved forward to investigate at his command. I unsheathed my own Balisarda slowly, silently, unsure what to do with it. Jean Luc couldn't know we were here. He would try to detain us, or worse—follow us. I gripped my knife tighter. Could I truly harm my brothers? Disarming them was one thing, but . . . there were too many. Disarming wouldn't be enough. Perhaps I could distract them long enough for the others to escape.

Before I could decide, the black cat brushed past me, yowling loudly.

Shit. Coco and I both made to grab it, but it darted out of our reach, heading straight toward the Chasseurs. The three in front nearly leapt out of their skin before chuckling and bending to scratch its head. "It's just a cat, Chasseur Toussaint."

Jean Luc watched it weave between their ankles with suspicion. "Nothing is *just* anything in La Fôret des Yeux." Hearing a disgruntled sigh, he waved the Chasseurs onward. "The Chateau could be near. Keep your eyes sharp, men, and your knives sharper."

I waited several minutes until daring to breathe. Until their footsteps had long faded. Until the fog swirled undisturbed once more. "That was too close."

Madame Labelle clasped her fingers together and leaned forward on her stump. The cat—our unexpected savior—rubbed its head against her feet, and she bent to give it an appreciative pat. "I would argue it wasn't close enough."

"What do you mean?"

"We don't know what awaits us at the Chateau, Captain Diggory. Surely there is strength in numbers—"

"No." I shook my head, unwilling to hear more, and stalked back to my spot against the tree. "They'll kill Lou."

Danger averted, Ansel burrowed deeper in his blanket. "I don't think the Archbishop would let them. She's his daughter."

"And the others?" I remembered Jean Luc's frightening smile, the way his eyes had glinted with secret knowledge. Had he told our brethren, or had he kept it to himself, content in his new position of power? Waiting to reveal the information until it best suited him? "If any suspect she's a witch, they won't hesitate. Can you guarantee her safety from them?"

"But the Archbishop warned them," Ansel argued. "He said if she died, we would all die. No one would risk harming her after that."

"Unless they know the truth." Rubbing her arms against the

chill, Coco sat back down beside him. He offered her half the blanket, and she wrapped it around her shoulders. "If Lou were to die before the ceremony, there would *be* no ceremony. There would be no danger. The royal family would be safe, and a witch would be dead. They'd kill her just to be rid of her blood."

Madame Labelle scoffed. "As if the Archbishop would ever incriminate himself with the truth. I'd bet my beauty he hasn't told them she's a witch. Not after Ye Olde Sisters. The implication would be too damning—not that it matters. Auguste will be forced to reprimand him regardless, which is probably why he and his merry band of bigots took to the forest so quickly. He's postponing the inevitable."

I hardly heard her. Jean Luc's smile taunted my mind's eye. He was close. Too close.

Keep your eyes sharp, men, and your knives sharper.

Scowling, I stood once more and began to pace. Touched each knife in my bandolier, the Balisarda against my heart. "Jean Luc knows."

"Isn't he your best friend?" Coco's eyebrows knitted together. "Would he really kill the woman you love?"

"Yes. No." I shook my head, rubbing a frozen hand across my neck. Restless. "I don't know. I won't risk it either way."

Madame Labelle sighed impatiently. "Don't be obstinate, dear. We'll be grossly outnumbered without them. Between the five of us, I'm sure we'll be able to whisk Lou away before this Jean Luc can touch her—"

"No." I silenced her with a curt swipe of my hand. "I said I won't risk it. This conversation is over."

Her eyes narrowed, but she said nothing. Wisely. Bending low to scratch the cat's ear, she muttered something under her breath instead. The creature stilled—almost as if it were listening—before slinking away into the fog.

DRIFTING

Lou

I woke to Manon stroking my hair. "Hello, Louise."

Though I tried to jerk away, my body didn't so much as twitch. Worse—stars dotted my vision, and the world spun around me. Forcing myself to breathe deeply, I focused on a golden leaf directly above my head. It was one of the many metallic blooms that crept across my ceiling and rustled in the breeze. Despite the open window, the room remained balmy and warm, each flake of snow swirling into silver glitter as it crossed the sill.

I'd once called it moondust. Morgane had gifted it to me on a particularly cold Samhain.

"Careful." Manon pressed a cool cloth against my forehead. "Your body is still weak. Morgane said you haven't eaten properly in days."

Her words spiked through my pounding head, accompanied by another dizzying wave of nausea. I would've gladly never eaten again for her to shut up. Scowling, I fixated on the golden light inching steadily across the room. It was morning, then. Two days left.

"Something wrong?" Manon asked.

"If I could move, I'd puke all over your lap."

She clucked sympathetically. "Morgane said you might have an adverse reaction to the medicine. It's not meant for such prolonged use."

"Is that what you call it? Medicine? That's an interesting word for poison."

She didn't answer, but the next moment, she waved a blueberry oatmeal muffin under my nose. I closed my eyes and resisted the urge to gag. "Go away."

"You need to eat, Lou." Ignoring my protests, she sank onto the edge of the bed and offered me a tentative smile. "I even made a chocolate hazelnut spread—with sugar this time, not the beastly kind I used to make with salt."

When we were children, Manon and I had loved nothing more than playing tricks, usually involving food. Cookies with salt instead of sugar. Caramel onions instead of apples. Mint paste instead of icing.

I didn't return her smile.

She sighed and touched a hand to my forehead in response. Though I strained to jerk away, the effort was in vain, and my head swam sickeningly. I focused on the leaf again, on breathing in through my nose and out through my mouth. Just like Reid had done when he needed to regain control.

Reid.

I closed my eyes miserably. Without Angelica's Ring, I couldn't protect anyone. The Lyons would die. The Church would fall.

The witches would crush the kingdom. I could only hope Reid and Ansel escaped the fallout. Perhaps Coco could help them—they could sail far away from Belterra, across the sea to Amaris or Lustere . . .

But I would still die. I'd made an odd sort of peace with my fate last night while the castle slept. Even if Morgane hadn't poisoned me—even if she hadn't ordered guards outside my door—I had no doubt she'd keep her promise if I somehow managed to escape. Bile rose to my throat at the thought of tasting Reid's blood. Of choking on his heart. I closed my eyes and willed back the sense of calm I'd conjured last night.

I was tired of running. Tired of hiding. I was just . . . *tired*.

As if sensing my growing distress, Manon lifted her hands in invitation. "I might be able to help with the pain."

Stomach rolling, I glared at her for only a moment before conceding. She set to examining my various injuries with gentle fingers, and I closed my eyes. After a moment, she asked, "Where did you go? After you fled the Chateau?"

I opened my eyes reluctantly. "Cesarine."

With a wave of her fingers, the pounding in my head and gnawing ache in my stomach eased infinitesimally.

"And how did you stay hidden? From the Chasseurs . . . from us?"

"I sold my soul."

She gasped, lifting a hand to her mouth in horror. "What?"

I rolled my eyes and clarified. "I became a thief, Manon. I squatted in dirty theaters and stole food from innocent bakers.

I did bad things to good people. I killed. I lied and cheated and smoked and drank and even slept with a prostitute once. So it amounts to the same thing. I'll burn in hell either way."

At her stunned expression, anger flared hot and insistent in my chest. Damn her and her judgment. Damn her and her *questions.*

I didn't want to talk about this. I didn't want to remember. That life—the things I'd done to survive, the people I'd loved and lost in the process—it was gone. Just like my life at the Chateau. Burned to nothing but black ash and blacker memory.

"Anything else?" I asked bitterly. "By all means, let's continue catching up. We're such great friends, after all. Are you still bedding Madeleine? How's your sister? I assume she's still prettier than you?"

As soon as the words left my mouth, I knew they'd been the wrong things to say. Her expression hardened, and she dropped her hands, inhaling sharply as if I'd stabbed her. Guilt trickled through me despite my anger. Damn it. *Damn* it.

"Don't get me wrong," I added grudgingly, "she's prettier than me too—"

"She's dead."

My anger froze into something dark and premonitory at her words. Something cold.

"The Chasseurs found her last year." Manon picked at a spot on my bedspread, pain shimmering hard and bright in her eyes. "The Archbishop was visiting Amandine. Fleur knew to be careful, but . . . her friend in the village had broken his arm. She healed him. It didn't take long for the Chasseurs to notice the smell. Fleur panicked and ran."

I couldn't breathe.

"They burned her. Eleven years old." She shook her head, closing her eyes as if fighting against an onslaught of images. "I couldn't reach her in time, nor could our mother. We wept as the wind carried her ashes away."

Eleven. Burned alive.

She gripped my hand suddenly, eyes shining with fierce, unshed tears. "You have a chance to right the wrongs of this world, Lou. How could you turn away from such an opportunity?"

"So you'd still have me die." The words left me without heat, as empty and emotionless as the chasm in my chest.

"I would die a thousand deaths to get my sister back," Manon said harshly. Relinquishing my hand, she loosed an uneven breath, and when she spoke again, her voice was much softer. "I would take your place if I could, *ma sœur*—any of us would. But we can't. It has to be you."

The tears spilled down her cheeks now. "I know it's too much to ask. I know I have no right—but please, Lou. *Please* don't flee again. You're the only one who can end this. You're the only one who can save us. Promise me you won't try to escape."

I watched her tears as if from another's body. A heaviness settled through me that had nothing to do with injections. It pressed against my chest, my nose, my mouth—suffocating me, pulling me under, tempting me with oblivion. With surrender. With rest.

God, I was tired.

The words left my lips of their own volition. "I promise."

"You—you do?"

"I do." Despite the gentle pressure, the coaxing darkness, I forced myself to meet her eyes. They shone with a hope so clear and sharp it might've cut me. "I'm sorry, Manon. I never meant for anyone to die. When it—after it happens—I—I promise to look for Fleur in the afterlife—wherever it is. And if I find her, I'll tell her how much you miss her. How much you love her."

Her tears fell faster now, and she clasped my hands between her own, squeezing tight. "Thank you, Lou. *Thank you*. I'll never forget what you've done for me. For us. All of this pain will be over soon."

All of this pain will be over soon.

I longed to sleep.

I had little to do over the next two days but drift into darkness.

I'd been buffed and polished to perfection, every mark and memory of the past two years erased from my body. A perfect corpse. My nursemaids arrived each morning at dawn to help Manon bathe and dress me, but with each sunrise, they spoke less.

"She's dying right before our eyes," one had finally muttered, unable to ignore the increasing hollowness of my eyes, the sickly pallor of my skin. Manon had shooed her from the room.

I supposed it was true. I felt more connected with Estelle and Fleur than I did with Manon and my nursemaids. Already, I had one foot in the afterlife. Even the pain in my head and stomach had dulled—still there, still inhibiting, but somehow...removed. As if I existed apart from it.

"It's time to get dressed, Lou." Manon stroked my hair, her dark eyes deeply troubled. I didn't attempt to move away from her touch. I didn't even blink. I only continued my unending stare at the ceiling. "Tonight is the night."

She lifted my nightgown over my head and bathed me quickly, but she avoided truly looking at me. A fortnight of inadequate eating on the road had forced my bones to protrude. I was gaunt. A living skeleton.

The silence stretched on as she stuffed my limbs into the white ceremonial gown of Morgane's choosing. An identical match to the gown I'd worn on my sixteenth birthday.

"I've always wondered"—Manon swallowed hard, glancing at my throat—"how you managed to escape last time."

"I gave up my life."

There was a pause. "But...you didn't. You lived."

"I gave up my life," I repeated, voice slow and lethargic. "I had no intention of returning to this place." I blinked at her before returning my gaze to the moondust on the sill. "Of seeing you or my mother or anyone here ever again."

"You found a loophole." She exhaled softly on a chuckle. "Brilliant. Your symbolic life for your physical one."

"Don't worry." I forced the words from my lips with extreme effort. They rolled—thick and heavy and poisonous—off my tongue, leaving me exhausted. She laid me back against my pillow, and I closed my eyes. "It won't work again."

"Why not?"

I peeked an eye open. "I can't give him up."

Her gaze dropped to my mother-of-pearl ring in an unspoken question, but I said nothing, closing my eyes once more. I was vaguely aware of someone knocking, but the sound was far away.

Footsteps. A door opening. Shutting.

"Louise?" Manon asked tentatively. My eyes fluttered open . . . whether seconds or hours later, I did not know. "Our Lady has requested your presence in her chambers."

When I didn't respond, she lifted my arm over her shoulder and hoisted me from the bed.

"I can only escort you to her antechamber," she whispered. My sisters drew back—surprised—as we walked through the corridors. The younger ones craned their necks to get a good look at me. "You have a visitor, apparently."

A visitor? My mind immediately conjured up hazy images of Reid bound and gagged. The horror in my chest felt deadened, however. Not nearly as painful as it would've once been. I was too far gone.

Or so I'd thought.

For as Manon left me slumped in Morgane's antechamber—as the door to the inner rooms swung open—my heart started beating again at what I saw there.

At *who* I saw there.

It wasn't Reid bound and gagged on my mother's settee.

It was the Archbishop.

The door slammed shut behind me.

"Hello, darling." Morgane sat next to him, trailing a finger down his cheek. "How are you feeling this afternoon?"

I stared at him, unable to hear anything beyond my wildly pounding heart. His eyes—blue like mine, but darker—were wide and frantic. Blood from a cut on his cheek dripped sickeningly onto his gag and soaked the fabric.

I looked closer. The gag had been torn from the sleeve of his choral robes. Morgane had literally silenced him with his holy vestment.

In another time, in another life, I might've laughed at the unfortunate situation the Archbishop had landed himself in. I might've laughed and laughed until my chest ached and my head spun. But that was before. Now, my head spun for a different reason. There was nothing funny here. I doubted anything would ever be funny again.

"Come, Louise." Morgane stood and gathered me in her arms, carrying me farther into the room. "You look dead on your feet. Sit and warm yourself by the fire."

She deposited me next to the Archbishop on the faded settee, wedging herself on my other side. The seat wasn't big enough for all three of us, however, and our legs pressed together with horrible intimacy. Heedless of my discomfort, she wrapped an arm around my shoulders and pulled my face to the crook of her neck. Eucalyptus choked my senses. "Manon tells me you won't eat. That's very naughty."

I couldn't force my head back up. "I won't starve before nightfall."

"No, I suppose you're right. I do hate to see you so uncomfortable though, darling. We all do."

I said nothing. Though I frantically tried retreating back into that welcome darkness, the Archbishop's leg was too heavy against mine. Too real. An anchor holding me here.

"We discovered this despicable man early this morning." Morgane eyed him with unabashed glee. "He was wandering around La Forêt des Yeux. He's lucky he didn't drown in L'Eau Mélancolique. I must admit I'm a bit disappointed."

"I . . . don't understand."

"Really? I should've thought it obvious. He was searching for you, of course. But he wandered a bit too far from his motley band of huntsmen." Though I hardly dared to hope, my heart leapt at the revelation. She smiled cruelly. "Yours wasn't among them, Louise. It seems he's washed his hands of you."

It hurt less than I anticipated—perhaps because I *had* anticipated it. Of course Reid hadn't accompanied them. He, Coco, and Ansel were hopefully safe at sea—somewhere far, far away from the death that loomed here.

Morgane watched my reaction closely. Unsatisfied with my blank expression, she gestured to the Archbishop. "Should I kill him? Would that make you happy?"

The Archbishop's eyes swiveled to meet mine, but otherwise, his body remained still. Waiting.

I stared at him. I'd once wished this man every version of a fiery and painful death. For all the witches he'd burned, he deserved it. For Fleur. For Vivienne. For Rosemund and Sacha and Viera and Genevieve.

Now, Morgane handed it to me, but . . .

"No."

The Archbishop's eyes widened, and a slow, malevolent smile broke across Morgane's face. As if she'd expected my answer. As if she were a cat examining a particularly juicy mouse. "How interesting. You spoke of tolerance earlier, Louise. Please . . . show me." With a flourish, she removed the gag from his mouth, and he gasped. She looked between us with fervent eyes. "Ask him anything."

Ask him anything.

When I said nothing, she patted my knee in encouragement. "Go on. You have questions, don't you? You'd be a fool if you didn't. Now is your chance. You won't get another. Though I'll honor your request not to kill him, others won't. He'll be the first to burn when we reclaim Belterra."

Her smile finished what her words did not. *But you'll already be dead.*

Slowly, I turned to look at him.

We'd never sat this close. I'd never before seen the green flecks in his eyes, the nearly indiscernible freckles on his nose. My eyes. My freckles. Hundreds of questions flooded my thoughts. *Why didn't you tell me? Why didn't you kill me? How could you have done those terrible things—how could you have murdered innocent children? Mothers and sisters and daughters?* But I already knew the answers to those questions, and another rose to my lips instead, unbidden.

"Do you hate me?"

Morgane cackled, clasping her hands together in delight. "Oh, *Louise*! You aren't ready to hear the answer to that question, darling. But hear it you shall." She jabbed her finger into the cut on the Archbishop's cheek. He cringed away. "Answer her."

Close enough to watch each emotion flit across his face, I waited for him to speak. I told myself I didn't care either way, and perhaps I didn't—for the war raging behind his eyes was also my own. I hated him. I needed him to atone for his heinous crimes—for his hatred, for his *evil*—yet a small, innate part of me couldn't wish him harm.

His mouth began to move, but no sound came out. I leaned closer against my better judgment, and his voice rose to a whisper, the cadence of his voice changing as if he was reciting something. A verse. My heart sank.

"'When thou art come into the land which the Lord thy God giveth thee,'" he breathed, "'thou shalt not learn to do after the abominations of those nations. There shall not be found among you any one that maketh his son or his daughter to pass through the fire, or that useth divination, or an observer of times, or an enchanter, or a . . . or a witch.'"

His eyes rose to mine, shame and regret burning bright behind them. "'For all that do these things are an abomination unto the Lord, and because of these abominations, the Lord thy God doth drive them out before thee.'"

A lump lodged in my throat. I swallowed it down, vaguely aware of Morgane cackling again.

Of course I do not love you, Louise. You are the daughter of my enemy. You were conceived for a higher purpose, and I will not poison that purpose with love.

Abomination. The Lord thy God doth drive you out before me.

You are not my wife.

"'But,'" the Archbishop continued, his voice hardening with resolve, "'if any provide not for his own, and specially for those of his own house, he hath denied the faith, and is worse than an infidel.'"

A tear escaped down my cheek. Upon seeing it, Morgane laughed louder. "How touching. It seems the whole lot of them are infidels, doesn't it, Louise? First your husband, now your father. Neither have provided you anything but heartache. Where is this tolerance of which you spoke?"

She paused, clearly waiting for one of us to respond. When we didn't, she rose to her feet, smile slipping in disappointment. "I'm surprised at you, Louise. I expected more of a fight."

"I will not beg for his affection, nor his life."

She scoffed. "Not *his*—I meant your precious huntsman's."

I frowned at her. Something vaguely urgent knocked at the back of my skull. Something I was missing. Some crucial bit of information I couldn't quite remember. "I . . . I didn't expect him to come after me, if that's what you mean."

Her eyes gleamed wickedly. "It's not."

The vague something knocked harder, insistent. "Then what—?"

The blood drained from my face. Reid.

Morgane's forgotten words drifted back to me through the heavy fog of my mind. Amidst my heartache—amidst my rage and hopelessness and *despair*—I hadn't stopped to consider their meaning.

The Lyons will rue the day they stole this land. Their people will writhe and thrash on the stake, and the king and his children will choke on your blood. Your husband *will choke on your blood.*

But that meant—

"I know I promised you the chance to light his pyre." Morgane's croon scattered the thread of my thoughts. "But I'm afraid you won't get the chance, after all. The king's blood runs in your huntsman's veins."

No. I closed my eyes, focusing on my breathing, but quickly reopened them as the darkness beyond my lids began spinning. Through sheer willpower—no, through sheer *desperation*—I forced my useless limbs into action. They twitched and spasmed in protest as I toppled, falling toward Morgane's outstretched hands, toward the promise of Angelica's Ring—

She caught me against her chest in a sick embrace. "Fret not, darling. You'll see him again soon."

At a wave of her hand, everything went dark.

CONSORTING WITH THE ENEMY

Reid

Madame Labelle pointed above our heads midafternoon. "Chateau le Blanc is there." We followed her finger to the mountain towering in the distance, perhaps two hours away. "We should arrive in time for the feast."

We had to take her word for it. No one else could see anything but trees. When Beau grumbled as much, Madame Labelle shrugged and sank gracefully onto her stump, folding her hands in her lap. "'Tis the magic of the Chateau, I'm afraid. None but a Dame Blanche can see it until we cross through the enchantment." At Beau's puzzled look, she added, "The bridge, of course."

Beau opened his mouth to reply, but I stopped listening, drifting to the edge of our hidden camp. In the forest, the faint smell of magic touched everything. But it burned less sharp here, somehow, mingled with the salt and trees. As if it belonged. I closed my eyes and breathed deep. Waves crashed in the distance. Though I'd never set foot in this place, it felt familiar . . . like Lou.

Her essence infused everything—the sunlight filtering

through the pines, the creek trickling beside us despite the cold. Even the wind seemed to dance. It swirled her scent around me, soothing my frazzled nerves like a balm.

There you are, it seemed to say. *I didn't think you'd come.*

I promised to love and protect you.

And I promised to love and obey you. We're both such pretty liars . . .

I opened my eyes, chest aching, to see Coco standing beside me. She stared out into the trees as if she too were holding a silent conversation.

"I can feel her here." She shook her head. Wistful. "I've known her since childhood, yet . . . sometimes . . . I wonder if I really know her at all."

I blinked in surprise. "You and Lou knew each other as children?"

Her eyes flicked to mine, searching my face as if considering how to answer. Finally, she sighed and turned back to the trees. "We met when we were six. I'd . . . wandered away from my coven. My aunt and I—we didn't get along much, and she'd . . . well—" She stopped abruptly. "It doesn't matter. Lou found me. She tried to make me laugh, braided flowers in my hair to make me feel better. When I finally stopped crying, she tossed a mud pie in my face." She flashed a grin, but it quickly faded. "We kept our friendship a secret. I didn't even tell my aunt. She wouldn't have approved. She loathes Morgane and the Dames Blanches."

"It seems Lou has a habit of endearing herself to her enemies."

Coco didn't seem to hear me. Though she still stared at the trees, it was clear she no longer saw them. "I didn't know what the Dames Blanches were planning. Lou never told me. She never said a word—not one—in all those years. And then one day, she just . . . disappeared." Her throat worked furiously, and she ducked her head to stare at her feet. "If I had known, I—I would've stopped them, somehow. But I didn't know. I thought she was dead."

An inexplicable urge to comfort her overwhelmed me, but I resisted. This wasn't the time to comfort. This was the time to listen.

"But you found her."

She chuckled without mirth, lifting her chin once more. "No. She found me. In Cesarine. Without Lou, I decided I needed some time away from my—my coven—so I tried my hand at pickpocketing in East End. I was shit at it," she added. "The constabulary arrested me the second day. Lou dropped out of the sky and saved my ass." She paused, shaking her head. "It was like seeing a ghost. A ghost with a disfigured throat. The scab had just fallen off, but it was still gruesome to look at." She lifted her sleeve, revealing her own scars. "Even for me."

I looked away. I could imagine it all too clearly. Her silver scar reared in my mind's eye—followed swiftly by the gaping wound at the dead witch's throat. I forced the memory away, bile rising.

"I wanted to kill her," Coco said bitterly. "Or kiss her."

I chuckled ruefully. "I can empathize."

"And even after—after everything—she *still* wouldn't talk about it. To this day, *two* years later, I don't know what happened that night. I don't know how she escaped. I—I don't know anything." A solitary tear leaked down her cheek, but she wiped it away angrily. "She kept it locked in tight."

Her eyes finally turned to me, beseeching. I didn't quite know what she was asking.

"We have to save her." The breeze picked up, ruffling her hair. She closed her eyes and lifted her face into it. Chin trembling. "I have to tell her I'm sorry."

My brows dipped. "For what?"

Lou hadn't mentioned a fight with Coco. But I now realized Lou hadn't mentioned much. She was an incredibly private person. The grins, the easy laughter, the tricks and coarse language and sarcasm—all defense mechanisms. Distractions. Meant to deflect anyone from looking too close. Even Coco.

Even me.

"I should've been there when Morgane attacked. I should've helped her . . . protected her. But I wasn't. Again." Her eyes snapped open, and she turned her sudden vehemence on me. "We argued at your ball. I told her not to fall in love with you."

I couldn't keep myself from scowling. "Why?"

"It's no secret Chasseurs kill witches. I don't like you, Diggory, and I won't apologize for it." She paused, seeming to struggle with herself a moment, before sighing heavily. "But even I can see you're trying. You and I are the best chance Lou has now. I don't think even she can walk out of that place twice."

"Don't underestimate her."

"I'm not," she snapped. "I'm being realistic. You don't know the Dames Blanches like I do. They're zealots. There's no telling what sorts of torture Morgane has inflicted on her."

Unease dropped in my stomach like lead.

"Whatever happens," she continued in a steely voice, "you get her out. I'll worry about the others." She glanced over her shoulder to where Madame Labelle sat beside Ansel and Beau. "Madame Labelle shouldn't need much help, but the other two will be vulnerable."

"Ansel has trained in combat." But my voice lacked conviction even to my own ears. At sixteen, the boy had yet to fight outside the training yard.

"So has Beau." She rolled her eyes. "But he'll be the first to piss down his leg when faced with a witch's magic. Neither of them have the protection of your Balisarda, and these witches aren't like Lou. She's been out of practice, hiding her magic for years. These witches will be highly skilled and out for our blood. They won't hesitate to kill us."

Everyone kept saying that. Everyone kept saying Lou was weak. My unease spread. She hadn't seemed weak when she'd bound me to the witch—when she'd nearly torn my spine in half and stitched my limbs together like a rag doll. If *that* was weak, the other witches must possess the power of God.

Madame Labelle marched up behind us. "What are you two whispering about?"

Unwilling to relive such a painful conversation, I took a page out of Lou's book and deflected. "How are we to form a strategy if we can't see the walls we're meant to breach?"

She tossed her hair over a shoulder. "Dear boy, I've already answered this question at least a dozen times. We won't be *breaching* anything. We will be walking through the front doors."

"And I've already told *you* that you won't be changing our faces."

Madame Labelle shrugged and looked toward Ansel and Beau with feigned nonchalance. "Too late."

Sighing in irritation—or perhaps resignation—I followed her gaze. Two young men sat behind us, but they appeared as strangers. When the taller of the two flashed me a sheepish grin, however, I recognized Ansel. He still had his straight nose and curly hair—black now instead of brown—but the similarities ended there. Beau too had completely changed. Only his disdainful sneer remained.

Raising thick, dark brows at my appraisal, he called, "Like what you see?"

"Shut up," Ansel hissed. "Do you want the witches to hear us?"

"No need to fret, dear," Madame Labelle said. "I've cast a protective bubble for the time being. In this moment, we cease to exist."

She returned her attention to me. I stared at her as if she'd sprouted another head. "Now, *dear*, let me explain this one last time: we cannot hope to enter the Chateau your way. Scaling the walls or whatever other nonsense you're contemplating simply won't work. The entire castle is protected by a thousand-year-old enchantment to prevent such endeavors from succeeding, and besides, that is *precisely* what Morgane will expect from you *têtes carrées*. Brute strength. A show of force. We would be playing right into her clawed hands."

Beau drifted closer. "Are they really clawed?" Savage satisfaction stole through me when I saw Madame Labelle had given him a bulbous nose and a wart on his chin.

"How is changing our faces going to get us inside?" Coco asked, ignoring him.

"We're too recognizable as we are." Madame Labelle gestured between me and Beau. "Especially you two."

"Why him?" Beau asked dubiously.

"He's almost seven feet tall with red hair," Madame Labelle said. "*And* he's gained a certain notoriety for killing Estelle—as well as sullying their precious princess. The witches will have heard of him."

Sullying their precious princess. Each word stabbed through my chest, but I forced myself to concentrate. "Men aren't allowed at the Chateau, so unless you plan on making us all women—"

"Don't tempt her," Beau muttered.

Madame Labelle chuckled and patted my elbow. "As fun as that sounds, Reid dear, men are allowed at the Chateau as consorts—especially during festivals such as Modraniht. Every witch in attendance will likely be toting a special someone on her arm. Don't worry," she added to Coco. "Many witches prefer female companionship. Truthfully, it'll be easier to sneak you inside than these brutes."

"I know. I'm *also* a witch, in case you'd forgotten." Coco crossed her arms, skewering Madame Labelle with a glare. "But do you expect us to just waltz up to the front doors and ask if any witches are available for the night?"

"Of course not. There are plenty of available witches traveling through these woods right now." She pointed through the trees, where a trio of witches had just appeared. Young. Slight. Doll-like features with dark hair and amber skin. Laughing freely—completely unaware of being watched. "But we need to hurry. We aren't the only hopefuls wandering the mountainside today."

As if in response, a skinny young man staggered up behind the witches and produced a bouquet of winter greens. The witches giggled—delighted and cruel—before flouncing away.

"Oh dear." Madame Labelle watched the boy toss the bouquet to the ground. "I almost feel sorry for the poor soul. He'll need to try harder than that to snare a witch. We have impeccable taste."

Beau made a noise of outrage. "Then how exactly am I supposed to snare one with the face of a toad?"

"By having devilishly handsome friends, of course."

Madame Labelle winked, and, faster than I'd believed possible, slipped the Balisarda from my bandolier. She flicked a finger at me when I lunged after her, and a peculiar sensation spread from the center of my face outward—like an egg had been cracked on my nose. Startled, I stopped moving as it slipped over my cheeks. My eyes. My mouth. But as it began to slide down my throat, I charged forward once more, clamping my lips against the magic.

"Almost there," Madame Labelle said cheerfully, dancing out of reach. The others watched my transformation with rapt attention. Even Beau forgot to look unpleasant.

After coating the tips of my hair, the magic finally vanished. Silence descended, and I expelled the breath I'd been holding. "Well?"

"This is bullshit," Beau said.

My hair had deepened to black. Stubble grew on my cheeks. Though I couldn't see the rest of the changes, the angle of the world looked different. As if I'd . . . shrunk. Gritting my teeth, I wrenched my Balisarda back from Madame Labelle, sheathed it, and stomped after the witches.

"Wait, wait!" she cried. I turned reluctantly, and she held out her hand once more. "Give it back."

I stared at her in disbelief. "I don't think so."

She waved her hand, insistent. "You might think those picks of yours were forged in holy water, but I know better. The Sword of Balisarda was made in the same water as Angelica's Ring." She jerked a thumb over her shoulder. "In L'Eau Mélancolique. By a witch."

"No. It was forged by Saint Constantin—"

"It was forged by Saint Constantin's lover, Angelica," Madame Labelle said impatiently. "Accept it. Move on."

My eyes narrowed. "How do you know?"

She shrugged. "Magic always leaves a trail. Just because we can't smell it on your Balisardas or Angelica's Ring doesn't mean a clever witch won't detect it—and Morgane is a clever witch. Do you really want to risk her discovering us?"

My hand gravitated back to my bandolier, and my fingers wrapped around the sapphire hilt by my heart. I savored its smoothness . . . its reassuring weight. Our Balisardas couldn't be magic. They *protected* us from magic. But everything else in my godforsaken life had been a lie. Why not this too?

Unsheathing the blade, I scowled up at the sky.

"You're expecting us to walk into Chateau le Blanc completely unarmed?" Beau asked in disbelief.

"Of course not. Take whatever nonmagical weapons you wish. Just leave the Balisarda at camp." She smiled sweetly. "We can collect it after we've rescued Louise."

"You're mad—" He broke off, stunned, as I placed my Balisarda in Madame Labelle's outstretched hand.

Without another word, I turned and headed after the witches.

They took one look at me and erupted into unintelligible squeals.

"His jaw could cut glass!" one of them trilled. Loudly. As if I weren't there. No—as if I was nothing but a prized cow, unable to comprehend a word they were saying. I tried not to scowl but failed miserably.

"Oh, look at his eyelashes," the second sighed. This one had the nerve to reach up and touch my face. I forced myself to remain still. To refrain from snapping its—*her*—wrist. "Do you have a sister, handsome?"

"He's mine," the third said quickly, batting away the second's hand. "Don't touch him!"

"*I* am the eldest," the first interrupted. "So I get first pick!"

Behind me, Ansel and Beau choked on silent laughter. I longed to knock their heads together, cursing Madame Labelle for pairing them with me.

I adopted as pleasant a voice as I was able. "*Mademoiselles*, may I introduce my brothers?" I jerked them both forward by the scruffs of their necks, and their grins vanished. "This is Antoine."

I shoved Ansel toward one of them at random. I grabbed Beau next. "And this is Burke."

The witch I paired with Beau wrinkled her nose. Though Madame Labelle had taken pity on him and removed his wart, he undoubtedly remained the least attractive of us. Undeterred—or just stupid—he shot the witch a charming smile, revealing a gap between his two front teeth. She stepped away from him, disgusted.

The first witch wrapped a hand around my arm, attempting to pull me close. "And what's *your* name, handsome?"

"Raoul."

Her fingers explored my biceps. "It's nice to meet you, Raoul. I'm Elaina. Have you ever been to the Chateau?"

I struggled to keep my face polite. Interested. "No, but I've heard it's beautiful."

"As are its inhabitants." Beau gave them a roguish wink. Everyone ignored him.

"You are in for *such* a treat!" The witch next to Ansel pushed past her sister to clutch my other arm. "I'm Elodie, by the way. Are you *sure* you don't have a sister?" She peered behind me hopefully.

"Hey!" the third sister protested when she realized I had no more arms to spare.

"That's Elinor," Elaina said, dismissive. "But Elodie is right—you couldn't have picked a better night to offer your services. Tonight is Modraniht, and tomorrow is Yule. Our Lady has planned a great festival this year—"

"We've traveled all the way from Sully to celebrate—" Elodie said.

"—because Louise has finally returned!" Elinor finished. She grabbed Ansel's arm and followed us through the trees.

My heart stopped, and I stumbled. Two sets of hands moved eagerly to steady me.

"Are you all right?" Elaina asked.

"You look quite pale," Elodie said.

"Who is Louise?" Beau asked, shooting me a sharp look.

Elinor's nose wrinkled as she looked at him. "Louise le Blanc. Daughter and heir of La Dame des Sorcières. Are you daft?"

"Apparently." Beau looked on with a bemused expression. "So, *mademoiselles*—what does our fair Lady have planned for us this evening? Food? Dancing? Will we get to *meet* the lovely Louise?"

"*You* won't," Elinor said. "You're not coming."

I stopped walking abruptly. "He goes where I go."

Elaina pouted up at me. "But none of us *want* him."

"If you *want* me, he goes." I pulled away from her, and her lips puckered slightly. I mentally chastised myself. "Please." I tucked a strand of black hair behind her ear and attempted a smile. "He's my brother."

She leaned into my touch, frown melting into a sigh. "Well, if you insist."

We resumed walking. Ansel cleared his throat. "So—er, what *can* we expect tonight?"

Elinor grinned coyly. "You needn't be nervous, Antoine. I'll take good care of you."

Ansel's face burned crimson. "No, that's not— I meant—"

Elinor laughed and nestled closer to him. "There'll be the usual gifts and minor sacrifices. Our mother passed a few years ago, so we'll honor our Lady in her stead."

"And the Goddess, of course," Elodie added.

"And then," Elaina said, eager, "after the feasting and dancing, Morgane will make her sacrifice to the Goddess at midnight."

Midnight. Numbness crept over my limbs. "Her sacrifice?"

Elaina leaned in conspiratorially. "Her daughter. Terribly wicked, but there you are. We'll be witnessing history tonight, you and I."

Elodie and Elinor both huffed protests at being excluded, but I didn't hear them. A ringing started in my ears, and my hands curled into fists. Beau clipped my heel in an innocent gesture. I tripped, breaking out of the witches' grip, before rounding on him.

"Sorry, Raoul." He shrugged and smiled easily, but his eyes held a warning. "You'd think I could control my own feet, eh?"

I took a steadying breath. Then another. Forced myself to unclench my fists.

One.

Two.

Three—

"Oh, look!" Elinor pointed to our left. A small group of people emerged between the trees. "It's Ivette and Sabine! Oooh, we haven't seen them since we were witchlings!"

Elaina and Elodie squealed in delight and dragged me and Ansel toward the newcomers. Beau trailed behind.

Upon closer inspection, I recognized Coco on the arm of one

of the newcomers. Which left only Madame Labelle unaccounted for. When Coco cast me a furtive, troubled glance, I nodded in understanding.

"Keep your mouths shut and your eyes open," Madame Labelle had warned. "I'll find you inside."

Vague, unsatisfactory instructions. No further explanations. No contingencies. We were a Chasseur, initiate, Lyon prince, and blood witch walking into Chateau le Blanc blind. Lou wasn't the only one who would die if things went badly tonight.

Elaina introduced me to her friends before curling her fingers around mine and resting her head on my arm. I bared my teeth in a smile, imagining she was Lou instead.

Lou, vibrant and alive. Flicking my nose and swearing at me affectionately. I pictured her face. Held on to it.

It was the only way I could continue without throttling some-one.

Elodie eyed one of the women beside Coco with obvious inter-est before patting my cheek. "Sorry, pet. If you'd had a sister . . ."

She strode away without a backward glance, and Ansel fell into step beside me. Under cover of the girls' prattling, he nudged my arm, nodding in front of us to where the trees thinned out. "Look."

A bridge stretched out before us. Impossibly long. Wooden. Fabled. Above it, towering over the peak of the mountain, sat Chateau le Blanc.

We had arrived.

MODRANIHT

Reid

There were witches everywhere.

My breath caught as they swept me into the snowy court-yard. It was almost too crowded to walk. Everywhere I turned, I bumped into someone. There were hags and babies and women of every age, shape, and color—all bright-eyed with excitement. All flushed. All laughing. All praising the pagan goddess.

A dark-haired woman ran up to me through the crowd, stand-ing on tiptoe to press a kiss to my cheek. "Merry meet!" She giggled before disappearing into the crowd once more.

A decrepit old witch with a basket of evergreens came next. I eyed her suspiciously, remembering the hag from the market, but she only placed a juniper crown on my head and croaked a bless-ing from the goddess. Little girls ran shrieking past my legs in a wild game of tag. Feet bare and faces dirty. Ribbons in their hair.

It was madness.

Elaina and Elinor—who had abandoned Ansel after realizing Elodie had traded up—pulled me in opposite directions, each determined to introduce me to every person they'd ever known. I didn't bother remembering their names. A month ago, I would've wanted them all dead. Now, a hollow sort of pit opened up in my stomach as I greeted them. These women—with their pretty smiles and shining faces—wanted Lou dead. They were here to *celebrate* Lou's death.

The revelry soon became intolerable. As did the undiluted stench of magic, stronger here than anywhere I'd ever encountered it.

I tugged away from Elaina with a strained smile. "I need the washroom."

Though my eyes roamed for Madame Labelle, I had no idea what face she'd taken—or if she'd even gotten inside.

"You can't!" Elaina clutched me tighter. The sun had sunk below the castle, lengthening the shadows in the courtyard. "The feast is about to start!"

Sure enough, the witches began moving toward the doors as if answering a silent call. Perhaps they were. If I concentrated hard enough, I could almost feel the faint whispering of it across my skin. I shuddered.

"Of course," I ground out as she tugged me forward. "I can wait."

Ansel and Beau stuck close to me. Coco had been dragged away as soon as we crossed the bridge, and I hadn't seen her since. Her absence made me uneasy.

Beau elbowed a plump witch aside to keep up. "Will our Lady be attending the feast?"

"*Excuse* you." She nearly leveled him in retaliation, and he skidded into me before righting himself.

"Good Lord." He eyed the witch's broad back as she shoved through a set of stone doors. Above them, an elaborate depiction of the waxing, full, and waning moons had been carved.

"I think you have the wrong deity," I muttered.

"Are you coming or not?" Elinor yanked me past the carving, and I had little choice but to follow.

The hall was vast and ancient—larger than even the sanctuary in Saint-Cécile—with vaulted ceilings and giant beams covered in snow and foliage, as if the courtyard had somehow spilled inside. Vines crept in from the arched windows. Ice glittered on the walls. Long wooden tables ran the length of the floor, overflowing with moss and flickering candles. Thousands of them. They cast a soft glow on the witches who lingered nearby. No one had yet seated themselves. All watched the far side of the room with rapt attention. I followed their gazes. The very air around us seemed to still.

There, on a throne of saplings, sat Morgane le Blanc.

And beside her—eyes closed and limbs dangling—floated Lou.

My breath left in a painful whoosh as I stared at her. Only a fortnight had passed, yet she appeared skeletal and sickly. Her wild hair had been trimmed and neatly braided, and her freckles had disappeared. Her skin—once golden—now appeared white. Ashen.

Morgane had suspended her in midair on her back, with her

body bowed nearly in two. Her toes and fingertips just brushed the dais floor. Her head lolled back, forcing her long, slender throat to extend for the entire room to see. Displaying her scar prominently.

Rage unlike anything I'd ever felt exploded through me.

They were making a mockery of her.

Of my wife.

Two sets of hands gripped the back of my coat, but they weren't necessary. I stood with preternatural stillness, eyes locked on Lou's inert form.

Elinor stood on tiptoes to get a better look. She giggled behind her hand. "She's not as pretty as I remember."

Elaina sighed. "But look how slender she is."

I turned to look at them. Slowly. The hands at my back tightened.

"Easy," Beau breathed at my shoulder. "Not yet."

I forced a deep breath. *Not yet,* I repeated to myself. *Not yet not yet not yet.*

"What's the matter with you three?" Elaina's voice rang unnaturally loud in the hush of the room. Shrill and unpleasant.

Before we could answer, Morgane rose from her seat. The murmured conversation in the room died instantly. She smiled down at us with the air of a mother beholding her favorite child.

"Sisters!" She lifted her hands in supplication. "Blessed be!"

"Blessed be!" the witches hailed back in unison. A rapturous joy lit their faces. Alarm tempered my rage. Where was Madame Labelle?

Morgane took a step down the dais. I watched helplessly as

Lou floated along behind her. "Blessed be thy feet," Morgane cried, "which have brought thee in these ways!"

"Blessed be!" The witches clapped their hands and stomped their feet in wild abandon. Dread snaked down my spine as I watched them.

Morgane took another step. "Blessed be thy knees, that shall kneel at the sacred altar!"

"Blessed be!" Tears ran down the plump witch's face. Beau watched her in fascination, but she didn't notice. No one did.

Another step. "Blessed be thy womb, without which we would not be!"

"Blessed be!"

Morgane had fully descended now. "Blessed be thy breasts, formed in beauty!"

"Blessed be!"

She stretched her arms wide and threw her head back, chest heaving. "And blessed be thy lips, that shalt utter the Sacred Names of the gods!"

The witches' cries rose to a tumult. "Blessed be!"

Morgane lowered her arms, still breathing heavily, and the witches gradually quieted.

"Welcome, sisters, and merry Modraniht!" Her indulgent smile returned as she stepped to the head of the middle table. "Draw near to me, please, and eat and drink your fill! For tonight we celebrate!"

The witches cheered once more, and they scrambled for the chairs nearest her.

"Consorts can't sit at the tables," Elaina called hastily over her shoulder. She rushed after her sister. "*Va-t'en!* Go stand by the wall with the others!"

Relief surged through me. We quickly joined the other consorts at the back wall.

Beau directed us toward one of the windows. "Here. I'm getting a headache from all the incense."

The position offered an unimpeded view of Morgane. With a lazy wave of her hand, she called forth the food. Soon sounds of clinking cutlery joined the laughter echoing through the hall. A consort beside us turned and said in awe, "She is almost too beautiful to look upon, La Dame des Sorcières."

"So don't look at her," I snapped.

The girl blinked, startled, before shuffling away.

I turned my attention back to Morgane. She looked nothing like the drawings in Chasseur Tower. The woman was beautiful, yes, but also cold and cruel—like ice. She had none of Lou's warmth in her. She had none of Lou in her at all. The two were night and day—winter and summer—and yet . . . there was something similar in their expression. In the set of their jaw. Something determined. Both confident in their ability to bend the world to their will.

But that was how Lou used to look. Now, she floated near Morgane as if sleeping. A witch stood by her side. Tall and ebony-skinned. Sprigs of holly braided through her black hair.

"A poor witch's Cosette," a voice murmured beside me. Coco. She watched Lou and the ebony witch with an unfathomable expression.

A small hand touched my arm through the window. I spun swiftly.

"Don't turn around!"

I stopped moving abruptly, but not before glimpsing strawberry blond hair and Madame Labelle's alarmingly familiar blue eyes.

"You look the same." I attempted to move my lips as little as possible. Coco and I inched back until we were pressed against the windowsill. Ansel and Beau fell in on either side of us, completely blocking Madame Labelle from view. "Why aren't you disguised? Where have you been?"

She huffed irritably. "Even *my* power has its limits. Between casting the protective enchantment on our camp and transforming all your faces—as well as *maintaining* those transformations—I'm spent. I could barely manage lightening my hair, which means I can't come inside. I'm too recognizable."

"What are you talking about?" Coco hissed. "Lou never had to *maintain* patterns in the infirmary. She just—I don't know—*did* them."

"Did you want me to alter your face permanently, then?" Madame Labelle skewered her with a glare. "By all means, it would be *much* easier for me to be done with it and have you all remain lecherous little cretins forever—"

Heat crept up my throat. "Lou practiced *magic* in the *church*?"

"So what's the plan?" Ansel whispered hastily.

I forced myself to refocus on the tables. The meal was quickly coming to an end. Music drifted in from somewhere outside.

Already some had risen from their chairs to retrieve their consorts. Elaina and Elinor would soon be upon me.

"The plan is to wait for my signal," Madame Labelle said tersely. "I've made arrangements."

"What?" I resisted the urge to turn around and throttle her. Now was not the time or place for vague and unhelpful instructions. Now was the time for conciseness. For action. "What arrangements? What signal?"

"There's no time to explain, but you'll know when you see it. They're waiting outside—"

"Who?"

I stopped talking abruptly as Elinor bounded up to us.

"Ha!" she cried, triumphant. Her breath smelled sweet with wine. Her cheeks flushed pink. "I beat her here! That means I get first dance!"

I dug in my feet as she pulled me away, but when I glanced back over my shoulder, Madame Labelle had gone.

I spun Elinor around the clearing without seeing her. It'd taken a quarter of an hour to trek to this unnatural place, hidden deep within the shadow of the mountain. The same thick mist from La Forêt des Yeux clung to the ground here. It swirled around our legs as we danced, matching the lilting melody. I could almost see the spirits of witches long dead dancing within it.

The ruins of a temple—pale, crumbling—opened up to the night sky in the middle of the clearing. Morgane sat there with a still unconscious Lou, overseeing minor sacrifices. A stone altar rose from the ground beside them. It shone pristine in the moonlight.

My mind and body warred. The former screamed to wait for Madame Labelle. The latter itched to throw itself between Lou and Morgane. I couldn't stand to look upon her lifeless body any longer. To watch her drift along as if she were already a spirit of the mist.

And Morgane—never before had I longed to kill a witch as I did now, to plunge a knife into her throat and sever her pale head from her body. I didn't need my Balisarda to kill her. She would bleed without it.

Not yet. Wait for the signal.

If only Madame Labelle had told us what the signal *was.*

The music played endlessly, but there were no musicians in sight. Elinor grudgingly passed me to Elaina, and I lost track of time. Lost track of everything but the panicked beat of my heart, the cold night air on my skin. How much longer would Madame Labelle expect me to wait? Where was she? *Who* was she expecting?

Too many questions and not enough answers. And still no sign of Madame Labelle.

Panic rapidly gave way to despair as the last sheep was slain, and the witches began presenting other tokens to Morgane. Wooden carvings. Bundled herbs. Hematite jewelry.

Morgane watched them place each gift at her feet without a word. She stroked Lou's hair absently as the ebony witch approached from within the temple. I couldn't hear their murmured conversation, but Morgane's face lit up at whatever the witch said. I watched the witch return to the temple with a sense of foreboding.

If it made Morgane happy, it couldn't be good for us.

Elaina and Elinor soon left me to add their gifts to the pile. I craned my neck to search for anything amiss, anything that might be construed as a signal, but there was nothing.

Ansel and Coco sidled up beside me, their distress nearly palpable. "We can't wait much longer," Ansel breathed. "It's almost midnight."

I nodded, remembering Morgane's wicked smile. Something was coming. We couldn't afford to wait any longer. Whether Madame Labelle gave the signal or not, the time had come to act. I looked to Coco. "We need a distraction. Something to draw Morgane's attention away from Lou."

"Something like a blood witch?" she asked, grim.

Ansel opened his mouth to protest, but I cut him off. "It'll be dangerous."

She slit her wrist with a flick of her thumb. Dark blood welled, and a sharp, bitter stench pierced the cloying air. "Don't worry about me." She turned and wove through the mist out of sight.

I checked the bandolier of knives beneath my coat as inconspicuously as possible. "Ansel . . . before we do this . . . I—I just want to say that I'm"—I broke off, swallowing hard—"I'm sorry. About before. In the Tower. I shouldn't have touched you."

He blinked in surprise. "It's fine, Reid. You were upset—"

"It's not fine." I coughed awkwardly, unable to meet his eyes. "Er, what weapons do you have?"

Before he could answer, the music stopped abruptly, and the clearing plunged into silence. Every eye turned to the temple. I watched in horror as Morgane stood, eyes shining with malicious intent.

This was it. We really were out of time.

I followed the witches as they moved closer, moths drawn to the flame. Gripping a knife under my coat, I maneuvered to the front of the crowd. Ansel shadowed my movements, and Beau soon joined him.

Good. They could protect each other. Though if I failed, they were as good as dead anyway.

Morgane was the target.

A blade in the chest would distract her just as well as Coco could. If I was lucky, it would kill her. If I wasn't, it would at least buy enough time to grab Lou and run. I prayed the others would be able to slip away undetected.

"Many of you have traveled long and far to pay homage on this Modraniht." Morgane's voice was soft, but it carried clearly across the silence of the glade. The witches waited with bated breath. "I am honored by your presence. I am humbled by your gifts. Your revelry tonight has restored my spirit." She searched each face carefully, her eyes seeming to linger on mine before continuing on. I released a slow breath.

"But you know this night is more than revelry," she continued, voice softer still. "This is a night to honor our matriarchs. It is a night to worship and pay tribute to the Goddess—she who brings light and darkness, she who breathes life and death. She who is the one true Mother of us all." Another pause, this one longer and more pronounced. "Our Mother is angry." The anguish on her face had even me nearly convinced. "Suffering has plagued her children at the hand of man. We have been hunted." Her voice rose steadily. "We have burned. We have lost sister and mother and daughter to their *hatred* and *fear.*"

The witches stirred restlessly. I gripped my knife tighter.

"Tonight," she cried passionately, lifting her arms to the heavens, "the Goddess will answer our prayers!"

Then she brought them slashing down, and Lou—still floating, still insentient—tipped forward. Her feet dangled uselessly above the temple floor. "With my daughter's sacrifice, the Goddess shall end our oppression!" Her hands clenched, and Lou's head snapped upright. Nausea rolled in my gut. "In her death, we shall forge new life!"

The witches stomped and shouted.

"But first," she crooned, barely audible. "A gift for my daughter."

And with one last flick of her hand, Lou's eyes finally opened.

I hesitated just long enough to see those blue-green eyes—beautiful, *alive*—widen in shock. Then I lunged forward.

Ansel grabbed my arms with surprising strength. "Reid."

I faltered at his tone. In the next second, I understood: the ebony witch had reappeared, and now she dragged a second woman—limp and immobilized—out of the temple. A woman with strawberry blond hair and piercing blue eyes that searched the crowd desperately.

I stopped dead, stricken. Unable to move.

My mother.

"Behold this woman!" Morgane shouted over the sudden din of voices. "Behold the treacherous Helene!" She grabbed Madame Labelle by the hair and threw her down the temple steps. "This woman—once our sister, once my *heart*—conspires with the human king. She birthed his bastard child." Shrieks of outrage rent the air. "Tonight, she was found attempting to force entry on the Chateau. She plots to steal our Mother's precious gift by taking my daughter's life herself. She would have us all burn under the tyrant king!"

The cries reached a deafening pitch, and Morgane's eyes shone with triumph as she descended the steps. As she drew a wickedly sharp dagger from her belt. "Louise le Blanc, daughter and heir to La Dame des Sorcières, I shall honor you with her death."

"No!" Lou's body spasmed as she fought to move with her entire being. Tears poured down Madame Labelle's cheeks.

I tore viciously from Ansel's grasp and lunged forward, diving for the temple steps—desperate to reach them, desperate to save the two women I needed most—just as Morgane plunged the dagger into my mother's chest.

THE PATTERN

Reid

"NO!" I fell to my knees before her body, jerking the dagger from her chest, fingers moving to stanch the bleeding. But I already knew it was too late. *I* was too late. There was too much blood for this wound to be anything but fatal. I stopped my frenzied ministrations and clutched her hands instead. Her eyes never left my face. We each stared at the other hungrily—as if in that brief moment, a thousand other moments might've happened.

Her holding a chubby finger. Her tending a scraped knee. Her laughing when I first kissed Célie, telling me I hadn't done it right.

Then the moment ended. The cold tingle of her magic left my face. Her breath faltered, and her eyes closed.

A blade touched my throat.

"Rise," Morgane commanded.

I exploded upward, catching her wrist and shattering it with ease—with savage pleasure. She screeched, dropping the dagger, but I didn't stop. I bore down on her. My free hand wrapped around her throat—squeezing until I could feel her windpipe give, kicking the dagger down the steps toward Ansel—

Her other hand blasted into my stomach—stunning me—and invisible bonds cinched around my body, pinned my arms to my sides. My legs went rigid. She struck me again, and I toppled over, thrashing against the bonds. The harder I struggled, the tighter they became. They bit into my skin, drawing blood—

"Mother, stop!" Lou spasmed again, shuddering with the effort to reach me, but her body remained suspended. "Don't hurt him!"

Morgane didn't listen. She appeared to be feeling for something in empty air. Her eyes darted outward as she tracked whatever it was into the crowd. With a vicious tug, two familiar people staggered forward. My heart dropped. Morgane pulled harder, and Ansel and Beau fell at the temple steps, struggling against invisible bonds of their own. Their faces had returned to normal.

"Her coconspirators!" A mad gleam entered Morgane's eyes, and the witches went wild with bloodlust—stamping their feet and screaming—as they struggled to converge on the temple. Magic shot past my face. Ansel cried out as a spell slashed his cheek. "The king's sons and huntsmen! They shall bear witness to our triumph! They shall watch as we rid this world of the House of Lyon!"

She jerked her uninjured hand, and Lou slammed onto the altar. The witches screamed their approval. I threw myself forward. Rolled and clawed and twisted toward Lou with every ounce of the strength I had left. The bonds around me strained.

"Nature demands balance!" Morgane swooped to retrieve the dagger from the steps. When she spoke again, her voice had deepened to an unearthly timbre, multiplied as if thousands of witches were speaking through her. "Louise le Blanc, thy blood is the price." Enchantment washed over the temple, burning my nose and clouding my mind. I gritted my teeth. Forced myself to see through it—to see through her.

Beau immediately slackened. His eyes glazed as Morgane's skin began to glow. Ansel alone struggled on, but his resolve quickly faltered.

"Let it fill the cup of Lyon, for whosoever drinketh of it shalt surely die." Morgane walked to Lou slowly, her hair billowing around her in a nonexistent wind. "And so the prophecy foretold: the lamb shalt devour the lion."

She forced Lou to her stomach. Ripped her braid back to extend her throat over the altar basin. Lou's eyes sought mine. "I love you," she whispered. No tears marred her beautiful face. "I will remember you."

"Lou—" It was a desperate, strangled sound. A plea and a prayer. I tore violently at my bonds. Sharp pain lanced through my body as one arm snapped free. I flung it outward, mere inches from the altar, but it wasn't enough. I watched—as if in slow motion—as Morgane raised the dagger high. It still gleamed with my mother's blood.

Lou closed her eyes.

No.

A terrible shriek sounded, and Coco leapt for Morgane's throat.

Her knife sank deep into the tender flesh between Morgane's neck and shoulder. Morgane screamed, attempting to pry her away, but Coco held on, pushing the blade deeper. She fought to bring Morgane's blood to her lips. Morgane's eyes widened in realization—and panic.

A full second passed before I realized the bonds holding me had flickered out at Coco's assault. I bolted to my feet and closed the distance to Lou in a single stride.

"No!" she cried when I made to pick her up. "Help Coco! *Help her!*"

Whatever happens, you get Lou out.

"Lou—" I said through clenched teeth, but a high-pitched scream silenced my argument. I spun just as Coco collapsed to the floor. She didn't get back up.

"Coco!" Lou screamed.

Chaos erupted. The witches surged forward, but Ansel rose up to meet them—a lone figure against hundreds. To my dismay, Beau followed him—but he didn't brandish a weapon. Instead, he shucked off his coat and boots, searching the crowd wildly. When his eyes landed on the plump witch from the hall, he pointed and bellowed, "BIG TITTY LIDDY!"

Her eyes widened as he kicked off his pants and began singing at the top of his lungs, "'BIG TITTY LIDDY WAS NOT VERY PRETTY, BUT HER BOSOM WAS BIG AS A BARN.'"

The witches nearest him—Elinor and Elaina among them—stopped dead in their tracks. Bewilderment tempered their rage as Beau slipped his shirt over his head and continued singing, "'HER CREAMERY KNOCKERS DROVE MEN OFF THEIR

ROCKERS, BUT SHE WAS BLIND TO THEIR CHARM.'"

Morgane bared her teeth and whirled toward him, blood flowing freely down her shoulder. It was all the distraction I needed. Before she could lift her hands, I was upon her. I pressed my knife to her throat.

"Reid!" It was the voice I least expected, the only voice in the world that could've made me hesitate in that moment. But hesitate I did.

It was the voice of the Archbishop.

Morgane made to turn, but I dug the blade in deeper. "Move your hands. I dare you."

"I should've drowned you in the sea," she snarled, but her hands stilled regardless.

Slowly, carefully, I turned. The ebony witch had returned, and an incapacitated Archbishop floated before her. His eyes were wild—with panic and something else. Something urgent. "Reid." His chest heaved. "Don't listen to them. Whatever happens, whatever they say—"

The ebony witch snarled, and his words ended in a scream.

My hand slipped, and Morgane hissed as blood trickled down her throat. The ebony witch stepped closer. "Let her go, or he dies."

"Manon," Lou pleaded. "Don't do this. Please—"

"Be quiet, Lou." Her eyes glowed manic and crazed—beyond reason. The Archbishop continued screaming. The veins beneath his skin blackened, as did his nails and tongue. I stared at him in horror.

I didn't see Morgane's hands move until they grasped my wrists. White-hot heat melted my skin, and my knife clattered to the floor.

Faster than I could react, she scooped it up and dove toward Lou.

"NO!" The shout tore from my throat—feral, desperate—but she had already thrust the knife upward and slashed, tearing Lou's throat open completely.

I stopped breathing. A horrible roaring filled my ears, and I was falling—a great, yawning chasm opening as Lou gasped and choked, her lifeblood pouring into the basin. She thrashed, finally free of whatever had been holding her—still fighting, even as she struggled to breathe—but her body stilled quickly. Her eyes fluttered once . . . then closed.

The ground gave way beneath me. Shouts and footsteps thundered in the distance, but I couldn't truly hear them. Couldn't even see. There was only darkness—the bitter void in the world where Lou should've been and now was not. I stared into it, willing it to consume me.

It did. I spiraled down, down, down into that darkness with her, and yet—she wasn't there at all. She was gone. Only a broken shell and sea of blood remained.

And I . . . I was alone.

Out of the darkness, a single golden cord shimmered into existence. It drifted out of Lou's chest and toward the Archbishop—pulsed as if in echo of a heart. With each beat, its light grew dimmer. I stared at it for the span of a single second. Knew what it was in the same way I knew the sound of my own voice, my reflection in the mirror. Familiar, yet foreign. Expected, yet startling. Something that had always been part of me, but I had never quite known.

In that darkness, something awoke inside me.

I didn't hesitate. I didn't think. Moving quickly, I swept a second knife from my bandolier and charged past Morgane. She lifted her hands—fire lashing from her fingertips—but I didn't feel the flames. The gold light wrapped around my skin, protecting me. But my thoughts scattered. Whatever strength my body had claimed, my mind now forfeited. I stumbled, but the gold cord marked my path. I vaulted over the altar after it.

The Archbishop's eyes flew open as he realized my intent. A small, pleading noise escaped him, but he could do little else before I fell upon him.

Before I drove my knife home in his heart.

A life for a life. A love for a love.

The Archbishop's eyes were still wide—confused—as he slumped forward in my arms.

The gold light dispersed, and the world came rushing back into focus. The shouts grew louder now. I stared down at the Archbishop's lifeless body, numb, but Morgane's scream of rage made me turn. Made me hope. Tears of relief welled in my eyes at what I saw.

Though Lou was still pale, still unmoving, the gash at her throat was closing. Her chest rose and fell.

She was alive.

With a brutal cry, Morgane jerked her knife up to reopen the wound, but an arrow sliced through the air and lodged in her chest. She screamed anew, whirling furiously, but I recognized the blue-tipped shaft immediately.

Chasseurs.

Led by Jean Luc, scores of them surged into the clearing. The witches shrieked in panic—scattering in every direction—but more of my brethren waited in the trees. They showed no mercy, cutting through woman and child alike without hesitation. Bodies everywhere fell into the mist and disappeared. An unearthly wail rose up from the very ground in response, and soon Chasseurs began disappearing as well.

Fury contorted Jean Luc's features as he notched another arrow and raced toward the temple. His eyes were no longer fixed on Morgane, however—they were fixed on me. Too late, I realized my hand still clenched the knife protruding from the Archbishop's chest. I dropped it hastily—the Archbishop's body falling with it—but the damage had been done.

Jean Luc took aim and fired.

LA FORÊT DES YEUX

Reid

I grabbed Lou and ducked behind the altar. Ansel and Beau scrambled after me, holding a barely conscious Coco between them. Arrows rained down on our heads. Morgane blasted most of them into ash with a wave of her hand, but one sank deep into her leg. She screamed in fury.

"Through there." Voice faint, Coco pointed into the depths of the temple. "There's . . . another exit."

I hesitated for only a second. Another volley of arrows distracted Morgane—it was now or never.

"Get them out." I slid Lou into Beau's arms. "I'll catch up."

Before he could protest, I dove out from behind the altar toward Madame Labelle's body. No arrows had yet pierced her, but our luck wouldn't hold. As the Chasseurs closed in, their range turned deadly. An arrow whizzed by my ear. Grabbing Madame Labelle's wrist, I hauled her into my arms. Tried to shield as much of her body as possible with my own.

Fire and arrow pursued me as I sprinted back into the temple.

Sharp pain lanced through my shoulder, but I didn't dare stop.

The sound of the battle died as I entered the uncanny quiet of the inner temple. Ahead of me, Ansel, Coco, and Beau raced toward the exit. I sprinted after them, trying to ignore the warm, wet substance spreading across my arm. The small moans of pain escaping Madame Labelle's throat.

She's alive. Alive.

I didn't look behind to see if Morgane or Jean Luc followed. I focused only on the small rectangle of moonlight at the end of the temple, on Coco's hair bobbing as she cleared it.

Coco.

Coco could heal her.

I caught up to them as they entered the shadows of the forest. They didn't slow. Lurching forward, I grabbed Coco's arm. Her eyes were dim, glazed, as she turned back to me. I extended Madame Labelle's broken body to her. "Help her. Please." My voice shook—my eyes burned—but I didn't care. I pressed my mother into her arms. "Please."

Ansel glanced behind us, breathing heavily. "Reid, there's no time—"

"Please." My eyes never wavered from her face. "She's dying."

Coco blinked slowly. "I'll try."

"Coco, you're too weak!" Beau shifted Lou in his arms, red-faced and panting. "You can barely stand!"

She answered by lifting her wrist to her mouth and tearing the thin skin there. The same acrid scent singed the air as she drew back. Blood coated her lips. "This will only buy us time until we reach camp." She lifted her wrist to Madame Labelle's chest. We watched, transfixed, as her blood dripped down, sizzling when it touched Madame Labelle's skin.

Beau watched incredulously as the wound knit itself back together. "How—?"

"Not now." Coco flexed her wrist and shook her head, eyes sharpening, as a man's scream sounded beyond the temple. The witches must've marshaled their forces, recovering from their initial panic. Though I could no longer see the clearing, I could imagine them using the only weapons they had at their disposal: their consorts. Human shields against my brethren's Balisardas.

Coco glanced back at Madame Labelle's pale body. "We need to find our camp quickly, or she'll die."

She didn't need to tell us twice. Ducking our heads, we raced through the forest and into the night.

Shadows still cloaked the pines when we found our abandoned camp. Though Madame Labelle had grown steadily paler, her chest still rose and fell. Her heart still beat.

Coco rifled through her pack and pulled out a jar of thick, amber liquid. "Honey," she explained at my anxious look. "Blood and honey."

Lowering Madame Labelle to the forest floor, I watched in morbid fascination as Coco reopened her wrist and mixed her blood with the honey. She applied it carefully to the puckered welt on Madame Labelle's chest. Almost instantly, Madame Labelle's breathing deepened. Color returned to her cheeks. I sank to my knees, unwilling to look away. Not even for a second. "How?"

Coco sat back, closing her eyes and rubbing her temples. "I told you. My magic comes from within. Not—not like Lou's."

Lou.

I lurched to my feet.

"She's fine." Ansel cradled her head in his lap across the camp. I hurried over to them, examining her pale face. Her gashed throat. Her gaunt cheeks. "She's still breathing. Her heartbeat is strong."

I turned to Coco despite Ansel's reassurance. "Can you heal her too?"

"No." She vaulted to her feet as if realizing something, pulling a bundle of herbs and a mortar and pestle from her pack. She set to grinding the herbs into powder. "You've healed her already."

"Then why isn't she awake?" I snapped.

"Give her time. She'll wake when she's ready." Breathing labored—ragged, uneven—she let the blood from her wrist drip onto the powder before coating her fingers with the mixture. Then she crawled to Lou's side. "Move. She needs protection. We all do."

I eyed the mixture with revulsion, angling myself between them. It smelled terrible. "No."

With a noise of impatience, she knocked me aside and swept a bloody thumb across Lou's forehead. Then Madame Labelle's. Then Beau's. Then Ansel's. I glared at all of them, pushing her hand away when she lifted it to my face.

"Don't be an idiot, Reid. It's sage," she said impatiently. "It's the best I can do against Morgane."

"I'll risk it."

"No, you won't. You'll be the first Morgane targets when she can't find Lou . . . *if* she can't find Lou." Her eyes flicked to Lou's inert form, and she seemed to crumple. Beau and Ansel both extended hands to steady her. "I don't know if I'm strong enough to ward against her."

"Anything will help," Beau murmured.

An empty platitude. He didn't know any more about magic than I did. I'd just opened my mouth to tell him so when Ansel sighed heavily, touching my shoulder. Pleading. "Do it for Lou, Reid."

I didn't move as Coco wiped her blood across my forehead.

We all agreed to leave the camp as soon as possible, but the mountainside proved just as dangerous as the Chateau. Witches and Chasseurs alike roamed the forest with predatory intent. More than once, we'd been forced to scramble up trees to avoid detection, unsure whether Coco's protection would hold. Palms sweating. Limbs shaking.

"If you drop her, I'll kill you," she'd hissed, eyeing Lou's unconscious form in my arms. As if I could've relinquished my grip on her. As if I'd ever let her go again.

Through it all, Morgane did not reveal herself.

We felt her presence hovering over us, but no one dared mention it—as if giving voice to our fear would bring her swooping down upon us. Neither did we mention what I'd done at the temple. But the memory continued to plague me. The sickening feel of my knife sinking into the Archbishop's flesh. The extra push it'd taken to force the blade between bones to the heart beneath.

The Archbishop's eyes—wide and confused—as his would-be son betrayed him.

I would burn in Hell for what I had done. If there even was such a place.

Madame Labelle woke first.

"Water," she croaked. Ansel fumbled for his canteen as I hurried over.

I didn't speak as she drank her fill. I simply watched her. Inspected her. Tried to calm my racing heart. Like Lou, she remained pallid and sickly, and faint bruises shadowed her familiar blue eyes.

When she finally let the canteen fall, those eyes sought mine. "What happened?"

I unloosed a breath. "We got out."

"Yes, obviously," she said with surprising bite. "I mean *how*?"

"We—" I glanced to the others. How much had they guessed? How much had they seen? They knew I'd killed the Archbishop, and they knew Lou had lived—but had they connected the two?

One look at Coco gave me my answer. She sighed heavily and stepped forward, holding her arms out for Lou. "Let me have her." I hesitated, and her eyes hardened. "Take your mother, Reid. Go for a walk. Tell her everything . . . or I will."

I looked from face to face, but no one seemed surprised at her words. Ansel wouldn't look at me. When Beau jerked his head, mouthing *get it over with*, my heart sank.

"Fine." I deposited Lou into her outstretched arms. "We won't go far."

Carrying Madame Labelle just out of earshot, I set her down on the softest bit of ground I could find and lowered myself opposite.

"Well?" She smoothed her skirt, impatient. I scowled. Apparently, near-death experiences made my mother irritable. I didn't mind, really. Her irritation gave me something to focus on other than my own growing discomfort. Many unspoken things had passed between us in that moment she lay dying.

Guilt. Anger. Yearning. Regret.

No, irritation was much easier to face than all *that*.

I recounted all that had happened at the temple in clipped, disgruntled tones, leaving my own role in our escape vague. But Madame Labelle was an inconveniently sharp woman. She sniffed me out like a fox.

"You're not telling me something." She leaned forward to examine me, lips pursed. "What did you do?"

"I didn't *do* anything."

"Didn't you?" She arched a brow and leaned back on her hands. "So, according to you, you killed your forefather—a man you loved—for no apparent reason?"

Loved. A lump formed in my throat at the past tense. I cleared it away with a cough. "He betrayed us—"

"And then your wife came back to life—also for no apparent reason?"

"She was never dead."

"And you know this how?"

"Because—" I stopped short, realizing too late I couldn't explain the thread of life connecting Lou and the Archbishop. Not without revealing myself. Her eyes narrowed at my hesitation, and I sighed. "I . . . saw it, somehow."

"How?"

I stared at my boots. My shoulders ached with tension. "There was a cord. It—it connected them. It pulsed in time with her heart."

She sat up suddenly, wincing at the movement. "You saw a pattern."

I said nothing.

"You saw a pattern," she repeated, almost as if to herself, "and you recognized it. You—you *acted* on it. How?" She leaned forward again, clutched my arm with surprising strength despite her trembling hands. "Where did it come from? You must tell me everything you remember."

Alarmed, I wrapped an arm around her shoulders. "You need to rest. We can talk about this later."

"*Tell me.*" Her nails dug into my forearm.

I glared at her. She glared back. Finally, realizing she wouldn't budge, I blew out an exasperated breath. "I don't remember. It all happened too quickly. Morgane slit Lou's throat, and I thought she was dead, and—and then there was just darkness. It swallowed me up, and I couldn't think clearly. I just—reacted." I paused, swallowing hard. "That's where the cord came from . . . darkness."

I stared down at my hands and remembered that dismal place. I'd been alone there—truly, absolutely alone. The emptiness reminded me of what I'd imagined Hell to feel like. My hands curled into fists. Though I'd washed away the Archbishop's blood, some stains went below the surface.

"Amazing." Madame Labelle released my arm and slumped backward. "I didn't believe it possible, but . . . there's no other explanation. The cord . . . the balance it struck—it all fits. And not only did you *see* the pattern, you were also able to *manipulate* it. Unprecedented . . . this is—it's amazing—" She looked up at me in awe. "Reid, you have magic."

I opened my mouth to deny it, but closed it again almost immediately. It shouldn't have been possible. Lou had *told* me it wasn't possible. Yet here I was. Tainted. Stained by magic and the death that invariably followed.

We stared at each other for a few tense seconds.

"How?" My voice sounded more desperate than I would've liked, but I needed this answer more than I needed my pride. "How could this happen?"

The awe in her eyes flickered out. "I don't know. It would seem Lou's imminent death triggered you somehow." She clasped my hand. "I know this is difficult for you, but this will change everything, Reid. You're the first, but what if there are others? What if we were wrong about our sons?"

"But there's no such thing as a male witch." The words fell flat, unconvincing, even to my own ears.

A sad smile touched her lips. "Yet here you are."

I looked away, unable to stand the pity in her gaze. I felt sick. More than sick—I felt *wronged*. My entire life I'd abhorred witches. Hunted them. Killed them. And now—by some cruel twist of fate—I suddenly *was* one.

The first male witch.

If there was a God, he or she had a shit sense of humor.

"Did she realize?" Madame Labelle's voice grew quiet. "Morgane?"

"No idea." I closed my eyes but immediately regretted it. Too many faces rose up to meet me. One in particular. Eyes wide. Frightened. Confused. "The Chasseurs saw me slay the Archbishop."

"Yes, that is potentially problematic."

My eyes snapped open, and fresh pain lanced through me. Jagged and sharp. Raw. "Potentially problematic? Jean Luc tried to *kill* me."

"And will continue to do so, I'm sure, as will the witches. Many died tonight in their foolish quest for vengeance. None will forget your part in it—especially Morgane." She sighed and squeezed my hand. "There is also the matter of your father."

If possible, my heart sank even lower. "What about him?"

"Word will reach him about what happened at the temple. He will soon learn your name . . . and Lou's."

"None of this is Lou's fault—"

"It doesn't matter whose fault it is. Your wife's blood has the power to wipe out his entire line. Do you really think any person—let alone a *king*—would allow such a liability to walk free?"

"But she's innocent." My pulse ratcheted upward, pounding in my ears. "He can't imprison her for Morgane's crimes—"

"Who said anything about imprisoning her?" She raised her brows and patted my cheek again. This time, I didn't flinch away. "He'll want her dead, Reid. Burned, specifically, so not a drop of her blood can be used for Morgane's foul purpose."

I stared at her for a long second. Convinced I hadn't heard her. Convinced she might start laughing, or a *feu follet* would flare and transport me back to reality. But—no. This *was* my new reality. Anger erupted inside me, burning away the last of my scruples. "Why the *fuck* is everyone in this kingdom trying to murder my wife?"

A bubble of laughter escaped Madame Labelle's lips, but I didn't think it was funny at all. "What are we going to do? Where are we going to *go*?"

"You'll come with me, of course." Coco stepped out from behind a large pine, grinning in unabashed delight. "Sorry, I was eavesdropping, but I thought you wouldn't mind, considering . . ." She nodded down to Lou in her arms.

Lou.

Every trace of anger—every doubt, every question, every *thought*—emptied from my head as blue-green eyes met my own.

She was awake. Awake and staring at me as if she'd never quite seen me before. I stepped forward, panicking, praying that her mind hadn't been affected. That she remembered me. That God hadn't played yet another cruel, sick joke—

"Reid," she said slowly, incredulously, "did you just *curse*?"

Then she leaned over Coco's arm and heaved bile all over the forest floor.

LA VOISIN

Lou

"I'm fine, really." I repeated the words for the hundredth time, but I wasn't really sure I was fine at all.

As far as I could tell, the innards of my throat were only being held in by a hideously disfiguring scar, my stomach rolled from my mother's abominable drug, my legs were numb from disuse, and my mind still reeled from what I'd just overheard.

Reid was here.

And he was a witch.

And—and he'd just said *fuck*.

Perhaps I'd died after all. That was certainly more plausible than Reid swearing with such delicious proficiency.

"Are you sure you're all right?" he pressed.

He'd completely ignored the bile spattering the ground in his haste to reach me. Bless him. And Coco—perhaps sensing Reid was a man on the edge—had handed me over willingly enough. I tried not to resent them for treating me like a sack of potatoes. I knew they meant well, but honestly, I was perfectly capable of moving on my own.

Admittedly, my head *was* spinning at Reid's sudden proximity, so perhaps it was a good idea for him to carry me, after all. I wrapped my arms more firmly around his neck and breathed him in.

Yes. It was a *very* good idea. "I'm sure."

Reid sighed in relief before closing his eyes and letting his forehead drop to mine.

Madame Labelle gave Coco a pointed smile. "Dear, I think I'd like to stretch my legs a bit. Would you mind accompanying me?"

Coco obliged, helping Madame Labelle to her feet. Though Coco supported a good deal of her weight, she still paled at the movement. Reid's eyes snapped open, and he stepped forward in concern. "I really don't think you should be walking."

Madame Labelle silenced him with a scowl. Impressed, I memorized the look for later use. "Nonsense. My body needs to remember what it's like to be a body."

"Too true," I muttered.

Reid frowned down at me. "Do you want to walk too?"

"I— No. I'm quite happy here, thanks."

"We'll talk later." Coco rolled her eyes, but her grin only widened. "Do me a favor and get out of earshot this time. I have no desire to overhear this particular conversation."

I waggled my eyebrows. "Or lack thereof."

Madame Labelle scrunched her face in disgust. "And *that* is my cue. Cosette, lead on, please, and do be quick about it."

My grin faded as they hobbled out of sight. This was the first time Reid and I had been alone since . . . well, everything. He too seemed to sense the sudden shift in the air between us. Every muscle in his body went tense, rigid. As if preparing to flee—or fight.

But that was ridiculous. I didn't want to fight. After everything I'd just been through, after everything *we'd* just been through, I'd had enough fighting to last a lifetime. I raised my brows, reaching a hand up to cup his cheek. "*Couronne* for your thoughts?"

Anxious, sea-blue eyes searched my own, but he said nothing.

Unfortunately—at least for Reid—I'd never been one to suffer silence peaceably. I scowled and dropped my hand. "I know it's difficult for you, Reid, but *try* not to make this any more awkward than it needs to be."

That did it. Life stirred behind his eyes. "Why aren't you angry with me?"

Oh, Reid. The loathing shone clear in his eyes—but not for me, as I'd once feared. For himself. I rested my head against his chest. "You did nothing wrong."

He shook his head, arms tightening around me. "How can you say that? I—I let you walk right into this." His eyes swept around us with a pained expression—then fell to my throat. He swallowed and shook his head in disgust. "I promised to protect you, but I abandoned you at the first opportunity."

"Reid." When he refused to look at me, I cupped his face again. "I knew who you were. I knew what you believed . . . and I fell in love with you anyway."

He closed his eyes, still shaking his head, and a single tear tracked down his cheek. My heart twisted.

"I never held it against you. Not really. Reid, listen to me.

Listen." He opened his eyes reluctantly, and I forced him to meet my gaze, desperate for him to understand. "When I was a child, I saw the world in black and white. Huntsmen were enemies. Witches were friends. We were good, and they were evil. There was no in between. Then my mother tried to kill me, and suddenly, that sharp, clear-cut world shattered into a million pieces." I brushed the tear from his cheek. "You can imagine my distress when a particularly tall, copper-haired Chasseur walked in and crushed what was left of those pieces to dust."

He sank to the ground, pulling me down with him. But I hadn't finished yet. He'd risked everything for me by coming to the Chateau. He'd abandoned his life—his very beliefs—when he chose me. I didn't deserve it. But I thanked God anyway.

"After I pulled you through that curtain," I whispered, "I said you should've expected me to behave like a criminal. I didn't tell you I was a witch because I was following my own advice. I expected you to behave like a Chasseur—only you didn't. You didn't kill me. You let me go." I moved to drop my hand, but he caught it, holding it to his face.

His voice was thick with emotion. "I should've come after you."

I brought my other hand to his face as well and leaned closer. "I shouldn't have lied."

He took a shuddering breath. "I—I said terrible things."

"Yes." I frowned slightly, remembering. "You did."

"I didn't mean any of them—except one." His hands covered my own on his face, and his eyes bored into mine as if he could see into my very soul. Perhaps he could. "I love you, Lou." His eyes welled with fresh tears. "I—I've never seen anyone savor *anything* the way you do *everything.* You make me feel alive. Just being in your presence—it's addictive. *You're* addictive. It doesn't matter you're a witch. The way you see the world . . . I want to see it that way too. I want to be with you always, Lou. I never want to be parted from you again."

I couldn't stop the tears from falling down my cheeks. "Where you go, I will go."

With deliberate slowness, I pressed my lips to his.

I managed to walk back by myself, but my body tired quickly.

When we finally reached the camp, the others were preparing dinner. Coco tended a small fire, and Madame Labelle dispersed the smoke into thin air with her fingers. Two fat rabbits sizzled on the spit. My stomach contracted, and I pressed a fist to my mouth before I could puke again.

Ansel saw us first. A wide grin split his face, and he dropped the pot he held and raced toward us, enveloping me as best he could in a fierce hug. Reid reluctantly let me go, and I returned Ansel's embrace with equal fervor.

"Thank you," I whispered in his ear. "For everything."

He blushed pink as he stepped away, but he kept a firm arm around my waist regardless. Reid looked as if he were trying very hard not to smile.

Beau leaned against a tree with his arms folded across his chest. "You know, this wasn't exactly what I had in mind when I said we could have fun together, Madame Diggory."

I arched a brow, remembering his naked chest shimmying in the moonlight. "Oh, I don't know. I thought parts of the evening were entertaining."

He grinned. "You enjoyed the performance, then?"

"Very much. It would seem we frequent the same pubs."

Madame Labelle's fingers still moved lazily through the air. The smallest trickle of magic streamed from them as the smoke disappeared. "I hate to interrupt, but our rabbits are burning."

Beau's smile vanished, and he leapt to slide the blackened rabbits off the spit, moaning bitterly. "Took me *ages* to catch these."

Coco rolled her eyes. "You mean to watch *me* catch them."

"Excuse me?" He lifted the smaller of the two rabbits indignantly. "I shot this one, thank you very much!"

"Yes, you did—right through the leg. I had to track the poor creature down and put it out of its misery."

When Beau opened his mouth to reply, eyes blazing, I turned to Reid. "Did I miss something?"

"They've been like this ever since we left," Ansel said. I didn't miss the satisfaction in his voice or the smirk on his face.

"The prince had some trouble adjusting to the wilderness," Reid explained quietly. "Coco was . . . unimpressed."

I couldn't help but chuckle. As the argument escalated, however—with no sign of either party backing down—I waved my hand to reclaim their attention. "Excuse me," I said loudly. Both whirled to look at me. "As entertaining as all this is, we have more important matters to discuss."

"Such as?" Beau snapped.

Ass. I almost grinned, but at the ferocity of Coco's scowl, I caught myself at the last second. "We can't hide in this forest forever. Morgane knows all your faces now, and she'll kill every one of you for helping me escape."

Beau scoffed. "My father will have her head on a pike when he learns what she's planning."

"And mine," I said pointedly.

"Probably."

Definite ass.

Madame Labelle sighed. "Auguste has failed to capture Morgane for decades—just as his ancestors failed to capture a single Dame des Sorcières in their long and gruesome history. It's highly unlikely he succeeds now either. She'll continue to remain a threat to all of us."

"But now the Chasseurs know the location of the Chateau," Reid pointed out.

"They still can't enter without a witch."

"They did before."

"Ah . . . yes." Madame Labelle cleared her throat delicately and looked away, smoothing her wrinkled, bloodstained skirt. "That's because I led them to it."

"You *what?*" Reid stiffened beside me, and a telltale flush crept up his throat. "You—you met with Jean Luc? Are you insane? How? When?"

"After I sent you lot off with those twittering triplets." She shrugged, bending low to scratch the blackened log at her feet.

When it moved, blinking open luminous yellow eyes, my heart nearly leapt to my throat. That wasn't a log. That wasn't even a cat. That—that was a—

"The matagot delivered a message to your comrades shortly after our disagreement. Jean Luc was less than pleased by a demon waltzing around in his mind, but even he couldn't ignore the opportunity I presented him. We met on the beach outside the Chateau, and I led them within the enchantment. They were supposed to wait for my signal. When I didn't reappear, Jean Luc took matters into his own hands." She touched the crusty bodice of her gown as if remembering the feel of Morgane's knife sinking into her chest. My throat throbbed with empathy. "And thank the Goddess he did."

"Yes," I agreed quickly before Reid could interrupt. His flush had spread from his throat to the tips of his ears during Madame Labelle's explanation, and he looked likely to further derail the conversation by throttling someone. "But we're worse off now than we were before."

"Why?" Ansel's brow wrinkled. "The Chasseurs killed dozens of witches. Surely Morgane is weaker now, at least?"

"Perhaps," Madame Labelle murmured, "but a wounded animal is a dangerous beast."

When Ansel still looked puzzled, I squeezed his waist. "Everything that happened—everything we did—it'll only make her more savage. The other witches, too. This war is anything but over."

A foreboding silence descended as my words sank in.

"Right," Coco said, lifting her chin. "There's only one thing for it. You'll all come back to my coven with me. Morgane won't be able to touch you there."

"Coco . . ." I met her gaze reluctantly. She set her jaw and planted a hand on her hip in response. "They're just as likely to kill us as they are to help us."

"They won't. You'll be under my protection. None of my kin will dare lay a hand on you."

There was another pause as we stared at each other.

"You don't have many other options, Louise, dear," Madame Labelle finally said. "Even Morgane isn't foolhardy enough to attack you in the heart of a blood coven, and Auguste and the Chasseurs would never find you there."

"Aren't you coming with us?" Reid asked, frowning. The back of his neck nearly blended into his coppery hair, and his hands remained clenched. Tense. I coaxed his fist open with a gentle brush of my knuckle, lacing my fingers through his. He took a deep breath and relaxed slightly.

"No." Madame Labelle swallowed hard, and the matagot rubbed its head against her knee in a startling domestic gesture. "Though it's been years since I've seen him, I think . . . I think it's finally time I had a conversation with Auguste."

Beau frowned. "You would have to be a complete idiot to tell him you're a witch."

Reid and I glared at him, but Madame Labelle only lifted an elegant shoulder, unruffled. "Well, it is good I'm not a complete idiot, then. You will come with me, of course. I can't just waltz into the castle anymore. Together, we might be able to persuade Auguste against whatever harebrained scheme he's undoubtedly concocting."

"What makes you think *you'll* be able to persuade him to do anything?"

"He loved me once."

"Yes. I'm sure my mother will be thrilled to hear all about it."

"I'm sorry, but I still don't understand." Ansel shook his head in bewilderment and looked to Coco. "Why do you think we'll be safe with your coven? If Morgane is as dangerous as everyone says . . . will they really be able to protect us?"

Coco barked a short laugh. "You don't know who my aunt is, do you?"

Ansel's brows furrowed. "No."

"Then allow me to enlighten you." Her grin stretched wide, and in the dying sunlight, her eyes seemed to glow brilliant crimson. "My aunt is the witch La Voisin."

Reid groaned audibly. "Shit."

ACKNOWLEDGMENTS

This story passed through many hands before publication, which means I have many people to thank for helping me shape it into something special.

To my husband, RJ—I quite literally couldn't have written *Serpent & Dove* without you. Thank you for your patience throughout this entire journey—for every night you brushed the boys' teeth and tucked them into bed when I was writing, and for every weekend you retreated with them to the basement when I was banging my head against my laptop. For all the dishes and laundry you washed when I was revising, and for all the emergency grocery runs you made when I ran out of 5-Hour Energy. You'll never know how much your support means to me. I love you. (P.S. You're now holding my book in your hands, which means . . . IT'S OFFICIALLY TIME TO READ IT.)

To my children, Beau, James, and Rose—If I can do it, so can you. Follow your dreams.

To my parents, Zane and Kelly—You fostered my love of

reading, and more important, you fostered my love of myself. Without your praise—and your total confidence in my abilities—I never would've mustered up the courage to pursue publication. I can't thank you enough for your unconditional love and support.

To my siblings, Jacob, Justin, Brooke, Chelsy, and Lewie—It would've been hard to take an eight-year-old writing poetry about Peter Pan seriously, but you always did. You never laughed at my writing dreams. Your enthusiasm means everything to me.

To my parents-in-law, Dave and Pattie: Thank you for all those days you volunteered to watch the boys. We love you.

To my forever friends Jordan, Spencer, Meghan, Aaron, Adrianne, Chelsea, Riley, Courtney, Austin, and Jon—Thank you for celebrating my weirdness and sticking around despite it. Life is hard—and publishing is harder—but I know you'll always have my back. See you at the party barn!

To my first critique partners, Katie and Carolyn—As the very first people to believe in my story, you two will always hold a special place in my heart. Thank you for your encouragement and critique—as well as talking me through my writer's block, helping me untangle complicated subplots, and reminding me these characters are special. Because of you, I finished my first draft; *Serpent & Dove* wouldn't be here today without you.

To my first beta readers, Mystique_ballerina, SomethingsHere, fashionablady, BadlandsQueenHalsey, drowsypug, Djwestwood, Arzoelyn, Mishi_And_Books, reaweiger, lcholland-82700, laia233, saturday—, JuliaBattles, and BluBByGrl—

Thank you for all your views, comments, and messages. I appreciated every single one.

To Brenda Drake, Heather Cashman, and the entire Pitch Wars team—Your incredible mentorship program ignited my writing career. Thank you.

To my Pitch Wars mentor, Jamie Howard—Without your vision, *Serpent & Dove* would be a much different story—and not in a good way. Thank you for believing in me and my story, and thank you for all the time and energy you devoted to us.

To my critique partners and sisters, Abby and Jordan—I adore you both. You came into my life at a critical juncture, and though we started as critique partners, we're so much more now. I consider you both sisters. Thank you for walking beside me on this crazy journey, holding my hand when I was unsure, and encouraging me to continue when it would've been easier to turn back. Writing can be an incredibly isolating career, but you make me feel less alone.

To my writing friends Lindsay Bilgram, Madeline Johnston, Destiny Murtaugh, Abigail Carson, Kate Weiler, Jessica Bibi Cooper, Hannah Whitten, Layne Fargo, Allison L. Bitz, Laura Taylor Namey, Monica Borg, E.K. Thiede, Kimberly Vale, Elora Cook, Christina Wise, Isabel Cañas, Kylie Schachte, Luke Hupton, Rachel Simon, and Lily Grant—Thank you for being such a supportive online community. You're all *wonderful*, and I'm so grateful I stumbled upon each of you when I did.

To my Francophile, Catherine Bakewell—Your knowledge of the French language and culture enriched this story—especially those curse words! Lou and I are forever indebted to your foul mouth.

To my wonderful agent, Sarah Landis—I knew about three seconds into our first phone call that you were the agent for me. Your enthusiasm is contagious, and more important, you have this knack for putting me at ease—a difficult feat for a worrier like me! Your transparency and general warmth have been invaluable as I navigate the publishing industry. Thank you for always being in my corner.

To my agent siblings, Erin A. Craig, Jessica Rubinkowski, Meredith Tate, Julie Abe, Jennie K. Brown, Ron Walters, Elisabeth Funk—Your publishing knowledge and experiences have been such an important resource for me. Thank you for sharing your insight and encouragement!

To my beta readers, Erin Cotter, Margie Fuston, Megan McGee Lysaght, Lindsey Ouimet, Kylie Schachte, Emily Taylor, E. K. Thiede, Carol Topdjian, Kimberly Vale, and Christina Wise—I can't thank you enough for taking the time to read early versions of *Serpent & Dove*. Your feedback—both the praise and the critique—was vital in shaping this story.

To my phenomenal editor, Erica Sussman—I'll never find the right words to thank you for your unending patience and vision. As a writer, there's always a small fear in handing your story to someone else. After our first brainstorming session, however, that fear disappeared. I trust you with my story completely—from my characters to my magic system to my world building. You are a true rock star. Thank you for loving this story as much as I do.

To my team at HarperTeen, Sarah Kaufman, Alison Donalty, Jessie Gang, Alexandra Rakaczki, Ebony LaDelle, Michael D'Angelo, Bess Braswell, Olivia Russo, Kris Kam, and Louisa Currigan—*Thank you* for believing in this story. I've been blown away by your skill time and time again, and I consider myself unbelievably lucky to be surrounded by such a talented team. Thank you for fulfilling my lifelong dream.